Savoring the Seasons

A CHILTON CROSSE NOVEL

TRACI BORUM

Savoring The Seasons

First Print Edition: June 2017

ISBN-13: 978-1-940215-91-4
ISBN-10: 1-940215-91-9

Red Adept Publishing, LLC
104 Bugenfield Court
Garner, NC 27529
http://RedAdeptPublishing.com/

Cover and Formatting: Streetlight Graphics

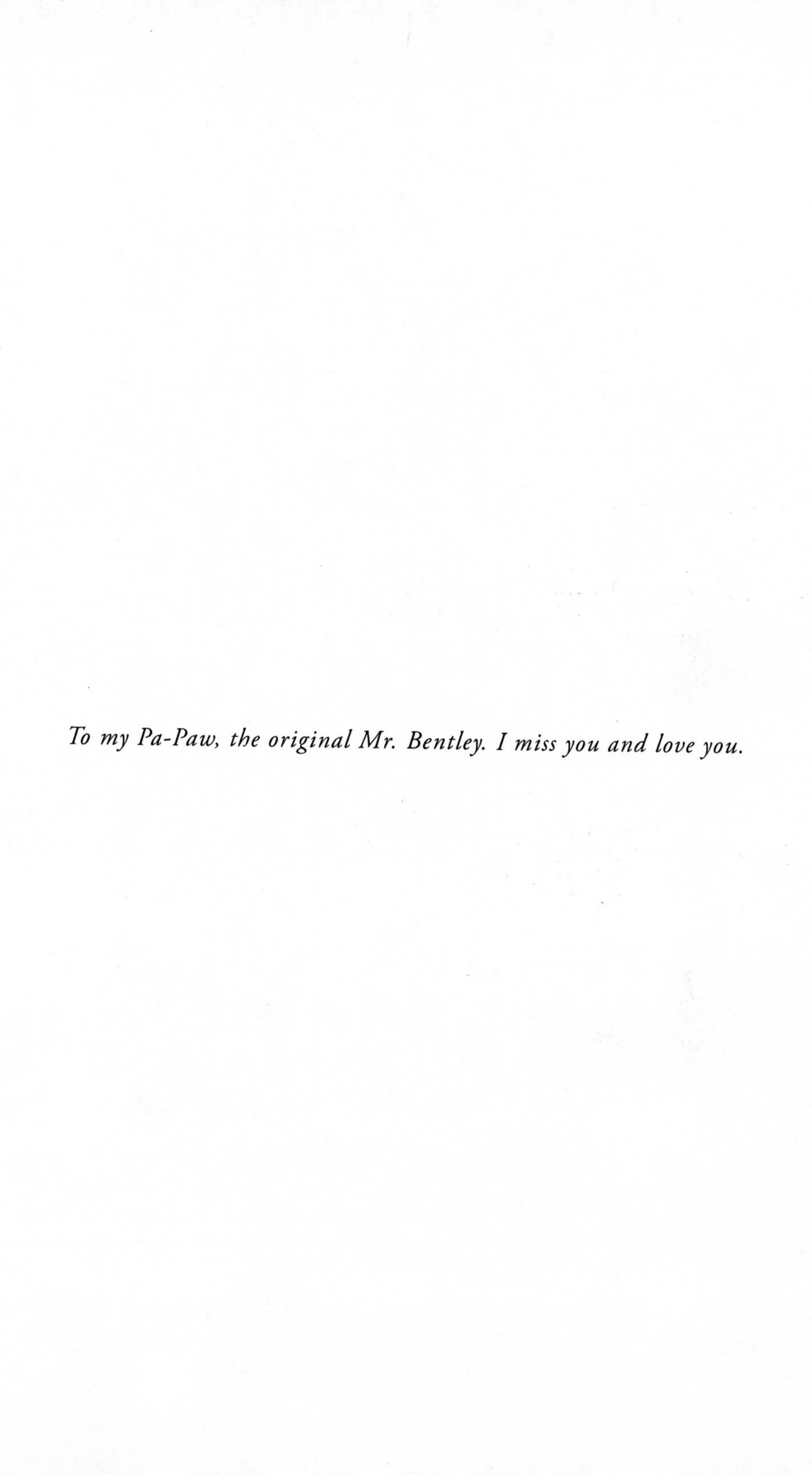

To my Pa-Paw, the original Mr. Bentley. I miss you and love you.

Chapter One

"Always remember why you bake—a birthday, a new baby, a graduation. What we do in the bakery goes deeper than measuring or sifting or icing. Ultimately, we're celebrating people."

As a little girl, Julia Bentley believed there were ghosts living in the walls of her father's Cotswold bakery. She would enter the building with him in the pre-dawn hour, wide-eyed, clutching his strong hand and shuddering at the spooky noises and creaks. But Julia's father would sit her down on a stool and reassure her that the centuries-old building was simply waking up with stretches and yawns. Then he'd bring the bakery to life—ovens whirring, pans clanking, radio playing—and banish the ghosts. Comforted, Julia would watch as he rolled up his sleeves to prepare delicious treats for villagers who were still tucked snugly in their beds.

During the daylight hours, intoxicating scents of baked bread and sugary treats infused the Chilton Crosse bakery, which thrummed with the light chatter of customers and the clinking of eager utensils against plates. With that familiar hum of activity, young Julia could practically feel the building's heartbeat. Warm sunlight streamed in through the diamond-paned window behind her as she sat coloring at a corner table. She loved observing villagers and tourists chattering away, pausing their busy days to fill their bellies with comfort food provided by her father.

As an adult, Julia stopped believing there were ghosts in the walls. She'd learned to savor the dark, early mornings, which had become her favorite hours. Those empty, pitch-black moments were no longer scary or eerie. Instead, they were all hers—a solitary refuge. With the whole world asleep, she was the only person in existence.

This morning, in the peaceful hush of her four a.m. hour, Julia reached for *Baker's Delight*, the old cookbook she'd discovered the night before while clearing out the flat above the bakery. She hadn't had time to open the book until now, and she gasped softly as she flipped through it, noticing what was written in the margins. Her mother's flowery handwriting graced nearly every page. Among the grease stains and flour stains and who-knows-what-other-kinds-of-food stains stamped inside the yellowed pages, her mother had scribbled little notes about each recipe: "Use non-salted butter." "Add a dash more sugar." "Let rise for thirty minutes longer." Julia paused when she saw a dog-eared page and knew immediately which recipe she had to try first, the "Lip-Smackin' Apple Tart" with her mother's starred note: "Alton's favorite."

In the silence of the bakery's kitchen, Julia squinted at the page and reminded herself, begrudgingly, to use her new reading glasses. "Granny glasses," she'd dubbed them the first time she'd tried them out in front of a mirror. Cheap, half-rimmed, and plain—but at least they served their purpose. Her eyes had decided to betray her a couple of months ago, but it had taken her several weeks to give in. Finally, she'd purchased her first over-the-counter reading glasses at the chemist's last week while picking up her father's medicine. Julia was tired of the squinting, tired of the headaches, and tired of denying she was almost forty (*in two days' time!*) and that signs of aging were inevitable. It helped to remember that some people, like her own mother, hadn't been allowed the privilege of reaching a milestone like forty.

Hours later, as she walked toward her cottage, Julia balanced a white bakery box and cookbook on one arm and used her other hand to release her hair from its band. Usually, by the time the bakery opened, the top of Julia's head ached, courtesy of the bun she always wore to keep her shoulder-length sandy hair out of the way.

Brandy, the just-graduated-from-university student who minded the counter, and Miranda, Julia's assistant, had taken over the bakery a few minutes ago, giving Julia her usual break so she could tend to her father.

Rosebud Cottage stood only a hundred meters behind Storey Road, the high street containing the long row of shops in Chilton Crosse.

Julia spent the majority of her days trekking back and forth between the bakery and cottage at odd hours—entering the bakery at four a.m., returning to the cottage to pick up her father midmorning, taking him back to the bakery, staying a few hours to help Miranda prep for the lunch crowd, and going back to the cottage for a quick nap if she could squeeze in the time. She ended her days by closing up shop and escorting her father to the cottage in the early evening. *Wash, rinse, repeat.* Six days a week.

This morning, as with nearly every morning, she heard the distinct sounds of a silky clarinet coming through an open cottage window. Even at ninety years old, her father could still play beautifully, except for an occasional squeak or pause while he took a breath or hunted for a note. She opened the creaky wooden gate and made her way up the stone path. They didn't have much of a garden to speak of, only a few shrubs and perennials. Julia didn't have time to tend flowers, and her father had never been the gardening type.

Inside, Julia headed for the kitchen. "Dad! I'm here!" The clarinet music halted long enough for her father to acknowledge her—"Good morning, love!"—then continued, picking up right where the song had left off.

The cottage was over a hundred years old, with low, beamed ceilings and cold stone floors—as rustic and quaint as every other cottage in this English village, Julia assumed. The kitchen stood at the back, small and unassuming, nothing like the bakery's kitchen. But it was still Julia's favorite room. She wasn't obligated to stand and bake for *other* people. Here, she could make a cup of tea, putter about, chuck some leftovers into the microwave, and keep things simple for herself and her dad.

She pulled her arms out of her fleece-lined jacket—April mornings still held a strong chill—threw it over a chair, then put the kettle on. Opening the box, she once again smelled that sweet-and-spicy apple scent and sliced her father a piece of the newly made tart. Earlier, she'd stolen a sliver fresh out of the oven to test it. Delicious! Plating the slice, Julia knew her father wouldn't eat all of it—his appetite wasn't what it used to be—but it was a habit she couldn't break, offering people generous portions.

She went to the cabinet and counted out her father's morning medications: blood pressure pills, vitamins, blood thinners, thyroid hormones, some of them to be repeated again at night. The list of necessary meds seemed to lengthen every year, but that was expected at his age.

Julia found a serving tray and added the tart slice, the medicine, a glass of water, and a fresh cup of tea with a hint of sugar. She wedged the cookbook under her arm and carried the tray through the hall to her father's bedroom.

"Good morning," she said with a tired-but-cheery smile. She couldn't wait to see his reaction to the tasty treat. The aspirin and long nap she craved could wait a little longer.

Alton Bentley laid down his clarinet and returned his daughter's smile. She set the tray carefully on the table.

"I have a special treat for you this morning." She always had to speak to her father in a volume one notch louder than usual to avoid having to repeat herself.

"Oh?" Her father's eyes widened.

Julia retrieved the cookbook from under her arm and flipped to the dog-eared page. "I was cleaning out the wardrobe in the upstairs flat last night, and I found this. It was Mum's."

She gave him the pair of glasses from his nightstand and patiently waited for him to fumble with them. When the glasses were firmly set on the bridge of his nose, she handed over the book.

The silver of his hair reflected in the lamp's light as he bent his head to examine the pages. Julia often marveled how a man his age could still have a nearly full head of hair. For a ninety-year-old, he looked at least twenty years younger, especially with his complexion, free of wrinkles except for a few creases around his mouth and eyes when he grinned. Whenever people asked his secret, he would always cite "a happy attitude and healthy living," adding that he had never smoked a cigarette in his whole life. He was especially proud of that fact.

He scanned the cookbook pages. "Mm. Yes. Mm-hmm." His expression softened. "This *was* your mother's." He tapped the page and looked up at Julia. "She special ordered it from a catalogue. Dormann's? Dorwell's? I remember it was in summer. During a blistering heat wave…" Her father was forever padding his stories with seemingly pointless details. Julia always waited through them until he wandered back to his main point, which he sometimes never discovered. She suspected that sorting through the details helped to prod his mind along the right path to reach the pertinent information. "In any case, this was her first cookbook, and she read it like she might a holy book. I caught her studying it one night, just after we'd learned we'd inherited the bakery. We hadn't even made the decision to keep it yet. But I think your mum knew we would end up back in Chilton Crosse. So night after night, she would jot down notes in this cookbook, practically memorizing the recipes. She would sometimes experiment with ingredients in our little kitchen. She wanted to learn, all on her own, how to bake. No help from me." His gaze returned to the page. "Alton's favorite," he muttered. "I don't remember her making this, but I suppose she must have..."

"Well, that's my second surprise." Julia proudly clasped the fork and raised it. "Apple Tart. Just for you."

Her father closed the book and exchanged it for the fork. "When did you—"

"This morning, first thing. I was eager to have a go. I followed Mum's suggestions in the margins—adding more brown sugar and a hint more vanilla."

Her father moved his attention to the tray and sectioned off the corner of the tart with his fork then brought it to his mouth. He chewed and nodded. "Delicious! Your mum was spot on. Thank you, love." His eyes turned misty behind his glasses. "I wish she could be here now, your mother. It seems the longer I'm without her, the more I miss her."

Julia wished she could feel the same. But she never knew her mother. Rose Bentley died in childbirth, right after having Julia, the "surprise" child her parents had later in life. All Julia ever knew of her mum were her father's pictures and memories.

"I know, Dad. I wasn't trying to make you sad."

"On the contrary!" He moved one finger to the corner of his eye to wipe a tear. "Anytime I think of your mum, it's a good memory. Always good. Thank you for the tart."

Julia transitioned into caretaking mode. "Now don't forget this pink pill." She pointed to it on the tray. Yesterday, she'd found it on the floor beside his chair. "It's an important one. I'll be back to check on you in a moment. Is there anything else you need?"

"No, I'm set." He winked.

"I'll just put the book here." But before she could place it on his table, her father protested with a wave of his free hand.

"No, no. That book is yours. Your mum would want you to have it."

"Are you sure?"

"Julia Rose"—he sometimes called her by her middle name, her mum's name, when he wanted her full attention—"She would be delighted that you're using those recipes. Shame that they were tucked away for all these years. They were meant to be used. They were meant to be *yours*."

Julia tucked the book back under her arm, eager to try out more recipes her mother had tested all those years ago. *What a treasure.*

Half an hour later, after helping her father into his socks and shoes—he could still mostly dress himself, though sometimes his shirt buttons didn't match up—Julia helped ease her father into the front seat of her van. No sense in forcing him to walk the distance to the bakery, even though he insisted every single day that he could easily manage the journey. But her father got enough daily exercise when one of his mates, usually George Cartwright or Mac MacDonald, would offer to take him for a leisurely afternoon stroll along Storey Road. The village had a way of helping Julia look after her father without even being asked.

Julia pulled her van in front of the bakery's shop front, a charming honey-colored limestone that matched the rest of the shops, and helped her father out of the van. After a couple of grunts, he managed to straighten up and pat her arm.

They waddled over to the blue chair, where he sat most days to greet the customers and tourists. Eleven years ago, when he'd retired from the bakery and handed Julia the keys, he'd insisted on still being part of the shop's life. He couldn't possibly retire and stagnate in a cottage alone, day after day. This greeter job fit him—and the village—perfectly.

In colder seasons or wet weather, Julia moved her father's blue chair inside the bakery's front door, so he could continue his duties in a warm, dry place. But these mid-April days allowed her father to remain outdoors, so long as he wore a coat and hat.

Brandy met them, bringing out the usual plate of samples—bite-sized scones and teacakes—ready to be distributed to passers-by.

"All set?" Julia asked her father, handing him the plate then covering him up to the waist with a blanket she'd grabbed from the van.

He adjusted his cap with his free hand. "Ready for the day!" He turned on the charm for his first customer. "Hello there, young man," he told a little boy wandering up.

Julia left her father to it, parked the van behind the bakery, then entered the kitchen through the back door. Part Two of her day always involved baking more scones, her fastest sellers, and helping Miranda set up the lunch menu—creating the soup of the day and preparing the sandwich ingredients with the freshly baked bread from the morning shift.

Miranda, a round-faced woman in her early fifties, was a model employee—never complained, never got in Julia's way. She simply did her job cheerily and quietly in the corners of the kitchen. Half the time, Julia forgot Miranda was there, chopping, stirring, assembling, plating, and generally minding her own business. Julia knew next to nothing about Miranda's personal life, only that she was married with one child. Julia had attempted small talk a few times over the years, but Miranda always politely evaded the chitchat, so at some point, Julia had stopped trying.

This morning, Miranda was absent from the kitchen, but evidence of her labor remained: an enormous pot of potato soup simmering on the stove and the makings of sandwiches in a pile on the countertop. Likely, Miranda was helping Brandy out at the counter, something she often did during busy surges.

Julia set down her bag and peeked through the circle window on the swinging door that separated her cave—the kitchen—from the rest of the bakery.

In an almost-full house, with only a couple of empty tables, she recognized several of the customers. Holly Newbury and Mary Cartwright waited in line at the counter. Noelle and Adam Spencer sat with their new baby boy at a far table. Julia watched the baby giggle at a funny face his father made. Even Mac had stopped in for a coffee this morning.

Julia geared up to make more scones but remembered to take a couple of aspirin first. The beginnings of a headache could sometimes transform into a full-blown migraine if she wasn't careful. But before Julia could reach for her bag, she heard a knock at the swinging door. She peered at the window and didn't see a head or even the top of a head. *Must be Brandy, needing something.*

Julia called, "Come in," as she rifled through her bag.

Mrs. Pickering stood in the doorway, her foot holding the swinging door in place.

Julia abandoned the aspirin. "Oh. Hello."

Mrs. Pickering owned the grocers five shops down. She, more than anyone, had her fingertips firmly on the pulse of the village. *Too firmly, sometimes.* Mrs. Pickering knew everything about everyone, and over the years, people had learned that the best—or worst!—way to spread any sort of news about the village was to inform Mrs. Pickering about it first. Julia's own dealings with her over the years had been thankfully sparse. After she'd overheard Mrs. Pickering speculating and making judgments about Julia's single status years ago, Julia only made trips to the grocers when absolutely necessary.

"May I?" Mrs. Pickering pointed to a corner chair, dusty from disuse.

Embarrassed, Julia snatched a dishtowel and did a quick wipe of the seat. "Certainly."

Julia folded the towel and found her stool, wondering what this was all about and how long it would take. She had work to do.

"I've had a—what do you call it?—a brainstorm." Mrs. Pickering clasped her hands together on top of her beige skirt. Her long nose and deep-set eyes contributed to a "beady" look that complemented her nosey tendencies. "It's been brewing for a while now, this brainstorm. As you're probably aware, the bakery's anniversary is coming up."

Yes, Julia was aware. Forty years ago in June, her father reopened his family's bakery, all on his own, with an infant daughter in tow. She knew the story very well.

"And I was thinking," Mrs. Pickering continued, "that perhaps we should commemorate the occasion. The whole village, I mean. Put on a celebration."

The first question Julia had, that was too rude to voice aloud, was *Why*? Mrs. Pickering had no particular ties to the bakery and rarely visited it. She also had no special connection to Julia or Julia's father beyond occasional, polite chitchat. Why would *she* want to initiate an anniversary celebration?

And then it hit her. Julia remembered that, for the first time in years, Chilton Crosse had no festival or celebration going on. Since the Dickens Christmas Festival nearly five months ago, no other celebrations—that Julia knew of, at least—had been set into this year's village calendar. So perhaps, a bakery anniversary was Mrs. Pickering's way of creating one from thin air. She was always at the helm of social, church, and festival committees. Things were making perfect sense now.

"Well, Mrs. Pickering. It's a lovely thought, but we really don't need to do anything elaborate—"

"This bakery has been a staple in the village for decades. We *need* to celebrate it. Trust me. It will be simple but elegant. And I know your father would enjoy the festivities. We should all be celebrating *him*."

She'd actually done it. Mrs. Pickering had played the father card. To say no to this idea, even to hesitate, would officially make Julia a bad daughter, make it look as though she were standing directly, knowingly, in the way of her father's happiness.

Julia tightened her grip on the dishtowel and took a deep breath.

"I've already jotted down some ideas." Mrs. Pickering produced a folded paper from her bag. "A committee would be formed, of course. That's the only way to get anything done in this village."

"Of course." Julia gritted her teeth.

"We could have a lovely banner made up for the front of the bakery. *Fortieth Anniversary!* My nephew could help with that. He's good at that sort of thing."

"Your nephew?"

Mrs. Pickering's eyes sparkled. "Yes. He's here in the village for an extended visit. I'm surprised you haven't met yet. But then, you're stuck back here in this kitchen all hours of the day and night." She clucked. "Tristan—that's his name—arrived last week. He's a remarkable young man, an enormous help to me, working around the shop. I'm delighted to have him here."

"I'm sure." Julia nodded.

Mrs. Pickering peered down at her list again, in committee-chairman mode. "Now. We could have music and, of course, food."

And who *will be making the food?* Julia saw herself slaving away, producing enormous volumes of treats and refreshments straight from the bakery's kitchen.

"Villagers could even bring a small token, a gift, for your father. That would be optional, though..."

Before Mrs. Pickering could continue, Julia gently interrupted. "It *is* a lovely idea, but I'll have to give this some thought. I'm just not sure whether—"

"Oh, but think of your father. Imagine the expression on his face when he realizes the whole village is celebrating *his* accomplishment. In fact, I think it's a good idea to keep it from him."

"What do you mean?"

"A surprise celebration! We could hold it all under wraps, keep it quiet, and do all the preparation and decorating behind the scenes. That's why I need your help and input to pull this off. Mr. Bentley won't know a thing about it until that very day."

It was pointless to resist. Mrs. Pickering had a spectacular talent for making it impossible for anyone to say no to her. She would nag and argue and convince and badger until she wore down her opponent. And at this moment, with her work day ticking away, Julia felt weak enough to say yes. Sometimes, it was easier to let Mrs. Pickering have her way.

And if Julia *did* actually picture her father's delighted face upon seeing a surprise celebration, she had no other answer than...

"Okay. I'm in."

"Wonderful! I thought it might be a harder sell than this." Mrs. Pickering's mouth pinched into a self-satisfied smile. She folded the paper and stood. "We can get together and discuss more details. Tomorrow, maybe?"

"Perhaps. I can let you know in the morning."

Julia realized one side effect of saying yes was being forced to spend more time with Mrs. Pickering. *This is for Dad.* It would have to become her mantra in order to survive the next two months. When Mrs. Pickering left through the swinging door, Julia reached for the aspirin.

Chapter Two

"Distractions will interfere as you bake. Phones will ring. People will interrupt. Dogs will bark. Welcome the distractions. There are more important things in life than sugar and flour."

THE ANNOYING JINGLE OF HER mobile phone woke Julia from a deep sleep and a weird dream, something to do with a giant spatula and a man with glowing, purple eyes.

"Hello?" she croaked into the mobile, half her face buried in her pillow.

"Um, hey, boss..."

She recognized the hesitant voice. "Hi, Brandy. What is it?"

"Miss Newbury is here to see you. I showed her to your office. I hope that was okay."

"Holly?" Julia ticked through the short list of reasons Holly would be in her office and then remembered. "Four o'clock appointment." She groaned, opening her eyes to see the clock on the dresser. *Quarter past four.*

With a gust of forced energy, Julia raised herself up. The meeting about Holly's upcoming wedding had been on the calendar for two weeks. "I'm on my way. Please give her a coffee or tea. And my apologies."

"Will do, boss."

They hung up, and Julia took a few seconds to consider her circumstances. She remembered driving her father to the cottage three hours ago, giving him a snack and his midafternoon meds, then settling him in to read the Louis L'Amour book she'd bought online. Then she'd finally gobbled down a quick sandwich, put some clothes in the wash, and... fallen promptly asleep.

She rose from the bed with a wobble and looked down at her attire. For the wash, she'd put in *all* her blouses and tops and borrowed a huge flannel shirt, a loud red-and-blue tartan from the stack of her dad's fresh laundry, with every intention of moving her garments from washer to dryer *before* her nap. But she must've forgotten. Aside from sopping-wet clothes, flannel was all she had.

Julia kicked into gear as she pictured Holly waiting at the bakery's office, tapping her foot against the desk with each passing moment. She went to transfer the clothes to the dryer and check on her father—sound asleep, with the western splayed out on his rising and falling chest.

She gently removed the book, keeping his place, and set it on his table. She would let him sleep through the afternoon, as she sometimes did. He could ring her if he needed something in the next couple of hours.

With no time for any sort of freshening up, Julia grabbed her bag and keys and sneaked out of the cottage. Along the path to the bakery, she tucked her unruly hair behind her ears while dodging the fat raindrops falling sporadically around her and wished she'd had time for at least a coffee. She sorted through the details of the upcoming meeting. Holly and Fletcher's wedding was set for late June. On the phone for the initial conversation, Holly had mentioned a wedding cake, which would take up the bulk of today's meeting—showing Holly a folder with laminated pictures of cakes Julia had created in the past few years, discussing various flavors and icings and decorations. Simple enough. Holly and Fletcher would have their reception at Joe's pub, so Joe would be providing the food for that.

Julia entered the back kitchen and passed through to the main bakery then rounded the corner of her tiny office and offered Holly a smile.

"So sorry I'm late." Julia settled into the chair behind her desk, a tight squeeze. "I'm still learning how to work the alarm on my mobile."

Holly returned the smile. "I know what you mean. And I forget to set it half the time, so I'm still using an old-fashioned alarm clock."

Julia felt particularly unkempt and frumpy, facing adorable Holly, perky and sweet, in her late twenties, wearing hoop earrings and a lovely blue jumper-skirt combination. And her hair was set in a perfect braid, not a single auburn strand out of place.

Julia noticed a steaming mug of hot coffee on her own side of the desk and made a mental note to thank Brandy. She took a sip and felt marginally better.

"Mildred says hello," Holly mentioned. "She wanted to come along today, but she and Dad are getting ready for their trip to Switzerland."

Holly's new stepmother, Mildred Newbury, was the woman who'd practically raised Julia in her toddling years. At the time, Julia's father had been consumed with the bakery and grief over his wife's death, and Mildred had stepped in, taking care of Julia when no one else could or would. Unmarried and living with her brother at the time, Mildred had adored Julia and not only babysat her but lovingly educated her. Julia still had fond memories of flipping through books, skipping stones at the bridge, taking walks in the woods, and catching butterflies with Mildred. When Julia was in school, she saw less of Mildred, and as an adult, time and responsibilities had continued to nudge them further apart. But Mildred would always hold a unique place in Julia's childhood.

"Tell her hello for me. I miss seeing her. We need to have lunch—maybe after her trip."

Julia pulled the thick folder of wedding cake pictures from a nearby bookshelf and got down to business. She explained the vast choices Holly would have for her cake, told her this was just an initial meeting, that nothing needed to be decided today, and that she could even change her mind up until two weeks before the wedding.

Holly pointed and nodded at certain pictures, held her gaze longer over others, and tilted her head as she imagined *this cake* or *that cake* as her own. It was the process Julia had observed dozens of times, brides selecting the perfect cake. Julia's role was to finish her coffee and be patient, give the customer space and time, and answer occasional questions.

As Holly flipped through the pages, Julia let her mind wander. The one and only time she'd been a bride, Julia wasn't offered the opportunity to pick out a wedding cake. At twenty-two, she'd thought it was romantic and impetuous to elope. Actually, the elopement was her ex-husband's idea, so she never *had* a wedding dress, a cake, or loved ones cheering her on. Instead, she and Braeden had a quick ceremony at the registry office on a Wednesday night and celebrated afterward at a London pub, splitting a mediocre raspberry cake. Looking back, it hadn't been very romantic at all.

Soon, Holly made up her mind on a two-tiered buttercream with multicolored floral décor. As Julia jotted down her selection, Holly tapped her mobile.

"Is it almost five? I'd better return to the bookshop." She scooted her chair back and beamed. "I'm excited about the cake. It's going to be beautiful, thank you. And… this probably sounds a little barmy, but locking in this choice—of the right cake—helps make the wedding seem more real."

"Not barmy at all. Selecting the right cake is an important step in the process. I'm glad you're happy."

They parted with a friendly wave and a plan to follow up in a couple of weeks.

Julia poured a second cup of coffee from behind the counter. She glanced at the main floor, saw that Brandy had the late-afternoon crowd under control, then slipped away to the kitchen. Miranda had left for the day, so Julia had the cave all to herself. She rolled her hair up into a messy bun, pushed Play on her antiquated CD player to hear her guilty-pleasures album—ABBA's Greatest Hits—then washed her hands and located her granny glasses. Last night, Julia had earmarked more recipes from her mother's book and wanted to try out a new orange cranberry scone recipe. As she always did, Julia laid out the ingredients beforehand on the large stainless-steel island in the middle of the kitchen: flour, caster sugar, dried cranberries, one orange, yogurt, butter, eggs, milk.

To Julia, baking had become as simple and natural as breathing in and out. She'd known it all her life. The process was comfortable, safe, easy. But there were still moments that gave her great pleasure, still tickled her senses, such as the rubbery feel of a bright raspberry rolled between her thumb and fingers before placing it atop a tart, the snowy dusting of icing sugar sifted onto a finished sponge cake, the smooth, shiny ribbons that flowed from a mixture of cupcake batter as she filled the baking tins, or the predictable rhythm of whisking heavy cream in a copper bowl. Her favorite aspect of baking, though, was the intoxicating scent that wafted from the ovens at a certain point in the baking process as the concoction bubbled to perfection.

As she measured out the flour, hoping this recipe would turn out as pretty as the picture in her mother's book, Julia's favorite ABBA tune came on. She sang along and moved her hips to "Dancing Queen."

From the corner of her eye, Julia noticed a dark shadow. She craned her neck and saw a man standing in the back doorway. Had she forgotten to lock the door? Gasping, she swiveled around to face him and, in the process, knocked over her measuring jug, filled to the brim with flour. Thankfully plastic, it landed with a *clop* and dusted the entire floor as well as her trousers.

"I'm sorry," the man said above the disco music, his hands raised. "I didn't mean to startle you. I knocked, but there wasn't an answer, so I turned the knob."

Before Julia could coax her thumping heartbeat down to a normal rhythm and figure out who this stranger was, he'd already bent down and began scooping the flour into one big pile with his hands, dusting his own trouser legs with the cloud of flour. All she could see of him was the top of his brown wavy-haired head.

His cupped hands were large enough to make a lot of progress in just a few seconds. Julia leaned over to shut off ABBA then found the broom in the corner.

"Here, this will help."

He patted his hands together to remove the excess flour from his palms before he stood. Julia busied herself by sweeping up the giant mound of flour he'd created. She got most of it into the dustpan in a couple of passes, knowing she could go over it later with a damp cloth.

Still a little out of breath, partly from the unexpected bit of exercise and partly from being startled, Julia set the broom and dustpan aside and glanced at the man. Mid-thirties, six feet tall, wearing a navy zippered jacket with khaki trousers. She noticed he had a light beard that framed his face perfectly—not one of those patchy beards that looked scruffy and haphazard. Julia's gaze lingered the longest on his eyes: chocolate-brown and warm. Kind eyes, knowing eyes.

She'd never seen this man around the village or in the bakery before. She had a gift for remembering faces, and this was one she surely would have recalled.

"Sorry again." He grimaced, glancing down at her shirt.

Julia realized, horrified, that the bottom half of her father's completely unflattering, utterly unattractive tartan flannel shirt was covered in flour dust. Even worse, she still wore her granny glasses with her hair in a messy bun. She promptly removed the glasses and hung them at her neck.

"It's fine. Easily fixed. At least it was flour and not the eggs I was about to pour in." She thought her joke had fallen flat until he chuckled under his breath.

"Speaking of eggs…" He smiled through his beard. "I nearly forgot why I'm here. I've taken over Hamish's duties for a while."

"What happened to him?"

Hamish was the university student who worked on Mr. Elton's farm. For the past several months, he'd been the one delivering fresh eggs to the back door of the bakery a couple of times a week.

"He broke his leg in three places. Something about jumping out of a barn window into a haystack. Not the brightest move, I guess."

"I suppose not." Julia snickered. "Poor guy."

"You might know my aunt. Elda Pickering."

Julia stared at him with wide eyes. "*You're* Tristan?"

Somehow, she had pictured Mrs. Pickering's nephew as a goofy, geeky, lanky boy with buckteeth, a pointy nose, and an obnoxious snort for a laugh. The last thing Julia had expected was this strapping, good-looking man standing before her. How was it even possible they shared the same genes?

"Tristan Hannigan. And you're Julia? That's what Hamish told me."

"Yes. Julia Bentley." She didn't know why, but she offered to shake his hand as though this were a job interview. By the time she realized what an odd, formal gesture it was, especially while covered in flour, it was too late. But Tristan played along and took her hand in a warm, strong grasp. Every little thing about the situation should've made Julia want to cringe and run away in horror. But something in Tristan's eyes—that same kindness—put her at ease, made her feel accepted no matter *how* frumpy she felt.

"It's lovely to meet you, Julia Bentley."

She released his hand and remembered she had scones to bake and customers to feed.

"Well," he said, probably sensing the shift in the atmosphere, "I've got these trays of eggs in the van." He pointed toward the door. "Guess I should get to them."

"I'll show you where they belong."

He disappeared through the back door while Julia made sure she had enough shelf space. After a couple of quick adjustments of items, she turned to see Tristan, jacket removed and taut muscles showing underneath his Rolling Stones T-shirt. He carried both egg trays, each holding two dozen eggs. Hamish usually had to make two trips.

"Over here." She pointed to the cupboard shelves.

With a quiet grunt, Tristan gingerly placed the trays where they belonged. She noticed a tattoo on his left forearm and couldn't help taking a peek. The tattoo was solid black, in the shape of perhaps a bird, but it was hard to tell at this angle. She wondered if it was his only tattoo or if he was one of those guys with ink all over his arms and chest, hidden beneath his clothing.

"What were you making when I interrupted?" He stepped toward the island, set out with bowls and spoons and measuring jugs.

"Orange cranberry scones."

"Mmm. Sounds good."

"I'm hoping so. It's a new recipe."

"If they're anything like the blueberry scones, they'll be amazing."

"You've tasted my scones?"

Tristan leaned against the island, relaxed, as though he intended to stay awhile. "The elderly man outside handed me a sample the other day. I hadn't planned on coming inside, but the sample was scrumptious. I'm a sucker for fresh blueberries. So I popped in for a half dozen."

"That's my father, the elderly man. He's sort of a mini-celebrity around here."

"He's a friendly sort of chap. We chatted for a bit before the next customer came along."

"Yeah, he's our village greeter."

After an awkward pause, Tristan stepped away from the island and clapped his hands together. "Guess I should go. More deliveries to make."

"Okay. Well. Thanks for dropping those by. The eggs, I mean."

"I'll see you around." He backed toward the door. "Or here again. Next delivery."

"Yep, here's where I am most days."

He waved, and Julia watched him go. She washed her hands then returned to her scones, forcing her mind to switch back to the task at hand. But as she measured out more flour and reread the recipe, she knew her mind was elsewhere. And it probably would stay there for the rest of the day.

Mrs. Pickering rang Julia's mobile at seven, just as she'd flicked off the bakery lights. The day had taken its toll, as it always did, and Julia looked forward to a hot bath and a good book.

"Julia! Good, I caught you. I was wondering if you might pop round to my shop this evening to pick up some notes."

Julia wished she'd had the good sense not to answer the call. "Notes?" She locked the back door with her free hand.

"I've done more brainstorming since our chat yesterday about the fortieth anniversary party..." Mrs. Pickering whispered this last part into the phone, as though the entire world were eavesdropping. "I've added a list of possible committee members and party details, and I wanted to get your input."

"Well, that sounds lovely," Julia lied. "Could I pick them up tomorrow, maybe? I was about to head home for the night. Or could you email them to me?"

"I don't know how to do that, dear. I don't even have an email account. This modern technology baffles me. I did need your opinion on a couple of things before moving forward." She sighed into the phone. "But I suppose they could wait another day..."

The idea of this "quick" meeting hanging over her until tomorrow was so unappealing that Julia told her, "No, no. Tonight is fine. Let me just go see to my dad first, and then I'll head your way."

"Perfect! I'll see you soon."

Julia clicked off and kissed her hot bath goodbye, at least for another hour or so.

In hindsight, Julia was grateful for the excuse to check on her father. It gave her a chance to change out of the floured flannel shirt she'd worn all afternoon into a freshly laundered blouse. At the mirror, she even combed out her hair and dabbed on a bit of lip-gloss to feel human again. She told herself it had nothing to do with the possibility that she would run into a certain nephew of Mrs. Pickering's.

Mrs. Pickering's office was even more compact than Julia's. It required squeezing into the chair facing a desk with no room to scoot back without hitting the wall. Mrs. Pickering passed three pages of notes across to her.

"These are yours. I've made copies."

Julia could only imagine how many notes she'd be receiving by the end of this if these three pages were only the brainstorming part. Dutifully, she skimmed the handwritten pages and noticed possible dates jotted down, committee members, meeting times (*weekly?*), and decoration and food ideas. Julia didn't know why Mrs. Pickering hadn't just made this a one-woman committee. She would control all the decisions in the end, anyway.

A quick knock at the doorframe drew Julia's attention away from the notes.

"Aunt Elda, where did you want the..." Tristan stood in the doorway and paused when he saw Julia. "Oh. Hi again. Sorry. I didn't know my aunt had company."

"You've met?" Mrs. Pickering asked.

Tristan nodded, keeping his gaze on Julia as he spoke. "Yes. I made a rather grand entrance at the bakery, delivering the eggs. Did your floor recover from the flour?"

"I think it'll survive. Thanks for asking."

"Flour?" Mrs. Pickering looked positively bumfuzzled, and Tristan seemed to be enjoying it.

"Just a little accident, no worries. Well, I'll let you get back to your meeting." For the first time since he'd arrived, Tristan transferred his gaze over to his aunt. "Where would you like that new shipment of crisps? On the shelf or in storage?"

"Check the quantities on the shelves first. I think we have enough there for now. Thank you, dear."

"Cheers." Tristan gave a wave to Julia, along with a grin, and disappeared.

"He's a special boy," Mrs. Pickering said, though Julia hardly thought of him as a boy.

"I know you're glad to have him in town. How long will he be staying?"

"Through the summer, at least. But I'll be twisting his arm to see that he stays longer than that. Now, where were we? Why don't we begin on page one?"

Julia sighed under her breath, her hopes for a brief meeting dwindling as she shuffled the pages to find the first one.

Chapter Three

"People tend to judge things by their outward appearances. That's human nature. But as bakers, we can surprise people. The frosting on a cake doesn't always have to be fancy or colorful or pristine. The drizzle on a scone doesn't have to be perfect. Sometimes, the most delicious treat in the world is ordinary looking on the outside. But it's the inside that matters most."

JULIA WAS *DETERMINED* TO MAKE this day like any other day, nothing special, nothing to celebrate. No parties or cards or presents—no acknowledgment of a fortieth birthday, just work, as usual. So far, the day had cooperated. She'd arisen before four a.m., walked the pitch-dark path to the bakery, and prepared for the day. She hadn't seen anyone the whole morning except Brandy, who had no idea it was her boss's birthday.

At ten, as usual, Julia walked the path back to the cottage to retrieve her father. But as she got closer, she realized she didn't hear the clarinet streaming from his bedroom window. Perhaps he'd just slept in. Her father had seemed noticeably lethargic the past couple of days. Julia was relieved that he had an appointment tomorrow with Dr. Andrews for a routine checkup and blood work. Maybe his meds needed adjusting.

Opening the cottage's front door, Julia smelled smoke! She heard some clanking in the kitchen and rushed in that direction. As she entered, the smoke alarm began to bleat incessantly. Her father stood at the kitchen counter, holding his hands over his ears and staring at the root cause of the smoke—two burnt pieces of toast, still smoldering.

"Dad, are you okay?" She rushed to the toaster to yank out the slices with the tips of her fingers.

He removed his hands from his ears. "What?"

"Are you okay?" She brought her face close to his.

"Yes, yes. Though I can't say the same for the toast."

Julia found a chair to stand on to silence the alarm. It took a couple of pushes of the button, but finally, mercifully, the bleating subsided. She stepped down and reached for her father, holding his arms to guide him to the chair. She sat across from him, leaning in, out of breath, touching his knee.

"Dad, what happened? Why were you making toast? You know I'll make it for you. I always do."

He shrugged and looked down at the floor like a scolded child. "I'm sorry, love. I was making you a birthday breakfast."

Julia followed his gaze to the table, set with empty plates and a single rose placed in a slender vase alongside a card labeled, "For Julia," in her father's chicken-scratch handwriting.

She fought the sting of tears and rose from her seat to hunch over him in a gentle-but-firm hug. "Oh, Dad. Thank you. It's lovely."

"But it's all *burned*," he mumbled into her shoulder.

She backed away and made eye contact, offering a bright smile. "No worries! I can make us some toast in a snap! Plus, look what I brought." She pointed to the white box she'd hastily tossed onto the counter when she'd first entered the kitchen. "Apple muffins. One for each of us."

His thin lips relaxed into a smile. "Happy birthday, my Julia."

"Thank you, Dad."

So that his thoughts would no longer linger on the burnt toast, she got right to work doing damage control. She chucked out the toast, sprayed some air freshener to remove the smoky odor, retrieved two plates for the muffins, and put the kettle on for tea. Minutes later, they had a small birthday feast.

"Open your card," he insisted between bites.

She swallowed her sip of tea and fumbled for her glasses, hanging at her neckline. The front of the card read: *Today is the day to celebrate THE BEST daughter in the whole wide world. Happy Birthday!* When she opened it, a paper cake and balloons popped up from the center of the card. She folded it back together and held the card to her chest. "It's precious."

More than anything, she was grateful that her father hadn't sought a card which plastered the number forty all over it, screaming at her a reminder of precisely how many years she'd been on the planet. Of course, it was highly likely her father didn't remember *which* exact birthday of hers this was. But that was entirely fine with her.

She recalled last year, when they celebrated his ninetieth birthday. After a small party given by his mates, Julia had tucked him in bed and asked him a question. "How old do you really feel today?" He'd squinted and considered his answer. "Well, this old body of mine feels ninety most days." He chuckled. "But my soul... well, that's another matter. I look down sometimes at these old, wrinkled hands, and they surprise me because, inside, I feel so much younger. But really, age doesn't matter in the scheme of things. It's just a number, marking time."

As they finished the birthday breakfast in silence and her father took his medications with strong gulps of water, Julia sensed the same rush of bittersweetness she always did on her birthday. It didn't only mark the day she was born. It also marked the day her mother died in childbirth. How could she ever be completely happy on the anniversary of her mother's death?

She knew her father felt a particular pinch of grief on this day each year, and yet, Julia never saw a single trace of sadness or wistfulness in his eyes, as though he'd selflessly promised himself long ago that he would never turn his daughter's birthday into a somber day. If he mourned, he did it in secret.

It was one of the million reasons she loved him.

Her father wasn't the only one to acknowledge Julia's birthday. Mildred Newbury, her second mum, took the time to stop by with a present before leaving for Switzerland. Julia had been absorbed with making rye bread later in the afternoon. Even with hundreds of doughs rolled out in the past several years, Julia still became rather hypnotized by the rhythm of kneading it. It took a moment before she heard the knocking at the cave's door—Brandy, letting her know Mildred was there.

Julia wiped her hands on a damp cloth and welcomed Mildred with a hug.

"It's been too long," Mildred said, her bright eyes squinting with a smile.

"I agree."

"We must get together for lunch or tea when Duncan and I return."

"What time do you leave on your trip?"

"We're headed to Gatwick now, in fact! Duncan's waiting for me in the car, but I insisted on popping 'round to give you this."

She handed Julia a medium-sized box wrapped in shiny gold paper.

"You remembered."

"Of course I remembered."

Julia removed the wrapping carefully and lifted the box's lid to discover a jewelry box, wooden and glossy.

"I know you don't wear jewelry, but perhaps you could use it for other things. Knickknacks, trinkets. I just had to get it.You'll see why." Julia twisted the knob on the side of the box. "That song from *The Sound of Music*. I remember how much you loved it as a little girl."

The memories were still vivid—Julia begging Mildred to rewind the video over and over again to hear "Do Re Mi" and "I Am Sixteen Going on Seventeen," but especially "My Favorite Things." She'd memorized every word of that song, and now, the lyrics played in her mind as she hummed along with the music box.

"It's beautiful. Thank you." Julia leaned in for another hug, careful not to get any flour on Mildred's pristine pale blue blazer. It was probably new, purchased for her trip.

"Well. You have a marvelous day." Mildred backed out of the hug and looked Julia square in the face. "Be good to yourself. You deserve it." Mildred was forever telling Julia not to work too hard, to take more frequent breaks. "You're a caretaker to that wonderful father of yours. You've made it look easy, but I know how draining it can be. Remember how I took care of my ailing brother all those years. The one thing I learned: You must take time for *yourself* to be at your best for him. Promise me. Step outside now and then, see the world, be good to yourself."

"I promise. I will." Julia had already begun trying, in small ways, to do just that—most recently, by attending the village's book club—but she still needed to work harder at finding time for herself. At *making* time.

When Mildred left, Julia took a sip of bottled water then lifted the rolling pin. Before she could refocus on her dough, she heard another knock at the swinging door.

"Come in!" she shouted over the bustle of bakery noise.

"Hi!" Abbey Newbury, Mildred's new stepdaughter and Holly's youngest sister, timidly walked through the door, bumping an empty basket against her thigh. Two months ago, Julia had hired her to deliver sandwiches and snacks around the village. Abbey was reliable and mature for her age and had lived her entire thirteen years in Chilton Crosse. She knew the residents and locations very well, so the job was a perfect fit.

"I just saw your stepmother," Julia mentioned. "They're off on their trip to Switzerland. Sounds exciting."

"Yes! They promised to take me with them the next time." Abbey's eyes sparkled with the possibility. "What's that?" She pointed to the music box, which still played.

"A gift from Mildred."

"I love that song." Abbey closed her eyes and swayed a little, mouthing the words. It seemed *all* little girls made a space somewhere in their childhoods for the Von Trapp family. Abbey opened her eyes when the music came to an abrupt halt. "Oh, I almost forgot. Mr. Butterfield placed another order for tomorrow. He wrote it down." She handed the basket over to Julia, along with a paper order and an envelope filled with several pounds.

"Thanks. Oh, and Brandy has your wages up front. Check with her before you leave."

"I'll be back tomorrow to pick up the new orders!"

Julia returned to the island, wishing she owned some sort of "I'm Baking. Do Not Disturb" sign. If she had another interruption, however well intentioned, her rye dough would dry out.

Those moments after the bakery closed at the end of a bustling day had been dubbed "the hour of calm" by Julia's father, years before. That hour contained the rare, quiet minutes when the bakery—filled with chatter and laughter and music and noise during business hours—was infused with a lovely, peaceful hush, and the usual closing-up duties began.

The busboy, Enzo, quietly cleared and cleaned tables. His dishwasher brother, Marco, clanked pans to prepare dishes and pots and pans for tomorrow. Brandy counted out the till while Julia looked over the day's receipts and glanced over Theresa's accounting.

Theresa had recently taken over as the bakery's bookkeeper. She had worked behind the counter for a couple of years then decided to pursue an accounting certificate. Last month, Julia had put her in charge of the bakery's accounts, payroll, and taxes. Previously, the paperwork had all fallen on Julia's shoulders. But it was nice having someone with fresh eyes, in house, to lift the burden. Not that Theresa was in house very often. She mostly worked from her cottage and sometimes took over Julia's office. But Julia rarely saw her these days, unless an issue arose.

Tonight, Julia's father sat in a corner, as he usually did, contentedly munching on a ham sandwich.

When Brandy finished her till duties, she collected her bag and coat and said goodbye.

"See you tomorrow," Julia called as Brandy shut the front door behind her.

She returned to her paperwork but glanced up again when she heard the bell jingle a second time. Brandy was heading toward the counter with someone, a man.

"He says he needs to see you," Brandy explained hesitantly to Julia as they approached. "I told him we were closed, but he says he has something for you. I thought it was okay to let him in..."

As he stepped closer, Julia recognized the man because of his eyes. It was Tristan, Mrs. Pickering's nephew. But there was something much different about him.

"Your beard," Julia said as he stopped across from her at the counter. "It's gone."

Tristan raised a hand to wipe his smooth chin. "Yeah, it gets too scratchy sometimes, so out comes the razor."

"How old are you?" The words shot out before Julia had a chance to censor them. Beardless, Tristan looked *years* younger than she'd first suspected (mid-thirties). "Oh. Sorry. Incredibly rude, asking a person's age."

Tristan grinned. He had perfect lips, not too thin, not too full. And Julia noticed a small cleft in his chin.

"Yeah, it's because of the beard. Or lack of. People tell me it adds a few years. I've never really thought about it. I just get lazy sometimes and don't shave." He shrugged. "I'm twenty-nine, to answer the question."

Julia tried to cover her shock.

Twenty-nine years old. Still in his twenties.

"But I'm turning thirty in August," he added quickly.

"And *I'll* be twenty-eight in May," Brandy chimed in, clearly ogling the dishy young man.

Feeling a weird social pressure to reveal her own age, as though it were her turn, Julia changed the subject instead. "You had something for me?"

"Oh. Yeah. From my aunt." Tristan stepped even closer and slid an envelope across the counter to Julia. "She said it was top secret," he whispered, leaning in. Their faces were inches apart. She got a faint whiff of his shaving cologne, spicy and intoxicating.

Julia cleared her throat then put her hand over the envelope, assuming it contained information regarding the bakery's anniversary. She glanced at her father, still in the far corner munching his sandwich. He couldn't tear his gaze away from the western he was reading.

"Okay, thanks," she told Tristan and backed away to slip the envelope discreetly into her bag.

"Can I get you a coffee?" Brandy offered Tristan, knowing there were strict rules about not serving customers after closing.

But the deed was done, so when Tristan tilted his head and said, "Well, if it's okay with the boss," Julia nodded politely.

"But be sure the door is locked," Julia suggested. "We don't want people thinking we give preferential treatment after hours."

"Even though we *do*." Brandy winked and went to do as she was told.

"I can see you're busy," Tristan acknowledged, eyeing Julia's paperwork. "I'll join your father for a bit, if that's okay."

"He'd love the company."

Brandy poured Tristan's cup and offered it with a smile and several blinks. Julia assumed she was trying to be cheeky, but it came across as though she'd just been poked in the eye with something sharp.

Tristan said, "Cheers," for the coffee and walked over to Alton's table. Julia could tell by his gestures that he was introducing himself then asking permission to sit. She watched her father wave him forward and close his book. A chat with a stranger was always good for her father. Although, knowing him, they might be there all night long.

Julia said goodbye to Brandy one more time as she left then attempted to return to her work. But between the lines of the ledger, Julia could only see Tristan's newly shaven face in her mind's eye.

Twenty-nine. Over a decade younger than Julia. An entirely different generation from her, in fact. One that played Pokémon, considered tattoos as body art, and had no idea what an eight-track was.

Since their first meeting yesterday morning, she hadn't had time to assess how she felt about Tristan, hadn't had time to analyze or absorb it. But her first impression of him had been strong. A stranger in town showing up at her back door, polite and self-effacing and kind—and rather dishy. His showing up at Mrs. Pickering's, being jovial and attentive… Julia had been instantly attracted to him.

But that was when she thought he was *thirty-five-or-so*, only a handful of years younger. But this? Eleven whole years between them? It seemed absurd, someone her age having even so much as a passing flirtation or fleeting attraction toward someone his age. And as she watched him laugh at something her father said, she couldn't help it. She saw Tristan differently than yesterday. Something *had* changed. And it was more than just the beard.

Crawling underneath the newly laundered sheets, Julia clicked off the nightstand lamp and brought the covers up close to her chin. She stared at the mosaic of moonlight reflected on the opposite wall and thought about her day. A monumental birthday. Forty. Lots of little surprises had presented themselves: her father's botched breakfast, Mildred's thoughtful gift, even Tristan's surprise appearance during closing.

Tristan.

She thought of other young people she knew. In fact, she was surrounded by them at her bakery. The brothers she employed as busboy and dishwasher, Enzo and Marco—all they seemed to care about were militant video games and a band called "Basement Jaxx," whom Julia had never heard of. And she'd often listened to them brag about women as one-night stands, conquests.

Brandy, also twenty-something, chatted during breaks on her mobile, mostly conversations involving Kim Kardashian and glitter nail polish—such completely different priorities than Julia at this stage of life.

Miranda and Theresa were the only employees even close to Julia in age. But Miranda was guarded and private, and Theresa's role in the bakery kept her off-site, offering fewer chances for Julia to find out what they might have in common.

Tristan. Twenty-nine.

Julia remembered herself at that age, newly divorced, feeling fractured and dismayed by her suddenly wide-open future. At twenty-nine, she hadn't been settled or content. She'd still pondered that restless, "What will my life become?" question. Also, her body was skinnier then, healthier. She missed that body sometimes. And thirty had still been over the horizon with so many possibilities before her. But the horizon of forty was an entirely different perspective. Nearly half her life was already lived.

She hadn't intended on letting depression seep in today. And until this moment, she'd done rather well keeping the maudlin musings at bay. Birthdays not only nudged a person to look backward but often to look hesitantly forward. Julia knew very well what her future looked like, what she would face in these coming years, in upcoming birthdays: her father's eventual passing, an empty cottage, the loneliness of the bakery walls, the temptation to shut herself away entirely.

But perhaps it was inevitable, marking forty with some level of sadness, wistfulness, regret, or anxiety. And surely it was natural, healthy, to examine one's life now and then. Sadly, Tristan, a bright new spot in her life, had triggered these musings.

Rolling over on her side with a deep sigh, Julia made a decision. She would leave Tristan to the young people, to the fawning Brandys of the world who could relate to him, who grew up knowing the same TV shows and video games. They would have plenty in common, plenty to discuss. Surely he would end up asking Brandy for a date, and surely, she would accept.

Julia wished them well. She would still have to conduct business with Tristan, of course, receive his egg deliveries and see him occasionally at Mrs. Pickering's. She could still be cordial, professional. But anything beyond that, anything that resembled serious interest or flirting, was completely out of the question.

Twenty-nine. And forty.

Whether Julia liked it or not, age did matter.

Chapter Four

"Never underestimate the power of chocolate to lift the spirits."

A DAY OFF FROM THE BAKERY was never really a day off. Julia usually spent Monday, the only day the bakery closed, catching up on paperwork, planning next week's menu, or visiting farmers markets for fresh produce in neighboring Cotswold villages. Plus, Monday mornings were book club mornings, and Monday evenings were her father's poker nights. They ended up nearly as full and busy as any regular workday.

Book club meetings forced Julia to get out into the village, to venture away from her cave, to interact with people outside of her role as the baker. Not that Julia had a great deal to contribute at these meetings—she mostly sat in the back row of chairs in Gertrude Middleton's cottage and nodded now and then as someone commented on a section of the current book. But she always showed up with treats in hand, scones or tarts or biscuits. And with each meeting, she knew the participants accepted her a little more. It showed up in warm smiles and nods, in genuine inquiries about the bakery or her father, and in gratitude for the snacks she brought.

Holly had started the book club last year when a film crew for the production of *Emma* arrived at the village. Since then, the club had made its way through *Pride and Prejudice* and *Little Women*. But this go-round, the selection was more modern. It was Mildred's idea to suggest *The Shell Seekers* by Rosamunde Pilcher, a Scottish author. Julia began the book on Saturday night and couldn't put it down. In fact, she was far past the "read the first two chapters" assignment by the time she arrived at Gertrude's this Monday morning, blueberry scones in hand.

Julia usually timed her arrival so that she wouldn't be late, but so that she also wouldn't be too early, in order to avoid several minutes of social chitchat. Mildred often arrived at the same time, and they used that small window to catch up. But Mildred was off on her trip with her new husband, and Julia was on her own.

Holly opened the door to greet her, and as Julia walked in, she saw many of the usual participants, among them, Mrs. Pickering, Lizzie Tupman (the pub owner's wife), Frank O'Neill (the art gallery curator and the only male who regularly attended the meetings), and Noelle Spencer, who'd brought her four-month-old son along. He slept soundly in his carrier, in spite of the noise and commotion.

Mary Cartwright, another regular, asked after Julia's father and commented on how delicious last week's teacakes were. Mary was soon pulled away by Mrs. Pickering, and Julia looked around to realize she was standing nearest to Gertrude, who was even less of a social butterfly than Julia. Somewhere in her eighties, Julia presumed, Gertrude Middleton was the crankiest woman in the village, but had softened a bit because of these very meetings, which took place in her cottage. Julia gave her a half smile and was about to have to approach her with the cursory "Good morning, Ms. Middleton. How are you enjoying the new book?" when, thankfully, Holly brought the meeting to order.

Julia found an empty seat and settled in.

"Before we start, I think there's some good news to share." Holly looked over at Lizzie and prompted her with a nod.

Lizzie ducked her head, but her grin grew wider. "Well, I might as well just say it. I'm pregnant!"

A burst of cheers and squeals echoed inside the small cottage's walls, and a couple of the ladies jumped from their seats to give hugs and congratulations. Julia didn't know what to do with herself, except to offer a warm smile in case anyone was looking in her direction, which they weren't. All eyes were on Lizzie.

"Joe and I have kept it a secret as long as we could. But you might've suspected by now." Lizzie clutched her stomach with both hands to produce a bump Julia hadn't noticed before. "We found out yesterday... We're having twins!"

More squeals and cheers erupted, and Julia almost wished she *had* arrived late to avoid the news. It wasn't that she wasn't happy for Joe and Lizzie. They were a genuinely adorable couple and desperately wanted children. She was happy that they were happy. But Julia didn't have much personal experience with children and never knew what to say to someone with Lizzie's sort of good news.

But mostly, this news tended to cast Julia as an instant outsider, "the one without children." That was especially poignant since Julia couldn't *have* any. Not that anyone would know that—not even her father was aware of the hysterectomy she'd been forced to have five years ago because of her endometriosis. Only Mildred, who'd driven her to the hospital in Bath, had known about that life-changing event.

Julia shifted in her seat and waited patiently for the congratulations to die down. Finally, it was back to business, and Holly started the book discussion.

When the meeting ended after a rousing exchange about Scotland and who had visited and who desperately wanted to, Julia made her way to the dining room to collect her bag and jacket. She paused beside the doorframe to fish out her mobile and make sure her father hadn't tried to ring her. He was on his own at the cottage this morning.

"Did you see her expression during Lizzie's announcement?" a voice asked in hushed tones from the other side of the wall. The voice, carrying through the open doorway, sounded very much like Mrs. Pickering's.

Julia glanced at her mobile—no calls—and kept listening.

"No, how did she react?" another voice asked, though Julia didn't recognize it.

"Poor dear," Mrs. Pickering clucked. "She seemed a wee bit shell-shocked. I mean, it's just one more young woman in the village having babies. Holly's marriage is coming soon, and Julia's making the cake, from what I hear. It's got to sting, getting older, watching her prospects dwindle away. She hasn't dated in... oh, at least a decade, I would think. You've got to feel quite sorry for someone like that..."

The other woman clucked, too, and Julia felt her face flush—with embarrassment or anger, she wasn't sure. Probably both. She wanted to leave, but her legs wouldn't let her. She stayed frozen in place, heart thumping.

"I hate saying it," Mrs. Pickering continued, "but she only has herself to blame, really. Holed up in that bakery, day and night, all alone. No social life to speak of. It's like she's stopped trying. She barely puts on makeup or does anything much to her hair..."

Before Julia could hear the inevitable word "pathetic" tacked on somewhere at the end, she caught sight of a door in the dining room that led to a back garden. Her escape.

Julia took the isolated road behind the busy shops and fumed all the way home. She strongly contemplated quitting the book club—no grand announcement, just quietly halting her attendance. The irony was she'd been rather proud of herself lately for getting out, for trying to be more social, only to be met with cruel words that two women assumed she would never hear.

But if she did quit, they would win—the Mrs. Pickerings of the world, the women casting judgment upon other women, not even knowing the other woman's mind or heart or even bothering to ask. Not even having shared a single conversation about marriage, children, or family.

It wasn't the first time Julia had overheard gossip concerning her life, her choices. People were mostly discreet or *thought* they were, but a few were bold enough to make judgments straight to Julia's face, disguising them as fake sincerity and concern, usually with a gentle pat on Julia's shoulder or a tilt of the head. These discussions usually began with bold inquiries about whether or not Julia was dating and ended with, "I just *know* the right man will come along for you someday. Don't give up hope." Or even, "I'm praying that you'll find the one soon. Don't lose faith."

Julia wasn't sure which was worse, the private gossip or the openly patronizing advice accompanied by an arm pat.

Not every villager shared Mrs. Pickering's views. Julia felt warmly accepted by women such as Mary and Holly and especially Mildred. They didn't judge her for what *they thought* her lifestyle should look like. She was safe with them, respected. They accepted her separately from her father—unlike many villagers, who saw Julia only as part of the long shadow he cast in the village. And because of their support, Julia could only hope she would find the courage to attend the next book club meeting, despite having to face Mrs. Pickering again.

"How many confirmed for tonight, Dad?"

"Eight, including myself. Plus you, if you're in!"

"I wish. But I've got some supply orders to look over."

It was the truth, but if she'd really wanted to play a hand or two, as she sometimes did at these weekly poker nights, Julia could have. The orders could wait. But she didn't want to play, not after the book club debacle. She'd been in a funk all day and couldn't shake it. She had let the gossip get to her. She'd let it seep into her bloodstream, into her thoughts, affecting the way she saw herself. She had almost started to believe the gossip was true.

So tonight, she would remain on the fringes of the poker game in the safety of her bakery, handing out some sandwiches and crisps and listening to the men talk rubbish and swap stories while she got busy with other things.

Her father had talked about hosting a regular poker game for years but never had the time until he retired. When he'd first suggested it to Julia, she was resistant, especially when the venue he had in mind was the bakery. *Too much work*, was her first thought. But eventually, she caved, and Monday nights became a regular game night. The number of players grew from three to ten as the village men used it as a wee break from their daily lives. Longtime friendships were formed over the shuffling of cards and betting of worthless tokens inside that bakery with the shades drawn and big band music playing through the speakers—her father's choice. He loved Artie Shaw, Benny Goodman, Tommy Dorsey. Last year, the vicar had even heard about the weekly game and asked to get in on the action. He was welcomed heartily.

Sometimes, Joe, the pub owner, could sneak away from his busy bar and play a round or two. When he did, he provided soup and ale, giving Julia a break from her refreshment duties. But he couldn't attend tonight, so Julia took over, putting sandwiches together and adding crisps to bowls spaced around the table.

In typical greeter fashion, her father was the one who insisted on opening the door to each secret knock—two quick raps, followed by a pause, followed by another two raps. The bakery remained officially closed, so the door had to be locked and unlocked each time to prevent tourists or uninvited guests from wandering in.

Earlier, Julia had squeezed tables together in the center of the main floor and added a tablecloth to prevent poker chips from falling between the slats. Eight chairs, sandwiches prepared, and they were ready to go.

The men filed in promptly at seven o'clock. Adam Spencer and Fletcher Hays arrived together, already in mid-conversation, soon followed by the vicar and Dr. Andrews, then George Cartwright, the postman. The last to arrive was Mac MacDonald, the village's gardener and handyman.

As they removed their jackets and took their seats, Julia whispered to her father, "I don't think anyone else is coming. Should I remove a chair?"

"No, let's give the last one a chance to arrive. He's just late."

Julia shrugged and distributed the sandwiches. The men begged her to sit and play the first hand with them, but she opted out. They decided to begin, not wait for the final player, and Julia settled at her post behind the counter. The order sheet suddenly seemed completely unappealing, so she drew out her Rosamunde Pilcher novel from beneath the counter and flipped to her bookmarked page.

The men ate sandwiches and exchanged banter then finally shuffled the deck. Well into the first hand, Julia heard the secret knock at the door. So that her father wouldn't be compelled to heave himself out of his seat and struggle to the door, she said, "I'll get it!"

She opened the door. Tristan stood on the other side, clean-shaven and neatly dressed in a black leather jacket and dark trousers. She hadn't seen him since his quick appearance to hand over Mrs. Pickering's notes to her a few days ago and hadn't expected to see him until tomorrow, during his routine delivery.

Julia's expression must have revealed her confusion because Tristan said, "I'm here for the game. Sorry I'm late. Got hung up at my aunt's."

"Oh. For poker night?" She wondered how he'd heard about it then remembered the jovial conversation he'd had with her father at the corner table. Her father had surely invited him.

Julia kicked into hostess mode. "Sure, come in."

She'd forgotten how tall Tristan was compared to her five-six frame. The top of her head came close to his shoulder. She shut the door behind him and locked it.

"I offered to bring something—food, wine, dessert—but your dad told me it was all covered."

"He was right." She smiled. "Everything's taken care of."

"*There* he is!" her father called out from across the room. "Join us, young man." He waved Tristan over and began the introductions as Tristan took his seat.

Julia made her way to the kitchen to remove Tristan's sandwich from the fridge and add some extra crisps to his plate. She hadn't known it was "his" sandwich when she made it half an hour ago. She tried to approach the poker table with stealth movements, as the second poker hand had just gotten underway and the room was hushed while the players assessed their cards, but Tristan looked up as she placed his sandwich and a coffee in front of him.

"Thanks," he whispered, his gaze lingering for a beat before he returned to his hand. He had the makings of a full house, she noticed.

Unexpectedly buoyed by his presence at the game, Julia decided to whip up a quick dessert—decadent chocolate brownies from scratch. Always a hit with the men.

An hour later, the players took a short break and devoured the brownies Julia set in the middle of their table. She'd sneaked a bite of her own before cutting into the warm pan oozing with melting chocolate. She always added half a bag of chocolate chips to the mix to make the brownies extra gooey. As much as she craved an entire slice, a small bite was all she could afford tonight if she wanted to keep off the five pounds she'd struggled so hard to lose last month. Her final goal was another ten, and only then might she *start* to be happy with her figure again.

As the boys ate and chattered, Julia returned to her novel, feeling serene. Her hostess duties mostly finished for the night, she could enter her book and visit Scotland in her mind. But as she cracked open the cover and found her place again, Tristan approached the counter with a brownie in his hand.

"These are incredible. What's the magic ingredient?"

Julia shook her head. "Top secret."

"C'mon, you can trust me." He took an enormous bite.

As she contemplated telling him, she studied his face and noticed something distinctive above his right eye—a two-inch scar that ended near his temple. She hadn't noticed it before. Julia wondered how he got the scar. *Perhaps a childhood accident, a tumble from a tall tree, a fall from a skateboard.*

Realizing she was staring, she blinked. "It's coffee, actually. In the brownies, I mean."

"Coffee?" He crinkled his eyebrows and raised the last bite of brownie to eye level, examining it as though he could actually see the coffee if he looked closely enough.

"Yeah, it brings out a stronger flavor in the chocolate."

Tristan shook his head. "Who comes up with that sort of thing, anyway? Like, did some chef just accidentally spill his coffee into a batch and say, 'Hey, I'll bake them anyway—they're delicious!'?"

Julia snickered. "That's probably *exactly* what happened. Most genius recipes are due to happy accidents rather than trial and error."

"You make it sound interesting."

"Naw, they're just brownies." Julia felt a blush rise to her cheeks and was glad when he changed the subject.

"I recognize that cover." He pointed at her book with one hand and polished off his brownie with the other.

Julia tilted it to the light, pondering how on earth he recognized the cover of a "women's fiction" novel. Then she remembered that Mrs. Pickering probably had it lying around the shop to read between customers.

"It's really good." She ticked the pages with her fingernail. "Most of it takes place in Cornwall. But the author actually lives in Scotland. I've never been to either place."

"My grandfather is Scottish. We used to visit him on holiday there when I was a boy. Beautiful country, Scotland. I'd like to go back someday—"

"Okay, lads! Time for a final hand!" Julia's father shouted with an enthusiastic clap from the poker table. He grinned as he counted up his poker chips. Her father always seemed at his most energetic during these games. He usually slept most of the day in preparation to be awake until ten p.m.

"Why don't you join us?" Tristan asked Julia. "Your father told me you play sometimes. He says you're really good."

"I don't know about that..."

She was about to turn down his offer, but suddenly, words on a page—even beautiful words creating beautiful pictures—didn't seem as interesting as cards, strategies, and interaction with people like Tristan. So she set the book down and pushed away from the counter. "Okay. Deal me in."

Tristan walked ahead of her and located an extra chair, squeezing it between his own and Mac's. The men welcomed her and gushed about the brownies—all gone, now, except for crumbs—and dealt her into the game. She enjoyed being part of these poker nights, feeling like one of the lads.

Her hand was questionable until she was dealt a deuce, and later, another deuce! She easily won the hand and enjoyed ribbing the men about it. But in the end, Mac won the whole night and received the prize. The person who won the previous week's game was required to bring a white elephant gift for the forthcoming week's winner. The prize was always something ridiculous, like an old, rusty hammer or pair of shabby, unwanted shoes, nothing useful or expensive. Tonight, Mac unwrapped his present from George—no doubt meticulously wrapped by his wife, Mary—to reveal a book of poetry with half the pages missing.

"I might actually use this," Mac joked in his thick Scottish accent. But as soon as he flipped the book's pages, another ten fell out, causing the men and Julia to chuckle and guffaw.

When the laughter died down, the players stretched and yawned as they pulled themselves up from the chairs. As they always did, they took a moment to help return the chairs and tables to their usual places for tomorrow.

On their way out, the men thanked Alton and Julia and gave various versions of, "See you next week."

Tristan was the last to leave, making a point to shake Alton's hand.

"I had a lovely time. Thank you for including me."

"Well, you're a member now," Julia's father replied. "You're welcome anytime. In fact, I fully expect to see you next week!"

Tristan turned to Julia, who held the door open for him. "Guess I'll see you tomorrow."

"Tomorrow?"

"I'm scheduled for an egg delivery. Promise not to startle you this time."

"Very thoughtful of you, thanks."

She caught a whiff of the cool April evening before shutting the door. She didn't spend enough time outdoors in the fresh, clean air, looking at nature. She made a mental note to change that.

"Such a nice young man." Her father lost his balance a little as he attempted to straighten a chair at one of the tables. The poker guys were helpful in moving them back, but they never got the chairs straight or even enough. Julia's lightning-fast reflexes helped catch him before he could topple backward.

"Dad, you know this is my job. Please, just sit for a moment. This won't take long."

He obeyed as she eased him into a chair.

"Now, what were you saying? About a nice young man?" She shuffled around the tables to wipe crumbs and straighten chairs as her father had taught her. She took great pride in the smaller details of the bakery: keeping the floors pristine, making sure the tables were uniform and neat. "It shows you care," he would always tell her.

"That Truman fellow."

"Tristan," Julia corrected.

"Is it Tristan?"

"Yes. He's Mrs. Pickering's nephew."

"Oh, yes, yes. I remember now. Nice fellow…"

Finished with the tables and chairs, she did a quick sweep-round with a broom. The men had been surprisingly neat tonight.

"What impresses you about him? Tristan."

Her father scratched his chin. "Has a good head on his shoulders. Sensible lad. Responsible."

"What makes you say that?" Julia paused her sweeping and watched her father search for his answer.

"Well, he's a military man. Royal Navy. Just like your old pop." He thumped his fist against his chest lightly, with pride.

"He is?" Julia was gobsmacked. She didn't take Tristan for a Navy man. He didn't have the regulation haircut, for one thing. She would've thought perhaps her father had confused Tristan with some other person, but she'd seen this confidence before. Her father's answer was sure.

"We discussed it the other night," he confirmed. "Swapped some stories."

Julia had seen her father do the majority of the talking that evening and had suspected *he* was the one telling most of the stories.

"Of course, my stories were from an entirely different age than his." He chuckled.

"Is Tristan on leave? Is that why he's here in Chilton Crosse?"

Probably due to the late hour and her father's tiredness, he had to cock his head to recall. "I don't think so. I don't remember." He rubbed his eyes.

"Let's get you home. It's late." Julia returned the broom to its spot behind the counter and found her keys and bag. "I'll bring the van 'round. You just sit tight. Promise?"

"Promise." He held his hand over his heart as his eyelids grew heavy.

She wondered how much longer they could have poker nights. They drained him so. But Julia knew he would never give them up. They were too important.

Chapter Five

"When two people share a cake or a treat, they share a moment. A connection is made, sometimes unexpectedly. Two forks, one dessert between them. We're not just baking treats. We're baking future memories."

JULIA STRAIGHTENED HER BACK AND realized how sore it was after ninety minutes of scrubbing and cleaning. But after all her work, the entire kitchenette was nearly finished, spic and span.

For the past few weeks, she'd devoted an hour here and there to clearing out the flat above the bakery. Today, it was the hour between the early-morning bakery prep and the opening. Over the weeks, Julia had dusted, emptied boxes, and chucked out all the rubbish. The space was beginning to take shape.

Not that she had any particular use in mind for it, except perhaps as a retreat for the occasional nap or a quick breather in between shifts. Once upon a time, the flat had served as her childhood playroom, a space where she could escape and play with her dolls or read Beatrix Potter while her father worked downstairs. But over the years, as she grew up and life became busy, the space became a cluttered storage area, a graveyard for unwanted books or knickknacks. While sorting things, Julia had discovered some treasures: her mother's recipe book, some beloved old toys, photos of her parents she'd never seen before, a couple of jackets and fedoras her father wore years ago. But most of the items were unusable, thick with dust, or not worth keeping at all.

Julia rubbed her lower back and crossed the room to stare out the window at the view behind the bakery. She thought she'd heard the plinking of rain on glass, and she was right. She craned her neck to see fat drops hitting the pavement below. She'd always loved the view from this window—miles and miles of rolling hills, sheep in pastures, stone walls segregating properties, a few cottages dotting the landscape. No tour busses or people bustling about, no commotion or activity. Just nature being nature, serene and peaceful under a muted gray sky.

One downside of the rain was that her father would have to stay inside the bakery today, handing out samples from his blue chair. He would balk, but the damp, chilly weather wasn't good for his lungs.

"I'm here!" Brandy called from below. *Is it already time?* Julia had lost track.

As she stepped down the narrow, treacherous staircase to the main floor, she heard the *ding* of the timer. The butterscotch bread pudding was ready.

Julia offered a quick good morning to Brandy at the foot of the stairs before heading through the swinging kitchen door to retrieve the sweet concoction. The luscious scent, heady and sugary, only grew stronger when she opened the oven door to a burst of lovely warm air. Julia left the bread pudding on a rack to cool and returned to Brandy, who was already arranging the trays of fresh scones and teacakes inside the counter's glass case.

"Been working upstairs? How's it coming along?"

"Slowly. But I'm making progress. Hard to do when it's raining outside. All I want to do is sleep."

Brandy looked up with an understanding nod. "It took me a grunt or two to get out of bed this morning, and an extra tap on the snooze button."

"Before I forget"—Julia snapped her fingers— "the lunch specials will be smoked ham sandwiches and vegetable soup." Brandy copied down the specials on the chalkboard each morning. Her handwriting was *much* clearer, much prettier than Julia's. She even dotted her *i*'s with little hearts.

"Got it. Oh, and today is Tristan's delivery day, isn't it?"

Interesting. Whenever Hamish had made deliveries, Brandy never paid attention.

Julia grinned. "Yes, I believe it is."

Brandy leaned in, her thickly lined blue eyes sparkling. "He's a bit of a dish, isn't he?"

Julia had no idea how to respond. Tristan worked for Julia. Well, sort of. It would be more than inappropriate for her to agree, even if she *did* happen to agree, on some basic human level.

"And did you notice the scar above his eye?" Brandy pointed to her own to demonstrate. "I think scars are sexy. They're so mysterious. He probably has some secret past..."

Julia tried to get things back on track. "Why don't you watch for Tristan and help him out with the delivery? I have to go and get my father anyway."

"I think I can handle that, no probs." Julia could imagine her primping furiously in anticipation of Tristan's arrival.

Later, in the early afternoon, when Julia was certain enough that the lunch crowd was taken care of and her father sat contentedly with a bowl of soup at his corner table, she sneaked away to the pub next door. The skies had broken wide with sunshine, and the only evidence of precipitation was the occasional puddle on the ground and a sweet lingering scent of rain.

Mrs. Pickering had rung her up an hour ago and insisted that Julia meet in person with Lizzie, the pub owner's wife, to discuss the banner for the fortieth anniversary party, even though their first committee meeting would be later this evening at the pub, and Julia could just as easily speak to Lizzie then. Rather than hand Mrs. Pickering the million reasons why tonight's meeting or even a phone call to Lizzie would suffice, Julia decided to give in and go to the pub. Sometimes, most times, that was the easier route with Mrs. Pickering. Just do whatever she asked.

Julia hadn't entered the pub in ages. She had missed its behemoth mahogany bar, comforting crackling fireplace, diamond-paned windows, and the buzz and chatter of people enjoying themselves by playing darts or cards or just having a pint. Julia didn't know how ravenous she was until the scent of shepherd's pie hit her senses when she opened the pub's door. She caught Lizzie's glance from across the room and waved.

"The bar?" Lizzie mouthed and pointed on her way to deliver a pint to a customer.

Julia nodded then made her way to a stool. The pub wasn't as active as it usually was—probably just a rare lull. Julia was familiar with lulls at the bakery, the waxing and waning. Some days, all the tables were filled without a place for everyone to sit, especially when the tourist buses came to town. Other days, only a handful of customers trickled in, and the pace was snail-like.

As she stretched up to sit on the high stool, Julia heard a cheer bursting from the other side of the bar. A darts game was going on, and she recognized both players: Fletcher (Holly's fiancé) and Tristan. They were oblivious to her, Fletcher patting Tristan on the back for a good toss. Then practically in synch, they reached down to take sips of their half-empty lagers.

That was when Tristan looked toward Julia and caught her eye. Before she could turn away, he tilted his head in recognition then raised a hand to wave. A beaming smile crossed his face.

She reciprocated with a shy wave, grateful when Fletcher handed Tristan more darts, pulling his attention back to the game.

"So!" Lizzie appeared from behind the bar. She had a way of doing that, appearing swiftly in front of people. She possessed a youthful energy that never seemed to slow down, even with pregnancy. Still in her late twenties, Lizzie had married Joe—at least ten years older—about three years ago. People in the village always regarded it as a good match because Lizzie brought lightness to Joe's more logical, sensible personality.

Julia was endlessly fascinated by the delicate, invisible force field that kept certain couples together forever—or that pulled them together in the first place. But Julia had no intention of diving in, experimenting with these Love Laws of the Universe. She enjoyed her role as observer too much. It was safer that way.

"I can't even remember why Mrs. Pickering asked us to meet," Lizzie confessed with an eye roll. "My brain is a little fuzzy these days." She was already doing that subconscious tic, that pregnant-mother thing of placing her hand on her stomach at certain times during any given conversation as though reminding herself about the little ones growing inside.

"She mentioned something about a banner?" Julia prompted.

"Oh! Right! She was very specific about what she wanted printed on it. I wrote it down." She fumbled around for a piece of paper buried inside her dress pocket and unfolded it. "'Celebrating Forty Years of Delicious Memories.'"

Although Julia despised the "forty" reminder again, she had to admit the sentiment was rather poetic. And her father would love it.

"I think there's a site online that sells quality banners, waterproof, specifically for shop fronts. I'll have Joe get the measurements for me, and we can decide on fonts and colors and the like..."

Raucous cheers came from the other side of the pub again, distracting Julia and Lizzie. Tristan and Fletcher must've ended another competitive game.

"Mrs. Pickering's nephew," Lizzie whispered to Julia. "He's rather fit, isn't he? That wavy hair and those perfect teeth... And did you see the scar above his right eye? Maybe he got into some brutal fight, defending the honor of a woman he loved."

Julia feigned offense with a half grin and raised her eyebrows. "Lizzie Tupman. You have quite the imagination. And you're a married woman. And soon-to-be mum of two!"

Unfazed, Lizzie stole another peek at Tristan. "Well, it does no harm to look, now does it? Married doesn't mean I'm dead." Her smile widened, and she and Julia probably seemed like a couple of snickering schoolgirls as Tristan glanced their way.

They wrapped up their meeting, and Lizzie offered to email banner examples to Julia. The order needed to be sent by next week for the banner to be created and shipped in time for the festivities.

"Oh, I wanted to order two shepherd's pies to go." Julia opened her bag to find her money.

"On the house." Lizzie patted the bar.

"No, no."

"That precious dad of yours hands out *how* many dozens of free samples per day? All year long? Let this be the pub's thank you. Besides, how many times do you bring refreshments to our book club without any compensation? It's high time someone did it for you." She winked and headed toward the back to collect the pies.

Julia's gaze wandered back to the darts game in time to see Fletcher head in the direction of the loo. Tristan took another swig of his lager, set it down, and walked toward Julia. She drew in a quick breath, her mind scurrying for something to say in the few seconds before he arrived.

"Hey." He stopped one stool away.

She swiveled to face him. "Hi."

He wasn't entirely clean-shaven this time—no beard but just a hint, a perfect shadow of stubble across his jaw. Of the three, it might have been Julia's favorite look. He wore dark jeans and a black knit shirt, which clung to his chest's perfect proportions. Not too muscular, not too skinny. *The body of a healthy twenty-nine-year-old.*

Julia could tell he wouldn't be staying long. Instead of taking a seat, he leaned on the bar with both hands. He was probably committed to a tie-breaking game upon Fletcher's return.

"How's your dad?"

"Doing well. He's happy the rain ended so he can resume his post outside."

Tristan grinned. "I'm glad the weather cooperated."

After a beat, Julia realized this was the most awkward she'd been with him since their first meeting. With Lizzie and Fletcher soon to reappear, Julia could practically hear the tick of an impatient clock, counting down the seconds until they weren't alone anymore.

"I was just about to take him back to the cottage for a nap—my father. I'll probably take one, too." She wasn't exactly sure why she added that last part.

"Early days, running a bakery, eh? I'll bet your work hours are all over the place. When do you start the day?"

"Four o'clock, usually."

"Blimey. Even the military doesn't arise until five."

Before Julia had a chance to expand on that, to segue into his naval experience and ask him more about it, Lizzie arrived with a large bag. "You're all set!" she proclaimed then paused as she placed it on the bar. "Oh. Hello," she told Tristan.

"Afternoon," he replied with a nod and a small salute. "I'll leave you both to it."

When he'd gone, Lizzie leaned in and mumbled through clenched teeth to Julia, "What was *that* all about?"

"Just shoptalk. Tristan makes deliveries to the bakery from Mr. Elton's farm."

Lizzie almost looked disappointed as she backed away. Had she hoped something clandestine was going on between Julia and Tristan? Something to gossip about or live vicariously through?

"Oh. Well, anyhow, here are the pies. Tell your dad hello from me and Joe."

"Will do. Thanks for the food! I'll see you again tonight."

"Tonight?" Lizzie frowned, confused.

"For the meeting! Right here, at your pub!"

"Oh, sure." Lizzie blinked hard and shook her head. "I'm so scatterbrained these days… must be all these hormones."

They said their goodbyes, and Julia purposely kept her eye on the door as she left, not turning to look Tristan's way, lest Lizzie was still watching. As she walked next door to the bakery to retrieve her father, Julia wondered why she'd had the compulsion to stretch the truth to Lizzie about her conversation with Tristan. It hadn't been all shoptalk, not really. Their conversations were never just shoptalk. They were filled with hints of other things, too, more personal things—about her father, about books, about Scotland. She only wished the conversations lasted a bit longer than a minute at a time.

Mrs. Pickering had actually brought her gavel with her. Julia had seen her use it in the big, boisterous committee meetings at the cavernous church hall when a gavel might actually be necessary to draw the attention of numerous chattering ladies. But here? Inside a cramped room at the back of the pub, where Joe had had to nudge chairs together to accommodate the seven ladies who'd arrived?

Mrs. Pickering tapped the gavel on the counter beside her, poised and waiting for the ladies to settle down and focus all their attention on her. She did a brief roll call, inserting a nod of her head with every present member as she checked off her list. "Holly." Nod. "Julia." Nod.

"Lizzie." *Pause, waiting for Lizzie to stop whispering to Holly*. Nod. And so forth.

Julia had half-expected Tristan to tag along at Mrs. Pickering's insistence and was surprised when he didn't appear. She pictured him stocking boxes in the back of Mrs. Pickering's shop then following an endless list of chores and duties she'd handed over before she left.

Mrs. Pickering clasped her hands together and welcomed the members to the first official meeting.

Julia's mind quickly zoned out as Mrs. Pickering delivered the same spiel she'd given last week when she'd first proposed the idea of the bakery's fortieth anniversary. Plus, she was still fuming on the inside about Mrs. Pickering's mean-spirited comments at the book club. Hard to reconcile this Mrs. Pickering—benevolently in charge of a committee planning a lovely surprise for Julia's father—with that other Mrs. Pickering.

Finally, the details got underway as Mrs. Pickering made the assignments. Lizzie was in charge of the banner. Mary and Holly were in charge of invitations with the strict understanding that it was all an enormous secret to be kept from Mr. Bentley, and the rest of the committee would work on decorations for the inside of the bakery, which would have to be put up the evening before. Special desserts would be created in individual cottages—Mrs. Pickering produced a sign-up sheet—and would be brought to the bakery on the day of celebration.

Julia's only job, thankfully, was to make sure her father would be out of the way until a very specific time, when people could be poised in their "surprise!" positions. Still, Mrs. Pickering had insisted that Julia attend all committee meetings in order to help finalize and approve the decisions.

Just before the meeting ended, Julia had a thought. "What about a cake?"

Mrs. Pickering looked baffled. "A cake?"

"An anniversary cake. I could make one."

"But, dear..." Mrs. Pickering's tone took on that of a schoolteacher talking to a child. "This is a party for you and your father. You shouldn't have to bake your own cake."

"It's no trouble," Julia insisted. "It could be a large sheet cake, all decorated. I know exactly what kind to make. It would be my contribution and my gift to my father."

"Well, when you put it that way..." Mrs. Pickering had nothing else to argue, and the other ladies seemed, by their nods, to agree heartily.

The final, and possibly most important, detail to finalize ended up being the date. A lively debate ensued, examining all the pros and cons about which day would suit the party best—a Monday, when the bakery was closed? But then Julia would have extra work, hosting everything on her day off. Another weekday, when the bakery was open? Fine, but there were still customers to serve, and they wouldn't want the party to interfere with the shop's regular business. Finally, Julia suggested a compromise—Sunday, always a half day for the bakery, opening at noon. But she could close the bakery for this special occasion. After the church service, Julia could come up with a cunning way for her father to linger behind while the committee members discreetly disappeared and convened at the bakery, waiting for the big moment.

"It's settled, then!" Mrs. Pickering said with a definitive nod. "I think we have ourselves the makings of a wonderful celebration." And with that, she pounded the gavel a final time, and the meeting was adjourned.

Later, at the cottage, Julia's father was already snoring softly. He'd told her that he would read a chapter and turn in early. Julia set down a half-full glass of water on his bedside table, tucked the covers around his bare arm, and clicked off the light.

Since she hadn't gotten a proper nap this afternoon, every limb in her body felt the weight of the day. But her mind was strangely sharp and alert. She milled about the kitchen for a while, cleaning crumbs, emptying the rubbish bin, and setting out her father's pills for the next morning. Then she brushed her teeth and changed into her pajamas but still found herself antsy. Tiptoeing back downstairs, she made a cup of Earl Grey, stoked the fire in the sitting room, and curled up with a fleece blanket on the sofa.

She stared into the fire and thought about the meeting. Julia had been flattered by the turnout, by people volunteering their time to help make the party a success. This village genuinely cared for her father, and through him, she knew, they cared about her. She'd made conscious efforts to become more involved in the village during the past year or so with the book club, with poker nights, and starting conversations rather than waiting for someone else to do it. Julia hoped, in time and all on her own, she might become as valuable to the villagers as her father was.

The meeting also brought to light something else for Julia—not only who had attended but who hadn't. Tristan. She'd spent the entire meeting actually swatting away the nagging idea that she wished he had come. She wished he had opened the door and sat down beside her—that he'd stayed around afterward for another fragment of conversation. Julia had begun to look forward to those ongoing fragments, piecing together more of him, more of who he was. She couldn't deny the internal smile it always produced, seeing him enter a room, knowing there was a likelihood he would approach her, start up a chat. She'd become used to it now, something to look forward to during her mundane routine.

Certainly, that was a huge part of his occupying her thoughts. Tristan brought a fresh excitement not just to her but to the entire village. He had cast a spell on almost every female in town. Julia had yet to run into one who wasn't enamored of him or didn't comment about him. He was the new kid, to be gawked over, talked about, analyzed. Surely, everyone's fascination with him had simply rubbed off onto Julia, that newness, that curiosity about a stranger.

It was contagious. That was all.

Satisfied, she finished off her tea and threw aside the blanket, feeling drowsy and ready for bed.

Julia gave the steaming tomato soup—Friday's soup of the day—another gentle, broad stir and left it to simmer. Miranda had been humming a show tune under her breath for the last few minutes while putting together sandwiches at the kitchen's island.

"That's it for the soup. I'll leave you to it, then." Julia reached for her bag.

"Have a good rest," Miranda replied, her focus still on the sandwiches.

Julia checked the time and realized it was early. She pushed through the cave's door to see that her father was happily settled outside. She saw him through the front window, still handing out his samples on this sunny day. Julia decided to take a quick detour before heading back to the cottage for a nap. A few mornings ago, she'd been interrupted by Brandy while cleaning the upstairs flat and remembered that a half-sorted box still remained on the coffee table. At the least, she could finish that up and discard the box, make a bit more progress on the room.

This was the fun sort of clearing out, the part where you could pause and linger on items you'd never seen before or hadn't seen in a long while, trekking down Memory Lane through photos or dusty knickknacks or bittersweet mementos. Upstairs, Julia set down her bag and stretched her hand into the box to shuffle through the items. If they were worthy of keeping, she'd take them back to the cottage with her to show her father. If not, she'd chuck them out.

Her fingertips grazed over a stack of books, some slender, some thick. She lifted them out and sat down on the sofa. Smiling, she saw pregnancy and baby books, lots of them, with dog-eared pages and notes scribbled inside margins by her mum. Julia assumed her father hadn't seen the books in at least forty years. She pictured him, all those years ago, grief-stricken, unable to bear chucking these books, so he'd placed them into a box, lifting it high onto the wardrobe's corner shelf to deal with later. He'd either forgotten about the books since or hadn't the heart to revisit them.

But here they lay, in Julia's lap. And it appeared that, just as she'd studied up on recipes for the bakery, her mum had studied up on how to *be* a mum for Julia's arrival. Julia flipped through the books and saw yellow highlights in certain chapters. She squinted to read the scattered margin notes—"Important!" "Remember this!" "Research this further"—and could practically feel her mother's anticipation and anxiety leap off the pages. The irony that her mother would never even get to hold her new child gripped Julia's heart in a way it hadn't before.

Setting the books aside, Julia held the final book in her hands, entitled *Words for My Daughter*.

Curious, Julia opened the cover and saw scribbling, not in her mother's handwriting: "For Rose, on the day of your baby shower. I know you'll have many insights and bits of wisdom to add to this book for your new daughter. Warmest regards, Mildred."

So her mother had made enough friends in the village to warrant a baby shower. And Mildred had been in attendance. Julia wondered who else had been there, where it had been held. Perhaps she could ask Mildred someday.

As Julia flipped through the book, it became obvious this was no how-to book like the others. This was a personal journal. Blank lines graced every page, sometimes with a prompt at the top, encouraging the mother-to-be to write down her deepest feelings. Julia scanned the pages briefly and saw that her mother had only filled out the first few pages. All the rest were empty lines.

Julia no longer cared about the bakery, a nap, or any other pressing matter that might've been important to her a minute ago. The journal was all that mattered. Julia put on her glasses and sat cross-legged as she returned to page one, where her mother had scribbled out a long message, an introduction of sorts.

"My Dearest Little One, I sit at the kitchen table writing this as you gently kick me from within. You're getting stronger each day. I feel it. Ready to meet the world.

"I can't wait to see you, to touch your smooth skin, to gaze into your tiny baby face. I wonder what features you might have of mine: cowlick at the brow, thin lips, thick eyelashes, petite fingers? Perhaps my stubbornness or my pathological need for structure and organization? Or maybe you'll have your father's crystal-blue eyes, his love for music, his natural joy. I hope you have his joy.

"I sit here and ponder who you'll become, what your career will be, who you will end up loving. I wonder what your life's journey will look like. Ultimately, my only wish for you, as I'm sure any mother's wish would be for her child, is health and happiness.

"But let me be honest. Life isn't always simple or easy. It's messy and confusing and heartbreaking at times. But it can also be very beautiful. I hope, every day of your life, you find the beauty, even in the midst of challenges. Search for it. Hold onto it. It will save you, give you hope.

"I don't know how much 'wisdom' I hope to impart in these pages. But I'll give it my best. I'll jot down life truths as I know them to be from my parents' experiences, from my own philosophies. Take them with a grain of salt, for each person's journey is their own. No one else can live this life for you. I only pray that it's a rich, precious, fulfilling life you lead. And I'll be honored to play some part in it.

"All my love and affection, Mum."

Tears splashed onto Julia's hands when she blinked, reading the last sentence again. Literally, some of her mother's very last words.

Her mother had no idea they would never meet, that the only words of wisdom she would ever impart to her child would be these, handwritten, on the page. If she *had* known, would she have worded anything differently? Did she have any idea how weighty this book would be, how important, how precious?

Julia wiped her cheeks and skimmed the next few pages. Her mother had written down bits of wisdom, some in paragraphs, some in phrases or quick sentences. Random and scattered topics, a stream-of-consciousness flow, in many cases. Some were practical bits—*Always take a sensible jacket with you wherever you go. Beige is always a safe color*—and some were poignant, deeper bits—*Don't ever be too stubborn to forgive someone. You might need it yourself someday.*

Julia imagined her mother jotting down the advice sporadically, as it came to her each new day, an ongoing conversation between mother and daughter.

"Knock, knock?" a voice said behind her.

Julia sucked in a breath and whipped her head around to see Tristan peeking through the cracked doorway. Jolted into reality, Julia removed her glasses then shut the book and lowered it back into her lap, attempting to force a smile.

"Oh, hi. Come in." She wiped beneath her eyes in case her tears had smudged her eyeliner.

Tristan walked around the sofa to face her then paused. "Oh. Sorry. You're clearly in the middle of something…" He'd obviously noticed her tearstained cheeks. "Brandy told me I could come on up. But I can come back later. I'm intruding."

Normally, under a circumstance such as this, caught off guard in her most vulnerable moment, Julia would have hidden her face, stood up to busy herself, and politely said something to the effect of, "Let me finish this, and I'll be right down," in her cheeriest fake voice.

But for some reason, she didn't really care whether Tristan saw the remnants of her tears. She was already vulnerable; her wall was down. And it would take too much effort and energy to erect it now. Julia didn't wish to wave Tristan away. She wished him to stay.

"You're not intruding," she said softly.

"Is everything all right?" His brown eyes filled with concern.

Julia nodded. "I just found something… unexpected." She stared down at the journal and rubbed the cover with her thumb. "Something amazing, actually."

Tristan came closer and moved the box to sit across from her. Their knees were almost touching. "During a clear-away? Those can produce the most remarkable tokens, can't they?"

"They can. This is my mum's." She tilted the cover toward him. "Well, it's mine now. She wrote it to me. She died when I was born. And she left me this. I didn't even know it existed until a few minutes ago. A journal, of sorts. To me. Her unborn baby."

"Blimey. What a treasure."

"It really is. Skimming through it, I just feel… if this makes any sense… equal parts happy and sad. Like, at the very same time."

"Yeah. It makes perfect sense to me."

Julia moved her gaze up to Tristan's eyes, and a softening in his expression told her he might've been through something similar. A great loss. It was a shared glance, an unspoken understanding.

Rather than elaborate on his statement, Tristan leaned forward and clasped Julia's hand—a kind, strong gesture between people who barely knew each other, who'd only ever held a few conversations together. But right now, Julia felt she *did* know Tristan. She could feel his pulse beating through his fingers. And her tears welled up again. She was so glad not to be alone in this moment.

"Thank you," she whispered.

He smiled, squeezed her hand, then released it.

Feeling immeasurably stronger, better, as though some of her burden had been supernaturally channeled to Tristan through his grasp, Julia wiped her tears again.

"You never said. What did you need from me?"

"Nothing urgent," Tristan said with a cluck. "I was delivering your eggs, and Mr. Elton wanted me to tell you he'd added some cheese to the order. No extra charge."

"Oh, that was kind of him. Please let him know."

Tristan rose from the table and backed away. "Will you be all right?"

"Yes, thank you. It's helped, someone being here. You being here."

"I'm glad."

With that, he disappeared out the door and down the stairs.

Chapter Six

"If something goes wrong—an egg drops on the floor, the batter is too runny—don't panic. It's the worst thing you can do. Breathe, take a moment, and figure out how to correct it. There's always a way."

JULIA STARED AT THE LAPTOP'S screen and clicked on the picture of the wicker hamper. She scrolled down to view the sample list of contents—jams, gourmet cheeses, biscuits, bread loaves, and wrapped chocolate mints. She frowned, realizing the extra planning and work it would take, this hamper idea.

She'd been curious about it for a couple of years, as tourists would often ask if the bakery sold hampers stocked for picnics. Chilton Crosse was dead center in the Cotswold Way, a long hiking trail that led from village to village with serene landscapes along the way.

Not that Julia had *any* extra time for a new venture, but she was tired of constantly having to turn down the tourists with a wince and an, "I'm sorry. We don't carry hampers. Maybe someday..." So this evening, she'd decided at least to open up to the idea, do some research. But as she did, Julia's business brain only saw the realistic downside—the inventory issues (Where would they stock all these hampers? Maybe the upstairs flat?), the overall cost, the burden of ordering the expensive gourmet goods each week and making sure they had enough. Or she could forgo the gourmet goods and pack the hampers with her special creations, which would still cost extra time and money. Perhaps she could hire another part-timer to handle this venture for her.

"Three deuces, would you look at that!" her father shouted from his chair in the center of the bakery. Julia watched him reach forward for the mound of poker chips with an enormous smile while the men offered their sulky congratulations.

Julia could have done her hamper research upstairs in the almost-cleaned-out flat tonight. It certainly would've been quieter. But the lads might need something, refills, second helpings on sandwiches (provided by Joe this time), or more crisps. She knew that if she wasn't immediately available, her father might attempt to fill her shoes, play host to the lads, struggle up from his chair, and do everything himself. So she remained behind the counter, perched on a stool, researching hampers.

Most of the usual suspects were in attendance: George, Joe, the vicar, Fletcher, Adam, Mac… and Tristan. He had actually been the first one to arrive, book in hand, an Elmer Kelton western for her father. He'd ordered it last week online, he said.

When she noticed him across the room as her father let him inside the bakery, she'd exchanged a lingering gaze with him, and then Tristan had lifted a hand to wave at her. It had only been a couple of days since he'd clutched her hand, and she wondered how she would feel, seeing him again. Awkward, regretful, nervous? But the first glimpse of him only brought the same comfort as before. She was glad to see him.

As usual, about this time of the evening on poker night, Julia was pressured into abandoning her work and joining the lads in their final two hands. Tristan had been the one to insist she join them and added a seat between himself and Fletcher. She couldn't possibly refuse.

After two rousing hands, Adam won the night and was awarded a rusty pair of pliers from last week's winner, Mac. As Adam tried to pry the pliers apart, he realized it was impossible and chuckled with the rest of the table. "Well, these are sure to come in handy. Gee, thanks, mate."

Mac laughed his husky laugh. "Aye. 'Twas nothing at all."

"You're not kiddin'," Adam agreed.

The party soon dispersed with the men eager to return to their homes and their wives. It had been a longer-than-usual poker night. Even so, Julia's father had remained at one of the tables with Tristan after everyone else left, talking his ear off about another western series he'd finished last week.

Her father pointed a withered finger at the book Tristan had just given him. "I skimmed over the back cover. Haven't read this one before. It's a good subject—about Texas Rangers and the War Between the States..."

Julia locked the front door and went about the business of sweeping the floor and rearranging the chairs, careful to tread quietly and leave her father and Tristan alone. She couldn't resist a glance toward them now and again. Her father used hand gestures to explain his knowledge of the Rangers, according to a history program he'd seen on the telly. He often had trouble remembering what his last meal had been but never had any trouble giving the specific details of novels he'd read or historical details he'd learned. Tristan listened patiently, nodding every so often to show his interest.

Julia went to shut down her laptop so she could take it to the cottage and continue her research at home. When she clicked the lid shut, she heard Tristan call, "Julia?" Then louder, more urgently. "Julia!"

She glanced up and saw Tristan's hands clasping her father's shoulders. The table had been pushed out of the way. Something was wrong. Fear shot up and grabbed Julia's throat.

She somehow found her sea legs and rushed to her father's side. Tristan had already backed away to give her space and told her quietly, "He's conscious, but his speech is slurring. I haven't heard him do that before."

She kneeled in front of her father with a weak smile and grasped his hands. They were ice cold. "Dad? How are you feeling? Can you talk to me?"

He focused on her face, but his eyelids looked droopy. "I feel sleepy. A little dizzy." All his *l*'s slurred slightly.

Julia mentally rifled through a list of stroke symptom tests she'd memorized for just such a possibility. She'd never had to use them before.

"Dad, can you smile for me? Try to smile. Watch me." Both corners of his mouth raised easily then dropped down again. His focus on her face was steady, his eyes getting a little brighter and clearer. All good signs.

"Are you numb anywhere?" She touched his arms. "Can you feel this?"

Her father nodded. "I feel it." The slurring lessened with every new word.

She leaned back and whispered to Tristan, "We should ring the doctor, just in case."

"Here." Tristan had his own mobile handy.

She kept one hand on her father's arm and tapped out Dr. Andrews' memorized number with the other, deftly, calmly, even though her insides were doing somersaults. "It'll be fine," she told her father while the phone rang. "I'm right here."

She got the answer-phone with Dr. Andrews' recorded voice telling her: "I'm currently out of the office or unavailable. If you have an emergency, please contact my associate, Dr. Ben Granger." Julia panicked and scrambled for anything to write on to record Dr. Granger's phone number. Tristan looked confused, but when Julia spoke the new number aloud, Tristan seemed to understand.

She hung up, and Tristan repeated the new number for her.

"Dr. Granger, here," a deep voice said after only one ring. He sounded groggy, and she knew she'd woken him.

"This is Julia. From the bakery."

"Mr. Bentley's daughter, yes." He sounded more alert.

"Well, I'm actually calling about my father." She lowered her voice and turned away from her father's hearing range. "We're at the bakery now. He's slurring, and he's a bit dizzy. I'm worried about a stroke."

"I'll be right over."

Julia clicked off and handed the mobile back to Tristan. She kept her focus on her father, feeling helpless. There was nothing she could do until the doctor arrived, nothing but stay with him, offer comfort.

"How can I help?" Tristan whispered.

"I think the front door is still locked. The doctor needs to get in."

"Right. I'll see to it." Tristan unlocked the door then returned to her side. He didn't hover or irritate, just kept a respectful distance.

As she patted her father's arm, whispered occasional words of easy comfort, she remembered a technique he had once used with her when she was a little girl. It had been a lovely summer's day in the village, and her father was taking her on a spin with the new bike he'd bought for her eighth birthday. They had walked out to a remote path behind their cottage. Her father coached her. "Hold tight to the handlebars! Keep your feet on the pedals! Watch the road in front of you!"

Julia made four passes on the long stretch of road with her father jogging behind, holding onto the bar behind her seat. She heard his comforting steps. On the fifth pass, halfway down the road, Julia felt confident, inspired, and craned her neck behind her to see her father. But she realized he'd removed his hand from the bar, though he was still jogging with her. When she turned her attention back to the road, the front wheel hit a rock and sent the bike—and Julia—flying.

She'd hit the ground hard, and the searing pain in her right wrist made her eyes flood with instant tears. Her father raced to her side, examined the injury, then abandoned the bike and scooped her up into his strong arms while she continued to cry.

"You're my tough little warrior. Did you see how far you pedaled all on your own?"

"But I fell!" She choked back tears, wiping them from her cheeks with her uninjured hand.

He chuckled. "That's part of life, my love: the triumphs and the falls. You can't have one without the other. It's what we do *after* the fall that matters. Now. What shall we sing? The Grand Old Duke of York?"

"No, Daddy. I hate that song. I want the goats song!"

"The goats song you shall have." Her father cleared his throat, still walking, and began to sing in the silliest of voices, not caring who in the village heard him along the way. He sounded very nearly *like* a goat. "The goats came marching one by one, hurrah, hurrah! The goats came marching one by one, hurrah, hurrah! The little one stopped to bask in the sun..."

Julia forgot all about her wrist and sang along, watching her father's funny face the entire way. The longer they marched, the sillier he got until they reached Dr. Andrews' office. That day, she'd received a cast for her fractured wrist, but her father covered it with stickers and drew cartoon faces with a green marker so that each time she gazed down at it, she smiled instead of winced.

As Julia came out of the memory, Dr. Granger arrived at the bakery.

"Thank you for coming, doctor." She stepped back to give him enough room.

Dr. Ben Granger had only been a part of the village for a handful of months, since last December, and his origins were an enigma. Although he was rumored to be Mary Cartwright's nephew, some people—Mrs. Pickering, particularly—insisted that he was the vagabond who'd wandered into the village in the middle of the night, collapsing on George and Mary Cartwright's doorstep. Whatever the truth, Dr. Granger had decided to stay in the village and become Dr. Andrews' associate. He'd rented a little cottage on the outskirts of the village last month.

"Please, call me Ben. I need to know what medications he's taking." He moved toward Julia's father as she rattled off the names and their doses.

"He's right on schedule with them," she reassured. "Had his last dose three hours ago."

Ben checked her father's vital signs then asked him questions—dates and the weather and his own name. When Ben snickered at one of her father's answers, Julia's body relaxed a little. Humor was usually a good sign.

Her father raised a finger of recognition to Ben. "You're the one with that painting. It was beautiful. A seagull in flight. Called 'Freedom,' wasn't it?"

Julia froze. "What's he talking about?" she whispered. "Is he hallucinating?"

Ben patted her father's arm. "That's right, Mr. Bentley. You have a spectacular memory." He swiveled to look at Julia and whispered, "He's not hallucinating. Last week, I had a painting delivered to the art gallery across the street. I remember waving to your father that day. He must've visited later to see it hanging in the gallery. He's spot on. It's a seagull oil painting called 'Freedom.' An original Joy Valentine."

Relieved, Julia watched Ben return to his patient. Likely, Mac or George had walked her father across the street to the gallery while she was busy inside the bakery.

Julia had nearly forgotten that Tristan was still standing close behind her. They weren't touching, but she could almost sense the heat of his presence like a strong magnet. She was relieved he had lingered after the poker game. She had been so used to handling her father completely on her own, but it was comforting, having someone else standing nearby, being there.

"Mr. Bentley, do you think you can stand?" Ben looped his stethoscope over his neck then raised his arms to create a safe basket for her father to lean into.

"I can surely try." He gripped the doctor's arms.

Julia's father was occasionally wobbly on his feet, but he also had an iron strength, which kept him from falling. She hoped that strength would help him now.

She caught her breath as her father raised up with a bobble or two but then stood with a firm stance, still clutching the doctor's arms. He grinned like a little kid who'd just received a prestigious award. His dark blue eyes shone bright with his accomplishment.

"I did it."

"Good. Very good," Ben said. "No dizziness? No unsteadiness?"

"None at all. Strong as an ox." He got a twinkle in his eye. "Did you know, I've never broken a bone. Not a single bone. Not in ninety years of living."

Ben shook his head and clicked his tongue. "Well, I honestly don't know that I've ever seen a patient like you before. That's quite astonishing. Let's make sure we keep it that way and sit you back down for a moment while I speak with your daughter."

Her father was able to return steadily to his seat, and Julia could breathe again.

Ben turned around and lowered his voice. "Although it's possible he had a very minor stroke, I'm inclined to believe his dizziness and slurred speech are due to the new medication. Those are the possible side effects. He seems clearheaded now, no slurring at all. I recommend rest tonight and a visit to the office first thing tomorrow morning. We can check his levels again, do some further testing."

"That's a great relief. Thank you for coming so quickly."

"If you have any other concerns, ring me, even if it's the middle of the night. I'll keep my mobile on. Can you handle things from here, get him home all right?"

"Yes, thanks."

Ben noticed Tristan, and they shook hands and made polite introductions as Julia knelt beside her father's chair.

"Let's get you to the cottage, Dad. It's been a long night."

As she helped him wriggle into his coat, she heard the front door close. Julia assumed Tristan had left along with Ben, but as she struggled to help raise her father out of his chair, she watched Tristan round the corner and approach her father on the other side to support his elbow.

"Why, thank you, young man." Her father grunted as he stood with both their help. "My book!" He tried to reach it.

"Dad, be careful!" Julia scolded. "You don't want to fall."

"I'll get it." Tristan fetched it, still steadying her father's arm. "I'll carry it for you."

With only a few steps to the front door and a few more to Julia's van parked out front—and with Tristan's help—the journey wasn't nearly as lengthy or nerve wracking as it might have been for Julia on her own.

Once she got her father settled in the van and safely buckled in, Julia looked toward Tristan. "Thanks for all your help. Really. You kept things calm."

"I didn't do much." He shrugged. "But I'm glad I could be here. Do you need help in getting him home?"

Julia opened her mouth to answer. Her first instinct was a knee-jerk-but-courteous "no thanks." But then she imagined herself struggling to walk her father up the cobblestone path to the cottage and then all the way into his bedroom. Suddenly, the prospect of help became very attractive, if nothing else, to save her aching back muscles. More importantly, she would feel horrid if her father ended up falling just because Julia refused a little help out of pride or awkwardness.

"Well, only if you're sure..."

"Positive." Tristan opened the van's side door and tucked his long legs inside the backseat while Julia started the engine.

During the brief drive, her father told a lengthy naval story to Tristan about a mishap on leave that involved meeting Julia's mother. He had become so enamored of her that the ship nearly took off without him. Julia had heard the story a million times, but she was particularly glad he told it now, so that she could hear for sure that the slurring had completely disappeared. And it had. The details, as always, were vivid and crystal clear. *Amazing, that long-term memory of his.*

Tristan and Julia got her father inside the cottage with no trouble or near falls. He was even steady enough to use the loo on his own, and when he returned to his bed, Julia was satisfied enough that she could tuck him in and leave him to sleep. Even though Ben's examination had eased her mind, she would be tempted to hover over her father throughout the night, like a new mother checking on an infant.

"Will you stay for tea?" she asked Tristan after she'd left her father's room with the door cracked open. "I was going to put the kettle on, anyway."

"Sure." He shook off his jacket, draping it over a chair in the sitting room.

Julia went to the kitchen to make the tea and add scones to a plate, grateful for a task. She needed something to do with her hands, something to channel her nervous energy. She paused in the hall to hear her father snoring through the crack then carried the tray into the sitting room where Tristan had started a gorgeous fire.

"Good thinking." She set down the tray. "I can't believe it's so chilly tonight."

"Even in May." Tristan dusted off his hands and found a place on the sofa.

Suddenly, Julia was aware of the clutter in the room. She and her father rarely had guests over, and between caring for her father and the bakery, she never had much time to clean. She did her best—kept the loo disinfected and the kitchen tidy—but there always seemed to be certain spots that were forever cluttered. She'd toyed once with the idea of hiring someone to help, but couldn't get over the idea of someone else cleaning up a mess *she*'d made. She cleared away the small stack of newspapers and junk mail from the adjacent sofa as casually as she could, trying not to draw attention to them, and sat down to pour the tea.

Under other circumstances, she would've been anxious having unexpected company in the cottage. People tended to judge one another by the condition of each other's homes: furniture style, general décor, cottage size, cleanliness. But none of it likely mattered to Tristan. Julia doubted if he'd taken special notice of these elements at all—the shoes near the fireplace, the wrinkled shirt draped over the arm of the chair, the coffee stain in the rug she couldn't completely scrub out. He didn't seem the type to judge.

"Sugar?" she asked.

"I take it straight, thanks."

They each took a cup from the tray. Tristan blew on the surface of his, and Julia added a cube of sugar to hers and stirred.

One sip was enough to send a calming warmth through her entire body, like a hug from the inside. Julia crossed her legs, careful not to spill the rest of her tea, and slid the thick quilt up over her legs and waist. It was the quilt she always used to cover her father whenever he fell asleep reading. She watched the fire's flames lick the air.

"I'm glad your father's okay."

Julia nodded. "I've never seen him that weak and dizzy. And never the slurring. It scared me."

"Well, I couldn't tell. You were brilliant with him."

"I wonder where it comes from, that autopilot reaction to a crisis," she mused. "Something just kicks in. I mean, way deep down I felt like a little girl, panicked, unsure I was doing the right things to help him. But there was this other part of me that took over, and I felt... sort of brave. Confident. Even though I was really the opposite."

"I've experienced that autopilot before, too. It's a weird feeling. I think it's our brains pretending everything will be okay, protecting us. We want to be strong for other people, even when the worst feels possible. You did it tonight—stayed calm because you wanted to convince your dad that everything would be okay."

"Like he used to do for me..." she whispered, remembering the bicycle injury, picturing her father young and strong. And brave. Julia blinked, shifted the blanket, and offered a segue to a new subject. "I'll bet you had some experience with crisis, yourself. In the Royal Navy."

Tristan looked confused, perhaps wondering how Julia knew about something they hadn't ever discussed.

"Sorry. Dad let it slip. I hope it was okay."

"Oh, sure." He waved his hand. "I went into the Navy right out of university. But just as a communications tech on a sub."

Julia's eyes widened. "'Just'? You were on a sub? That's not 'just.' That's pretty amazing." She wasn't sure why she'd imagined Tristan on land or on a carrier. A sub seemed so... dangerous. Adventurous. Julia hated water. And the idea of being submerged—even voluntarily, even safely—made her shiver.

"Yeah, that part was exciting, at first. But then, like anything, you just get used to it." Tristan took another sip of tea. "My position was mostly tech related—analyzing radio signals and passing the data up along the chain of command. Nothing glamorous. But as a whole, I loved it, being part of something bigger than me. I enjoyed the order, the structure. I needed it."

Julia thought of her own job, her own days, combining sugar and flour and eggs to make cakes and biscuits and tarts, which now felt a little small in comparison to a naval career. Was she doing something bigger than herself? Helping other people on a grander scale? It didn't feel that way most days.

"So, are you still active?" she asked. "In the Navy, I mean."

The gossip around the village about Tristan—courtesy of Brandy—was either that he was running away from a personal crisis and trying to find himself or that he was a lazy drifter who would rather stay with his aunt than get a real job. Julia wondered how many villagers had heard about his impressive naval background.

Tristan shook his head. "I had to quit four years ago. Since then, I've sort of bounced around from job to job."

Julia found herself oddly disappointed. "Had to quit" implied he'd gotten into some sort of trouble, might've been forced out. And "bounced around" seemed to verify Brandy's drifter theory.

Julia stopped cold, realizing she was as bad as all the gossips in the village, making assumptions. She didn't *know* Tristan's whole story. And even if she did, and even if it confirmed all her assumptions, so what? Wasn't he allowed to make a few mistakes? She'd certainly made her share.

"I'm working on something, though. A new software idea, a project. That's why I'm here in the village, trying to save on the cost of rent for a bit. My aunt's suggestion." Tristan shrugged. "Don't know if I'll succeed. The odds aren't great for start-ups, but it's something I've been working toward for a couple of years, an idea to help make it easier for patients and their physical therapists to communicate outside the office. It would be a user-friendly format, with question-and-answer capability and some built-in resources and links for the patient, that sort of thing."

Ambitious, creative, and philanthropic. Clearly, ***not*** *a drifter...*

"That sounds really interesting." Her gaze drifted to the scar above his eye. She wanted to ask him more about the origin of the idea. Had something in his past prompted the idea? It sounded so specific and specialized. But her questions felt like prying.

Julia leaned over to place her empty cup on the table and shifted the blanket back over her waist.

"What about you? Have you always been here, at the bakery?" Tristan set his cup next to hers.

"Mostly. My father reopened it on his own when I was a baby, and my earliest memories are of helping him in the kitchen. He taught me everything I know. The bakery has been in the family for generations, so I guess it's practically part of my DNA." As she said the words, it dawned on Julia that Tristan knew about the bakery's anniversary from his aunt—the *fortieth* anniversary of the reopening—and now he was surely doing the math in his head, calculating Julia's age. But even so, the realization didn't appear to faze him.

"I worked in the bakery after school as I got older. But then I attended university in London and stayed awhile."

"But you eventually came back?"

Because I got divorced was the real answer. But rather than dive into those deep and murky waters, Julia said, "Yeah, I guess I just missed it here." *Which was also true.* "The village, the bakery, my dad. And when he retired a few years ago, he gave everything over to me."

"Sounds ideal. As in, meant to be."

Julia thought about it for a moment and had to agree. Her life, however she got here to this place, whatever decisions and twists or turns had brought her back to the village, were somehow destined to be. And for the first time in a long time, Julia peered at her own life from the outside looking in and felt... grateful.

For the next minute, neither she nor Tristan spoke, and the fire's crackling was the only sound in the room. The comfort of good conversation—a rarity in her life—and the comfort of warm tea and a hot fire made Julia yawn. She tried to suppress it but couldn't.

"I should probably go." Tristan stood up. "You've got an early day tomorrow."

She started to remove the quilt, but Tristan said, "No reason to get up. I can see myself out. Stay put, enjoy the fire."

He found his jacket and stretched his arms into the sleeves.

"Thanks again for everything," she told him. "You'll never know what a help you were tonight."

"Glad to be of service." His warm eyes shone back at her in the fire's glow.

And then he was gone.

Julia shifted on the sofa and pulled the quilt higher, tucking it under her chin. She heard her father snoring again in the next room, so she closed her eyes and let sleep come.

Chapter Seven

"Surprise the customer with a flavor they don't expect, a texture they're not anticipating. Those little enticements will keep them coming back for more."

"WHY DOES THE BUTTER *HAVE* to be cold?" Abbey pushed the cutter into the soft dough to create the final scone.

"Well, it depends on the texture you want. Some people want their scones a little more cakey and dense, so they use softened butter. But after lots of experimenting, I like my scones a little lighter, so I use cold butter. There's something about the heat of the oven that makes the butter sort of… expand," Julia explained.

"There's a lot of science in baking, isn't there?" Abbey carefully lifted a doughy circle and placed it onto the baking sheet. She stood on a step stool at the bakery kitchen's center island so that her petite thirteen-year-old frame could reach the counter. Her blue T-shirt was newly decorated with flour handprints.

"That's true. Baking involves experiments and setbacks and careful calculations of ingredients and temperatures. And if just one component is off, the final product could completely fall apart."

"Fascinating." Abbey bumped up her glasses with the back of her hand before placing another circle onto the baking sheet.

Last week, Abbey had approached Julia to see if she might teach her how to make scones, as part of Abbey's Hobby badge for the Girl Guides. Abbey said she'd always been interested in baking and that she and her sister even had baking days together every Saturday for the past few years. But now, Holly was busy with wedding plans and with

Fletcher. So Julia agreed to help out with Abbey's badge, squeezing in a time slot on a busy Tuesday between afternoon shifts.

"When's Mildred returning from holiday?" Julia asked.

"They added on a few extra days, going to a couple more countries. End of next week, I think."

"I know they're having an amazing time. Your step-mum didn't get to travel much before she married your dad."

"That's what she told me. She'd never stepped foot out of England until last year!"

Julia could relate. She never traveled either—no time for it. She and her father had gone on the odd holiday to Ireland or Wales when she was a child. But she'd never left the borders of Britain. Someday...

The timer dinged for the first batch of scones.

"I'll get them." Julia grabbed a hot pad and moved toward the oven.

"Good timing. Mine are ready to go in!" Abbey announced.

Julia set down the freshly baked scones, filled with chocolate chunks per Abbey's request, and let Abbey place the other sheet pan carefully into the oven.

As Abbey shut the oven door, someone knocked at the back door.

"Come in," Julia called.

A ray of sunshine pierced the tiled floor as Tristan nudged the door open with his elbow, carrying his egg delivery.

"Tristan!" Abbey darted to open the door wider for him. "I'll help."

It seemed absolutely everyone in the village knew Tristan by now.

"Hey, Abbey. Thanks for the help." Tristan moved toward the cupboard, and Julia helped him find a place for the eggs while Abbey shut the back door.

Julia gingerly removed the top tray from his stack and placed it onto a cleared-off shelf.

"How's your dad this morning?" Tristan asked in a lowered voice.

"Fine, thankfully." They had nothing to hide from Abbey, but for some reason, they were whispering while they worked with the eggs, which made every word and gesture seem particularly intimate. "The doctor gave him a look-over this morning, did some tests, and adjusted his meds again. He's been great all morning. Alert, telling jokes."

"That's a very good sign." Tristan grinned.

The task over, they turned to see Abbey removing scones with a spatula.

"Those smell incredible." Tristan joined Abbey at the island.

"You can have the very first one!" Abbey offered.

Julia handed a napkin to Abbey, who folded a scone into it. "Don't eat it yet. It's *very* hot."

"Is this chocolate? My favorite."

"Yes. And I made them!" Abbey bragged.

"Well then, they're probably extra sweet."

Tristan's charm at work again, Julia thought, seeing Abbey's smile grow wider. It was nice having a real gentleman in the village. Julia had begun to notice the little things—how Tristan, without even thinking, opened doors for people, slid out chairs, paused to let someone pass through a doorway before he did. Those patient, thoughtful gestures made him seem like an old soul trapped in a young body and almost lessened the age gap between them.

Tristan thanked Abbey for the scone and headed toward the door while Julia walked with him to say goodbye.

"Hey, do you have an hour to kill today?" Tristan shoved his hand into his jeans pocket. He seemed suddenly shy. "There's someone I want you to meet."

"Who?" she asked, intrigued.

"It's a surprise. But I know you'll like her."

Her? Even more intrigued, Julia ticked off her mental to-do list—quick nap, return to work, close up shop, eat something, back to the cottage—which all sounded incredibly bland compared to this mysterious proposal.

"I might have a little time after I finish up with Abbey. I could get my dad settled at the cottage then meet you?" She could certainly abandon her nap for today.

"You could just text me when you're ready."

Julia paused. "I... well, I don't really know how."

"How to what?"

"How to text. I've actually... Well, I've never texted before." She said it with a strong degree of shame as though she'd just admitted an unforgivable defect in her character. Really, though. *How* could she have never texted before? What did that say about her technological skills? Or even the state of her social life? She had no one to text anything *to*.

Abbey came to the rescue and scooped up Julia's mobile from the chair. "Here! It's *so* easy." She brought the device close to Julia so they could both view the screen. "You tap this icon and then this one for a new message." She brought up a blinking cursor, and Julia realized she would need her glasses for this little impromptu lesson. She lowered the glasses down from the top of her head and adjusted them on the bridge of her nose.

"But first, we need Tristan's contact info," Abbey said.

She sounded so well versed in all this techno stuff that Julia should've felt even more ashamed. But instead, the humor of the situation made Julia giggle. "I can't *believe* a thirteen-year-old knows so much more about this than I do."

"Don't feel bad." Tristan drew his mobile out of his pocket. "It's her generation. Abbey's grown up with this stuff since she was a baby. Unlike us." That was actually true, Julia realized. Even in Tristan's childhood, certain technology was still in its infant stage, especially texting, which made Julia feel infinitely better.

Tristan asked for Julia's number. At least she knew *that* much! Then Abbey tapped his info into Julia's mobile, and that was it.

Before Abbey could continue her tutoring, a *ping!* made Julia blink.

"That's me," Tristan said.

Julia saw a text pop onto her screen inside a colored bubble.

Hi there!

"Just reply here." Abbey tapped the screen and handed over her mobile. "Use the tiny keyboard."

"That *is* tiny. Goodness." Julia decided on something brief, but it still took an embarrassingly long time to type out with her thumbs, so she switched to using her index finger, which still took forever. "This is harder than it looks. I see people just tapping texts at the speed of light. How do they do it?"

"Lots of practice," Abbey said. "You should see my sister, Bridget. She could probably enter a speed-texting contest. Her thumbs move so fast they're blurry!"

Julia finally managed, *Hello Tristan*, found an exclamation point, then tapped Send. She heard a *ping* at Tristan's end.

"See? Easy peasy." Tristan clicked off his mobile and returned it to his pocket. "I'll see you soon? I'll text you in a bit."

"Right."

As he went through the door, the new batch of scones was ready, so Abbey rushed to the oven to silence the timer's annoying buzz.

If Julia could control the weather, if she could choose a perfect day to be played over and over again all year through, this one just might be it: early May, cool-but-warming temperatures, crisp blue skies without a single cloud, and flowers. Blossoms everywhere. She identified the heavenly honeysuckle immediately. Her father had taught her, as a little girl, how to squeeze the sweet drop of nectar from the pistil, straight onto her tongue. Everywhere Julia turned, things seemed lush and green and colorful. The village was the best version of itself on days like these. Julia had been hibernating in her windowless kitchen, and suddenly, one day, she'd awakened to spring in all its glory.

She settled her father at the cottage for a nap then took a few minutes to have a shower, tousle her freshly dried hair, slip on some jeans—loose now, from dropping another three pounds —and change into her favorite peach jumper. She should've been drowsy from skipping a nap, but instead, she felt invigorated. She stepped out of the cottage and decided to walk down Storey Road, the village's high street. Normally, she took the back route, trying to avoid the crowds and tourists. But not today.

Carrying her box of chocolate scones, she walked the length of the street and soaked in every detail—the honey-colored limestone shop fronts, the tourists flocking to the stone gazebo in the street's center, Mary Cartwright's laughter from across the street, and the cooing sounds Noelle whispered to Adam Jr. in his pram as Julia passed them.

"Hi," Julia said quietly as she tapped Noelle's arm. "Have a good day."

"You, too." Noelle smiled.

The shops provided all sorts of treasures to draw in the tourists: an art gallery, a dress shop, the pub, a toyshop, and Holly's new bookshop at the end of the street. Julia hadn't yet visited it, her excuse always being "too busy." But that excuse was wearing thin. A lot of her old excuses were starting to wear thin. She made a mental note to stop by this week and pick up a new book for her dad.

Reaching the edge of Holly's shop, Julia recalled her mission, meeting Tristan at Mr. Elton's farm. That was where his recent text had asked her to go. No other information offered, just, *Meet me at Elton's Farm.*

She quickened her pace, heading toward the outskirts of the village on a path that led up a hill, cutting through towering trees and spacious fields dotted with sheep and rustic stone walls. She couldn't imagine what was in store for her. Who did Tristan want her to meet?

Tristan waited beside the farm's wide wooden gate and nudged it open as Julia approached. He followed her through then pulled the gate shut with one hand, holding a thermos in the other.

"Beautiful day," he observed, leading the way.

"I was thinking the same thing all the way here. Oh, I nearly forgot. These are for you."

She handed him the box, and he leaned in for a whiff. "More scones?"

"Abbey insisted you have the extras."

They walked in silence along the dirt path toward Mr. Elton's large stone farmhouse. The expansive fields on either side were a stunning emerald green, and the leaves on nearby trees shivered in the breeze. A dog barked somewhere in the distance.

Julia and Tristan moved past the two-story farmhouse toward the chicken coop, which Julia had seen many times before. In fact, she'd seen everything many times before, having dealt with Mr. Elton on a business level for decades. Surely Tristan knew this. But he seemed to be taking her on a tour of the entire farm. *Patience*, she told herself. She needed to relax and enjoy the suspense.

Soon, the worker's cottage came into view, a matching stone cottage, significantly smaller than the main house.

"That's mine." Tristan pointed to the cottage. "Well, for now, at least. I moved my stuff in over the weekend." An older-model Toyota was parked to the side, which Julia assumed was Tristan's car.

"Weren't you staying with your aunt, at her cottage?"

"That was only temporary. When Mr. Elton offered me full-time work last week, he offered the cottage, too. Nice little place."

"Sounds like you're staying awhile."

"I think I might be."

After another long walk past some hay-baled pastures where a couple of Elton's men worked the fields, Julia's patience hit its limits. She huffed with a smile and turned to Tristan. They paused in the grass as she set her hands firmly on her hips. "Okay, I'm here, and you've got me dying of curiosity. Who did you want me to meet all the way out here?"

Tristan chuckled. "Sorry. Wasn't trying to keep you in suspense. We're getting closer, but let me call her." He handed the scones back to Julia and cupped one hand to his mouth. "Maggie! C'mere, Maggie!" He whistled through his teeth.

Seconds later, Julia saw something race toward them, a blur of black and white—a short, stocky dog with little legs moving so fast they couldn't be seen. When the dog came closer, it jumped up, diving headfirst into Tristan's outreached arm. He dropped his thermos and caught the dog, holding on tight as it licked his cheeks with great enthusiasm.

"Meet Maggie."

The dog paused her licking as if she understood precisely what Tristan had said. Her mouth curled up into a broad smile as she panted at Julia. The huge triangle ears in combination with the stubby legs gave the breed away immediately.

"A Corgi!" Julia scratched the dog's soft head. Maggie closed her eyes and freely accepted the rubs from both of them.

"Maybe not full-bred—don't know for sure—but definitely mostly Corgi. I got her last year at a rescue center." Tristan shifted Maggie in his arms. "My mate was the one who wanted a dog, but I ended up getting her. Couldn't resist that smile."

"She's beautiful. Those colors..." Maggie's chest and paws were a bright white, her face a reddish-tan, and the rest of her was all black. The edges of Maggie's eyes looked like they'd been perfectly painted with black eyeliner. "And she's spoiled rotten, apparently."

"I've missed her. There wasn't room at my aunt's cottage," Tristan explained. "She hates dogs anyway—the shedding, the barking. So when

I moved to the farm, I made a quick trip back to London, where my mum was keeping an eye on Maggie."

"She'll probably be useful on the farm," Julia noted. "Aren't Corgis herding dogs?"

"Yeah, you should've seen her when she met the flock of sheep. She started racing around, nipping their heels, bossing them around. She herds the cows as well. Mr. Elton said he should probably pay me double wages for bringing on a work dog."

Maggie, still panting, had calmed into a trance state, her eyes half-closed. "You're getting heavy." Tristan bent over to set Maggie down. "Want a drink?" He unscrewed the thermos lid and poured clear water into it. Maggie lapped it up with the same enthusiasm she'd used to jump into his arms. When she'd finished every drop, she barked her thank you and raced back to wherever she'd come from.

But a few meters later, she turned to bark at Tristan.

"I think she wants us to follow." Tristan capped the thermos then relieved Julia of the scones again, and off they went, obeying the bossy Corgi.

Julia wasn't quite sure whether her lower back would let her keep up, but she quickened her pace to match Tristan's brisk walk. Just around the corner, in an open valley, they saw a group of about twenty sheep, contentedly grazing.

"We could sit here?" Tristan suggested, finding a tall oak tree at the top of the hill.

He removed his jacket before Julia could protest and set it on the ground for her. Underneath, he'd worn a white button-down shirt that made his tanned skin look even more tanned.

They sat in the shade, and the breeze found them there, lifting Julia's hair from her face and making her drowsy. The sun sifting through the branches created speckled shadows on the ground. Julia heard Maggie's commanding barks, ordering the sheep to step in line as she raced to gather them up and lead them who-knew-where.

"She's going to be so happy here." Julia smiled. "This is probably paradise for her."

"Yeah, it already feels like home."

Julia didn't know if Tristan meant for Maggie or himself.

"So you live in London, then? Well, I mean, originally..."

Tristan nodded, crossing his legs at the ankles. He picked at some grass blades. "Yeah. I actually grew up there, outskirts of London, a place in the country. Then university, then the Royal Navy, then... Well, I ended up back in London in a tiny flat, working odd jobs to make ends meet. That's when my aunt suggested Chilton Crosse. Her offer was irresistible. London has always been too crowded for me. Guess I'm not cut out for big-city life."

"Yeah, I loved London's culture and fast pace in my twenties, but then it became sort of suffocating. I was just a number there, never made any real friendships, never felt very grounded." Saying the phrase "in my twenties" *to* a twenty-nine-year-old made Julia aware of her age again.

But Tristan didn't seem to notice. "So you moved back to the village, then?"

"Yeah, after the divorce."

"You were married?"

"After university. We lasted seven years. And then I came back home after the breakup. It was a good place to heal, think things over."

"No kids?"

"No kids. We tried, but... things just didn't work out..."

"I'm sorry." Tristan's voice dropped to a respectful whisper.

Why had she spilled out such personal information, practically told him her entire life's story? She never talked about her past this way with anyone. And she'd only barely stopped short of telling him about her two miscarriages and the later hysterectomy. Even Julia's father didn't know about her miscarriages. She thought it might sting too much, knowing he'd almost had grandchildren to spoil. Julia blamed her openness with Tristan on the relaxed setting, a smiling dog, a soft breeze, and lush grass all around. And a sensitive man who was willing to listen.

Attempting to shift the focus back to Tristan, she said, "You mentioned last night that you'd quit the Royal Navy. Were you just tired of being on a sub?"

"I wish." His gaze was on the ground as he carved a line into the dirt with his thumbnail. "Life took an... unexpected detour. I was forced to quit."

"Oh." Julia felt nosy for asking and selfish for pushing the personal discussion toward him. Obviously, her first instinct had been right. He'd gotten into some trouble and didn't want to talk about it. "You don't have to explain."

"No, it's okay." Tristan rubbed the dirt off his fingers and reached down toward his right ankle. He edged up his trouser leg, revealing a long, jagged scar that began at the middle of his shin and kept on going. Julia wondered where it ended. When he got to the knee, Tristan pushed the trouser leg back down and turned to look at her. Sunshine sifted through the branches and highlighted Tristan's face, making him blink. "I was in an auto accident four years ago."

The scar above his right eye suddenly made perfect sense.

Julia tried not to stare, tried not to look too interested or to hang on his every word, but she couldn't help herself. She wanted to know more. She wanted to know everything.

"I was on leave for two weeks to see my parents. I went for a ride in my older brother's car. It was a brand-new convertible. 'The color of champagne' was how he described it. He was so proud of that car." Tristan's gaze moved to the field, where Maggie was napping, taking a break from her herding duties. "It was a day like today, gorgeous and bright. My brother was driving. We had the top down, and he drove us outside London on this empty country road so he could give the car some speed. We were listening to the new Travis album and joking around, just daft stuff between brothers, having some laughs. We hadn't seen each other in a year because he was in medical school at Oxford. Anyhow, he swerved hard to miss this dog crossing the road. Next thing I knew, the car had rolled a few times into a field and came to a full stop. When I opened my eyes, I smelled smoke and heard the engine hissing. And I heard this... whining... somewhere in the distance. And I remember thinking: It's the dog. The shaggy one Corbett avoided in the road. He's whining for us, like he knows something's wrong. Or maybe he even felt bad for causing the accident."

Julia swallowed, realizing her breathing had grown shallow.

"So I was trapped in the car, but I managed to look over at my brother. He was unconscious, and his head was bleeding. I tried to reach for my mobile, but my arm was broken. I had no way to ask for help, no way to rescue my brother or even myself. Right before I lost consciousness, I heard another car pull up and a woman scream. I woke up in the hospital three weeks later with a huge cast on this leg, ankle to hip, and one on my arm, too. Mum said I'd had emergency surgery and almost didn't make it. My brother was already gone. He died at the scene."

"Tristan," she whispered. "I had no idea..." Instinctively, she placed her hand on his arm, the one with the tattoo.

Tristan's eyes glazed over with tears. Julia wondered if this was the first time he'd talked about it, really talked about it. She felt guilty for asking him the question that had led him back to that place in his memory. "I'm so sorry." She said it for her own guilt, and she said it for what he'd been through, his injuries, his brother. She said it for everything.

Tristan wiped his eyes with the back of his hand. "Thanks. It still feels fresh sometimes."

"I can't even imagine..." She removed her hand to let him finish his story. She could tell he had more to say.

"So that surgery was just the first of nine. My leg was basically shattered, so they had to reconstruct it, and then there was physical therapy. It was grueling. Like nothing I've ever been through. Really painful."

Julia made the connection. Tristan's software program, offering patients and physical therapists an easier way to communicate was born out of his own experience with the accident and multiple surgeries.

"I wanted to quit so many times, but I always thought of my brother. He wouldn't want me to quit. So I pushed through the pain, and I did it for him. He's the reason I can walk again. And so, during my last week of therapy, I got this to remind me."

He tilted his arm toward her, revealing the full tattoo, the blackbird that she'd seen—and quietly judged—a couple of weeks before.

"Is that for your brother?"

"Yeah, Corbett. His name means 'raven.'"

Julia didn't tear up at Tristan's story. Perhaps she was too gobsmacked. But seeing that tattoo and hearing Tristan explain it made Julia's eyes well up. "That's really beautiful," she said through quivering lips.

"I didn't mean to make you cry. I shouldn't have told you everything."

She extended her hand again, touched the raven, and ran over the ink with her index finger. "No. I'm glad you did. It's part of who you are, part of who you've become."

She looked up to see his chestnut eyes staring into hers.

Julia heard a sudden rushing sound, a mini steam train headed their way, and glanced up to see Maggie racing toward them, tongue lolling.

"Hey you," Tristan said as Julia removed her hand from his arm. Maggie came to a dead stop in front of him, gazing into his face. Tristan leaned forward to rub Maggie's fur. "Did you have a good time? Did you give those daft old sheep all the right commands?"

Maggie barked her answer in between pants and made Tristan and Julia laugh in synch. *Corgi comic relief.* On cue, Maggie rolled over in the dirt, edging her way onto her back until she was completely flipped over in front of Tristan.

"What's she doing?"

"Tummy rubs," explained Tristan, giving Maggie what she wanted.

Julia joined him. "This dog. She knows exactly what she's doing, doesn't she?"

"Sometimes I'd swear she's a little person trapped inside a dog's body."

"No doubt."

Julia was grateful for Maggie's happy energy but most grateful for her timing. Julia wasn't quite sure what else she would've said to Tristan about the accident. She still needed to absorb the information, process it. But she knew one thing. Tristan's story had forced her to realize that her preconceived perceptions—about Tristan, about anyone—were usually inaccurate.

People were complicated and layered. The face they showed the world was only the smallest inkling of who they really were deep inside. People were the sum of their parts, the results of circumstances, hardships, life experiences. And knowing more about Tristan only made her want to keep peeling back the layers.

Chapter Eight

"Sometimes, the euphoria of a perfect bite can mimic the euphoria of love. The senses are heightened, and the result is a smile."

"Here's your tea." Julia set down Mac's to-go cup on the kitchen island then took her own mug to a corner stool to wait.

She had called Mac this afternoon, the moment she knew something was wrong with one of the ovens. Not a great time for an oven to go out—a busy Saturday at the bakery—so Mac had dropped everything to come and take a look. Though he was best known for his gardening skills, Mac was a whiz at everything else, too. Town gardener *and* town handyman, indispensable to Chilton Crosse.

"Thanks, lass." Mac grunted as he pushed his torch deeper into the oven in search of the problem.

Sitting down, Julia took a sip of her tea, adjusted her glasses, and pulled out her mobile. It had jingled in her pocket when Mac first arrived.

Until a few days ago, when Abbey had shown her how to text, Julia had never cared a whit for her mobile. She used it to stay in touch with her father, for emergency purposes only. But lately, after receiving daily texts from Tristan, she'd kept it close to her, in her pocket or bag or on a surface nearby, ever aware of its presence. That jingle was becoming very familiar.

She hadn't actually seen Tristan in the days since she'd met Maggie on the farm. She and Tristan had missed each other the couple of times he'd made his deliveries to the bakery, and Brandy had been the one to let him in. But the texting had made him not feel so far away. The texts often contained mundane, silly little bits of observations—the weather, work-related tidbits, comments about village life, and sometimes pictures. Though Julia hadn't figured out yet how to snap and share a photo, Tristan had sent her a couple of Maggie smiling widely.

Despite herself, Julia couldn't stop looking forward to Tristan's texts. It was becoming too hard to deny that there was something developing between them, an unexpected companionship, an ease and comfort between new friends that rarely happened in Julia's experience. She didn't go around telling people the intimate details of her life. And she imagined Tristan would say the same. *A life-threatening accident, a divorce, the loss of a brother, a mother.* The deepest, heaviest topics usually reserved for the most intimate of friends.

But the sensitive information seemed safe with Tristan without her even having to ask him—as though she'd just handed Tristan a key to something very personal and important, and he had exchanged his key with her. And now they trusted each other to hold onto it, keep it protected.

Julia tilted the screen and read Tristan's message. *Emergency meeting tonight? Apparently top secret. My aunt won't spill. She wants me there.*

Mrs. Pickering had rung Julia a couple of hours ago with a lilting excitement in her voice: "I've had another brainstorm. We need to make this fortieth celebration bigger, grander! I've called a special meeting for tonight. Can you be there?"

Julia couldn't think of a reason to say no, so she had agreed.

She texted Tristan back: *No idea what she's up to.*

Julia heard the oven door slam and looked up to see Mac wiping his hands on a cloth.

"What's the damage?" she asked, bracing for the worst. Those big commercial ovens usually had expensive repairs with hard-to-find parts.

"Not too bad. It's the door's seal causing the heat to escape." Julia always loved the way Mac trilled his Scottish *r*'s. Over the years, his accent had become only slightly easier to understand. "A gasket needs replacing. I'll see if a mate of mine has the part. He lives a couple of villages over. If he has it in stock, I can replace it later tonight."

"You're a lifesaver! It's been impossible working with only one oven all day. Thanks, Mac."

"No guarantees," he warned. "But I'll ring you when I know about the part. Thanks for the tea." He shoved the cloth into his back pocket, scooped up the paper cup, and went on his way.

The mobile vibrated in Julia's hand again, but before she could view the screen, Brandy stuck her head in through the swinging door. "Your hampers were just delivered."

"Oh, good!" Julia had ordered five hampers and some goodies to go with them for a test run of the whole picnic-tourist niche. She could try them out next week. "I'll be out to look at them in a sec."

Brandy backed out, and Julia peeked at Tristan's response. *With my aunt in charge, anything is possible. I don't know if that's a good thing or not.*

Julia snickered softly then tapped out: *You said it, not me.*

Tristan sent back a winking smiley face in reply.

Maybe it was the "emergency" status that caused it, but the meeting room at Joe's pub seemed more crowded than usual. Everyone on the committee was attending, plus a couple of curious spouses or relatives. Even Cora and Grace, sisters who'd lived together for most of their lives in Moonbeam Cottage, were in attendance. In their sixties, they were both employed at the primary school—Cora as the headmistress, Grace as a teacher—and thus, had very little time for village life and committee meetings. But they adored Julia's father. They'd been part of the welcoming committee when he first arrived at the village. Julia suspected they'd heard about the party and asked to be part of the planning.

Joe had set out extra chairs in short rows, allowing Mrs. Pickering enough room to stand at the front of the room with her gavel and her multiplying notecards.

Julia sat in the second row next to Abbey and glanced casually around for Tristan as she chatted with Holly and Abbey. But she saw no sign of him.

Mrs. Pickering tapped her gavel on the counter and shouted over the voices. "This meeting is called to order! Order, please!" She always reminded Julia of a strict schoolteacher who might punish her students arbitrarily.

Finally, the volume simmered down to a hush. At this point, Tristan dodged sheepishly into the room and avoided his aunt's stern gaze. Julia watched him wander to the opposite side of the room and stand alongside George Cartwright against the wall.

"As you know," Mrs. Pickering started, "Alton Bentley's bakery will celebrate its illustrious fortieth year of business next month. And the aim of this committee is to make his celebration the best it can be, worthy of a man of his character and work ethic."

"Hear, hear!" Joe said from the back, producing grins all around.

Mrs. Pickering continued, "To that end, I've devised a four-tiered plan to create a grand celebration. In no specific order—I haven't yet decided what that will be—here are the tiers." She shuffled the cards in her deck. "The first tier involves a street parade."

Parade? What happened to "simple but elegant?" Julia waited for the punch line. Surely she was joking.

"I've already spoken with the headmistress at the school." She nodded at Cora. "And she's making plans to have the children's band and choir participate."

Apparently, not *a joke.*

"And I'll accept other suggestions for parade participants, but I need those by this evening so I can begin contacting people."

Julia peeked around the room to see what other villagers' opinions were, but their expressions were much like her own: stoic, neither supportive nor alarmed. Julia wondered at precisely what point in earlier years Mrs. Pickering had wormed her way into the position of Most Influential Person in the Village. And she wondered when people stopped standing up to her—if they ever had in the first place.

"Now. For Tier Two." Mrs. Pickering shuffled her cards again. "Dependent upon the weather, I thought we could employ a skywriter to—"

"Skywriter?" Julia couldn't help herself.

"Yes, dear. A small plane, whose purpose it is to write an enormous message across the sky." She accompanied her next phrase with a sweeping hand gesture. "It could say something like, 'Happy Fortieth Anniversary. And a Happy Forty More.'"

Julia felt her mobile vibrate in her pocket and simply couldn't resist breaking Mrs. Pickering's MOBILES-OFF policy during meetings. When Mrs. Pickering returned to her notes, Julia peeked at the screen. A text from Tristan: *A celebration or a circus?*

Julia stopped herself from snickering aloud and incurring Mrs. Pickering's wrath.

After an awkward silence, Mrs. Pickering cleared her throat and carried on. "The third tier would consist of what we'd already mentioned in our last meeting: abundant food, gifts of appreciation for Mr. Bentley, and of course, the decorations provided by our subcommittee, headed by Mrs. Cartwright." She glanced in Mary's direction. "And the final tier would consist of..." She gave a dramatic pause and peered around the room. "Fireworks."

Another text from Tristan, simply: *????*

Again met with silence and stoicism, Mrs. Pickering's smile sank into a frown. Julia hoped someone would rescue them from this madness.

"So. What does everyone think? I would like input now, please." Mrs. Pickering folded her hands over her notecards and waited.

"Aunt?" All attention in the room moved to Tristan, who shifted his weight. His tone was respectful but steady and sure. "I think perhaps fireworks would be... against some sort of code? Aren't they illegal inside the village?"

Nods and murmurs all around as attention turned back to Mrs. Pickering.

"Oh. Well. Certainly, we'd need to check into that. Wouldn't want to do anything illegal, would we?"

"And I have an idea about the skywriter," Julia called out, feeling rather emboldened. "Instead of that, could we have a banner across the sky? Like, a small plane flying a banner behind it? Same impact, but just less... dramatic. And dangerous."

More nodding heads as Mrs. Pickering mused over it. Finally, she said, "Well, Julia, this party *is* for your father's bakery. Certainly, any input you give is appreciated." Others gently weighed in, offering possible ways to tone down the parade to an acceptable level, mentioning concerns about the length of time the entire celebration might take, and even how it might deter tourists from shopping if it went on too long.

"Valid concerns all. Very practical," Mrs. Pickering admitted. "Perhaps we should form subcommittees now, while we're here together, to put these plans into action and iron out the potential difficulties."

Julia thought she heard the whole room groan, but Mrs. Pickering must not have noticed. She appointed cochairs of each new subcommittee and gave them their separate tasks. The villagers spent the rest of the meeting in these smaller committees, mostly chatting about things *other* than the party while Mrs. Pickering's attention was turned away as she went around from group to group.

After another gavel tap, she announced, "I think we've made great progress here. I'd like thoughts and suggestions presented to me over the weekend. Phone only, please. I don't do email. We'll convene again next week."

As people filtered out, Julia stayed to chat with Lizzie about the banner that would attach to the awning outside the bakery. They'd agreed on the crisp white one with colorful lettering that Lizzie had emailed this morning. Julia said goodbye and shifted the bag on her shoulder as Tristan stepped into view.

"Hey," he told Julia. "So I guess this will be quite the production."

"Apparently so. But I do think my father will be dazzled by it, in the end."

"Tristan!" Mrs. Pickering called from the doorway. "Remember that shipment of jams. They need to be on the shelves this evening."

"Will do," he told her with a wave then faced Julia again. "My aunt hasn't come to terms with my being full-time at the farm. She keeps giving orders, and I can't say no to her. Doesn't leave me much time to work on my software program... Oh, listen. I've had a brainstorm of my own about something."

"They run in the family?" she teased. "These brainstorms?"

"Well. Let's hope mine is a bit more... levelheaded than my aunt's. It's about your website."

"I don't have a website."

"Precisely. And I think you need one for publicity. You should have a presence on the web, especially for tourists Googling the village and wanting to know about your place."

Julia hung on his last two words. She secretly loved that someone—finally, someone—considered the bakery to be *her* place. Julia had run it for over a decade now. But she didn't think anyone had noticed.

"Anyway, I don't want to be presumptuous, but I did a little online search last night, and every shop in the village has a website except the bakery."

It wasn't an insult; it was true. Julia, as in so many areas of her life, was behind the times. Similar to the hamper idea, the website idea had rooted itself somewhere in the shadows of her mind as a possibility someday. But she hadn't known where to begin.

"So, I was thinking," Tristan continued. "I'd like to create some mock-ups, different designs and layouts, see what you think."

"Isn't that a lot of trouble?"

"Not at all. I love this sort of stuff. It brings out the geek in me." Tristan grinned.

Julia had never, not once since she'd met Tristan, considered him a geek. "Well, if you're sure..."

"When's a good time for you? I can have something ready to show you by tomorrow."

"Sometime after the bakery closes, at the cottage? Say, eight o' clock?"

"I'll be there." He pushed his arms into the sleeves of his jacket. "Guess I'd better head off. Duty calls."

"Have fun."

"Always," Tristan replied with a wink.

Sundays were usually exhausting for Julia, marking the end of her workweek. Sundays involved prepping and baking—alone, since Miranda had the day off—church, then opening the bakery at noon, then more work, and closing up. Finally, blissful sleep, knowing tomorrow was more or less hers.

But this particular Sunday night, she felt energized. After closing the bakery, she'd brought her father home and immediately made a sticky toffee pudding—her personal favorite—humming as her dad sat on the living room sofa playing "In the Mood" and other Glenn Miller hits on his clarinet. Occasionally, he would miss a note or squeak one out then pause and find the right note again.

As the pudding baked in the Aga, Julia did a quick sweep around of the cottage, setting out a vase of wildflowers she'd picked from a nearby field earlier in the day. Her attire was casual. Jeans and a forest green blouse seemed appropriate for a casual meeting about webpages with Tristan.

Close to eight o'clock, she called from the kitchen as she pulled the pudding from the Aga. The sticky goodness bubbled in the tin and smelled like heaven. "Dad, do you want a slice now?"

"Slice of what?" he yelled back from the sitting room.

"Sticky toffee pudding!"

"Sticky what?"

Julia stepped closer to the doorway. "Sticky... toffee... pudding."

"Oh, *that's* what I've been smelling. Yes, surely I'll have some."

He resumed playing as Julia whipped up the toffee sauce, removed the dense pudding from the tin to a large white plate then drizzled the boiling sauce over it. Somehow, she was able to hear the knock at the front door above the sound of the clarinet. She pictured Tristan on the other side, and her heart jumped.

Walking through the kitchen, she made herself breathe. *Keep things casual and cool. He's just here on business. A website. That's all.*

She opened the door to see Tristan in a black leather jacket and carrying a laptop at his side.

Casual and cool.

"Hey," she said louder than normal, her voice competing with the clarinet.

Tristan passed through and waved at Julia's father in the sitting room.

Alton removed the clarinet from his lips. "Hello there, young man!"

"Good evening, Mr. Bentley." Tristan turned back to Julia and whispered, "Something smells amazing."

"I made a little treat for us. Have a seat, and I'll get you a slice."

Tristan approached the sofa with his laptop. "Mr. Bentley, you're really talented. How long have you played?"

Julia noticed that Tristan had developed the habit of speaking a decibel or two louder than he normally would to help her father hear him the first time.

"Thank you, son. You can't go wrong with a little Tommy Dorsey." He looked up at Julia for guidance. "How long now?"

She paused before entering the kitchen and did the math in her head. "Since university, right? So… more than seventy years?" Her father nodded. "Dad used to play in the naval band."

"It's important to keep the lip up, or you'll lose it," her father warned. "It's why I try to play every day. Plus, it's good for the lungs." He tapped his chest lightly with his fist.

"Well, it's impressive." Tristan took a seat on the empty sofa adjacent to her father's love seat. He removed his jacket then opened up the laptop on the table. "I'm not very musical. I took piano lessons as a child, but I guess they didn't take."

Julia heard the conversation continuing effortlessly forward as she slipped into the kitchen to put everything together. She'd already brewed some tea, so within a couple of minutes, she was carrying out a tray full of saucers and plates and pudding.

"Here, let me help," Tristan insisted, standing to take the tray from her and setting it on the table.

She handed a plate to her father as Tristan helped himself. "More sauce?"

"You know me too well." Her father watched while she drizzled more sauce onto his slice.

"Delicious," Tristan said even before he swallowed his first bite.

"You're so good for my ego." She grinned and joined Tristan on his sofa, tucking one leg underneath her. She hadn't brought out a plate for herself. She'd made too much progress with her weight loss to give in now. Soon, she'd have to buy new jeans.

"What's that thing you've got?" Her father pointed to Tristan's laptop.

"Oh, it's a computer," Tristan said. "Called a laptop. It's portable."

Her father smirked. "I don't get all this… technology. In my day, we didn't need all this telecommunications stuff. You young people have it all figured out, though. Too smart for your own good."

Tristan dipped his head and took another bite of pudding. After swallowing, he said, "I don't know about that. But technology can be pretty amazing."

"Dad, Tristan was an IT specialist in the Navy. That means he's really good with computers. He's here to help us create a website. For the bakery."

Her father crinkled his eyebrows. "Website. Why does the bakery need a website?"

Tristan answered, "Well, it will bring even more visibility to the bakery. Having an online presence... a space on the Internet where anyone in the world can see information about your bakery. It's just a good way to advertise, a smart way to enhance the business, to stay current. And it will probably bring in more customers."

Her father raised his eyebrows high. "More customers! Good thinking. I'm all for that. Julia, this one's a keeper."

Julia felt her cheeks go warm.

"I'll let you two get to work. Don't mind me." Her father put his empty plate back on the tray—Tristan leaned over to help steady it—and then searched for his latest western paperback, tucked in between the sofa cushions.

In two minutes her father was nodding off, something he often did after eating. Rather than wake him and move him to the bedroom, it was best to let him slumber there.

Tristan set aside his now-empty plate, took one more sip of tea, then leaned forward to adjust his laptop, still open on the table. As he started tapping the keyboard and moving his finger around the mouse pad, Julia inched closer to the screen and, therefore, closer to Tristan so she could get a better look. She realized she was squinting, so she found her glasses, which she now consistently remembered to place on top of her head or to hang at the collar of her blouse. She needed them too often these days, and she'd finally accepted it. She'd even bought more stylish glasses from the emporium just yesterday. The rims were a deep purple, her favorite color.

"Now, these are only mock-ups." Tristan clicked something, and a window opened up to show a gorgeous Wedgwood-blue background with the words "Rose's Bakery, a Chilton Crosse Treasure" in big bold font across a banner.

"Oh. Wow," she whispered. "It's so professional."

Though the bakery's awning did indeed say "Rose's," named after her mother, people always simply referred to it as "the bakery."

"I like everything about it," she said as Tristan scrolled further down. She saw a picture of the bakery's outside and several of the inside—*when had he done all this?*—and even a listing of menu items. "You've done so much work! I had no idea." She looked at him, his face glowing from the screen's light.

"It's nothing, really." Tristan shrugged and shifted to look at her. "The pictures were a breeze. I just snapped them with my mobile. And I borrowed a menu from Brandy. Remember, I *enjoy* this sort of thing. Hard to believe, but it's true."

"Well, you're very good at it." She elbowed him gently as they turned back to the screen at the same time.

"Rose," Tristan mused, looking over the banner. "That's your mum's name?"

"Yes. My dad named it after her. The bakery has actually been in my dad's family for a couple of generations. But he didn't want to be part of the family business. He had other plans. So he joined the Navy and later met my mum. When my grandfather died, he left the bakery and this cottage to my father."

"This was all forty years ago? When your dad took it over?"

"Yeah. He could've sold the bakery to someone else, I guess, but by that time, my mum had gotten pregnant with me. I was the great surprise. So Dad and Mum decided to settle down, keep the bakery, and make a life here in the village where he'd grown up. But then… she died in childbirth just a few weeks before the grand reopening."

"I can't imagine how your dad endured all that. I guess that's why this fortieth anniversary is particularly special. Perseverance in the face of tragedy."

"True. I wonder sometimes why Dad didn't just give up on the bakery when she died, why he didn't sell it after all. But I think he chose to press on for her, to open it in her memory. It's what she would've wanted."

"It must be hard on you, though."

"How so?"

"Well, it's just... bittersweet, isn't it? For you and your dad, this anniversary."

Julia nodded. *Bittersweet.* That was precisely what it was.

Tristan cleared his throat and returned his attention to the laptop. "So. I did a couple more sample pages." He tapped again. "Just to give you some color and font choices."

Julia took it all in, let her gaze wander over the screen. She pictured him up late, working on this for the bakery and her father. And for her.

"That's my favorite color," she said when he reached the last sample, a deep aubergine with light pink accents. "That's the one." She pointed. "But what do *you* think? Marketing-wise?"

She heard a rhythmical wheezing coming from the other sofa. Her father had leaned over a bit on his side, book flat against his chest, snoring soundly.

"That's my cue," she told Tristan. "This won't take long. Do you want a refill?"

"No, I'm good. Do you need a hand with him?"

"It's okay. Once he's awake, he's pretty steady on his feet."

Julia hung her glasses at her neck and stood to help her father. It took a moment to wake him, but once she did, he was willing and ready to sink into bed. After a light stumble getting up from the sofa, things went smoothly as they took methodical, shuffling steps toward the bedroom. She helped him with his nightly routine: removing his shoes, finding clean pajamas, helping him with some buttons, waiting for him to brush his teeth, then tucking him in.

"G'night, Dad." She clicked off the light.

When Julia entered the sitting room again, she noticed the fire had died down, so she went to stoke it. Tristan was still hard at work. He'd brought the computer to sit in his lap and was tapping away. When Julia joined him on the sofa again, Tristan kept his eyes on the screen and moved the laptop between them, so that it rested on his right thigh and her left thigh. She had to inch closer to him to keep the computer from wobbling.

"I adjusted the color on the menu, made it easier to read against the black font. What do you think?"

She wasn't required to read any text, so she left her glasses hanging on her shirt. "I like it." Honestly, she couldn't remember what the color had been before he changed it.

"And later, we can get you a domain name."

"What's that?"

"It's your address online. And if you want people to find you easily, you can use something like rosebakery-dot-com. You can totally customize it. There's a small fee per year, but it's worth it."

"I don't have any idea how to do that, set up a domain."

"No worries. I can help you with it."

When Julia turned to thank him, she hadn't realized *how* closely they were sitting. He had swiveled his neck to look at her, too, and their faces were inches apart, cheeks glowing in the fire's reflection.

"Thanks. For setting this up," she whispered.

Tristan's glance lowered from her eyes to her mouth as he whispered back, "Glad to help."

When his gaze lingered on Julia's lips, she knew he was going to kiss her. She couldn't back away if she tried—the pull between them was too strong. She let him lean in as she closed her eyes. Their shoulders touched as she felt his soft lips brush hers then press a little firmer, still gentle. His light beard was ticklish, but the heat of the kiss, the tenderness, were all she could feel. As she responded, leaning in deeper, she heard her father's voice.

"Julia! Water, please..."

His request had broken the mood, and Tristan backed away with a generous smile. Julia snickered and shook her head. "Sorry about that..."

"I'm not."

"I meant, about my dad."

"Well, I was talking about the kiss."

Julia's own smile broadened as she regretfully shifted the laptop over to Tristan's lap and stood to attend to her father. Probably for the first time in two years, she'd forgotten to set out a fresh glass beside his bed, a nightly ritual.

"Julia!" her father called again.

"Coming, Dad!"

"I need to get going, anyway." Tristan snapped the computer shut.

"Are you sure?"

He fetched his jacket. "Yeah, I've got about ten more things on my aunt's to-do list before I can hit the hay. Long day at the farm tomorrow."

They met around the back of the sofa, and Tristan leaned down to kiss her forehead. "Sleep tight." Then he was gone.

So much for casual and cool, Julia thought, moving her fingertips up to graze her lips.

Chapter Nine

"There's a certain kind of heritage that infuses old recipes, passed from generation to generation. Like someone from the past is reaching forward, to whisper their wisdom to you through a recipe stained with time."

THIRTY SECONDS AFTER SHE OPENED her eyes, Julia remembered the kiss. She replayed it in her mind and buried her face deep into her pillow with a wide smile. A twenty-nine-year-old had kissed her last night, just leaned in and kissed her. Straight on the mouth, no reservations. If Julia's father hadn't interrupted, the kiss might've been even longer, more passionate.

She hadn't been kissed in… she tried to recall. *Three years? Four?*

Immediately after her divorce, Julia had plunged herself into work, leaving no room for dating at all. A few years ago, she'd developed a crush on a guy in the village that never amounted to much—only two dates before he'd set his sights on someone else. It wasn't easy finding a single man within the bounds of Chilton Crosse or even building a relationship once you did find one. Besides the time factor, there were all those prying eyes and loose lips in the village.

But then Tristan had come along, kissed Julia, and awakened a sleeping giant somewhere inside her. During those few seconds, it all came rushing back. She remembered precisely what it felt like to be touched, to be *wanted*, and to want someone back. She didn't realize how much she'd missed it.

But as the morning wore on, as she showered and dressed, went downstairs to check on her father, prepare his medication, and start breakfast, harsh reality began to win the battle over the sleeping giant.

A twenty-nine-year-old had kissed her. Did it work in reverse? Would Tristan wake up today and think, *I kissed a forty-year-old.* Would he regret it?

All the old insecurities seeped in again, and Julia was too weak to fight them off. It was easier to believe Tristan regretted the kiss, that he'd done it in the first place because he was lonely or because the moment was relaxed and his guard was down. Maybe she was lonely, too, or just bored with her life and in need of a quick distraction.

After breakfast, when she applied her makeup, Julia saw the truth in physical form. The cruel bathroom lighting emphasized the creases around her eyes, the deep parentheses around her mouth, the noticeable streaks of gray hair growing near her temples, all announcing in big capital letters that she was teetering on the precipice of middle age.

How had a kiss so easily tricked her into feeling younger than she was, a teenager, a youthful person? It was only a mirage.

"Can I get you anything? Some breakfast or tea?" Joe called from the bar as he polished a glass.

Recently, Joe had started opening his pub earlier with a breakfast menu, which thankfully hadn't made any noticeable dent in the bakery's breakfast sales, probably because their offerings were completely different. Julia baked scones and muffins and quiches, while Joe provided heartier breakfasts, such as bubble and squeak or greasy fry-ups.

"Not for me, thanks. But Dad would like a coffee. Decaf, please."

She helped her father ease into the wooden chair beside the pub's fireplace then tilted the tweed cap on his head. He was the first of his mates to arrive.

"All good?" she asked him.

"All set!" he said with a clap. "You have fun at your… What was it?" He patted her hand.

"Book club."

"Yes, that's it."

She leaned over to kiss her father's scratchy cheek. "I'll pick you up in a couple of hours. Call if you need me for anything."

On Mondays, when Julia attended her book club at Gertrude's

cottage, her father sometimes visited the pub to chat on and on about the old days with his mates. Today, Julia had brought him to the pub a little early. Holly had sent an email to the book club members, asking that they arrive twenty minutes ahead of time to discuss details for Lizzie's surprise baby shower. Even Joe, her husband, didn't know anything about it.

As she left the pub, Julia thought about Tristan again. She recalled his "long day at the farm" statement last night and knew she likely wouldn't see him at all today, perhaps not even at tonight's poker game.

Earlier, during her ambling journey to the pub—her father had felt strong enough to insist on walking instead of using the van—Julia had caught herself glancing around Storey Road for a hopeful glimpse of Tristan. Despite her original concerns and doubts about the kiss, Julia seemed to have no real power over her feelings. She wanted to talk to Tristan, see him, gauge his reaction to last night. She yearned for a quick call or email, something, anything from him, to tell her where she might stand, where his head might be. The suspense was almost unbearable.

Her mobile jingled in her pocket, and she glanced at it. A text from Holly, reminding everyone about the baby shower meeting. Disappointed, Julia ignored the text and went on her way.

Hair pulled back, wearing a plain blue T-shirt and comfy jeans, Julia sifted through the remaining boxes in the flat above the bakery, determined to finish the job today. When she'd stopped by the pub after her book club ended, her father was in the middle of a lengthy, meandering story about the time the naval bandleader accidentally flicked his baton *into* the band during a performance. It had frightened the bass player, who flinched and leaned toward the alto saxophone player, who then toppled over while the band carried on playing. The five friends around the table were captivated. Her father used hand gestures to explain in vivid detail. It was a story Julia had heard a thousand times, always a bit more melodramatic and embellished than the time before. She sometimes wondered which version was the most accurate. Julia had waited patiently by the bar until the story ended and asked her father if he was ready to leave. But he hadn't been. He still had stories to tell and another coffee to drink. So she'd ordered him some lunch and tried to figure out what to do with her afternoon while he stayed put. The upstairs flat offered the perfect distraction.

Julia came upon an old shoebox full of memories: first and second-prize ribbons from her school-day achievements, hand-painted drawings for her father, even a pair of glitter shoelaces that were once all the fashion. And photos, dozens of them.

She moved to the old sofa and thumbed through the stack. Most of the photos were of little-girl Julia blowing out birthday candles, catching a ball, trying out new roller skates, icing a cake, delivering a plate to a customer's table. A few also included her father ho-ho-ho-ing in his Father Christmas costume, guiding Julia's hands to place something into the Aga, or reading Julia a story on his lap. And the last photo was of her very pregnant mother, standing underneath the bakery's awning—probably the last photo ever taken of her.

Much like the newly discovered journal, these photos were a treasure worth more than gold. Not just paper or ink, but so much more. They didn't deserve to be tucked inside a dusty, forgotten shoebox for the *next* forty years. She should frame them, display them, or at least place them into an album to flip through now and again. But first, she would show them to her father, let him walk down memory lane with her. He probably hadn't seen these pictures in decades.

Later in the day, before Julia started sandwiches for poker night, she sat down with her father at a table inside the bakery and produced the shoebox.

"What's this?" He adjusted his glasses.

"I found it upstairs when I finished cleaning today. Some old things, from years ago..."

He'd already brought out the first item with his wrinkled hands—a stick-figure drawing Julia had done of her father making a mince pie.

He chuckled. "Look at this. Sweet..."

Then he drew out the pictures, one by one, and explored them carefully, pausing on certain details, as though permanently memorizing them. And with every image came an accompanying story. "I remember this," he would say, pointing a bony finger at the photo. "This is the day you first showed an interest in baking," or "On this day, you fell and scraped your knee and vowed you'd never roller skate again," or "The Father Christmas costume. It's the very same one I used last Christmas at the festival. It still fits!"

Julia sat down next to him, hearing his stories, soaking them up. *He* was living history, much more so than these pieces of paper he held. He came to the last photo of his pregnant wife and took the longest pause. "Rose," he whispered, touching her belly with his index finger. "So beautiful."

"She really was."

"You favor her." He turned to face Julia. "It's the eyes, their shape and color. The older you get, the more I see of her in you…"

Julia slipped her arm around his shoulders and gave a gentle squeeze, tipping her head against his and trying not to cry.

"I wish I'd known her," said Julia. "She feels like the missing piece sometimes."

"She loved you. She used to pat on her stomach and talk to you every night before bed."

Julia leaned out of the hug, but her hand remained on her father's arm as he told the story.

"She even read books to you, played music for you, sang to you. She was never more proud of anything in her life than having you. You were her greatest achievement. And it's true. She would be so proud of you today. Running this bakery, taking care of your old dad…"

Julia chuckled. "Dad, you're no trouble. I don't know what I'd do without you. And—"

A knock at the front door—the secret knock—startled her. "It's a little early for the guys to arrive." She checked her watch. "I'd better see who it is."

Julia drew in a deep breath before she opened the door.

"Oh. Tristan."

"You look surprised. Did I get the wrong night? For poker?"

"No, no. It's tonight." She stepped aside to let him in. His hair looked damp, and he smelled freshly showered.

"I'm too early. Bollocks, I didn't check the time before I left. Today was busier than usual. Mr. Elton had a thousand different jobs for me, and I didn't get a break, not even for lunch. So when I wrapped up the day, I got changed and rushed to get here. I actually thought I was late."

A long day, no break. That could certainly explain the lack of texts. Julia closed the door behind him.

Tristan leaned down and looked into her eyes with concern. "Are you all right?"

Julia remembered the emotion she'd experienced over the pictures a moment ago. It must still be showing in her face, that wistfulness. She nodded. "Oh. I'm fine. We were just looking at some old photos of the bakery and my mum. Guess I'm too sentimental sometimes."

He reached for her hand and held it tenderly. "Nothing wrong with being sentimental. It's probably the thing I like most about you. Your heart."

His statement struck her—that someone she'd barely known for a handful of weeks could make that particular judgment about her. She wondered if many people in the village could say the same and mean it. Even with her growing up here, so few of the villagers truly knew her or cared to try to know her.

"That's a lovely thing to say," she told him.

"It's only the truth."

He continued to hold her hand. Julia stole a quick glance at her father, still absorbed in the pictures.

"And how was the *rest* of your day?" Tristan asked. "I missed talking to you, even just texting. I've sort of gotten used to our daily chats."

"Me, too." Now, she wished she'd at least texted him once today to break the ice instead of waiting on him to be the initiator. She'd let her stubbornness—and her fears—stop her from reaching out, making the first move. It all seemed silly now. "My day was good, nothing too exciting. Just the book club then a final clear-out of the upstairs flat. And now, poker night. The usual."

"Is that Tristan? Come here, young man. I want to show you some photos," her father called.

Julia released Tristan's hand as they walked toward the table then offered to make them both a sandwich as Tristan sat down with her father.

Back in the kitchen, she smiled. *No regrets about the kiss, about anything.* That was what Tristan's body language had told her and the words-between-the-lines, too. That was all she needed to know.

Soon, she brought turkey sandwiches and crisps over to the table. Her father was storytelling again, holding up a certain photo.

"... the icing was dark green, and so a couple of hours later, when Julia brushed her teeth, she realized her tongue was green. She called me from the bathroom—'Daddy, Daddy!'—I thought the cottage was on fire. But when she stuck out her tongue, I couldn't stop laughing long enough to reassure her that it was only the icing that turned her mouth green. She hadn't contracted some hideous disease..."

He and Tristan chuckled together as Julia handed her father a napkin.

The laughter was contagious. "I don't think I've eaten green icing since," Julia admitted.

The other men began to arrive, and the poker game got underway as Julia served more sandwiches. She chose not to play tonight. She needed to catch up on her reading. This morning's book club was the first time she'd ever failed to do the required reading, and she was utterly unprepared, praying she wasn't called upon to answer a question.

She read a couple of chapters, offered refills and seconds to the players between hands, then decided to whip up a quick batch of ginger biscuits. By the time they had cooled, the night had already ended. Her father won and received an ugly gnome figurine from Adam. "I'll find a prime spot for it in the cottage," her father had beamed, holding it high for everyone to see.

"Oh, I don't *think* so," Julia had countered, seeing the gnome's evil grin. "Maybe in your room, far, far away from me."

Tristan was the last to leave for the night, insisting on helping straighten the tables and carry dishes to the sink.

Saying goodnight to her father, Tristan found his jacket, then Julia walked him to the front door. When she opened it, Tristan grabbed her hand in a natural, fluid gesture and pulled her gently into the cool night air. She closed the door behind them and stood with him at the bakery's entrance under the awning.

The atmosphere suddenly felt intimate, personal. The sky was dark except for the clear sliver of a moon, and they had the entire street to themselves. Everyone had closed up shop and gone to bed long ago.

Tristan held both her hands and interlocked their fingers. She couldn't see his face very well in the shadows.

"Let's do something this week," he said softly.

Julia felt those same nerves as last night begin to rise in her throat. "Like what?"

"Go somewhere, do something fun. I just want to spend some time with you. Not spontaneous or accidental. I want to spend time with you on purpose."

Thankfully, he couldn't see her blushing cheeks in the shadows. "Okay. But we both have such crazy work schedules."

"So something easy, just an hour or two we can squeeze in somewhere."

Julia pondered it then thought of the perfect place on the outskirts of the village, where only tourists ever went. "Have you been to Chatsworth Manor yet?"

"No, what's that?"

"This grand, refurbished hotel right outside the village. It's been the site for lots of films. It's got a fancy restaurant and these massive Italian gardens. I haven't been there in a while. It's lovely."

"Perfect. We'll pick a day and go for it. Visit the gardens, maybe grab a meal, take a break from real life."

"Yes." A couple of hours away from the bakery, away from the drudgery of everyday life. *Something to look forward to. Something with Tristan.*

She watched him lean in closer as he pressed his warm lips to hers.

"Good night," he whispered as he backed away.

She watched him go, feeling that teenager-y feeling creep in once more.

Chapter Ten

"Deep talks shared over a savory meal... well, that's the best possible kind of companionship."

Julia swiveled her hips in front of the full-length mirror, swishing the lavender sundress around her ankles.

"Oh, that's a lovely choice." Mrs. Bennett stood at a respectful distance, her hands clasped together at her waist. "If it's too long for you, we have another size..."

But Julia wasn't convinced it was lovely. She'd spent the past twenty minutes in Mrs. Bennett's boutique struggling to find a couple of new outfits to add to her bland wardrobe—not an easy task, considering she loathed shopping. She never kept up with the latest fashion trends. Julia had already tried on at least ten outfits this afternoon—blouses, dresses, jackets. But nothing worked. Nothing. It only confirmed why she never shopped for clothes. She was running out of time and patience.

"I'm just not sure..." Julia told the mirror, trying out a new angle. But she already knew a different angle wouldn't solve the problem. A thin, pastel sundress simply wasn't *her*. Someone like Holly or Noelle or Lizzie could easily pull off this dress. They were young and pretty and innately feminine. But Julia had never considered herself the girly girl who loved dresses or shoes or nail polish. Certainly, she wanted to look respectable, maybe even to look pretty sometimes. She *did* wear skirts to church because she had to, but otherwise, she'd never invested much effort in her appearance. She didn't have time for it.

Mrs. Bennett snapped her fingers. "Wait a minute. I think I have the perfect outfit." She disappeared around the corner.

While she waited, Julia fiddled with the sundress's many buttons. In a couple of minutes, Mrs. Bennett returned, holding a long blouse with a navy-and-cranberry paisley pattern, not a pastel in sight.

"It's all the rage," Mrs. Bennett explained, handing the hanger to Julia. "It's a relaxed-fit blouse that hangs right below the hips. It's comfortable and feminine, but you can still wear jeans with it. Best of both worlds."

Intrigued, Julia thanked her and slipped back into the dressing room. When she re-emerged and glanced in the mirror, she brightened. "Hey. I think I actually like it."

The three-quarter-sleeve blouse swished with Julia as she pivoted. Even better than the color and fit, this blouse suited Julia, as though someone had designed it with her in mind.

"I'll take it!" she told Mrs. Bennett.

"Wonderful. I have a few different patterns available in the same size. Would you care to look?"

"Why not?"

As she followed Mrs. Bennett to the rack, Julia heard the tinkle of the front doorbell.

"Oh, Mrs. Spencer. So lovely to see you," Mrs. Bennett told Noelle, who pushed a pram with Adam Jr. inside.

Julia waved to Noelle from across the shop then turned back to Mrs. Bennett, who was already holding out the other blouses for Julia's approval. Similar to the one she wore, these contained various patterns and an appealing combination of colors.

In the corner, Adam Jr. began to fuss and squirm, and his fussing soon evolved into loud, squawking wails.

Mrs. Bennett had to raise her voice to speak over him. "Would you like me to ring these up for you?"

Julia mouthed, "Yes."

"I'm sorry about this," Noelle shouted, searching for something in her bag to calm her screaming son. Her voice competed with his. "He's been keeping me up nights. It's colic. We finally had a break this morning, so I thought I'd take him out."

Julia walked over to the pram and smiled at Adam, touching his quivering fist with her finger. "It's okay, little one." She didn't know what to say to Noelle. If Julia were a mother, too, maybe she would have the right words of comfort. *My baby did this, too. It won't last long. It's a stage. You're doing a brilliant job with him. Hang in there…*

But being childless, not having experienced a colicky baby, all Julia could say was, "I can't believe how fast he's growing." *The fallback cliché.*

Noelle forced a smile and picked up her son to soothe the crying by rocking him. Julia wondered how sore Noelle's arms already were, probably having rocked and carried him all night long.

When that still didn't do the trick, Noelle told Mrs. Bennett with an oh-well shrug, "We'll try again later," then patiently placed Adam, still screaming, back into his pram. She pushed it out the front door as Julia held it open.

The silence was thick and immediate as the door closed behind Noelle.

Julia remembered she was still wearing the new blouse and went to collect her old T-shirt from the dressing room. "I'll just wear this out, if that's okay," she told Mrs. Bennett, who was tapping the prices into the till.

When Julia returned to the counter and fished around for her credit card, she thought about Noelle's baby and about babies in general. It wasn't until she'd woken up after her hysterectomy at thirty-five years old that the sobering notion had truly hit Julia. She would never be a mother. Although it wasn't something she'd craved the way other women seemed to, suddenly being stripped of the chance to experience motherhood had left her with a sadness she hadn't anticipated. It had been thrust upon her, this childless life, and when the possibility of becoming a mother was actually removed, it became something she missed without even knowing she missed it.

But soon, life and work and duty crept in as they always did. Her work was the best medicine, and Julia had resolved to accept her childless life without emotion or regret. Since then, she'd only experienced the occasional pinch of "what if?" when seeing a pregnant woman or a new mother with a child. But the pinch always passed quickly.

Now, at forty, Julia couldn't *imagine* fitting a child into her life, even if it were possible. She already had enormous, taxing responsibilities with the bakery and her father that consumed nearly every waking moment. She couldn't afford even to get sick or take a real day off if she wanted.

Besides, the creaks in her joints, the soreness in her back at the end of a day, and the noticeable slowing down of her body almost made her grateful not to have children. Some women could handle it—women were having babies older and older these days. She'd just read online about a fifty-five-year-old new mother. But Julia couldn't fathom the physical strength and endurance it would take, raising a newborn or dealing with a colicky baby that kept her up all night. The window of motherhood had closed for Julia long ago, and she had made her peace with it.

She paid for the blouses and collected the rest of her shopping bags—two new western novels for her father, bought at Holly's bookshop, and a pack of new clarinet reeds, special-ordered from the emporium across the street. The clock on Mrs. Bennett's wall told Julia she had barely an hour until her picnic with Tristan at Chatsworth's gardens. She still had so much to do—pick up her father at the bakery, along with the hamper and goodies to go with it, take him to the cottage for his nap, and put the hamper together—before Tristan arrived.

Julia stretched her arms out to the edges of the quilt and folded the corners together, hoping it would be large enough for a picnic. As she folded, she hummed "I'll Be Seeing You," the tune her father had played earlier this morning during her break.

Julia couldn't remember the last time she'd hummed. Humming meant she was relaxed, enjoying her task, enjoying life at that particular moment. It wasn't the new outfit or the beautiful spring day that was the source of the humming. It was Tristan. Only a day and a half had passed since he'd kissed her under the moon. She couldn't wait to see his kind eyes, to hear his quiet chuckle when something amused him, or to see the outline of his muscles as he filled out a shirt. She wanted him nearby, wanted him in the same room, wanted more of him.

Setting down the quilt and moving on to the contents of the hamper at the kitchen table, Julia thought about the change in herself since Tristan's arrival. She'd never been the type of girl whose entire world revolved around a man. She'd experienced too much heartache, knew how fragile and temporary relationships could be. Why depend on something that could evaporate from one day to the next? Better to be self-sufficient. *Safer that way.* Besides, she'd been on her own so long, she'd forgotten how to factor another person into her life's equation.

But she couldn't deny it. There was something different in the air these days, a fragrant tinge, a lightness, a brightness. Same cottage, same job, same village. But her life had shifted from mundane and predictable to exciting and hopeful. It reminded her of a new bread pudding recipe she'd experimented with one Christmas. She'd made three versions of it, tweaking the ingredients each time. The first batch, following the recipe to the letter, was merely acceptable. The second batch was awful—entirely too much vanilla. But the third was *the one.* She'd added a light sauce with nutmeg and orange-flavored liqueur, which immediately vaulted the original recipe to new heights, adding seasoning and depth. Much like Tristan had done with her already good, already satisfying life. He had added seasoning to her dull days.

Julia was old enough to know that her feelings had everything to do with endorphins, hormones, and brain chemistry. Attraction and affection were a drug—intoxicating, addictive. *And usually fleeting.*

Even so, a strong part of her seemed to deliberately, consciously embrace that intoxication, eager to see where this thing with Tristan might lead. It didn't mean the other, rational part of her didn't nag away at her. The logical portion of her brain still held legitimate fears and doubts about the path ahead and the probability of heartache or failure.

But today, she and Tristan would have a picnic. Today, she wouldn't overanalyze or fret or be sensible. Today, she would happily place herself under Tristan's delicious spell.

As she walked with Tristan along the path to Chatsworth Manor, Julia peered at the canopy of arched trees that lined the way while the sun winked down at her through the branches.

This second week of May was unusually warm. Julia had even abandoned her jacket at the cottage when Tristan arrived minutes ago. He had complimented her new blouse then insisted on carrying the hamper, though Julia had told him it wasn't *that* heavy. As they took off for the manor, Julia led Tristan down the back road, behind the shops, and up the hill to the outskirts of the village.

"Hold up a sec." Tristan set down the hamper and stretched his right leg behind him, the leg with the scar.

"Does it hurt?"

"Just sore. Need to stretch it sometimes. I still get these cramps and shooting nerve pains now and then. They come and go. I'm used to them."

"We should've taken the van." Julia watched him wince. She wondered if he thought of his brother and the accident, even subconsciously, every time his leg held any pain. A forever reminder...

"No, a walk does me good. I need to stay active." He stood straight again and gave her a reassuring smile. "See? All better."

Tristan picked up the hamper with his left hand and found Julia's free hand with his right. "I had no idea this place was here. It's enormous." Tristan gazed toward the manor as they moved closer.

Chatsworth Manor had originally been built in the fourteenth century, as Julia recalled. Seeing it through Tristan's eyes, she noticed its particular grandeur—three stories tall, beautiful slate-colored stonework with delicate gables topping off the roof. The structure had been renovated and recently highlighted in last year's filming of Jane Austen's *Emma*.

As they approached the entrance, Julia led Tristan behind the manor to the edge of the Italian sunken gardens, which were open to the public. Cypress trees lined the way, and a large ceramic fountain sat prominently in the middle with chunky manicured hedges all around.

"Spectacular," Tristan mused. "I can't believe this is part of your village. I wonder who built it."

"I don't really know the history of it. I think it was some duke who wanted a country home for his new bride."

So that Tristan could receive the best, broadest glimpse of the gardens, Julia continued around the edges toward the very back to a secluded spot overlooking the manor and gardens. The sun poured a spotlight onto the manicured grass, making it look even deeper green than it was.

"How about here?" Julia paused at an open patch of grass between two trees.

Tristan agreed and set down the hamper then helped Julia unfold the quilt.

She moved the hamper to the quilt's edge to give them more room and sat down next to Tristan.

"I didn't tell you about the hamper idea, did I?" Julia opened its latch. "For the bakery."

"I don't think so."

The sweet scent of grapes and fresh bread hit her senses as she removed the contents: smoked ham sandwiches, fresh fruit, crisps, bottled water, and a couple of homemade brownies for dessert, with paper plates and napkins tucked away at the bottom. She explained about the hampers, her idea to make them available because of the demand from tourists. She would officially start selling them next week.

"I can add them to your website when you've decided for sure." Tristan popped a grape into his mouth. "I think it's a great idea. Very forward thinking."

Julia unwrapped a sandwich from the cling film and placed it, along with some crisps, onto a plate for Tristan then made a plate for herself. She took her first bite of sandwich and felt a cool breeze on her cheeks. She closed her eyes and swallowed. "I can't remember the last time I had a picnic. It feels naughty, like I should be working or doing something productive. I wish we could do this every day." She opened her eyes, hoping she hadn't been too forward. But Tristan's half smile told her otherwise.

"Count me in." He moved his hand to tuck a stray hair from Julia's cheek behind her ear.

A child's screeching drew their attention to the center of the gardens below. A chunky toddler struggled in her father's arms. From this distance, it was hard to recognize the faces of the couple—tourists, probably, viewing the gardens.

"Maggie would love it here." Tristan took a bite of his sandwich.

"She'd probably end up herding the tourists."

Tristan snickered. "True. Best to leave her at the farm."

"You know, you should bring her to the cottage sometime to meet my dad. He had a Corgi when he was a little boy."

"Oh yeah? I could bring her on a weekend, maybe."

Julia shifted and reached for a crisp. "You're so good with him. My dad, I mean. Not everybody has the patience to sit through his long-winded stories."

"He's amazing. I admire his attitude. He just keeps chugging along, grateful for everything. I hope I love life that much if I get to be his age."

Julia's mobile rang from her pocket. "Sorry. I always need to keep it on, just in case..."

"Your dad."

Julia nodded. But the screen showed a text from Mildred. Abbey had probably informed her that Julia knew how to text now. The message included three new pictures of their stop in Germany, along with: *Home tomorrow. Will be jet lagged. Get together Friday for tea?*

"Something good?" Tristan ate another crisp.

Julia realized she'd been smiling at the screen. "It's from Mildred Newbury. I guess you haven't met her yet. She's been out of the country the last few weeks. Mildred is Abbey's new step-mum."

"Newbury. Is she related to Holly at the bookshop? Fletcher's fiancée?"

"That's the one. Holly and Abbey are sisters. And there are two more Newbury sisters, twins. One's at university, and the other has a blossoming film career. They're my favorite family in the village. They've suffered a lot with the loss of their mum, but they've pulled together. And Mildred fits in with them perfectly. She actually helped raise me. She didn't have any children of her own, and when Mum died so suddenly, Mildred stepped in and took care of me while my father dealt with the bakery. I don't know what I would've become without Mildred. She's really the only mum I've ever known."

Before she could get emotional, Julia returned her attention back to the screen and tapped out her reply to Mildred with one thumb: *Yes!!*

"You're getting pretty good at that texting thing."

"I still make all these daft mistakes, though. I'll never be used to the keyboard. I'm usually fumbling all over the place. And I still don't know how to snap a photo."

"Oh, that's an easy one. Here." Tristan dusted off his fingers and took her mobile. His fingers grazed hers. He tapped on a little camera icon, and a live image of their picnic lunch showed up on her screen. "Ready for a picture."

Julia tapped the button and heard a picture-snap sound effect.

"You just took a photo of your own shoe," Tristan teased. "Here, let me show you something cool." He clicked another button, and suddenly, she could see a live image of herself and Tristan on the screen.

Tristan stretched out his arm as far as it would go. "Say 'cheese.'" They tilted their heads together and smiled toward the camera while Tristan snapped the photo.

"Our first selfie." He switched the viewer back to the picnic lunch.

"Okay, let me try."

Julia focused the camera on a ladybug crawling onto the quilt, moved in closer, and snapped the picture.

"How do I see the one I just took?"

Tristan showed her, and a beautiful vivid red ladybug appeared on her screen.

"Look at that! You don't know what you've done. I'll be snapping pictures all the time."

"It's addictive." Tristan found his own mobile then scooted closer to Julia on the quilt until their hips touched. He scrolled through dozens of photos: some of Maggie, one of Julia's dad sitting in his blue chair, some of Mr. Elton's farm, some of Tristan's aunt and the shop, one of magnificent clouds in the sky. He switched to a different feature that let her see how many pictures he'd stored in total. Hundreds, it seemed. He scrolled swiftly through them.

"It's a photo journal. It's hard for me to delete them. I've got years' worth in here. They sort of chronicle events in my life." After more scrolling, he stopped and clicked on one of them—an image of himself in a hospital bed, arm in a cast, leg in a cast, raised high, head bandaged.

"From the accident," she whispered.

"I know it's weird, but I keep it as a reminder of what changed my life. I don't dwell on it every day, but I also don't want to forget."

He scrolled through a couple more photos and tapped on one to make it full-size—Tristan, with one arm around another man, two inches taller, with nearly identical features.

"Your brother? You favor each other..."

"Mum took it the day before the accident. It's hard to look at this one sometimes. We had spent that entire day hiking on our parents' land, laughing, telling stories, catching up. It felt like when we were little boys, carefree and happy. No idea what would happen the next day. We didn't know it would be our last full day together."

"You said it changed you? The accident?"

Tristan lowered his mobile and stared out at the gardens. "Yeah. I tend to see my life as before and after the accident. I can't help it. That day was a profound marker in my life, but I didn't know it until much later. At first, when the accident happened, I was numb, just processing everything. I woke up from a three-week coma to my mother's face, tears streaming down her cheeks. It took her several minutes to finally tell me my brother was dead and that I'd missed his funeral. I channeled all my emotions into anger for a while. I was belligerent, hard to live with, always in a bad mood. Feeling sorry for myself. I missed him. And I didn't understand why he had to die. And maybe..."

"What?"

"Maybe I felt guilty for being the one to make it out alive. Maybe it should've been me."

Julia slipped her hand through his arm and squeezed it. She knew exactly what he meant—feeling guilty for being alive at someone else's expense.

Tristan shifted on the blanket, placed his warm hand on top of Julia's. He looked her in the eye. "And then, the best thing happened to me. After the sixth surgery, the doctor told me I might not ever walk again, and if I did, it would be with a severe limp."

"That's the best thing?"

"Yeah. Because I channeled my anger into proving him wrong. Physical therapy gave me something to battle, a physical way to face the rage. I worked every day, hours a day, usually through excruciating pain. But as my body healed, the grief didn't. It was a different kind of pain that stayed behind." Tristan glanced down at his hand touching hers. "You asked how it changed me. Well, I felt strong, but also fragile, kind of... anxious. As though anything could be snatched away from me without warning. I started feeling that way about my parents, my mates. I saw them differently. They were more valuable to me. And I also realized my own life could be taken from me as fast as Corbett's was—that tomorrow could always be my last day. Every single day matters. It's cheesy. But it's true." His voice cracked.

"Not cheesy at all." Julia shook her head.

She brought her other hand to encircle his arm then rested her head on his shoulder. She felt him swivel his neck and kiss the top of her head.

"Sorry I brought up something sad on such a beautiful day," Julia whispered.

"I like talking about my brother. Sometimes, I think I don't do it enough. Thank you for letting me talk about him. Not many people do."

Julia closed her eyes, letting another breeze touch her cheeks. She wanted to stay like this the entire afternoon, feel the warmth of Tristan's body through his sleeve, stay this close to him.

But the sound of his mobile ringing broke her thoughts.

Tristan groaned. "My turn. Seriously, next time we should both accidentally leave our mobiles at home."

As he peered at the screen, Julia lifted her head and backed away a little to give him some privacy. She took a sip of her bottled water.

"Mr. Elton. He wants me there now. Something about a delivery. And if I don't get there first, he'll start handling it on his own. He's a stubborn old man." Tristan looked Julia in the eyes and sighed. "Sorry. This was supposed to be a relaxed afternoon. No deadlines, no thinking about work."

"It's okay. He needs you. You should go."

"When can I see you again?"

Realistically, after skipping her nap today, Julia would be a zombie tonight. She'd been behind on her sleep for days and hadn't been able to catch up. It was starting to impact her memory, her body. Her younger self would have forgone her own needs and insisted, "Tonight!" as an answer to Tristan's question. But Julia got the sense he wasn't going anywhere and that one night apart wouldn't alter his feelings for her, whatever they might be. So she said, "Tomorrow, definitely. Maybe we could meet up after work or something."

"Sounds good."

They'd only finished half their meal, so they wrapped up the other halves of sandwiches, crisps, and fruits and tucked them back inside the hamper. "Take the picnic with you," Julia insisted. "You can eat the rest on a break later on."

"Are you sure?"

"Completely. I'm full. Plus, I'm surrounded by food, all day, every day. If I get hungry, I can always find something."

They stood to fold the quilt together, then Tristan picked up the hamper. They walked on in silence, holding hands past the property line of the manor until they reached the fork in the road, where one led to the bakery and the other led to Mr. Elton's farm.

Tristan faced her. "I enjoyed today. Just... being with you."

A smile started somewhere in her chest, inching upward toward the curl of her lips. "The feeling is extremely mutual."

Rather than wait for him, Julia took hold of Tristan's shirt and pulled him closer. And when he leaned down, she kissed him. She tried not to keep smiling as she kissed him, but it was impossible. Was she living a dream? Who was this person, making her hum, making her smile, making her take such initiative, yanking her firmly out of her comfort zone?

He returned the kiss, stroked her cheek with his free hand, and then whispered, "Mmm. That was nice." He leaned in, forehead to forehead. "We should do more of that."

"Count me in."

He waved goodbye and started off to Mr. Elton's, hamper in hand. Julia lingered for a moment, watching him leave, then hugged the quilt to her chest, knowing she could happily face whatever else the day had to offer.

Chapter Eleven

"Baking is hard work. Early mornings, constant repetition, solitary confinement. But it's also joyful work. It's making new discoveries, enjoying the small details, and seeing customers smile. If the joy ever disappears, it's time to quit."

JULIA GENTLY SHOOK THE SEMICLOSED umbrella free of excess water then tilted it against the stone wall at the entrance of Foxglove House. Before she could even raise her hand to ring the bell, Mildred had opened the front door.

"Here you are!" Her face beamed as she leaned toward Julia for a tight squeeze. "It's dreadful out here," Mildred proclaimed, ushering Julia inside the grand house, which smelled of strong tea and sweet fabric conditioner. "Let's get you out of this raincoat."

The two-story estate, home to Duncan Newbury, inarguably the wealthiest man in the village, stood on the outskirts of Chilton Crosse. Julia had only ever visited the estate a handful of times. She'd spent most of her visits over the years with Mildred at her small cottage, where she'd lived with her brother before marrying Duncan.

While Julia followed Mildred down the long hall toward the spacious French-style kitchen, she marveled at the broad wooden staircase, the beautifully decorated parlor next door, and the elaborate moldings near the ceilings. She was ecstatic for Mildred to have such a beautiful home to call her own.

"I brought us some lemon teacakes." Julia took a seat at the kitchen table. "Maybe they'll brighten up a dreary day."

The rain pattered against the French-doors leading to the lush gardens.

"Oh, lovely." Mildred took the box Julia offered. "That reminds me. I have something for you, too. There was this lovely little shop in Sorrento that sold landscapes and jewelry boxes and coasters—every item hand carved, made of wood." She produced a plastic bag and removed a box, which she slid across the table. "For you..."

Julia removed the tissue paper inside the box to reveal a handcrafted set of wooden coasters, each one detailing a different scene of the Italian countryside. "Oh, Mildred. These are incredible."

"Aren't they? Duncan couldn't get me out of that shop. I wanted to browse all day. I ended up buying a landscape for the parlor, and I got the girls each a jewelry box. And we watched a man at work, there in his little corner, carving the wood. A figurine, I think..."

"Amazing. Thank you. I love them." Julia tucked the coasters back inside, careful to replace the tissue on top.

Mildred set out the tea while Julia adjusted the silver charm bracelet she'd bought at Mrs. Bennett's boutique. It was the first bit of jewelry she'd purchased in ages. She never wore rings or bracelets while baking. They got in her way, so she normally ended up not wearing them at all. But she'd spotted this bracelet and couldn't resist.

"I'm so glad you're back," she told Mildred. "And you had a marvelous trip?"

"We *did*." Mildred paused and swiveled around. Her skin was tanned, her cheeks flushed with a healthy glow, evidence of her happy travels. "The trip of a lifetime. Part of me never wanted to come home. We kept adding on stops, extending our stay, city by city. But still, it's good to be home. I need my routine again. And I actually missed my soppy English garden."

Mildred continued her preparations and soon brought the tea tray to the table. She poured Julia a cup. "I never knew the world could be so lovely. Or so fascinating. All these old, established cultures with such history—their monuments, castles, ruins, and stunning landscapes. I kept trying to picture people hundreds of years ago, living right there where I stood. It took my breath away more than once. And since Duncan has traveled the world a few times over, I had a seasoned guide everywhere I went."

This was a new Mildred sitting across from Julia. Marriage had been good for her. And travel had been good for her. Even her posture seemed different—confident, assured. She was happier than Julia had ever seen her.

Mildred's hand froze, a sugar lump raised in midair between them as she studied Julia. "Something's different. You look… thinner. You've lost at least a stone, haven't you?"

Mildred had been the first one to realize it or, at least, to say anything. Julia couldn't help smiling. "Yes! Thirteen pounds, almost a stone. I feel so much better."

"You look amazing. What brought it on?"

"A couple of months ago, I noticed how sluggish I felt. And my clothes weren't fitting as easily. So, I cut down on sugar—not easy to do when you handle it all day—and I started walking instead of taking the van so much."

"I'm impressed! I might need to pick your brain for diet tips. I think I've gained the weight you lost during our trip. We ate like kings every day. Rich foods, dessert with every meal…"

With that, Mildred launched into more details about her travels—Switzerland and Germany and France, with a spur-of-the-moment jaunt to Italy. She fetched her mobile and scrolled through pictures, stretching across the table for Julia to see. With each picture came a new story—lunch at Maximilians, a coin toss into the Trevi Fountain, an entire day spent browsing the Louvre.

Usually, Julia became easily bored, or easily jealous, hearing of other people's extensive travels. But Mildred described the sights in such vivid detail that Julia felt as though she were taking a trip with her to each new place.

Pausing for a sip of tea, Mildred grimaced. "Oh my. I've completely dominated our chat with my travel stories, haven't I?" She glanced at the clock behind Julia. "Nearly an hour, gone!" She shook her head. "Can you forgive me? I didn't want your visit to be so *me* centered."

"Nonsense! I came to see you and to hear all about your trip. I'm enjoying it. Really."

"Well, you're being gracious. Let's talk about something else." She leaned forward to refresh Julia's tea. "Tell me all the goings-on in the village. I feel like I've been gone for an age! What have I been missing?"

"There's not too much excitement at the moment. Let's see... the book club is in full swing. Lizzie's pregnancy is going smoothly so far. Did you know she's having twins?"

"Holly told me about it! It's marvelous. I'll bet Joe is over the moon."

"He can't stop smiling. The book club is having a baby shower for her, by the way. Week after next."

Julia's mobile vibrated inside her jeans pocket, and she tilted the screen to check it. *Tristan*. The urge was nearly overwhelming to click open the message and respond that minute, but she would have to wait. Mildred was her focus right now.

"And your father? How is he?"

Julia slid her mobile back into her pocket. "Very well. We had a minor scare several days ago. He got disoriented. But Dr. Granger saw him immediately, and it was all just a meds issue, not a stroke, as we'd feared."

"What a relief!" Mildred removed a second teacake from the box. "Speaking of your father, how's the planning going for his secret anniversary party? Holly told me about some of it this morning. Do you think he suspects?"

"I don't *think* he does. I don't know how we'll keep it a secret from him with the way this village talks and with the circus the party is becoming. But so far, so good."

"Circus?" Mildred bit into a teacake.

"You know Mrs. Pickering. She's formed a committee. And she's always trying to outdo herself, always making events more about *her* than anyone else. If you can believe this, she tried to order fireworks for the big day and a skywriting plane."

Mildred nearly choked on her teacake. "She didn't!"

"She absolutely did. We talked her down a bit at the last meeting. No fireworks and merely a banner-carrying plane. But we'll still have a street parade with children, music, and who knows what else."

"Oh my. Well, your father will certainly enjoy the spectacle. He loves a good party, that man."

"Yes. Which is why I decided to stop stressing over something I can't control. I know he'll love it. A day to remember. That's really all that matters in the end."

"Agreed." Mildred gave a warm smile. "Oh! I've been hearing about a new face in the village. Abbey won't stop talking about this Trisham fellow? Mrs. Pickering's nephew?"

"Tristan." Julia nodded.

"Yes! Tristan. Abbey says he's absolutely dishy. She talked about him like he was a character in a romance novel. I believe Abbey has a little crush on him. I'll bet all the girls do. Have you met him?"

Julia stayed poised, found her poker face. "He took over Hamish's job a while ago. Delivering eggs to the bakery from Mr. Elton's farm."

"And? What's he like?"

Under normal circumstances, Julia would have let down her guard and spilled all to Mildred, right then and there. Every last detail—her first meeting with Tristan, her initial reservations, the change toward him as she realized how mature and sensitive he was, and how her feelings for him had kept multiplying day by day, something she couldn't control if she tried. In fact, she was brimming over with the desire to tell *someone* all about Tristan. But something wouldn't let her, not even with Mildred.

"Abbey's right. He is rather dishy," Julia conceded. "And he seems to be a nice help to his aunt. And he's been really good to my dad. They have long conversations at the bakery about books and things."

Omissions are not lies, Julia told herself.

"So he's nothing like his aunt, then, eh? I wonder how long he'll stay in the village."

"No telling." Julia sipped the last of her tea. "Listen, I hate to leave, but it's about time for Dad's nap."

"Of course. I've kept you too long, haven't I?"

"Not at all. I've enjoyed catching up. I missed you while you were gone."

They rose at the same time. Julia collected her handbag slung over the chair.

"Thanks again for those gorgeous coasters. Really thoughtful of you."

"You're very welcome. And thanks for the cakes. Duncan will love one when he gets home tonight. Lemon is his favorite." Mildred peered out the window. "Well, the rain has slowed to a depressing drizzle."

Mildred retrieved Julia's coat at the front door, and they hugged their goodbyes. Julia collected her umbrella and sprinted to the van, eager to let the heater warm up her ankles.

Inside, Julia looked at Tristan's text—a picture of the work boots he wore with Maggie resting her head on top of them, eyes shut tight, with the message: *Seeking shelter from rain under a tree with Mags. Just thinking about you. Missing the scent of your strawberry shampoo and that beautiful smile. Wondering when I can see it again.*

Julia read the message a second time, the warmth from her ankles spreading up to her whole body. He missed her after barely a day apart. She imagined Tristan and Maggie under that tree and wished she had time to pop in for a surprise visit. But what she'd told Mildred was true. Julia was late to pick up her father and return him to the cottage then get back to work.

She texted regretfully: *Wish I could be there now, but duty calls. How about tomorrow? Missing you, too. :-)*

Rather than wait for a response, she buried the mobile inside her pocket then shifted the van into gear to head for the bakery. On the way, she mulled over her conversation with Mildred. *Why* had she so purposefully hidden the Tristan situation from her dearest, closest friend, the only mother figure she'd ever known? Of anyone in the village, Julia could trust Mildred with this information. Mildred wouldn't have been judgmental or overly sappy. And she certainly wouldn't have told another soul. She would've been supportive, happy that Julia was happy.

Was Julia afraid that telling someone would make it real, would somehow prick a hole in this perfect, delicate balloon? Or was it just too early to call it a relationship at all? It felt somehow right, keeping this thing between herself and Tristan for the moment—sacred, intimate. If everyone in the village knew, or even if only Mildred knew, then it might feel less... special.

Besides, Tristan, to her knowledge, hadn't told anyone either. Perhaps he was leery of his aunt finding out. She would surely have more than an opinion or two! Or perhaps, like Julia, he simply wanted to keep the new relationship between the two of them, not an illicit secret to be ashamed of, but something too precious to share with the masses.

And deep inside, Julia wasn't entirely sure that Tristan wasn't a mirage—something she saw that really wasn't there, something that could disappear at any moment.

"More tea?" Julia held the kettle, poised, beside her dad's cup.

"No thanks, love. I'm good." His hands were clasped together across his broad barrel chest, fingers tapping in a very specific pattern and rhythm along with his right foot. Julia had seen her father's tapping thousands of times in her life. It was a tic, a habit. But it wasn't random the way some people scratched their chins or fidgeted in their seats. Her father's finger tapping came from something familiar and specific. He was playing his clarinet—tapping imaginary keys with his fingers. She always wondered which song was playing in his head but never asked. He seemed unaware he was doing it, and even as a little girl, Julia never wanted to draw his attention to it, never wanted to break him of a habit so meaningful. It would be like trying to wake someone from sleepwalking. Best to let them continue on.

She refilled her own cup then added sugar.

"What does your day hold?" her father asked, still tapping. They sat at the cottage's kitchen table for breakfast.

"It's surprisingly light. Some errands and some calls to make. And then I want to try a new recipe out for the guys at poker tonight. Do you think they'd mind being my guinea pigs?"

"Mind?" He chuckled. "They'd be the first to volunteer!"

"And Tristan said he might drop by the cottage this afternoon for a bit. He has a little surprise for you." She pictured her father's delighted expression upon seeing Tristan walk up with Maggie panting on a leash. Tristan had been too busy with work to drop by over the weekend but said he'd be sure to visit today.

Julia drank her tea and realized that, for the first time in years, she had slept late on her day off. Of course, late meant seven a.m., but it was still the best sleep she'd had in ages.

"Julia, are you happy here?"

Her father's question jarred her out of her serenity. He wasn't tapping anymore. Instead, he had reached out to hold the handle of his cup.

"Why do you ask? Do I seem sad?"

His eyes shifted to her, the wrinkles near the corners deepening as he smiled. "No, love. Just the opposite. I sense that you're happy. You seem particularly settled right now. But I guess I'm wondering if you feel..."

"What?"

"Stuck here. In the village. With me, with the bakery. Am I holding you back? Have I held you back all these years?"

Julia studied his dark blue eyes and leaned forward to touch his wrinkled hand. "Dad, I'm not stuck at all. I'm here because I want to be here. With you. And the bakery. What brought this on? Tell me."

He shrugged one shoulder, his gaze roaming back to the table. "I suppose that with the fortieth anniversary of your mother's passing, I've been looking back at my life a little deeper. And I wonder sometimes... if I did the right thing opening the bakery all those years ago, taking on a huge responsibility and leaving you alone so often. You were only a baby. I'm sure I neglected you with my long work hours. I was trying to learn how to run the place. And then having you work in the bakery as a little girl and a teenager." He looked up at Julia and tilted his head. "Did I ever even ask if that's what *you* wanted? I don't remember asking."

"Oh, Daddy. I've never regretted anything about my life. Well, maybe my marriage." She chuckled and saw the corner of her father's mouth rise. "But the bakery, this life, even coming back to the village after the divorce... I wanted to be here. I still want to be here."

"Are you saying that to make an old man feel better?"

"Hardly. Do you remember that time when I tried to show you I was ready to wait tables? What was I, only eight years old? And a total klutz. And you warned me that I was too young, but I insisted. I probably even threw a tantrum in the corner until you gave in."

"You certainly did. It was a whopper." He raised an eyebrow.

"And then, when you gave in and let me try, I accidentally dropped that entire tray of clotted cream and scones all over the floor, right in the middle of the bakery. Broke the dishes, made a fool of myself. You were right. But I wouldn't listen. See? I have a stubborn streak in me. I probably get it from you, in fact. And I don't do something unless I *want* to do something. I'm committed to the bakery and to our life here. I'm content here, Dad. I am."

He gave one decisive nod to show that her words had reassured him, and they unclasped hands. "I suppose another reason I'm asking is because of the future."

"How so?" Julia sipped her tea and wondered where he was about to steer the conversation.

"Although I have every intention of making it to a hundred years old, the fates don't always allow us what we wish. One day, things will change whether we like it or not. Everything is already in your name, as you know..."

Julia nodded. When he'd retired years ago, they'd had this same conversation, and he'd insisted on putting both the bakery and cottage in Julia's name. He claimed it was for his own sake, his peace of mind, but she knew he was also doing it to offer her some security. But he was younger then. His leaving her didn't seem as near. Or as real.

"Has anything changed, Dad?"

"No, no. I just wanted to make sure you were still okay with it all. That you didn't feel... obligated to stay on here after I'm gone."

Julia shifted, tapped her mug with her fingernails. "You know I hate talking about this, Dad. I don't wanna think about it."

"But sometimes we must, love. I'm in my final season of life. We both know it."

True. But it didn't mean Julia had to dwell on it. The thought of not having her father in her life was unbearable. He was her only family. Her kin. The only one who fully understood her, who had loved her every day of her life.

She rose from her seat and took her cup to the sink. "Tristan will be here later this afternoon." She rinsed the cup and set it aside.

"You've already mentioned it."

"Have I?"

"Julia, I already told you. I'm not going anywhere. Not for a good long while."

"I know, Dad." She turned to kiss the top of his head and squeeze his shoulder. "And neither am I."

Chapter Twelve

"Now and then, let someone else into the sanctuary of your kitchen. Baking is a lonely business, but it doesn't always have to be."

"I ALWAYS TURN THE DOUGH COUNTERCLOCKWISE then roll it. Turn then roll it again. That way the thickness stays even all the way to the edges."

Miranda nodded and watched as Julia demonstrated.

"Want to have a go?"

"Sure. More flour first?"

"Good instinct. Yes, it's important to keep the dough floured up. But not too much."

She watched Miranda sprinkle flour from a height then grasp the rolling pin in both hands, moving it along the dough exactly as she'd watched Julia do, smooth and steady.

Julia sipped her bottled water and thought how odd it was, having someone else inside her kitchen this early, before the bakery even opened. In fact, when Miranda had knocked on the back door an hour ago, it startled Julia until she remembered their scheduled meeting.

Last week, when Julia had returned from her picnic with Tristan, Miranda had approached her with a question. Could she be given more hours at the bakery in addition to her duties during the lunch shift? She needed the money and was also interested in becoming involved in the baking process.

"My daughter—she's sixteen—tasted the chocolate scones I brought home last week, and she asked me to help her make some. She never asks me anything these days—always tapping away on that mobile phone of hers, never talking to me in complete sentences. So when she asked about the scones, I thought maybe it was something we could finally have in common. My daughter loves that Nigella show. And Jamie Oliver. And I thought... maybe Julia could teach me something about baking, and I could pass it on to my daughter. And then start helping out more at the bakery."

Julia was honored by the idea and more than willing to teach some techniques, but she'd had to bite her cheek to keep from revealing the stark truth. Baking at home for oneself, or even on the telly for the public, was not nearly the same as baking six days a week for dozens upon dozens of people. The responsibility was hefty and daunting. Rewarding, yes. But also daunting.

Julia had happily offered Miranda the extra hours and set about to train her by using some basic recipes—scones, muffins, biscuits—to see how Miranda handled them on her own. Perhaps they could later graduate to tarts and puddings. Besides, what was wrong with a little extra help? If it all worked out, and Miranda turned into a reliable baking assistant, it could free Julia up during the week a bit, give her a flexible morning or two. If nothing else, Julia could stop worrying about future emergencies that might potentially bring the bakery to an inevitable standstill.

"Is this still too thick?" Miranda tilted her head toward the dough.

"No, it's perfect. Use your thumbnail to check the height." Julia showed her how. "Now, grab one of the cutters, coat it in a bit of flour, and twist it into the dough. This way." Julia cut out the first circular scone and placed it onto the parchment paper.

"Easy enough."

"I'll leave you to it," Julia replied. "I need to check on something up front."

She'd thought she heard Brandy enter the bakery, and she was right. Brandy waved and smiled, and Julia wondered if Brandy ever had a bad day in her whole life. She seemed eternally cheery and upbeat. And this morning was no different.

"Hi, boss! I'll put the coffee on..."

Julia met her behind the counter and mentioned that Miranda was helping out today with an extra shift.

"Oh, and we'll need that hamper display ready before we open," Julia reminded her.

Today was the first day hampers would be officially on sale at the bakery. Julia had told Brandy about the pricing and inside-of-hamper options they'd be offering. Brandy had thought it a spectacular idea. And Tristan had already added the photos and price listings to the website as of last evening. It was a go.

"It's the first item on my list." Brandy smoothed out her skirt. "Hey, do you know if...?"

Julia paused and searched Brandy's expression, which had shifted from cheery to shy and introverted. Very un-Brandy-like.

"Do you know if...Tristan... might be dating anyone?"

The question made Julia swallow hard, and she hoped Brandy hadn't noticed.

"I mean, I haven't *seen* him with anyone," Brandy continued. "Around the village. And I was just sort of... wondering if you'd heard anything."

Julia felt another lie of omission coming on. What choice did she have? Telling Brandy anything now would be prematurely letting the cat out of the bag. And worse, it would validate the truth—that, essentially, Tristan had chosen Julia over Brandy. And Julia certainly didn't have the heart to tell her that.

"Err, well... I don't really keep track of that sort of thing, sorry. I'm not out in the village enough to notice."

"Of course. Naturally. I feel silly for asking..."

"No, don't feel silly. I wish I could tell you more. But I can't."

Brandy shrugged and grasped the coffee pot. "You know, if I'm honest with myself, I already know the answer. At the least, he's just not that into me, or else something would've happened by now. He would've shown *some* interest." She fidgeted with the coffee filters. "Oh well..."

Julia didn't know what else to say. *The right one will come along someday? There are lots more fish in the sea? You're young and have plenty of time to find someone?* Every possible cliché felt completely patronizing, especially under these circumstances.

So Julia did the most humane thing she could think of. She told the bit of truth she was allowed to tell, even revealing some insecurities to herself that she hadn't voiced aloud. "I've been in your place before lots of times, especially at university. Guys are kind of… flaky in their twenties. They don't know what they want. Or who they want."

"Yeah, that's probably it. These boys. Guess I'll have to keep waiting around until one of them matures."

"That's the spirit." Julia was grateful to have a legitimate reason to leave—an important errand to run. "Listen, I'll be right back. There's something I need to do. Miranda can take charge of the kitchen while I'm gone."

"Sure, no probs."

Julia pushed the swinging door and located her handbag. Miranda whistled while she worked, placing the scones on the pan.

"Will you be all right for about twenty minutes?" Julia asked her. "I need to pop out for a bit. I'll be across the street."

"Sure. All good here. I'm about to bake this batch of scones. I already feel like Nigella." Miranda beamed.

Julia wondered if, after her ten thousandth batch of scones, the experience would feel quite so glamorous. "You can ring my mobile if you need me. And Brandy will help you with the display case. She knows what to do."

"Perfect. And take your time. I'm having fun!"

"I'm glad," Julia said, and she meant it. She tried to recall the last time she'd experienced that same new, energetic spark about baking that Miranda possessed. But the bakery had been part of Julia's life for her entire life. And as with any long-term job, the original excitement inevitably waned over time.

Julia went to the front door and opened it to an unusually warm, late-May morning. Her destination, the art gallery, only stood a short distance across the street. But on a day like today, Julia wished she could abandon all her plans and keep walking, breathe in the heady fragrances of flowers blossoming, feel the breeze on her cheeks, watch the sun brighten up the limestone shop fronts as it rose higher into the sky, creating long shadows everywhere. It was the kind of day to inhale, to appreciate, to wander around in. Perhaps she could squeeze time into her schedule later to do just that.

But for now, she was on an important mission. For weeks, as people had discussed and planned for the bakery's fortieth anniversary, Julia had panicked a little more every day. What would she give to her father as a commemorative gift? Nothing seemed adequate enough. A new book? Too mundane. A new fedora? Too generic. She'd even considered buying a new chair for him to sit in and pass out samples but wasn't sure he'd give up his old one. Too risky.

But this morning, inspiration had finally struck. As Julia struggled out of bed in the pitch-black of the morning, she thought of *the* perfect gift for her father. She couldn't believe she hadn't considered it before now.

Last year, when Noelle Spencer had been pregnant with her son, she'd gone into a painting frenzy, perhaps afraid she wouldn't have time to do any painting once her baby was born. She spent weeks at her gallery, painting a storefront series. It was her way, she said, of acknowledging how welcoming Chilton Crosse had been when she first arrived from California nearly four years ago.

Noelle had completed the series in December, hanging the eight-by-ten frames along the gallery's second-floor wall, where her famous Aunt Joy's paintings were also displayed. When Julia and her father visited them, it had taken a few minutes for him to wobble up the stairs, but her father insisted on going. His eyes positively lit up when he saw "Rose's Bakery." Noelle had captured every detail so perfectly, each limestone brick, the crisscross windows, the delicate awning, and even Alton Bentley's famous blue chair, sitting at the corner.

This morning, Julia hoped to purchase that painting. Noelle had recently mentioned at the book club that she might be placing the shop paintings up for sale sometime in the future, either individually or as a completed series. Julia remembered making a small mental note to inquire about it, but this morning, she knew she'd better be proactive, lest someone else snatch up the bakery's painting.

The only possible hitch was the price tag. Noelle's original oil paintings sold for hundreds, sometimes thousands, of dollars—as well they should. She'd received the artist's gene straight from her aunt, Joy Valentine, the much-heralded "Painter of the Cotswolds." In fact, this gallery had originally been Joy's, the most famous tourist attraction in Chilton Crosse.

Julia had added to her savings account over the past few years and was determined to pay Noelle's price, whatever it was. How often would her ninety-year-old father celebrate a fortieth anniversary for his life's work? The cost would be entirely worth it.

So at four this morning, before work, Julia had sent Noelle a brief email explaining her desire to buy the painting. Not surprisingly, Noelle had been up, too, with little Adam and had responded almost immediately. She wanted to give Julia half off the price, but Julia's pride wouldn't allow it. So they bargained politely back and forth until Noelle finally insisted on a significant discount, asking Julia to consider it as Noelle's small contribution to the fortieth anniversary party. With that, Julia caved and accepted the discount.

The gallery's distinctive smell, oils and turpentine mixed with coffee, immediately hit Julia's senses as she turned the doorknob. It had been months since she'd visited this space.

"Be right with you!" Frank yelled from the back. Julia didn't know Frank, the gallery's curator, very well. She only saw him occasionally at the bakery and at the weekly book club, usually the only male in attendance.

"Oh! Julia!" Frank stopped cold in the doorway when he saw her. He held a stack of receipts in his right hand. "I completely forgot. Noelle told me you wanted the bakery painting. I was supposed to wrap it up for you. I got entirely consumed with something else. My deepest apologies..."

"That's okay. I have a few minutes to spare. I'll just look around the gallery for a bit. Seems like you've added some new pieces since the last time I came."

Frank straightened his tie, which was already straight, and Julia realized she'd never seen him with a single hair out of place or even the smallest wrinkle in his attire. "Yes," he admitted. "We're chuffed to feature a new artist, Jeremy Cummings. I discovered his work in Bath on a recent trip. His colors are so vivid. Please, look around while I get your purchase ready."

Julia found her credit card inside her bag. "That's fine. I'll give you this now, so you can process it. Noelle and I already discussed the price."

"Will do." He took the card from her and gave a firm nod.

Julia wandered from painting to painting, amazed at the talent on canvas. She could barely draw a stick figure. And though her father insisted that baking was creative in its own right, Julia felt completely stumped when it came to this kind of artistic expression. How did artists capture real life—people and animals and landscapes—so vividly, so accurately? It was clearly a gift, one that even the artist probably didn't fully understand.

She heard Frank slip upstairs for the painting then back down again to his office. It would be awhile before he methodically wrapped it in brown paper and wrote up her order and receipt, so Julia went upstairs, passing a couple of tourists on their way down. She had the second floor completely to herself. But before she could step in front of the first painting—a Joy Valentine original—her mobile vibrated in her pocket.

Tristan. *Where are you now? I just tried the bakery.*

Julia typed her response. Abbey had shown her how to increase the font size, so she no longer needed glasses for this task. *At the gallery. Second floor.*

Be right there.

Julia smiled at the thought of an unexpected meeting with Tristan in a public place. More and more each day, while she was busy doling out her father's medicine, making him breakfast, doing inventory at the bakery, or trying out a new recipe from her mother's book, Tristan was always there along the fringes of her thoughts. Always. And because of that, she had already started to wonder if this could be evolving into something real and lasting. And the thought of that possibility made her heart rise with excitement and fall from fear at the same time.

A minute later, she heard, "Hey, beautiful!" and turned to see Tristan, hopping up the last step to meet her.

"That was fast!"

Tristan smiled and leaned in for a slow kiss. He smelled like fresh air and sunshine.

"I wanted to catch you before I went to my aunt's. No particular reason."

But that's the nicest reason of all, she mused.

"Why the gallery?" he asked.

They held hands as she explained. "Remember that series I told you about, the paintings Noelle did of the village, the individual shop fronts?"

"Yeah, I kept meaning to come see them but haven't had a chance yet."

"Well, I'm purchasing the bakery painting from her today as an anniversary gift for my dad."

"Brilliant! He will love that."

"Yeah, I think he really will. So you haven't seen any of Joy's paintings?"

"Not yet. But my aunt told me all about them. She knows the whole history, told me about how Joy was a recluse, holed up in her cottage for a decade. And when she died, her niece found all these paintings in the cottage."

Julia led him to the first one, still holding his hand. "This is one of them." Dr. Granger's donation of the seagull painting. "Joy Valentine is still a legend. She made our little village famous."

"I can see why. These are incredible." Tristan squinted. "The detail is remarkable."

Julia wasn't sure if it was Tristan or herself who pulled away first upon hearing Frank plodding up the stairs. Perhaps it was a mutual pulling away as they turned around together.

"I have your order filled out..." Frank looked up from the paper. "Ah, hello. Tristan, isn't it?"

"Yes. Frank? Nice to see you again."

As they shook hands, Julia wondered where they'd first met but realized that everyone in the village knew Tristan by now.

"My aunt has told me all about your gallery," Tristan explained. "This was my first chance to come and see the pieces."

"Ah, the Valentine collection." Frank nodded. "Enjoy yourself, and do take your time browsing. Her work is meant to be savored." He dragged out "savored" as though savoring the word itself. He turned to Julia. "I have your receipt ready, and the painting is all wrapped up downstairs."

"Thank you. I'll be right there. I want to finish browsing a bit."

"Certainly. Enjoy."

She waited until Frank left the room again before finding Tristan's hand. They moved in silence from painting to painting, except for the occasional "Mmm" or "Blimey" or "Look at those colors." Within moments, they'd reached the opposite wall, the shop paintings, and the blank space the bakery used to occupy.

"Well, I guess it's time." Julia sighed. "I need to go and see how Miranda's doing."

"Miranda?" Tristan faced her, grabbing her other hand.

Anytime he touched her, with even the slightest graze, Julia's brain seemed to freeze for a fraction of a second before functioning again. She assumed it was because she hadn't been used to being touched, not in a long, long time. It still felt so new.

Finding her answer after a beat, she explained, "You've met her, I think? She helps out with lunch, but she wants to try her hand at baking. I'm teaching her some basics in case I need a bit of time off or an emergency ever happens."

"Good call. It's too much pressure, being the only one running the shop."

"Speaking of pressure, will you be at tonight's meeting?"

Tristan's small grin widened. "You mean I have a choice?"

"Well, you're not technically *on* the committee..."

"But my aunt insists I'm there for 'moral support.' What she really means is, I'm a relative who's obligated to agree with everything she says."

"See? Pressure."

Tristan leaned in for another kiss, lingering this time, making Julia dizzy, making her want to stay. It took everything in her to pull away, to leave this blissful comfort zone for a busy, mundane day. But she couldn't *completely* lose her mind and abandon all her senses every time she was around Tristan. She had a painting to retrieve.

"I'll see you tonight, then," she whispered.

"I'll be there."

Chapter Thirteen

"Don't take fresh ingredients for granted. Smell them, touch them, turn them over in your hand and really look at them. Appreciate their qualities and what they're about to do for your recipe. Don't get so busy that you forget to savor the small things."

"YOU'RE ALL SET."

Julia took a step back to glance over her father's appearance—fedora angled just right, shoes laced up, walking cane in hand, light jacket around his hunched shoulders. They stood inside the cottage's entryway, waiting for Mac.

She noticed something odd about her father's shirt.

"Oops, let me make an adjustment." His buttons were all mismatched. She began at the top and unbuttoned the entire shirt. She usually tied his laces and buttoned his shirts—his fingers weren't nimble enough anymore to do those activities swiftly or correctly—but this morning, he had insisted on buttoning his shirt himself.

He chuckled. "This is what I used to do for you decades ago. You never did seem to match up the buttons."

Julia smiled. "I'm happy to return the favor."

"Now, tell me again where I'm headed?"

She had already told him twice at breakfast, but she told him again now, patiently, as though it were the first time. "Mac is coming to pick you up for a concert. A Dixieland band in Cirencester. He thought you'd enjoy it. Then later, George and Dr. Granger are stopping by for some cards."

"Cards?"

She stepped back to assess her handiwork. "Cards or dominoes. I can't recall which. That was Mary's idea. I think George is getting a bit restless, phasing out his full-time hours at the post office. He's headed for retirement."

"Well, I have a full day ahead."

"Your social calendar is fuller than mine! Are you up to it? If you get tired, you can always back out. They'll understand."

He shook his head. "No, no. I need to be out and about. It's good for me. And what are your plans for your Monday off?"

"Doesn't feel like a day off so far. I've been up since six. I sneaked out to the bakery to make a sheet cake for Lizzie's baby shower. I'll take it to the book club meeting in a few minutes."

"Lizzie Tupman. That's right. She's having a baby."

"She's having twins! Double trouble. And then, after the baby shower, I'll head off to the farmers market in Cheltenham."

"I know how you love a good farmers market."

"I really do. I haven't been to this one in a while. I'm taking along Mum's book of recipes. There are some specific ingredients I'll be on the lookout for."

"I wish I could go, but I would only slow you down. Will Tristan be joining you?"

"Tristan?" She adjusted the brim of her father's hat and diverted her eyes. "Um, yes, actually. I'm picking him up after the book club. Why do you ask?"

He made a *tsk* sound and gave another chuckle. "Julia Rose. You don't think this old man can see. But it's right there in front of me. How can I *not* see?"

"What do you mean?"

"You. And Tristan. There's something going on between you two young people. Tell me I'm wrong."

"Well, one of us is *considerably* younger than the other. By over a decade."

"What's wrong with that? Your mum and I were eleven years apart. And you're dodging the issue."

Julia looked her father squarely in the face and sighed. "Okay, you're right. Let's just say that Tristan and I are… getting to know each other well. I enjoy his company."

"That proves my theory. I've never seen you happier. I've suspected Tristan was the reason."

She should've known her father would see right through her. Ridiculous to try to hide or deny it. Surely, he'd caught the occasional handholding, the cheeky glances, or the laughter and whispering they often shared in her father's presence. But she'd assumed he hadn't been paying attention.

Julia dipped her head. "Dad, I don't know if it has any… staying power, this thing, whether it will last. Whether it *can* last."

"Is he leaving the village?"

"Not anytime soon. In fact, it seems he wants to stay for the foreseeable future. But I worry sometimes about the bigger issues. The realistic things: our age gap, what we both want for the future, the prying eyes of certain villagers and how they might judge us—"

"Rubbish to what other people think. It's not their business anyway. Do you enjoy spending time with him?"

"Yes."

"Does he treat you well?"

"He absolutely does."

"Are you friends? And can you be yourself with him?"

"Yes and yes."

"Well then." Her father grinned. "There's your answer, I think. Julia, enjoy this journey. Let it play out all the way. Even if you're not sure of the outcome."

"I think you've read that in a fortune cookie somewhere," she quipped. "But really, Dad, it's the outcome that scares me. I feel like protecting myself. Where will the journey lead? Heartache or happiness?"

"You'll never know if you stop your travels short. You have to keep moving forward. It's the only way." Her father winked. "I do sound rather like a fortune cookie, don't I?"

"That's only because you're full of great wisdom." She leaned in to kiss his cheek and heard a knock. "Mac's here." She backed away and patted her father's coat pocket. "I added a few extra quid to your wallet this morning, in case you need them."

"Thanks, love. You take excellent care of your old man."

Julia opened the door for Mac and saw the lingering mist hovering on the grass. The sky was a muted gray.

"Hello, lass." Mac tipped his cap to Julia then shifted his eyes to her father. "Are you ready for some Dixieland, Alton?" he asked in his gruff Scottish accent, hand extended to help her father out the front door. Julia stepped aside for them.

"Always ready for that." Her father joined his mate on the stone path, and off they went.

I can't believe I'm tasting BABY FOOD. Blech.

Julia sent the text to Tristan as discreetly as she could. She hated the rudeness of people texting in public gatherings, but she couldn't help herself, texting during Lizzie's baby shower. Tristan's texts were her only link to sanity at this point.

From the moment she'd arrived at Gertrude's cottage, Julia had been hit with *everything baby*. The décor (balloons, centerpieces, gift bags at each chair), the conversations (teething, formula, breast pumps), and the gift opening (burp cloths, bottles, stuffed toys, nappies).

After cutting into Julia's cake, the group had soon moved on to baby games. Mrs. Pickering was in charge.

My aunt's idea, right? Tristan texted back. *As gross as it sounds?*

So much worse.

Blimey. She made me look up shower games online. No idea baby food tasting was on the list.

So this is your fault?

"Julia? It's your turn, dear." Mary Cartwright had leaned in to warn her.

Julia shoved her mobile back into her pocket and plastered on a smile, realizing all eyes in the group were focused on her. She dipped her glossy plastic spoon into the least-gross-looking dollop on her plate, something orange, and did a quick pretend lick.

"Squash, maybe? I really have no idea," she said with a shrug and a grin.

"Correct!" Mrs. Pickering said from across the room, happily shaking one fist in the air then marking down a point for Julia. She might actually win this thing. It was her second correct guess in a row.

Gertrude was next. She had participated the first time around and proclaimed the baby food "absolutely revolting." This time, she simply shifted her pet poodle named Leopold in her lap and shook her head. She had already disposed of her plate. "I'll pass."

When it was safe, Julia peeked at Tristan's newest text: *I'll make it up to you. Promise.*

She smiled and returned her mobile to her pocket as Mary leaned in again. "This is such a ridiculous game, isn't it?"

Julia nodded, glad for a comrade in arms.

"I believe George will be at your cottage by one o'clock today for cards," Mary whispered. "He was going to bring lunch."

"My father's really looking forward to it."

"So am I. Truth be told, I need a break. As you know, George is phasing out at work. And as much as I love him… well… I'm not used to having a man about the cottage during the day. He follows me around and makes comments or offers constant suggestions. I've been laundering his shirts for over forty years, yet he knows a better way. Men!"

Julia snickered along with Mary. "Oh, I keep meaning to tell you something. Dr. Granger was a great help a few weeks ago with my father. I thought Dad was having a minor stroke, and I called Dr. Andrews. But your nephew was on call and came right away. He did some tests, asked my father questions, and put all our fears to rest. He was so kind. And knowledgeable."

Mary beamed. "Ben seems to be settling into village life nicely, doesn't he? I worried about him when he first arrived. But something changed for him on Christmas Eve. I'm not sure what happened, but I saw hope in his eyes. A renewal of some kind. And it was Ben's idea to stay in Chilton Crosse, to rent the cottage and partner with Dr. Andrews. I think he's here to stay."

Suddenly, it was their turn again. Julia wondered how much longer she could endure this silly game.

But Julia had to remind herself why she was there. This was for Lizzie, who appeared to be genuinely enjoying the party. She sat across from Julia, balancing her plate on her swelling tummy. It truly *was* delightful to see the village growing right before Julia's eyes. New babies, new residents, a new generation. All part of the extended village family, history in the making. Lizzie caught Julia's gaze and gave a little wave with her free hand. And Julia was glad she had come.

An hour later, the party had wound down, and its attendants discarded paper plates and cups, helped with silverware, and gathered Lizzie's million new presents to place into her car.

At the sink, drying the last of the glasses, Julia heard comments in various rooms, some about her delicious cake, others about how quickly Lizzie was growing.

Mildred entered the kitchen and patted Julia's arm. "We need to do lunch this week."

"Yes! Things have been hectic, as usual. But we'll make time."

Mrs. Pickering suddenly appeared and nudged between them, handing Julia another glass to be cleaned. "You certainly did seem consumed with your phone during the party, I noticed. A new friend perhaps?" Mrs. Pickering's tone contained a nudge-nudge, wink-wink.

Before Julia could fashion a response that wasn't entirely sarcastic or regrettably rude, Mildred stepped in for the save. "Mrs. Pickering! I finally got to meet that nephew of yours while I was leaving the Indian restaurant yesterday. He's a handsome young man and a gentleman to boot. Holding the door open for me, even offering to go inside in search of a box to help carry my bags."

Mrs. Pickering sighed. "He *is* incredible, isn't he? My sister raised him well, in spite of that annoying husband of hers..."

Julia kept busy with the dishes, smiling, wondering what Mrs. Pickering's beef was with Tristan's father. Mrs. Pickering didn't elaborate, so Julia made a mental note to ask Tristan later.

"Well, that's done." Julia switched off the tap and faced Mrs. Pickering. "It was a lovely shower. I know Lizzie was thrilled with everything."

"Must you rush off so soon? I think a few of us were going to stay here, discuss the next book to read..."

"Oh, sounds fun, but I really must get going. It's a busy day."

Julia leaned in to hug Mildred then found her handbag in the next room.

On her way out the door, she couldn't help picturing Mrs. Pickering's face if she only knew *who* Julia was rushing off to meet.

When Julia had walked out of her cottage at six this morning, mist had hovered on the fields, and the sky had been a melancholy gray. But by the time she'd arrived in her van to pick up Tristan at Elton's farm, the mist had dissipated, and a brilliant sun shone high overhead. *A peerless, pristine day.*

"Do I need to bring anything?" Tristan asked as he approached the passenger side. Julia had lowered all the windows to breathe in the crisp spring air.

"Just your handsome self," she said, watching him climb into the van. Today, he wore khaki trousers and a black jumper. He looked exceptionally good in black.

"Hey," he whispered, turning to her and leaning across the gearshift.

She received his kiss and felt him touch her cheek before he backed away.

She readjusted herself in the seat and grasped the steering wheel. "Are you *sure* you won't get bored today? I mean, it's just browsing stall after stall of breads and meats and veg. And maybe some desserts. It's not too late for you to say no."

"I'm looking forward to this." He clicked his seat belt. "I don't care what we're doing. I can't believe we have most of the day to ourselves. No interruptions, time away from the village. I think we need this."

Julia shifted into gear and heard Maggie's barking in the distance as she pulled away.

"So, you survived the shower?"

"It wasn't too bad in the end. Lizzie seemed to enjoy it."

"And I'm sure your cake was a hit."

"You'll be able to taste some tonight, in fact. Your aunt was bringing some home for you. Where does she think you are right now?" She glanced over at Tristan with a grin.

"Working, I suppose. I didn't say otherwise."

"Let's hope she doesn't check up on you."

"Entirely possible. I'd better turn my ringer off."

A baker's heaven!

Julia hadn't been to this particular farmers market in several months and had nearly forgotten how blissful it was, seeing stall upon stall packed with the freshest ingredients—seasonal fruits and vegetables, butter and cheeses, homemade breads, spices and jams—anything and everything she could possibly want.

Her only problem with any farmers market, besides the claustrophobia of dealing with the overwhelming crowds, was practicing her power of resistance. She could easily end up buying something from each and every stall. In fact, Julia's only hard-and-fast rule for visiting any farmers market was to bring along her own canvas bags—only two, so that she wouldn't be tempted to overspend. And, she had to keep specific menus and dishes in mind, which would also help her stay within budget.

She and Tristan had to park a couple of streets away, and as they approached the stalls on foot, Julia heard the growing sounds of crowds and smelled the mixtures of all the ingredients wafting her way, emitting a unique, luscious scent. She inhaled deeply.

"Look at that smile." Tristan side-eyed Julia as they approached the first stall.

"What?"

"You. It's adorable. You're in heaven, aren't you?"

"I can't help it."

"That's what's adorable."

As they waited behind an elderly couple at the first stall—seasonal fruits of apricots and strawberries—Julia felt Tristan reach down for the two empty bags lassoed around her wrist.

"I'll free you up so you can sample things. I can be your cupbearer."

"My what?"

"You know, those lads whose job it was to hold the royal cup for a princess or queen. Today, I'll be your cupbearer."

"Didn't they also have to taste the wine to make sure it wasn't poisoned?"

"Hey, if you need me to taste something for you today, I'm totally up for that."

The elderly couple moved along, and Julia was able to scan all the offerings before her. She consulted the list of ingredients she'd scribbled out this morning.

"I'll take five apricots and this basket of strawberries," she told the man after some careful consideration. While he bagged them up, she moved to the sampling display and dabbed a bit of apricot jam onto a small bite of toast. "Mm." She turned to Tristan. "Want some?"

He opened his mouth, and she popped the rest of her toast into it.

"Mm. Good!" he said through a mouthful.

The man at the stall handed over her selections and took her money. She inserted her purchases into the bag Tristan held then led him on to the next stall and the next.

The structures stood so close together that there wasn't much time for aimless wandering or chitchatting with Tristan. But sometimes, when they got stuck behind a particularly slow customer who couldn't make up his mind, she and Tristan would talk and hold hands or even steal a quick kiss. *Heaven, indeed.*

During one standstill at a fresh-bread stall (the most popular one), Tristan received a text, and Julia offered to hold the bags while he checked it.

Tristan glanced at his mobile and chuckled then texted back. As he waited for a reply, he explained to Julia, "It's Gavin, an old school chum of mine."

"From university?"

"Yeah. He and another mate, James, found me a couple of days ago. I guess they got my number from my mum or something. They're trying to cook up a reunion of sorts. I haven't seen them since we graduated."

Julia did some quick calculations and realized Tristan had only been out of university for a handful of years. His friends hadn't had time to go bald, to become totally unrecognizable, or even to settle down into the lives they would have for the rest of their lives.

But for Julia, university seemed a lifetime ago—eighteen years, to be exact. She'd lost all contact with any of those people she was once close to, including her ex-husband. She wondered what they were all up to now, what their lives looked like…

Tristan read his mate's reply silently and chuckled again. Probably an inside joke Julia wouldn't understand. Old friendships contained a shorthand all their own.

After Tristan tapped out his reply, Julia asked, "Are you going? To the reunion?"

"It's not really an official reunion, just a few mates getting together in Cornwall in a couple of weeks. But I'm not going."

"Why not?"

As people rubbed shoulder to shoulder past Tristan, who stuck out a little at the back of the bread line, he inched even closer to Julia. "It wouldn't be the same, I guess." She felt his breath on her neck. "Seeing them now, I mean. I was a different person at university. These blokes only knew me as an arrogant athlete, someone who could down several pints in one sitting and skip class the next morning. I barely passed my final term, in fact. I'm not proud of that. But that's not who I am anymore. And I don't even think they know about the accident. Or Corbett. Not unless my mum told them."

Julia didn't know what to say. The Tristan she'd gotten to know in these past several weeks had never gotten pissed at the pub and wasn't arrogant in the slightest. He was describing a totally different person than the Tristan she knew.

"They just wanna get together and rehash the old days." Tristan shrugged. "But I don't need to go back there or to have to explain about Corbett. I'm politely turning them down." He began texting again.

"Next!" the woman behind the stall yelled, jarring Julia back to the market, back to her original mission.

She stepped up and pulled her focus back to the bread.

Only a few stalls later, Julia found she had filled both bags to capacity. And there were still about seven more vendors to visit.

Julia paused to check her notes again and realized she'd fulfilled every item on her wish list. She would just have to window-shop the remaining stalls. If she found something she *couldn't* live without, she would indulge as long as she could squeeze it into the couple of small pockets in one of the bags.

That something ended up being truffle butter. Her father loved it, and the tub she bought was small enough to fit. *All finished!*

By the time Julia and Tristan had reached the final stall, Julia's stomach rumbled mightily. Reading her mind, Tristan led her over to the row of tables on the outskirts of the market and found the last vacant one. "I'll go grab us some food." He stared at the two bags he'd just set on the table, bulging with produce and bread and cheeses. "Err, not that we don't have plenty here, but you know. A proper lunch."

"I know what you mean. I'm famished."

"I saw a couple of stalls with ready-made Indian. Or burgers? Which do you prefer?"

"You choose. Anything sounds good."

In the twenty minutes it took for Tristan to stand in line and purchase the food, Julia had sifted through her stash of goodies and made extensive notes as to precisely which ingredients she would use in a variety of upcoming dishes—goat cheese salad with walnut vinaigrette, strawberry-and-cream scones, French onion soup, savory courgette muffins, and the list went on. Her menu for the next week was easily set.

"Hope you're hungry," Tristan said as he laid out a spread that could easily serve five people.

"What did you do?" She smiled as he handed her plasticware.

"A buffet! I wasn't sure what you liked, so I found a bit of everything."

"You certainly did." Julia tucked her notes inside her bag as she made room for Tristan's food. He took each item out and placed it before her.

"Oh, and I got these." He produced a small, tight bundle of roses from out of nowhere. Orange, yellow, purple, red. A rainbow of color. "For the princess."

Julia accepted the bundle, bringing them up to her nose and breathing in the rich scent. "They're beautiful."

"Even the flowers are the best and freshest around, it seems. I'm really impressed with this place."

Tristan took the seat across from Julia as she set the flowers on the table to serve as a makeshift centerpiece. She couldn't recall the last time a man—besides her father—had bought her flowers. Braeden never did, never once. She hadn't even had a wedding bouquet.

"Thank you for the flowers."

"My pleasure." He handed her a plate and napkin.

The table brimmed with food, not an empty space left. Julia and

Tristan picked and chose their meals—a bit of curry, a couple of sausages, even some fish and chips. A proper buffet.

Julia was relieved Tristan had chosen to sit in the spot across from her, rather than sneak into the seat beside her. She never understood why some couples sat side by side during a meal. It made it so much harder to face each other and talk.

"So, was Gavin disappointed? That you said no to the reunion?"

"He hasn't texted back yet," Tristan said between bites of chips. "Knowing him, he'll increase the pressure. He was always hard to refuse. He's half the reason we got into so much trouble in those days."

"What sort of trouble?" Julia spooned out some chicken curry onto her paper plate.

"Oh, just the regular sort. Sneaking into a professor's drawer to try and steal an exam—unsuccessfully. Or playing pranks on some guys in the hall—short-sheeting beds, cling film on the toilets. Mostly harmless."

"Mm," she replied, still trying unsuccessfully to picture *that* Tristan. She'd known blokes like him at university. And though she tried to steer clear of them—bad news, her father always called them—she seemed helplessly attracted to them. Braeden was actually a perfect example.

"What sort of student were you?" he asked. "Wait, don't answer. I'll bet you had high marks, followed the rules, never skipped a single class." His tone was teasing, not mocking.

Julia played along. "If you must know, as I student, I was... well, let's just say your assessment is incredibly accurate." She grinned. "I've always been a rule-follower. It's in my nature, I guess. I hated the thought of getting into trouble, of having attention drawn to me, especially negative attention. And I actually loved university. Green lawns, cozy corners to read in, libraries filled with books, students studying everywhere, or practicing guitar or rehearsing a scene from a play in hallways. I fit in there."

"I can see that. I wish I'd taken it more seriously while I was there." His tone turned reflective, pensive. "I didn't appreciate it the way I should have. Wasted my parents' money. I'll always regret it." He *tsk-ed* before grabbing another chip.

"Did you date a lot at university?" Julia easily imagined him with a beautiful girl on each arm.

"I wouldn't call it a lot. Nothing serious, at first. But then I spent the last couple of years in a steady relationship. With Cynthia. We met through Gavin, actually. She's his twin sister."

Julia paused with surprise, and something struck her. *Is Cynthia part of this upcoming reunion? And is she the real reason Tristan said no?*

Tristan took a sip of bottled water. "After graduation, Cynthia got a job in New York right away, and we never saw each other again. We tried to do the long-distance thing, but she started dating a bloke at her firm, and I was in the Navy by then. The breakup was pretty mutual. I think she eventually married the guy and stayed in New York."

Julia wondered what "pretty mutual" meant.

Before she could press any further, he said, "Okay. Your turn." He raised his eyebrows.

"My turn, for what? About university?"

"I've told you about my ex. I want to hear about yours. You were married for a short while?"

"Yeah, nearly seven years."

"You met at university, too?"

"We took an economics class together and hung out afterward, studying together, that sort of thing. We were friends at first."

"What was he like, this guy?"

Julia had to stop and remember. She didn't consciously think about Braeden or their relationship these days. He was in the past, and he usually stayed there.

"Well, I'd say he was on his best behavior with me at the start. You know, the courting phase."

Tristan nodded.

"And then after university, we were both staying in London to pursue careers and decided to get married."

"Decided? Didn't he pop the question?"

"Not really. I just remember it as this conversation we were having at a pub one night. About the future, about London. And I think he just mentioned it as a possibility, getting married."

"How romantic."

"It's embarrassing, looking back now. See, you're not the only one with regrets. I realize now how much I settled with him. We got married—we eloped, actually—and lived more like flatmates than husband and wife after that. Marriage weirdly ruined the relationship. He grew distant really fast, immersed himself in his career, found new mates to spend time with—women, included—and so I was on my own much of the time. I rarely saw him. It's hard to maintain a healthy relationship that way."

"No doubt."

"Those were actually some of the loneliest days of my life. We tried to salvage things a couple of times, even attempted to start a family. My idea, big mistake. Things didn't work out, then he had a couple of affairs, and that was the end."

"Blimey. I'm sorry," Tristan said softly across the table.

Julia hadn't intended to spill these private facts to Tristan today, over a picnic table at a farmers market with people bustling all around. It seemed too public a place for such intimate details, which was partly why she decided to stop the rest of the story in its tracks—the hysterectomy, which meant she wasn't able to have children, a piece of information that, in fact, had the potential to change everything between herself and Tristan. It would affect whatever future they were building. Or would it? She had no idea how Tristan might react to that sort of news. It was a detail he deserved to know about someday, but it still seemed too early for that kind of revelation.

"Yeah." She shrugged. "The marriage should've never happened in the first place. I was too young, and we weren't good for each other. But sometimes it makes me wonder…"

"Wonder what?"

"Well, I'm afraid, sometimes, that I equate all marriages with mine. Believing that they're *all* hard, cold, or unfulfilling. Or lonely. I try not to think that way, but it's the only marriage I've known."

"That makes sense." Tristan had stopped eating. He wiped his chin with his napkin and stared across at Julia. "I'm sorry he hurt you."

She saw compassion in his eyes but, thankfully, no pity. "It seems a lifetime ago, really. It's what you said before—I don't even recognize that Julia anymore when I look back."

"Well. I like the Julia I see right now." Tristan smiled, reached for her hand.

Julia mirrored his smile, grateful this Tristan had met this Julia.

Chapter Fourteen

"Sometimes a disaster will happen. A cake will burn. You'll forget an important ingredient. A sauce will come out all wrong. But don't let it frustrate you. Don't give up. Start all over again and learn from your errors. Persistence builds character."

Julia balanced the wrapped baguette on top of the container she carried in order to knock at the door of Moonbeam Cottage without dropping everything. The bread's fragrant smell had intoxicated her senses all the way up the stone path. She hadn't eaten a significant meal all day—only bits and snacks here and there. Brandy had called in sick, and although Miranda had been able to step in at the counter, it meant that Julia had to take over the full lunch duties without a significant break in her day.

Julia considered knocking again after a significant pause and chided herself for not calling first. She had just assumed the sisters were home this time of the night, especially with one of them ill. At yesterday's book club meeting, Mary had mentioned that one of the sisters, Grace, had contracted a severe case of bronchitis. So today, when deciding what to do with the leftover food—normally, it went to Julia's employees, or sometimes a soup kitchen in a nearby village—Julia had decided to bring some of it to Grace and Cora. She had tested the soup earlier, a new recipe out of her mum's book that included the fresh vegetables she'd bought yesterday at the market. It might've been the best soup Julia had ever tasted. In fact, she was surprised to have any of it leftover at all. Customers had raved about it all afternoon.

As Julia raised her hand to knock again, the door creaked hesitantly open, and Cora's face appeared in the crack of the doorway.

"Oh. Hello, Julia," she said, clearly surprised. She flicked on the porch light and widened the door.

"Hi, Cora. I'm sorry to disturb you. I really should've rung you up first. I have something for Grace. I hear she's been ill."

The confusion on Cora's face melted away, replaced with an appreciative smile. She opened the door fully, revealing her whole frame, clad in a crimson cardigan and khaki skirt. "Oh, that's very kind of you. Yes, it's the worst bronchitis yet. My sister has had bouts since she was a little girl, but this particular one was worrisome. Dr. Granger—isn't he such a nice young man?—made a house call and told us yesterday Grace has turned a corner. Thank God."

"Wonderful news."

"Oh, look at that. I've left you standing at the door too long. Please. Come in." She stepped aside.

Julia had visited the cottage only a couple of times, and it always felt strange being there. Cora—Mrs. Clementine—had worked as the school's headmistress back when Julia was a little girl in school, and she was regarded as a stern-faced and overly strict administrator. Julia never was sent to her office for misbehavior but had heard all the stories of those who had. Mrs. Clementine's greatest weapon wasn't a paddle or a whip. It was her disappointment. It pierced straight through to a student with a mere squint of her sharpened eyes, a loud *tsk*, a slight shake of a head. That—and the threat of a call to a parent and possible suspension—was always punishment enough. As an adult, even two decades out of school, Julia still had to make the conscious shift to speak to Mrs. Clementine—Cora, as she insisted on being called now—without trepidation.

She followed Cora inside to the warm glow of a fire, the scent of fresh roses, the immaculate living room. Julia cringed inside, thinking of her own cottage at the moment—not a *complete* mess, but very... lived in. She'd been too busy for even basic tidying up in the past day or so.

"Let me take this from you. It smells delicious."

"It's a vegetable soup with ingredients fresh from the market. There's plenty here for both of you. And some bread, baked this morning." Julia handed it over carefully.

"So thoughtful. Please, have a seat." Cora gestured toward the sofa with her free hand.

"I'm afraid I can't. I need to get back to my father."

"How is he these days?" Cora held the container to her chest. "I haven't had a chance to visit the bakery with Grace's illness..."

"He's well. Staying active and busy."

"He's fortunate to have a daughter like you taking excellent care of him. I'm glad you have each other."

"So am I."

Of all people, Cora probably understood more than anyone about the unorthodox living arrangement of a forty-year-old daughter living with her elderly father, having lived with her own sister for most of her sixty-something years.

Julia heard a series of coughs floating out from a nearby room.

"Oh, bless her soul," Cora said. "There she goes again."

Julia thought she detected a flicker of an eye roll from Cora. She wondered how the two sisters were getting along during Grace's illness. Even in the best of times, they had the reputation around the village for squabbling and twittering with each other constantly. Julia had seen it for herself, bickering under their breath, frustrated gestures as they tried to keep their sisterly arguments private, even in public. They had lived in this cottage together, their childhood home, for decades. Most of the village knew the backstory well, that Cora had married briefly in her twenties, but when her husband unexpectedly died, she moved back in with Grace. And so they had remained ever since.

"I'd better tend to her," said Cora.

"It was nice seeing you. Give her my best." Julia stepped backward toward the door.

"Have a nice evening. And thanks again for all the glorious food. So kind of you."

Julia closed the door behind her, stepped back into the night air, and inhaled. The cool breeze refreshed her lungs, and she heard a nightingale's call in the distance. Raising her head, she noticed diamond stars winking at her through a thicket of trees.

Her mobile buzzed, snapping her out of her trance. She retrieved it and walked down the stone path, back to her van.

A call from Tristan.

"Hey," she answered, hoping he could hear the smile in her voice.

"Hey back. I haven't seen you all day."

"It's been insane." Julia opened the van's door and *plonked* down into the driver's seat. "I'm knackered. Every bone in my body."

She heard him yawn at the suggestion. "Same here. Mr. Elton has been cracking his whip all day. Not even a break for dinner. Speaking of..."

Julia tapped the mobile's speaker—a trick Abbey had recently shown her—and set the device in her door pocket then pulled away from the cottage toward home.

"Come to dinner tomorrow," Tristan said. "At my cottage. I'll cook for us."

"You'll cook?"

"Don't sound so alarmed. I do a little dabbling now and then. You won't be disappointed. If you are, we can order a takeaway as a backup."

Julia chuckled. "Okay. I'll be there. What can I bring?"

"Just your beautiful self. I'll take care of the rest."

"No dessert? I make a killer lemon tart."

"You make a killer everything. But really, I have a whole menu planned, everything under control. This is your night. I don't want you to lift a finger. Let me cook for you. Your only role is to enjoy. Hopefully. If all goes well, that is."

They discussed what time to meet then said goodbye. Julia ended the call with a contented sigh. Once upon a time, she wouldn't have dreamed of ending her grueling workday with an offer of dinner in a cottage with a handsome younger man. And the fact that this was her current reality left her grinning all the way home.

Arriving empty-handed at Tristan's cottage the next evening made Julia feel half-naked. She had been tempted to grab the box of tarts from the bakery before leaving work earlier, breaking Tristan's rule and bringing something to this date other than herself. But in the end, she chose to go against her nature and show up with nothing in hand. As promised.

But it didn't dawn on her until she stood at Tristan's door that bringing treats or soups or snacks to people's cottages or to any sort of function had become a social crutch for her, a way to start the conversation. *Something to offer, something to hide behind.* And here she stood with only her handbag, feeling like something was desperately missing.

But she reminded herself of the rare jolt of confidence she'd felt an hour before, getting ready for this date. She wore a long skirt, bought for Noelle's wedding a couple of years ago, and tonight, it was cinched up at the waist with a pin because of the weight she'd recently lost. The burgundy material flowed down past her knees, and she had decided on a short-sleeved jumper to go with it. Peering into a full-length bedroom mirror, Julia couldn't deny it. She had never felt so feminine, so confident in her own skin. She'd even added some jewelry and spent extra time this evening on her hair, creating sweeping fringe and loose curls to frame her face. When she'd left for the evening after settling her father in for the night, she'd kissed his cheek and he had told her, "My darling, you're radiant. You look like your mother."

Tristan opened the cottage door after only one knock. He wore slacks and a dark green long-sleeved shirt Julia hadn't seen before. She wondered if it was new, special for this occasion. Even though she'd seen him nearly every day for the past couple of weeks, she noticed now that his hair was growing longer, with subtle waves making it look thicker. She fancied it this length. Not too short, not too long.

Clean-shaven and smiling, Tristan leaned his hand against the doorframe to look her up and down. "You look amazing."

"Thank you."

She had planned to sweep past him through the doorway, but he leaned down for a kiss, and she reciprocated. His lips were warm and soft, and they tasted of butter.

"You *have* been cooking." She backed away and licked her lips.

"Testing the sauce." He winked. "It's coming along. Ready in a few minutes."

He shut the door behind them, and before Julia had a chance to view the cottage, Maggie came bounding in from another room, tongue wagging.

"Down," Tristan warned before Maggie could have the chance to jump up on Julia's skirt.

Maggie obeyed and plopped down at Julia's feet, giving Julia the chance to bend over and rub her head. "Sweet girl. Have you had a good day?"

Maggie responded with a joyful bark and more tongue wagging.

"Okay, time to go," Tristan told Maggie. "Back to your bed." He pointed at the cushy pillowed disc near the wood-burning stove at the opposite wall, and Maggie trotted over to it.

Julia surveyed the room—cozy and small, with very little décor on the walls, one sofa, a slate floor, and one enormous window that revealed a brilliant setting sun. "It's so homey."

"We like it, though I'm hardly ever here. That's why it looks so sparse. I haven't even had a chance to unpack all the way."

A timer beeped in the kitchen. "That's me." But before he went, he gestured over to a small table near the window, already set with a crisp white cloth and place settings. There was even a single rose in a small vase in the table's center.

"For you, madam." He walked over to pull out Julia's chair. She looped her bag on the back of it and smoothed out her skirt to sit.

"The service gets an A-plus so far."

"There's more to come..." Tristan promised.

And with that, he was off to the kitchen, from which mixtures of sweet and savory scents had begun to waft. Julia folded her hands together and took in the glorious view outside the window on this almost-June evening: clusters of trees, hills and valleys, old stone walls. She heard Tristan clanking pans and opening the Aga's door while she watched the tall grass in a nearby meadow wave lazily in the breeze.

Soon, Tristan appeared with a full plate and a glass of water. Earlier, when he'd called from the kitchen to ask her drink order, she'd said, "Just water." He set the plate down before Julia, a large, steaming chicken breast covered in a golden sauce with flecks of bright green herbs. Beside the chicken lay five baby-sized potatoes, also steaming. The smell was incredible.

"Rosemary chicken with new potatoes. I'll be right back."

He disappeared into the kitchen again, and when he sat down across from her with his own plate, she told him, "I'm so impressed with you!" Her fork was poised. She could hardly wait to tuck in.

"It's a Jamie Oliver dish. I followed a tutorial online. He promised it was 'a succulent showstopper.' We'll see!"

She cut into the chicken with almost no effort before the meat fell apart. "So tender." She speared a bite with her fork and brought it to her lips. "Here goes…"

The chicken melted in her mouth. The tangy sauce was light and full of flavor, likely due to the herbs. "Oh, wow," she said after chewing and swallowing the first bite. "It's really amazing."

Tristan chewed his own piece. "Not bad, if I do say so…"

Next, Julia tried the potatoes, and they were the same—tender and packed with flavor. "My father would love this. Can I have the recipe?"

"Of course. Or maybe I can make it for him sometime."

"Even better."

As they ate, Julia asked about how his software idea was coming along. He hadn't mentioned it in weeks.

Tristan shrugged. "It's stalled a bit. But I'm still committed to it. Mr. Elton and my aunt have me working like a dog lately. Some days, I don't have a moment to think about the software. I need to refocus, get back to work on it."

"A break is good sometimes, though. Maybe you can get back to the project with fresh eyes."

"Good point." Tristan took a sip of water. "So, my aunt just reminded me today, it's only a couple more weeks until the final meeting, and then it's your dad's party. Does he suspect anything?"

"Not that I'm aware of. I've almost let it slip once or twice, but I caught myself," Julia admitted. "I hope we can pull this off."

"The whole village is talking about it. I saw Mac yesterday at the market, and he asked me how he could help."

"Lizzie told me the big anniversary banner was delivered to the pub yesterday. Joe's storing it out back for us. Maybe Mac could help us put it up when it comes time? He's good at things like that. He has ladders and such."

Tristan grinned and chewed another bite. "Good idea."

Julia cut another potato in half and shrugged. "I admit, when your aunt first approached me with this anniversary idea, I thought it was a little barmy. I mean, Dad's not the type to make a fuss about himself.

He'd probably just let the anniversary go by unacknowledged if he had it his way. But people are genuinely getting chuffed about this. I think it gives them something to look forward to."

"Well, your dad *is* an icon in this village. I've heard that tourists have started to take selfies with him outside the bakery in his blue chair. He's probably famous online, and we don't even know it."

Julia chuckled at the idea. "He'd be thrilled by that. Or confused. He still doesn't understand the Internet or what all the fuss is about."

She popped the next delicious potato into her mouth and noticed it was the next to last potato. And she only had two bites of chicken left on her plate.

"Something wrong?" Tristan asked.

She must've been frowning, so she covered it with a half grin. "Nothing. It's silly."

"Go on, what is it?" Tristan lowered his fork and waited, gazing across at her.

"Well, something just occurred to me. I'm probably not doing this right. I mean, aren't women supposed to eat like birds? Pick daintily at their food, leave half of it on the plate..."

Tristan tilted his head. "Who says?"

"Well, society, I think. It's just that... It's been awhile since I've done this, been on a proper date. And I'm out of practice. I mean, look at this plate! I've gobbled it up in a few minutes' time! I'm afraid the Queen—and certainly your aunt—would *not* approve."

"Nothing wrong with a healthy appetite. And I don't care what society thinks. An empty plate only tells me you really enjoyed what I made you, that you weren't just being polite."

"I wasn't. It really is delicious."

Tristan finished the last bite on his own plate and set his utensils down with a *clank*. "See, I beat you to it. You can still be considered dainty. Ready for some dessert?"

"There's more?"

"Indeed. Do you have room?"

"I'll make room." Julia took her final bite, and then Tristan cleared both plates with a sly smile. She wondered what else he had up his sleeve.

Across the room, Maggie yawned in her bed, stretching her stubby paws out then curling them back underneath her for another nap.

"The grand finale," Tristan announced as he re-entered the room, presenting a stacked mountain of something dark on a plate. "Double-chocolate brownies."

Julia moved aside the vase to make room as he set down the dessert between them. He'd also carried smaller plates and dessert forks, which he distributed now.

"Also Jamie's recipe," he confirmed. "But I decided to add something special to it." He sat across from her and paused, waiting.

Realizing this was her cue, Julia grasped the brownie perched on top of the stack and set it on her plate then dented the brownie with her fork for a significant bite.

When she closed her mouth to chew, the dark chocolate hit her taste buds immediately, strong and rich—almost too rich—and then something else she couldn't place came after. Something… bitter? It took great effort to keep from cringing.

"Well? What do you think?" Tristan's eyes shone with eagerness. "I haven't tried them yet."

"Mm." She swallowed the bite quickly and raised her eyebrows, frantic to search for a word to describe the brownie without actually lying. "The flavor is… intense."

"That's from the coffee." He beamed.

"Coffee?"

That explained the bitterness. She reached for her water, hoping he wouldn't realize she was trying to wash it all down in one gulp.

"You told me, remember? It's your secret. To bring out the chocolate flavor." He took the next brownie for himself and chomped down on half of it in one enormous bite. Julia watched his expression shift from delight to horror as he chewed. He wrinkled his nose, and the corners of his mouth turned downward, as though he'd just tasted the strongest lemon in the world. He turned his back on Julia to spit the bite into his napkin.

"That's bloody awful!" he said between gulps of water. "Why didn't you tell me?"

Julia held her palm up to her mouth, unable to contain her laughter.

Her giggles echoed off the stone floor. "I'm sorry. I was trying to be kind," she said, still laughing.

Tristan's frown grew stronger as he stared at the brownie plate. "What did I do wrong? I followed the recipe to the letter."

"I'm guessing it was the coffee?" Julia lowered her hand back to her lap, pacing her breathing, trying to suppress additional giggles bubbling up.

"Too much?" He winced.

"Probably. It only takes a little splash…"

"Splash? You mean, like, brewed coffee?" His eyes widened. "Blimey. I used espresso grains instead. A half-cup of them."

Julia's giggles returned, and she put her napkin up to her face. "I'm sorry. I don't mean to laugh. The effort was really sweet."

"Sweet and bitter, you mean. I'm such a git." Tristan's expression had relaxed. He ran a hand through his hair, and his smile broadened. "I didn't think to research it. And I couldn't ask you the amount without ruining the surprise."

"It's fine. Really. And you are anything *but* a git. You are kind and thoughtful and… creative."

"Creative. A nice way of saying 'you're a bloody git.'"

Julia giggled again. "Would you stop that?" She clutched his hand across the table. "The gesture was incredibly kind. No one's ever cooked for me before."

"After this, I don't think you'll ever let me cook for you again."

"Not true. You can cook for me anytime you want."

The giggles dissipated for good, and gratitude came over Julia in a sudden wave as she pictured the intensity on Tristan's face, pouring espresso grains into the brownie mix, trying *so hard* to get it right under the tremendous pressure of knowing that baking was her livelihood, her expertise. He'd taken a great risk to impress her.

She removed the napkin from her lap, rose from the table still holding his hand, and approached Tristan. He stood to join her.

"I think you're bloody wonderful," she said.

He leaned down to kiss her, soft and sweet, as she raised her hands to his shoulders then to his cheeks.

Just as the kiss was starting to become passionate, Julia heard the whines and moans of a certain Corgi. She ignored Maggie at first, but it became impossible. Julia and Tristan parted with frustrated laughter as Maggie's whimpers came closer. She had settled at their feet.

"What *is* it?" Tristan asked Maggie, looking down. Maggie stared up at him with round, sad eyes. "I think she has to... go out," he mouthed to Julia then gave her one more quick peck on the lips. "Duty calls." He went to open the back door for Maggie.

Tristan returned to Julia's side and replaced his hands on her waist. "There's a Part Two of this date if you're up for it. I thought we might watch a film. You're always saying you never get to see anything."

"You don't have a telly here." She looked around the room.

"But I have a laptop and the latest Bond already downloaded. But only if you like Bond..."

"Of course I do!" This time she didn't have to lie. Her father had been a fan since the Bond series began, and he'd taken her to see several of the films in nearby Bath when she was a teenager. And of course, he had read all of Ian Fleming's books multiple times. But in the last few years of Julia's running the bakery, they hadn't had time to see *any* films, not even the newest Bond. She had no idea who the current actor even was.

"You're up for it, then?"

"Totally." She went to gather up her plate and fork and glass then followed him to the kitchen, where she watched him promptly chuck the brownies straight into the rubbish bin.

Julia went to the sink to rinse her plates, but Tristan insisted he would do it all later. "This is your night, remember?"

She caved, and they abandoned the dishes and moved to the sitting room. Tristan opened the door to let Maggie back in then got settled on the sofa with Julia to watch the laptop he'd set on the coffee table. Maggie tried to climb up on the sofa, but Tristan told her, "no." She wasn't allowed on the furniture. So Maggie circled at their feet and chose the perfect spot to lie down with a generous sigh.

Tristan tapped Play then stretched his arm around Julia. But they both discovered soon enough that the sofa was stiff and terribly uncomfortable. Tristan suggested a new strategy and situated a throw pillow at one end, then lay down on his side and patted the sofa.

Julia leaned into Tristan, lying beside him, feeling his hand wrap around her waist. "Can you see the screen?" she whispered. They'd already missed the first five minutes—some intense car chase scene—but she didn't care.

"Perfectly."

She rested her arm on top of his, and he squeezed her tight in response.

"Your hair smells good."

She closed her eyes, knowing she could stay this way for hours and hours, Bond or no Bond.

In what seemed like a moment, Julia was startled awake by a buzzing noise. She'd apparently been *so* content in Tristan's arms that she'd drifted off to sleep.

"Sorry. I thought it was off." Tristan leaned toward the table, moving Julia slightly forward with his body. As he paused the laptop, Julia noticed by the counter bar that the film was nearly over. She wondered if Tristan had fallen asleep, too.

He held his mobile in front of them both to view the screen, a text from an unknown source, with only the digits of the number to identify it. Julia assumed it was a wrong number or spam and that Tristan would ignore the message and resume the film.

But glancing at those first few words on the screen, she realized it wasn't a stranger or telemarketer at all.

Pleeeease reconsider, the message said. This was someone Tristan knew.

He shifted to rise up into a sitting position. Julia moved with him then scooted apart a little to give him some space on the sofa. Maggie yawned audibly at her feet.

"Who's it from?" Probably too nosey of her, but she didn't care. Surely they were at the stage where they could ask a question like that without feeling squeamish.

Tristan didn't answer. He kept one arm at Julia's waist and used his other hand to tap the screen, revealing the full message. Then he grunted under his breath.

"It's nothing. Well, it's something, but it will be nothing."

"How do you mean?"

He lowered his mobile and turned to face her. "This morning I got a text from Cynthia."

"Your ex?"

"Yeah. I'm not sure how she found my number. We haven't spoken in years. She likely pried it out of her brother."

"Gavin."

"Right. Anyway, she texts this morning, asks me to join the reunion."

"Oh. I didn't realize she would be there, too."

"Neither did I." Tristan made deeper eye contact, as though checking to see whether Julia believed him. "I only just found out today with her first text. Apparently, she's returned from the States, moving back to Cornwall—that's where the twins are from. I'm sure Gavin told her about the reunion and that I had turned him down."

"Or maybe the reunion was her idea."

Tristan shrugged. "Doesn't matter. I'm not going anyway."

As though to prove this point to her, he set his mobile down on its face.

Unconvinced, Julia felt the warm glow inside her turn a little cold. "Well, maybe you should go. To the reunion, I mean. If it's what you want."

Tristan gazed at her. "Cynthia doesn't change anything. I still don't want to go. In fact, seeing her text makes me want to go even less. I have no desire to see any of them, especially Cynthia."

"I just..." Julia shifted on the sofa, faced him squarely. "I don't want you to feel like you can't go because of me. You can do whatever you want." She only half-meant the words as they came out. The part of her falling deeply for Tristan felt oddly possessive, wanted him to break away entirely from his past and only focus on her, on them. But that wasn't a realistic or mature expectation in any relationship.

She also fought off the entirely jaded part of herself, the part that wanted to jump to the worst of conclusions. *Why didn't he tell me earlier about her text? Would he have told me if I hadn't been sitting right here? Maybe he secretly wants to go. Maybe he's curious about her, wants to see her again. Why* wouldn't *he be curious?*

But Julia remembered something. Tristan hadn't asked for these texts. He wasn't encouraging them. This wasn't his doing.

Julia hated these doubts creeping in. She exhaled and looked at Tristan.

"I appreciate that," he told her. "But I already responded this morning, right after her text. I told her I wasn't coming. She's just being obnoxious now." He shrugged toward his mobile then picked it up again.

He paused then typed out a message. He read it aloud: "Sorry, mind made up. Have other plans. Have fun with the gang." He pressed Send. "I meant every word. See?"

He did it to make her feel better, Julia knew, to obliterate any insecurities with one press of Send.

"Okay," she said, hoping it all would be.

Tristan set his mobile down and leaned in to kiss her. As they usually did, his kisses distracted her, fuzzed her mind, dizzied her senses.

Maggie began to whine, and the whines soon turned into growls and desperate whimpers. Tristan pulled reluctantly away. "Again? Great timing, little one," he told Maggie then looked at Julia. "She's either jealous of us, or she needs to go out."

"Could be a bit of both."

"Sorry for all the interruptions."

"Is that the time?" Julia saw the clock on the mantel. "I didn't know it was so late. I really should get back to my father."

"We can finish the film another time. I fell asleep during half of it anyway."

"Me, too. It was all those lovely carbs you fed me."

"I still owe you a dessert to make up for the disastrous brownies."

Tristan stood and held out his hand to help Julia to her feet. She retrieved her bag from the chair as Maggie followed them out the door.

Tristan let Maggie wander in the front garden while he leaned against Julia's van and touched her bare arm, sending welcome shivers up to her shoulder. "Hey, I meant to ask you this over the meal. I'm going back home in a week or so, to visit my parents in London. Do you want to come?"

This—more than the scrumptious meal, more than the awful brownies, or even the Cynthia text—surprised Julia so much that her mouth fell open a little. The question was so utterly unexpected.

"Well, I..."

"I wanted to visit with my mum and thought you might need a break, away from the village. It would only be a quick day trip. I wanted to give you plenty of notice, in case you needed help with your father. We could go on your day off. But don't feel pressured. I *can* take no for answer." She saw his grin in the evening shadows. "Just consider it, and tell me later."

She sensed that he was trying to downplay the invitation, probably for her benefit, feeling her out, unsure of what it all meant to her. *Meeting Tristan's parents.*

"I'll definitely think about it." She nodded.

They said their goodnights with a final kiss, then Tristan opened her door and waited for her to climb into the van, making sure her long skirt was tucked in before shutting the door.

Julia checked that Maggie was out of harm's way before driving off at a snail's pace. Tristan bent over to scoop up Maggie and used her paw to wave goodbye from both of them.

On the drive home, Julia tried to process the mental whiplash of a lovely date, a text from an ex, then an invitation to meet Tristan's parents. It all seemed a bit overwhelming after a long day, and the only thing she craved right now was a soft pillow in her own bed. She would have time for all the rest tomorrow.

Chapter Fifteen

"Don't ever feel guilty about keeping some ingredients secret. They can make a recipe exciting, have people buzzing. There's a time and place to reveal a secret ingredient if you choose, but you have to be careful who to trust with it."

Helping Alton Bentley walk down the church aisle on Sundays was always a fifteen-minute social event. Julia held her father's bony elbow, inching behind him along the slate floor toward their usual pew. It was impossible to do so without being greeted by at least ten people along the way. She had accepted long ago that her father was the village celebrity, even at a church service. But Julia enjoyed staying behind, walking in his shadow, letting him be the star of the show. She was comfortable in that role and always had been.

"Looking dapper today, Mr. Bentley!" observed Lizzie, holding onto her growing belly.

"Morning, Lizzie."

"A beautiful sunshine day, isn't it?" George Cartwright asked.

"Certainly is, George. Certainly is. Great day to be alive."

Her father soaked up the attention, loving it. His bright expression said it all. Julia almost felt as if they were on parade.

Julia and her father usually attended Sunday morning church unless he was feeling particularly knackered or unsteady on his feet. Those days, they stayed home because Julia couldn't risk him falling. But this morning, he'd arisen early. In fact, an hour ago, as Julia walked into the cottage from the bakery, where she had spent hours prepping the after-church lunch menu, Julia found her father sitting on his bed, attempting to loop his tie around his neck. His fingers fumbled with the fabric, so Julia sat beside him and swiftly tied it for him. Then she made him breakfast, gave him his pills, hurried to change her own clothes, and drove him to the church.

"Is that a new hat, Mr. Bentley?" asked Mrs. Pickering.

"About five years old but new enough to me. Time is all relative, you know." This received a chuckle from Mrs. Pickering and some others standing around.

And so it went, all the way down to the second-to-the-front pew, their usual spot.

But even then they weren't yet free and clear to sit. The vicar, as he always did, came to greet her father with a firm handshake and a "looking well, this morning, Alton."

Michael, the vicar, had been in his clerical position for about ten years, taking over the duties from his own father, also a vicar at Chilton Crosse for decades before. Michael and his wife, Rachel, were near Julia's age, she assumed, quite young for their positions in the church. But the village saw past that, likely due in part to Michael's being the vicar's son, and accepted him warmly.

"Thank you," Alton told the vicar. "And there's your lovely wife." He turned his attention to Rachel and held out a withered hand, which she accepted.

"Good to see both of you," Rachel replied, looking toward Julia.

Julia didn't know Rachel well, except for the persona she presented to the village: wife of the vicar, schoolteacher, always put-together, always smiling, always helpful and gracious. Sometimes, Julia mused over what might lurk beneath the vicar's wife façade, and a strong gut instinct told her she and Rachel would be great friends if they ever had the chance to know each other.

The vicar and Rachel took their positions up front while Julia helped her father sit down. He gripped the pew in front of him for extra leverage.

Dr. Granger was substituting today for the pianist, and when the vicar gave the signal, Ben placed his hands on the black-and-white keys and filled the church with beautiful music.

The only thing missing from this restful scene—for Julia, at least—

was Tristan. He'd attended the service on a couple of occasions, sitting with his aunt in the row behind them, but Julia hadn't heard from him this morning. She knew that Maggie had taken ill last night, vomiting a few times, so perhaps that had kept him at home, worrying over her.

Just as Julia had firmly accepted the fact that she wouldn't be seeing Tristan, he appeared at her father's other side and sat down in their pew with a grin. "Good morning," he whispered, leaning over her father to greet them both.

"Hi," Julia whispered back.

Her father and Tristan shook hands. "Hello, young man."

Julia wondered if Mrs. Pickering would be insulted, having her nephew sit elsewhere this morning. She smiled at the thought then felt immediately guilty for it.

Normally, Julia regarded church as a calm, restorative break in an otherwise busy workday. She would close her eyes and listen to the beautiful hymns Rachel sang or focus intently on the scripture the vicar would read, absorbed in the words of wisdom.

But with Tristan sitting so nearby, a new distraction arose, and she struggled to stay focused on the service. She didn't have quite enough self-discipline to shove away the image of his chocolate eyes, the echo of his laugh, the small tuft of chest hair at his neck. She blinked hard to banish those details from her mind, to focus on the vicar's reading of a passage in Ecclesiastes.

But in the end, it was futile. As she listened to the service, little bits of Tristan would filter through her mind. Pointless to stop it, so she made room for them both.

When the service ended, the same polite social chatter that swarmed Julia and her father at the start happened again—people milling about, saying goodbyes, wishing one another a good week, and issuing invitations to Sunday lunch. Inevitably, her father always received more than one, and today was no different. Mary and George came to their pew and invited them both to Mistletoe Cottage for shepherd's pie. Ben, they said, would also be joining them.

Alton accepted, but Julia declined, as she always had to, because of the bakery. So Mary and George took over Julia's duties and helped her father out of the church, agreeing to escort him back to his cottage in a couple of hours.

Julia swiveled to exit the pew and saw Tristan standing before her.

"Hi there." She looked up into his boyishly handsome face. Tristan found her hand—dangling between the pews, hidden from people's sight—and held it. "How's Maggie doing?"

"Better. She quit heaving about three a.m. and slept the rest of the night. She's her old self this morning."

Julia noticed the bags underneath his eyes from the long night.

"I'm glad. Was it something she ate?"

"Probably. That pasture is filled with bugs and grass and who knows what else."

"Tristan! There you are!" Mrs. Pickering called.

Julia quickly slipped her hand out of Tristan's grasp, an unconscious reflex.

"Will you be having lunch with me?" asked Mrs. Pickering of her nephew. "You know I don't like eating alone."

"Um, sure. I have time for a quick bite. Mr. Elton's got my day lined up for me, though."

"No rest for the weary? Even on a Sunday?" She reached out to smooth a wrinkle in her nephew's shirt. "That man works you much too hard."

"It's fine, Aunt Elda. I don't mind hard work."

As they were about to exit the pew, Julia spied Noelle and Adam in the aisle. Noelle held her son, who looked drowsy but content. He hadn't made a single peep during the service.

Adam and Tristan shook hands, and Julia said hello to Noelle.

"Look at this growing boy." Tristan extended a hand to Adam Jr. "Bigger every time I see him."

The baby gazed into Tristan's face, unblinking, mesmerized. Then little Adam grinned, as big as Julia had ever seen him grin. When Tristan leaned closer and offered his pinkie, Adam Jr. grabbed on tight and then let out an enormous, hearty giggle that bounced off the church walls.

This, of course, made everyone nearby laugh with great amusement, and they watched Tristan lean in and receive another giggle, this time big and breathless. The baby's eyes were wide with amusement then squinted shut as he laughed, and it became a game.

"Isn't that too adorable?" Mrs. Pickering said from behind. "Tristan will make the most incredible father someday."

That statement erased the smile on Julia's face. Thankfully, no one saw it disappear, especially not Tristan, who was still fully engaged with his current mission of making Adam Jr. giggle. He was on a roll.

Julia heard her pulse beat fast in her ears and knew it was time to leave. She gave a cursory wave and said to whomever might be listening, "Happy Sunday, everyone. I need to open the bakery."

Noelle and Mrs. Pickering turned to acknowledge her, wishing her the same, but Tristan was still talking to the baby. Julia took the chance to slip away to the other end of the pew, unnoticed.

Outside, she decided to send Tristan a preemptive text so he wouldn't question why she'd bailed without even saying goodbye.

Had to run. Work today. See you sometime?

It had been weeks since Julia had started her day with a migraine. But this morning was one of them. It pounded at her temples before she even opened her eyes. She wondered if it had been the extra-busy Sunday workload the day before. Two busloads of tourists had stopped at the bakery, creating a rush and an all-hands-on-deck push for much of the afternoon. Or maybe it had been that she'd stayed up too late reading the final chapters of *The Shell Seekers*. Or maybe it was none of the above.

Tristan had rung her twice after church yesterday and texted once, late last night. Julia had ignored all of his efforts. Well, not ignored. Just chose not to respond. Later, if he asked, she would blame work—legitimately so.

But lying in bed this morning, nursing her headache, Julia knew it wasn't work that had her avoiding Tristan. It was Mrs. Pickering's very accurate "father" remark.

Tristan *would* make an incredible father. He had all the qualities—patience, thoughtfulness, a calm nature, a playful spirit. She'd seen it in the flesh after church with Baby Adam. Tristan knew just what to do, how to put a baby at ease, how to speak its language, how to connect on an organic level. *All very natural for him.* Yes. He would be an amazing father someday.

Julia turned on her side and cupped the pillow under her chin, feeling the migraine pound in her brain to the beat of her heart. These past weeks, she had avoided the baby talk with Tristan, not because she thought he shouldn't know about her situation, but because she'd never expected things to go quite this far. Every time he texted or called her, every time he came by or bent down for a kiss, there was a part of her completely gobsmacked to see him still there, still in her life.

But if things continued on—as she now hoped they would—the talk must take place. It was unavoidable. But at what point was it appropriate to lower the boom? After "I love you" was said? Or well before then? What was the etiquette for this?

Julia let herself go there. She pictured what that conversation might look like, imagined the words she would choose. Then she conjured up the particular expression on Tristan's face when he realized the truth—that a future with Julia meant sacrificing his chance at being a father.

With a groan, Julia shifted again, flat on her back, and massaged her temples. She decided to go to the other extreme, to play out the other possible scenario in her head. Perhaps, it would be the right decision to end their relationship altogether. Before things had a chance to get messy or complicated. Just rip off the bandage. She would be doing Tristan a favor, really, sparing him greater hurt down the road, allowing him to move on before he became too attached. Before both their hearts were fractured into a thousand pieces.

She felt the prick of tears and forced them back before they worsened her migraine. She couldn't do this right now. *No decisions today...*

An hour later, Julia sat in her dressing gown at the kitchen table and stared out the window at the gray day. The migraine medication she'd gulped down was starting to take effect, dulling the edges of her headache. She could open her eyes and look at the world now without wincing.

She heard her father snoring and knew it would be at least another couple of hours before he awoke. She had some rare solitude on her hands this morning before the book club meeting. But she didn't feel like doing much with it.

Julia raised her mug to her lips and paused. She thought she'd heard a soft knock at the front door...

There it was again. Who would be here this time of the morning? She racked her groggy brain for any appointments she might've forgotten about, but nothing came up. Today was her only genuine day off, so there shouldn't *be* any knocking at her front door.

She cinched her flannel dressing gown at the waist with a sigh and combed out her wavy hair with her fingers, hoping to answer the door before the next series of knocks woke up her father.

When she opened the door, Tristan stood on the other side.

He cocked his head when he saw her. "Hey. Is everything okay? You look..."

"Atrocious?" she answered for him. Julia remembered the dressing gown, the frizzy hair, the probable bags under her eyes and cringed, which made her head pound again.

"No. Not at all. Just... not yourself."

"I woke up with a migraine." She took a step backward to let him inside.

Tristan shut the door behind him and turned to her. He raised his hand to stroke her cheek, and she closed her eyes. His touch was tender and soothing.

"What can I do?"

"This is working pretty well." She gave a half grin, her eyes still shut. Before she knew it, Tristan had gently brought her close for an embrace. Pressed against him, Julia savored the rise and fall of his chest as he rubbed her back with his hand.

"I was worried about you." She heard the deep reverberations of his voice echo inside his chest when he spoke. "I didn't hear back from you yesterday. I thought I should come check on you."

"Sorry I didn't text back. Things were pretty crazy yesterday."

"With the bakery?"

Julia nodded into his shoulder.

"You work too hard sometimes. I know you love your job, but don't forget to be good to yourself."

She backed away to look at him, many of her earlier fears melting away at the sight of him.

"What about you?" She sensed something underneath his gaze, something she couldn't identify. "Is everything all right?"

Tristan shrugged in response and looked down at his hand, which was stroking her arm.

"Tell me," she prompted. "Something's bothering you."

"You've got enough on your plate. It's foolish. Really."

"Nothing you could say is foolish." It was her turn to comfort him. She squeezed his waist. "Tell me."

"Well, yesterday. It's just..."

"Oh, no. Is it Maggie? Did she have a relapse?" She felt doubly guilty for not responding to Tristan's text...

"She's fine. It's not Maggie. Like I said, it's a foolish thing. Petty. Not even worth mentioning." He wouldn't make eye contact with her.

"Why don't you let me decide? Please, Tristan. Go on..."

He puffed out a sigh. "Well, yesterday after church, when I held your hand. And then you pulled away when my aunt came 'round. You did it the other day, too, with Frank. At the gallery. And it just became obvious, what I already knew."

"What do you mean?"

"That you don't want this to be public. This... whatever we have between us. You don't want other people to know."

Julia knew this conversation might come up someday. The migraine strengthened.

"Tristan—"

"No, it's okay. I get it. This is your village, not mine. You're this really private person, which I respect. And you've told me before how gossipy things can get around here."

"That's true. Once something is out there to one person, it's out there to everyone. There's no controlling it."

"But..." He finally looked her in the eye. "Is that so bad? That people know? What harm would it do? It just makes me wonder..."

"What?" She moved her hands to his chest.

"It makes me wonder if you're ashamed of us. Or maybe ashamed of me."

Julia swallowed hard. She wasn't ashamed of Tristan. Of *course* she wasn't. If anyone, she was, perhaps, ashamed of herself—the image of a forty-year-old woman falling for Mrs. Pickering's good-looking, younger nephew? People would laugh at her, think she was pathetic, even more pathetic than they did now, with no man at all. And what if they didn't last? The only thing worse than experiencing a blossoming romance under the village's microscope was experiencing a painful breakup under it.

But how could she explain all that to Tristan? "It's not you. I would never be ashamed of you. C'mere." She grasped his hand and bought some time by leading him to the sofa, calming her mind, figuring out how to process her thoughts well enough to express them on the spot. They sat down, knee-to-knee, and held hands, threading their fingers. She found the words. "I don't know if this will make sense, but what we have… it's special to me. Too special to make public right now. I *like* the idea of us being us, together. Just us. I like the idea of meeting you without anyone else knowing. Well, my father knows…"

"He does?"

"He suspected it last week and called me out on it. He's more perceptive than I gave him credit for. I told him that we were seeing each other. And he was thrilled. He adores you."

She saw the relief on Tristan's face.

"I'm glad he knows."

"But my father is different. He doesn't judge. He only wants the best for me. But some of the people in this village can be pretty heartless. I've been the subject of gossip, even recently, and I was gutted. I'm sorry if I gave any impression that I was ashamed of you. It's not true. It's more that I wanted to keep this between us, protect what we have for now, at least. Can you understand?"

Tristan nodded. "I get it. I think I let the silence get into my head yesterday—you disappearing from the service then not hearing from you. I thought you were having second thoughts or something."

Julia shook her head. "No, not second thoughts. I really *was* busy with work. But I can't deny that sometimes, this just seems…"

"Seems what?"

"Too good to be true. And it makes me nervous, like it's something that could disappear. I never expected you to walk into my life. I'd convinced myself I was content with things—working at the bakery, making scones, going to bed early, and taking care of my father. That was enough for me. But here you come along, and… I sometimes still don't know what to do with that."

Tristan raised her hand to his mouth and kissed it while he stared straight into her eyes. "I care about you. So much. You know that, don't you?"

"I feel the same way."

"Well, good. 'Cause I personally have no trouble climbing the bakery's roof right now and shouting about us from the top of it. But I respect what you're saying. You've lived here longer, and you know these people. If you wanna stay private for now, let's stay private. I like having you all to myself anyway." He raised his eyebrows with a grin and leaned toward Julia. She met him in the middle for a kiss.

Even though Julia could still sense inevitable dark clouds on the horizon, for the moment, all was right with the world again.

Chapter Sixteen

"Baking can be surprisingly therapeutic. When you have an important life decision in front of you, try baking bread or creating a tart. One part of your brain will stay busy, occupied with recipes and measuring out ingredients, while the other part will be free to mull things over, hash things out. You'll often find the decision made somewhere between the mixing and the baking."

"Is this the last of it, boss?" Enzo wiped his dusty hands on his T-shirt then pointed to the box on the floor. Julia had paid her busboy brothers, Enzo and Marco, to haul off the rubbish from the bakery's upstairs flat and to move the keepsakes to the cottage.

"That's it, thanks. You can both take a long break after this."

"The vendor just pulled up with paper supplies. We'll stock those first and then take our break."

"Okay. And help yourself to a couple of biscuits downstairs. I just made them."

Enzo lifted the box with a soft grunt, leaving Julia alone in the empty flat. She stood in the center and swiveled on her heels to get a slow, panoramic view, to see the space through new eyes. Now that it was finally empty, save for a shabby sofa and coffee table, what could it become?

Once upon a time, she had considered leasing it out to a university student or even to one of her bakery employees. But something had told her to keep it in the family. It would be all too easy to let the flat revert back again into a storage unit, a place where, over the next decade, old books or photos or knickknacks or mementos she couldn't bear to chuck out could gather dust. But she didn't want that. She'd worked too hard to clear the flat out. She might as well turn it into something worthy of her efforts.

Julia let herself daydream a little. The old, battered sofa, reupholstered with a fresh, clean fabric... The thick, sixties-inspired orange curtains replaced with something modern and neutral... The bare walls painted and covered with prints of landscapes or cityscapes or even family photos... A blank canvas, all of it, waiting to be filled with anything she wanted. It would take time and money, of course. Perhaps she could start the renovations after the anniversary party, when all the buzz and activity had died down a bit.

Julia realized something. This would be the first time, ever in her life, that she'd had the chance to update *any*thing, to make it all her own. The cottage had essentially stayed the same since they'd moved in forty years ago—same wall colors, same flooring, and same furniture, with the exception of the sofas. This was true of the bakery as well. Her mother, weeks before she'd passed away, had been in charge of choosing the décor, the tables and chairs, the wall colors, the flooring, even the design of the main counter and shelves. When Alton had inherited the bakery from his father and decided to keep it rather than sell it, Rose didn't want to sit on the sidelines. She wanted to be Alton's partner. The bakery badly needed an update after decades of being a family business, so he'd asked Rose to take over all the decorating. Thankfully, she'd had beautiful style.

But that was decades ago. Recently, Julia had begun to look at the bakery through a fresh perspective, to consider the possibility of new flooring and fresh paint and even maybe all-new furniture. Perhaps it was Tristan's new website and her own hamper idea that had first sparked these ideas. Julia felt the need, lately, to stay more current with the times, to be more relatable to modern customers. The world was clearly changing, and shouldn't they change a little with it? Julia had considered telling her dad what she thought, but it never seemed the right time to bring it up. Plus, would it hurt his feelings, even a little, that she wanted to make significant changes? Even though he'd handed the bakery over to her, he was still a part of it. His opinion mattered.

But at least the flat could be a start, something she could improve upon. Julia walked to the window and peered down at their cottage, a stone's throw away: her home as a child and her home for much of her adult life. In fact, other than a room shared with two other girls at university and a sparse, tiny flat in London shared with her mostly absent husband, Julia had never really lived in a space of her own.

Could this flat be it? Her own space? A gentle retreat from the burdens of the bakery, a place to nap or read or just sit and think, take up a new hobby, breathe deeply? She always spent so much of her day meeting other people's needs—the customers, her employees, her father—that, perhaps, she could use this flat as a magic rabbit hole of sorts, a place to shed her duties and her troubles at the door, if only for an hour now and then.

She hugged herself at the thought. Yes. Her own little corner of the world.

Julia squirmed in the bakery's office chair and stared at the question mark she'd drawn a few days ago into her activities calendar. *Sixth of June. This coming Monday.* The day Tristan had asked her to go to London to meet his parents.

Even during her busy workdays, the question hovered. And when she was given a spare moment here or there, Julia *had* considered it, mulled it over. She'd even pictured herself there, at Tristan's childhood home, meeting Tristan's mum and dad. But every time she did, all she felt was dread.

She tried to downplay the weight of it, a trip to London with Tristan to meet his loved ones, to see where he'd grown up. But it *was* weighty. It meant something. On the one hand, if she turned him down—would *any* excuse actually be valid enough?—it might create an invisible dent in their relationship, a question mark all its own that they might not recover from. On the other hand, if she accepted, it could mean something she didn't necessarily intend for it to mean: the unspoken promise of a future with him.

Meeting the parents, not meeting the parents. They were equally significant in different ways. Which answer could she live with?

Either way, Julia didn't have the luxury of time to put Tristan off much longer. Today was already Wednesday, and a decision was imminent. It would be impolite, at the least, to keep him waiting any longer. He'd been exceptionally patient—no pressure, no quizzing her, no discussing it. But the London Question still lingered, like the countdown of an obnoxious clock. *Tick, tick, tick, tick...*

Julia uncapped a marker and doodled over the question mark, creating an eternity symbol in its place. With a frustrated grunt, she fetched her mobile and began to type out a text that included *both* versions of her answer to Tristan, just to view them in black-and-white. Maybe that would offer some clarity.

Tristan—about Monday's London offer—I have too much on my plate. Won't be able to go. So sorry.

Totally lame. Still, she carried on with the other possible answer, to compare:

Tristan—about the London trip offer... the answer is yes!

Too eager?

She erased and tried again: *Tristan—I've considered it. Yes, I really want to go to London on Monday.*

She punctuated it with a smiley face, the way Abbey had shown her, then read over both responses again, imagining Tristan's reaction to each.

This wasn't helping at all. She needed counsel, and she needed it fast.

Julia found Mildred at the back of Foxglove House, hard at work in her garden. After a series of unanswered knocks at the front door, Julia had grown impatient and rounded the estate toward the gardens, the venue where Mildred and Duncan had married last year: manicured lawns displaying gorgeous green hues, seasonal peonies blossoming, birds singing their little hearts out. Pastoral and idyllic on an early summer afternoon.

Mildred crouched on her knees, head down, hands combing the soil, so absorbed in her gardening that Julia had to call her name twice to get her attention.

"Oh. Hello!" Mildred swiveled toward Julia and shielded her eyes from the sun with a gloved hand. "This is unexpected."

"I'm interrupting you. I can come back another time..." Julia took a step backward, half-relieved for an excuse to put off this conversation. She could feel herself chickening out with every moment.

Mildred pushed off from the grass and stood with a wobble and a smile. "Nonsense. You came all this way. I'm glad to see you." She stepped closer to Julia and leaned in for a quick kiss on the cheek then backed away to study Julia's face. "Is something on your mind? You look troubled."

"Do I?" Usually, Julia had better control over her social face, the one that often masked her exhaustion or her mild anxiety at being in a crowd. But she could never hide much from Mildred. Sometimes a blessing, today a curse.

"I'll get us some lemonade." Mildred removed her gardening gloves. "We need refreshment on this unusually warm day."

"May I help?"

Mildred folded her gloves and waved them. "No, no. You just enjoy this rare bit of sunshine. I won't be a minute."

Julia took advantage of a moment alone in someone else's elegant garden. She wandered along the cobblestone path leading to a smaller cottage, Holly's life-sized playhouse, once upon a time. Then Julia moved along the sculptured shrubs and heard the buzzing bees and the leaves rustling through the wind in a nearby tree.

Julia stopped and closed her eyes. She needed this, a brief moment to collect her thoughts.

"Let's have a picnic!" Mildred soon exclaimed from far away.

Julia opened her eyes and saw Mildred walking to the center of the lawn with a tray in both hands and something tucked under one arm.

"Here, let me help!" Julia rushed to her side, relieving Mildred of the tray, which contained two lemonade glasses and a plate of assorted biscuits.

Mildred unfolded the hefty quilt she'd carried and shook out its creases.

"A proper picnic." Julia waited for the blanket to float up and settle down onto the grass before placing the tray down at the corner's edge.

"I haven't had a picnic for ages. Sometimes I'm so busy with tending to the garden that I forget to sit down and enjoy it!"

They lowered onto the blanket, both cross-legged, and Mildred handed over one of the glasses. "It's a marvelous day, isn't it?"

"It really is." Julia took a sip and let the lemonade's tartness tickle her tongue.

Mildred began their chat with small talk—Abbey's stellar exam results, Duncan's new business acquisition, the twins' accomplishments. Bridget was doing well at university, and Rosalee had a significant role on her newest film set.

"Oh, and Holly and Fletcher have decided to purchase my old cottage on Bramble Road, the one I shared with my brother. It's stood empty all these months with only a couple of interested buyers. I didn't think Holly would want it—surely, it's too small—but she took another look, called it cozy, and said it would be perfect for the two of them. Isn't that lovely? They'll move in after the wedding."

"It's the perfect idea."

Finally, after the small talk died down and Julia had drunk half her lemonade, she scrounged around for the courage to utter the real reason she'd come for a visit. "I have something to tell you."

Mildred attempted a casual expression, but her bright eyes gave her thoughts away—that she'd been dying from the start to know why Julia was here. She set down her glass, shifted on the blanket to make stronger eye contact with Julia, and waited.

"You remember Tristan? Mrs. Pickering's nephew?" The only way to do this was to start at the beginning, with everything Mildred didn't know.

"Yes, of course. I saw him just yesterday, stocking a shelf at his aunt's market. He reached the highest shelf for me to retrieve a bag of bread flour. Lovely young man."

Julia cringed inside, as she always did whenever "young" was mentioned as a main descriptor of Tristan. But she continued. "Well, Tristan and I have actually developed a… strong friendship over the past few weeks. I've gotten to know him quite well, in fact—"

"You're dating!" Mildred gave a small clap and offered a smile that stretched to both cheeks.

Julia dipped her head. Mildred's clap had broken the ice.

"Yes," Julia confessed with relief. It felt cathartic to admit it. She raised her head up to look Mildred hesitantly in the eye, unable to hide her own smile. "Yes, we are dating."

"I'm in utter shock!" Mildred put her hands to her mouth for a brief moment then lowered them. "I thought he was just your delivery boy. Why have you been keeping this all to yourself?"

Julia tilted her head with a teasing frown. "Mildred. You know this village. Would you want *your* brand-new romance splashed around as fodder all over town, especially when it's Mrs. Pickering's nephew you're dating?"

Mildred snickered. "No, indeed. In fact, I kept my relationship with Duncan tightly sealed in the beginning. I was so worried it would get out."

"Precisely. You even hid it from the girls, as I recall. And you didn't even tell *me* until just before it became public knowledge, remember?"

"Fair enough. So, go on. How did this develop with Tristan? Details, please. I'm hungry for them." Mildred took another quick drink of lemonade, set down her glass again, and gave Julia her undivided attention.

"We met weeks ago—you were on holiday by then, I think—with his first delivery to the bakery. Tristan had quite a full beard, so I assumed he was somewhere near my age. I admit there was an attraction. But when he shaved the beard later, I realized how young he was. How *much* younger..."

"Go on, then."

"Guess."

Mildred searched the blue skies for her answer. "Early thirties?" She cringed.

"Even worse. Twenty-nine."

Mildred widened her eyes.

Julia said what Mildred was likely thinking. "Eleven years, my junior. Eleven! Our ages aren't even in the same decade."

"My, my."

"So I did the sensible thing. I fought my attraction to him. I promptly shoved Tristan from my mind and went about my busy days. But we kept being thrown together—his deliveries, Mrs. Pickering's meetings, even my father's poker nights. I saw Tristan everywhere, and I guess my resistance crumbled."

"What finally made you change your mind about him?"

"So many things." Julia recounted for Mildred the multiple times Tristan had surprised her—the ways he'd chipped away at Julia's stereotypes of him, the long talks he had with her father, the ease she felt in his presence more and more, the small gentlemanly gestures that were a natural part of him, his admirable experience with the Royal Navy. And even the accident. Julia didn't want to betray Tristan's confidence, so she remained extremely vague on the details and didn't mention his brother, the tattoo, or the multiple leg surgeries.

"And so, it turns out that Tristan wasn't the immature young lad I'd assumed him to be. He's an old soul, really. My assumptions about him were all dead wrong."

"He sounds like a wonderful human being." The giddiness and novelty had worn off, and Mildred's expression had turned thoughtful. "And anyone who's that good to your father must be a good man."

"They genuinely enjoy each other's company. They play chess sometimes, talk about books. Tristan doesn't patronize Dad the way some people tend to patronize the elderly, as though they're not smart or they don't have any feelings. Tristan treats him as a human being, as a mate. It's very comfortable between them. You know Dad was in the Navy, too, so they have that in common."

"Precious. And so, Tristan's age is no longer an issue between you?"

"Well..." Julia shifted on the blanket. "Yes and no. I still have reservations about his age, mostly about how people might judge us. But I don't see him as a twenty-nine-year-old anymore. I just see him as Tristan."

"Your Tristan."

Julia could feel herself blush. "Yes. My Tristan."

"You might not want to answer my next question. But I have to ask..."

"What?"

"Well, bluntly, do you think this is love? Or at least, heading in that direction?"

Love. Julia had tossed around the word in her mind from time to time, trying it on, seeing how it fit. But anytime she came close to confessing her feelings to herself, either an interruption would distract her, or she'd create a distraction so she could avoid the answer.

"That's such a huge question," Julia admitted. "Part of me thinks it's too early for that word. How on earth can anyone fall in love in a matter of weeks? It only happens in films, doesn't it?"

"It happened to your father. You know the story."

Julia *did* know the story, by heart. Her father met her mother during his final day on leave in Cornwall. He'd spotted her on a cobblestone street, struggling to carry bulky armfuls of groceries to her cottage. Alton stepped in and lifted the bags out of her hands, and they chatted all the way there. At nineteen, Rose still lived at home, caring for an ailing mother, who offered Alton tea and biscuits as a thank you. Alton lingered the entire afternoon, talking with Rose outside her family's cottage near the sea until he suddenly realized the time and scurried back to the ship with barely a moment to spare. He had managed to jot down Rose's address, and so they exchanged letters every week for the next six months and married soon after. He always told Julia, "I fell deeply in love with your mother in a single afternoon, over a few cups of weak tea."

"True," Julia told Mildred. As she recalled the details, Julia knew there were some remarkable similarities between her parents' story and her own. "They had an age gap between them—eleven years, too. And I know that they struggled for years to have children. But that was after they were married. They didn't know it beforehand. They dealt with it together, as a team. It wasn't some secret one of them held from the other."

Julia had only planned on discussing London with Mildred, not this. Not her worst fears and biggest insecurity. But the opportunity was here, and Mildred was her safe place. Julia picked at a loose string on the blanket and rubbed it between her thumb and finger. "You know that I had a hysterectomy a few years back." She abandoned the string and made eye contact with Mildred, who nodded. Her eyes held nothing but compassion.

"I remember."

"So here's this incredible new man in my life, a young man, with plenty of time and energy ahead of him. Tristan deserves a family, or at least, the opportunity for one. And that's something I can't give him, Mildred."

Julia's lip quivered. *This* was why she'd rather have kept it bottled inside. And if it was this hard to tell Mildred, she couldn't even imagine saying the words to Tristan. Mildred reached down to clasp both of Julia's hands in her own.

Julia found the strength to finish. "I know that adoption can be an option, but that usually takes years. And the harsh truth is—I don't think I *want* to be a mother in my midforties. I settled this issue years ago in my mind and heart, that I wasn't meant for children. And I was okay with it. I still am. Does that sound selfish?"

Mildred cupped Julia's cheek in her hand. "Oh, my dear. Not selfish at all. It's realistic. Entirely understandable. I never had children either and came to terms with it years ago, just as you have. And then, here in these twilight years of mine, I have the delightful surprise of stepchildren. Four of them!" She chuckled. "Life never really pans out the way you think it will, does it?"

"Not at all." Julia gave a hint of a smile.

Mildred lowered her hand back to the blanket. "So you haven't yet told Tristan any of this? About not having children?"

"He knows about my divorce but not the miscarriages, not the hysterectomy. I didn't plan on hiding them, but at the time, it was just... too early. I mean, we haven't been seeing each other all that long, and I didn't want to ruin things, to risk scaring him off. 'Hi, my name is Julia. I'm not only middle-aged, but I also can't have any children. Wanna date me?'"

Mildred chuckled, and it was contagious. Julia wiped her eyes and breathed out a sigh. "But saying it aloud to you, it feels selfish to have hidden these issues from Tristan. Maybe I should've told him already. But it's so hard for me to talk about."

"Precisely. My dear, you're a very private person, and there's nothing wrong in that. It takes time for you to trust people, to open yourself up. And it sounds like you've been unusually open with Tristan in these short weeks. Don't be so hard on yourself."

"The thing is—I never expected Tristan. Or having to confront the child issue again. I was just minding my own business at the bakery one day, and in walks this handsome, sincere, sensitive man, this... surprise that caught me off guard, shook me out of my comfort zone. And I haven't steadied myself yet. He keeps on surprising me." Julia remembered her initial purpose for being at Mildred's in the first place. "In fact, he's asked me to go to London next week with him. A day trip."

"What's in London?"

Julia winced. "His parents."

Mildred's eyes went wide again. "That sounds..."

"Serious, right? Meeting the parents?" Julia bit at her bottom lip and waited for Mildred to offer guidance.

"Well, when you say it *that* way." Mildred chuckled. "But hold on. Maybe it doesn't have to be so serious. Tell me precisely how Tristan worded the question. And his tone."

Julia tried to recall. "He was pretty casual. He mentioned it as an afterthought after one of our dates—that he was already planning on a trip to London, a trip to see his parents, wondered if I might want to tag along."

"Well, that doesn't sound so scary. How did you respond?"

"I didn't give an answer. I didn't know what to say. He told me to think about it, no pressure."

"And have you decided?"

"That's why I'm here. I needed someone to talk to. London might be a huge decision in the grand scheme of things. And I'm nervous about making the wrong one."

Mildred shifted on the blanket and straightened her back. "Well. Here's what I think. As for the hysterectomy issue, that certainly is a necessary conversation for you two to have. Tristan deserves to be told and soon. But give him a chance to surprise you again. Don't automatically assume you know how he'll respond. As for London, I'm not sure it's the right time to broach the subject. Would a few more days really make that much difference? You could put off the talk until after London, to minimize the complications. One thing at a time."

"That makes sense. Plus, seeing how London goes can help me figure out where we stand afterward, where things could be headed."

"Right. And as for your meeting his parents, consider something.

Tristan knows your father very well. And they've spent hours together, talking, getting to know each other. Does that bother you, feel scary to you?"

"Not one bit."

"Right. So consider meeting his parents in the same way. Tristan knows your father well, but you've never even met his parents, don't know much about them."

"True."

"So, treat London as a sort of balancing out of things. Tristan, for weeks, has been in your universe in this village, watching you work, learning about your life, your history. He's been to your workplace, even to your cottage?"

Julia nodded.

"And no doubt, he's heard many of your childhood stories straight from the source, from Alton. So, you might think of London *not* as meeting the parents"—Mildred punctuated with air quotes—"but as a way of making things even. Tristan's been on your home turf this entire time. It's only fair he'd want you to visit his."

"I hadn't thought of it like that. Things are a little lopsided, aren't they? I mean, Tristan knows so much about me. And, other than him telling me some scattered details, I really haven't experienced his past at all. Not the same way he has mine."

"Precisely. It's only fair. Why not let this be just what it is? A quick sprint to London with Tristan? A casual outing. Who says this trip has to be a game changer?"

"You're using a lot of sports metaphors today."

Mildred snickered. "Am I? Duncan's been teaching me about rugby lately. It's quite complex..."

"Well, the metaphors are working for me. I'm feeling so much better now. I just needed to talk things out, get out of my own head."

Julia leaned in for a hug, never more grateful for a maternal figure in her life. She adored her father and respected his opinions, but Julia simply couldn't hash things out with him the same way she could with another woman.

"Anytime, my dear," Mildred whispered, squeezing Julia in return. "And if you decide to accept Tristan's offer for London, I'm free to help out with Alton while you're away. Whatever you need. It's been ages since we've caught up. I could show him my pictures from Europe. That would keep us occupied for a good long while."

Julia rocked back on her heels. "Thank you. I'll definitely consider it."

"Mildred!" a voice said from behind them. "I got the highest marks in the class! On my maths exam!"

They turned to see Abbey running fast and waving a paper in her hand. This was Julia's cue to leave. She'd spent more time here than she'd planned. She had another new recipe to try at the bakery for this afternoon.

"Oh, darling, I'm proud of you," said Mildred as they both stood to meet Abbey and examine her paper.

"Hi, Julia!" she said with a grin.

"Hi, sweetie." Julia put a hand on Abbey's shoulder. "Congrats on your marks!"

"Thanks. You look like you're leaving. Can you stay?" Abbey pleaded.

"I'm sorry, but I really must go. Duty calls..."

"I'll come by tomorrow to round up some more sandwich orders for you."

"Perfect."

Julia hugged Mildred once more, and Abbey joined in at her waist for a group hug. Julia waved goodbye and headed toward the front of the estate, a significant weight lifted.

She had walked instead of bringing her van this time, and when she reached the main road behind the bakery, Julia paused. Producing her mobile, she skimmed both texts to Tristan again. Sucking in a breath, she deleted the first message, letter by letter, and watched it disappear. The only message remaining was the "yes" text she'd written earlier. The one with the smiley face.

Julia hovered her thumb over the Send button, sucked in a breath, and pressed it.

Chapter Seventeen

"Don't ever let your nerves stop you from experimenting with techniques or ingredients. Have the courage to try something new. If you stay too firmly in your comfort zone, you might miss out on the best recipe of your life."

JULIA RAISED THE FLOWER-PATTERNED SKIRT against her hip to compare it to the one she wore, twisting before the full-length mirror to decide which would be better. Solid fabric or patterned, bold colors or neutral? Nothing seemed right for her trip to London. She'd been at this for thirty minutes, and time was running out. And worst of all, she'd suddenly turned into one of *those* girls: fussing over which outfit to wear, spending more time than needed on her makeup and hair and shoes, worrying over every little superficial detail.

"Enough," Julia proclaimed.

She returned the flowery skirt to her wardrobe and chose the dark green one she was already wearing. What difference would it make, anyway, which skirt she chose?

Last night, drifting off to sleep, Julia hadn't experienced a single nerve about the coming day. She'd dutifully arranged all the plans. Mildred would watch over her father, Noelle would take the scones to today's book club with Julia's apologies for missing, and Julia would return this evening in time for the poker game and to give her father his pills. She had even whipped up a batch of maple scones late last night, something to hand to Tristan's mother. All was in order.

But when a dove's gentle coo outside the window had nudged her awake this morning, a shot of adrenaline quickly followed. *To London, with Tristan.* Why had she agreed to it? This morning, in daylight, it all felt too rushed, too soon. Why disturb the delicate balance she and Tristan had already established? She wished, for a moment, he'd never even asked her. But she had made a commitment to go, and she wouldn't back out, even if part of her wanted desperately to make up an excuse and stay behind. It was too late for that. She was obligated now.

She heard the beginning notes of her father's clarinet floating up to her bedroom, reminding her that he still hadn't eaten breakfast. Time to abandon her primping—and her incessant doubts—and take care of him before Mildred arrived.

Downstairs in the kitchen while she scurried about, her father stopped his playing and joined her, teetering toward the table and settling into his chair with a grunt.

"What does today hold for us?" he asked.

"I'm going to London," she reminded him as she pressed the lever on the toaster and watched the bread sink. "Tristan's picking me up in"—she glanced at the wall clock—"about twenty minutes."

Julia had first mentioned the London trip to him on the same day she'd sent the "yes" text to Tristan. Her father's only reaction had been to raise his eyebrows and then to say, "Good. You need a nice break from things." She wasn't sure if the "you" had been plural, as though she *and* Tristan needed the break together.

"Mildred will be here any moment," she added. "She'll be spending the day with you. Isn't that nice?"

The toast popped up, crisp and brown, and Julia removed the hot slices with her fingertips and set them on a plate before her father, then she turned to wait for the egg to finish poaching.

"Mildred. Visit from an old friend. Yes. It will be good to see her." He crunched into his toast.

Julia added the egg to his plate with a spatula then moved to the cabinet and counted out his morning pills.

"It will all work out," he mumbled.

"What's that, Dad?" Julia held the multicolored pills in her palm and started to double-check them.

"Today. With London. No need to be nervous, meeting his parents."

Julia closed her fist around the pills and swiveled around to face him as he pierced the egg with his fork, letting the yolk ooze out toward the toast. "You think I'm nervous?"

He chuckled. "You forgot my jam and butter. You *never* forget my jam and butter."

"Oh! For the toast!" She opened her palm again and let the pills slide gingerly onto the counter, careful not to let them roll away. "Sorry. I'll get them."

"It's fine, love. Forget about them. Sit here."

Julia scooted back the empty chair and obeyed.

Her father placed his ice-cold hand on top of hers. "Tell me." He looked into her eyes and waited.

There was no use in Julia pretending her father was wrong, in pretending she wasn't a basket case this morning. And it would simply waste time, trying to find a suitable lie to cover her nerves. "It's just... meeting people for the first time isn't easy." She smiled. "I'm not like you. I'm not a social butterfly, easygoing and naturally friendly with everyone. I take some warming up to, I think." She'd never mentioned it out loud before, this specific insecurity of hers. "What if they don't warm up to me? Tristan's parents. It's a lot of pressure, this little trip."

Her father blinked and smiled in return. "My sweet girl, don't you know? Tristan is smitten with you. And that's what his parents will be able to see for themselves. The rest will fall into place."

"I'm glad you have faith in me. But what's your secret, Dad? How are you always so comfortable around people, even perfect strangers?"

He pondered for a moment. "Well, I don't really think about it too much. I suppose I don't work at it. I try to relax and be myself. People can always sense when someone is trying too hard."

"That sounds simple, but 'be yourself' is a challenge for someone like me. It just is."

"I know, love. But if you show them what you show to *me* every day—your kindness and good will and patience and thoughtfulness—that will be plenty. That *is* who you are. You just need to believe it about yourself."

A sharp rap on the front door startled Julia back to reality. "That must be Mildred. She's early."

Julia released her father's hand and stood to kiss the top of his head. "Thanks, Dad. For the advice." She located the jam and butter in a flash and set them before him then raced to open the door.

"Don't you look pretty?" Mildred said a minute later, leaning in for a quick kiss on the cheek.

"Thank you. It took forever to decide what to wear."

"It's the right choice," Mildred confirmed. "Perfect for your skin tone."

"Thanks. Listen, Dad's eating breakfast, and I'm about to give his morning pills. Really, there's nothing much else to do today. If you'll just feed him lunch… I've put some sandwiches in the fridge for you both. And then he'll probably take a long nap later on or read his new book. In case I don't return in time, I've set out his evening pills in the kitchen, behind the toaster."

"We're all set, then." Mildred clasped her hands in front of her. "How are *you* feeling? About London?"

"Better, now. I've had some iffy moments, but it is what it is. I'll do my best to enjoy it."

"That's the spirit."

They walked to the kitchen where Mildred greeted Alton, half-finished with his breakfast, and Julia checked over his pills one last time and placed them in front of him.

"We'll do fine," Mildred assured. "I've brought all my holiday photos to show him. And later, your father can teach me how to play chess if he's up for it. Now, go. Do whatever you need to do before Tristan arrives."

"I owe you," Julia mouthed to Mildred, out of her father's earshot, and left the kitchen knowing her father was in the best possible hands. *One thing less to worry about…*

"You're quite the good driver." Julia watched Tristan carefully navigate the crowded M4 toward London.

"You had your doubts?" he asked.

"Not at all. It's just that it occurred to me—you've never driven me anywhere. It's nice." She recrossed her legs on the passenger side and smoothed out her skirt then clasped her fingers together. Her hands were free since she'd set the box of scones in the backseat, alongside the two bundles of flowers Tristan had placed there—one for his mum, and the other for a "special purpose," he'd told her. But she already knew the second bundle wasn't for her. Tristan had earlier presented Julia with her own beautiful bouquet when he arrived at her cottage door a few minutes before. Mildred had snatched them up with a wicked smile and told Julia she'd put them in water.

"I admit to being a bit out of practice," Tristan said. "I've only been driving for a year."

"Only a year?"

"Well, since I had the accident, I mean."

"Oh." When Tristan had offered to take his car, he'd offered so casually that Julia hadn't stopped to consider his relationship to driving and how it was likely tainted forever because of what he'd been through.

"It was physically impossible for me to drive for a couple of years afterward with all the surgeries and nerve damage then the physical therapy. But when the doc gave me the all clear, I dunno… I just had this reaction. I'd get behind the wheel and start sweating and panicking and having flashbacks about Corbett in his driver's seat. I couldn't even start the engine; I was so paralyzed. So I took another year off from driving."

"And then you tried again?"

"Yeah, pushed through and faced the fear. Mum was great. She rode with me a few times until I could get my courage back. I knew I couldn't walk everywhere the rest of my life. And I'm not rich enough to afford a limo." He smirked.

"Not *yet*," Julia corrected. "With that software idea of yours, limos might just be in your future. You never know."

Tristan chuckled. "Highly doubtful, but nice of you to have such faith in me. But I actually do have some news on that front. There's an investor interested in my project: one Duncan Newbury."

"Mildred's husband? Oh, that's fantastic." She turned to squeeze his arm. "Why didn't you tell me earlier?"

"I didn't want to jinx it. He's looking at my proposal this week. And if he agrees to invest, it would free me up to work on the project with a lot less stress about where the funding will come from. I could devote more time to it, get the prototype finished sooner. And when it's ready, he could help find the buyers, put together a business plan, contact the hospitals, and so forth."

"That's amazing news. Your parents will be so proud of you." Julia had expected him to chime in and quickly agree, but he pursed his lips instead. "Won't they?" she asked. "Be proud?"

"Mum will. But Dad... I think it would take about ten years of my topping the Forbes list for him to admit I've been successful at something." He kept his eyes steady on the road and drove with one hand. With the other, he searched for Julia's hand and grasped it. "He doesn't have much faith in this project of mine."

"But I thought things were okay with you and your dad. I mean, you don't talk about him much, so maybe that's why I assumed..."

"It's complicated," Tristan acknowledged. "It's mostly tied to Corbett. He was Dad's favorite."

Julia squeezed his hand, not knowing what else to do.

"He's never said the word 'favorite,' of course," Tristan clarified. "He would never be that obvious. But it was just understood in the family, unspoken. Corbett was this force of nature. He was charismatic and good at everything. And he was the firstborn, which apparently makes a difference. He and dad just got each other. Corbett never flaunted it, always downplayed it. But then he decided to follow in my dad's footsteps, to become an anesthetist, and that was it. The favoritism was cemented. So I spent time living in my big brother's shadow, couldn't really find my own way. I guess that's why I made a mess of things at university, nearly flunked out."

"But then you enrolled in the Navy. Surely that must've meant something to your dad."

"Well, I enrolled after a huge row with him. He somehow got hold of my end-of-term school report and chewed me out, told me I'd wasted his money, that I wouldn't make anything of myself. I went out and promptly enrolled in the Royal Navy. A knee-jerk reaction. I needed something drastic to shake him up, to prove I wasn't a do-nothing. But it still wasn't good enough. He didn't believe I could stick with it. He thought I'd be out within the year, but I showed him I was serious, stayed in, made it a real career."

"And then the accident happened..."

"Right. And it nearly tore the family apart. My parents even separated for a while."

"Oh. I didn't know."

"Well, they're fine now. At least, they act like they're fine. But when the accident happened, they seemed to blame each other and maybe themselves, a little. The convertible had been Dad's gift to Corbett. For the longest time after the crash, Dad wouldn't speak to Mum. Just pushed his feelings down and grieved on his own, took extra shifts at the hospital. Mum busied herself taking care of me while I recovered. But then when I moved out, tried to find my life again, she left my dad for a couple of months. I guess she'd had enough."

The lingering silence told Julia that Tristan was tired of talking about such a heavy subject. This was supposed to be a road trip, not a therapy session.

"Do you want me to change the subject?" she asked.

"Yes. Please. Put me out of my misery." Tristan gave a half smile and cleared his throat.

"Okay. So. I know a lot about your parents, but what do they know about me? I need to be prepared for what I'm walking in to."

"Oh, that's easy. They know you're amazing and beautiful and warm-hearted, and..."

Julia nudged his elbow with hers. "Seriously."

"No, really, they do. I've told them you're a friend, but I'm sure they suspect more. And I've told them the basics—that you're a baker, that you work your arse off, that you take excellent care of your father, who's also amazing..."

"What if I don't match their expectations? You've made me sound perfect."

"Aren't you, though?"

Julia leaned in closer, placed her head on his shoulder. For the first time all day, she was genuinely glad she'd accepted Tristan's invitation. If she'd chickened out, stayed behind, she would've missed this talk, this moment.

"You're too good to me," she whispered then closed her eyes.

Chapter Eighteen

"Remember that our baked goods are an important part of people's lives—occasions such as weddings, funerals, parties, committee meetings. These treats we bake can help to break the ice between people, give them something to discuss when they're having trouble finding the words. We offer them something in common, if only for a moment."

"YOU SAID THIS WAS A country cottage." Julia peered through the windscreen as Tristan rolled the car up to his parents' house. "Looks more like a grand estate!"

It wasn't quite as immense or stately as Mildred and Duncan's home, but it was close: a gorgeous two-story structure with strong Tudor details and extensive gardens in front with every color of the rainbow in bloom.

Tristan shut off the engine. "Well, that's what Mum always called it, her country cottage. It's really not as pretentious as it looks..."

Julia pictured a young Tristan romping around in the vast surrounding countryside with his brother, climbing over stone walls and rushing home for lunch or tea. She wondered if the inside of the house matched the pristine formality of the outside. She and Tristan gathered their goodies from the backseat and walked up the stone path to the imposing front door.

"We look like we're trying too hard." Julia noticed she was standing straight-backed and grasping her box of scones with both hands. Tristan stood beside her and held his mother's bouquet firmly in front of him.

Tristan looked them both over and nodded. "Agreed. How's this?"

He tucked the stems under one arm—careful not to crush the

blossoms—and put his other hand on his hip in a dramatic slouch, overly casual.

"You're ridiculous." She chuckled.

He straightened up, retrieved the flowers, and pressed the doorbell. He kissed Julia on the cheek and whispered, "They will adore you."

Julia heard heels tapping on the other side then the unlatching of a lock. She blew out a breath and prepared a smile.

A woman with shoulder-length ash-blond hair answered the door. She wore a pressed khaki suit and coral shell. Her entire face lit up when she saw Tristan. "You're here!"

Tristan stepped forward for a tight embrace. Julia waited patiently, moved by their fondness for each other. Their strong connection was clear.

When Tristan backed away, he said, "For you," and handed his mother the bouquet.

She raised the flowers to her nose and inhaled deeply. "Lilies. My very favorite. Thank you, son."

So this was Mrs. Pickering's younger sister. Julia would never have believed they came from the same gene pool. Where Mrs. Pickering was fussy, cold, and ancient, her much-younger sister seemed relaxed, friendly, and energetic. Where Mrs. Pickering's expressions were permanently judgmental and sour, her sister's were open and warm. Julia noticed something familiar in her eyes—they were shaped and colored like Tristan's. He and his mother also shared the same slender nose. Julia determined that Tristan's mum was somewhere in her midfifties. Not terribly much older than Julia, in fact.

Tristan took a step backward and placed his hand around Julia's waist. "Mum, this is Julia."

"Mrs. Hannigan. So nice to meet you." Julia extended her hand.

"Lovely to meet you, as well. And call me Fran. Please. Come in this house, you two." She moved aside. "You didn't bring Maggie?"

"Maybe next time," said Tristan. "She's still getting used to the farm, and I want her to feel secure there."

"I miss that little ball of fur. She has so much personality."

After Fran closed the front door, Julia handed her the box. "I almost forgot. These are for you."

"More presents? You didn't have to bring anything but yourselves today."

"They're maple scones," Julia explained as Fran accepted the box with her free hand. "Tristan told me they're your favorite."

"And they are! Mm, these smell delicious. You baked them?"

"I did. Just last evening."

A tall, slender man with a salt-and-pepper beard appeared from another room and came to stand beside Fran, both hands inside his trouser pockets. He wore a Wedgwood-blue long-sleeved shirt and dark trousers. His smile was genuine but small, and Julia wondered if this situation was as challenging for him as it was for her.

"Son." He removed his hand from his pocket to extend to Tristan, who caught it in a formal shake.

"Father. I want you to meet Julia."

The man shifted his focus to Julia, his steel-blue eyes searching her face. "Julia. Welcome."

"Dr. Hannigan. Lovely to meet you."

"Call him Oscar. He's fine with it," Fran insisted. "Look, honey. They brought presents with them. Wasn't that thoughtful?"

"Very kind," Oscar agreed and offered to remove the flowers and scones from his wife's grasp. "I'll find a place for them."

Julia assumed this was Oscar's excuse to disappear for a few moments and let his wife handle the initial welcoming duties. As Fran led them into another room, Julia absorbed everything about the house: the dark wood floors, the rich oriental rugs, the grand staircase, the fresh flowers perched inside an elegant crystal vase on a hall table.

The parlor Fran entered was decorated in a strong Italian style with terra-cotta walls and overstuffed, sunshine-yellow sofas. There was even a painting of an Italian vineyard above the fireplace.

"It's a beautiful room," Julia noted as she sat on a sofa with Tristan while Fran took the straight-backed seat beside it.

"Oh, thank you. I decorated it myself. Well, with a little help from the Internet. I've found the most perfect decorating website." Fran used her hands to explain. Her excitement was obvious. "I even based the paint colors on some photos online. I was so pleased with how it all turned out."

"Have you been to Italy?" Julia asked.

"A few times, yes. We went on holiday to Tuscany before Christmas, most recently. That's where I bought the painting." She pointed to the mantel behind her. "Have you been? To Italy?"

Julia snickered and shook her head. "I've never been anywhere. Not outside the UK, at least. Someday, maybe."

"Well, if you ever have the chance, Italy is the most beautiful place on earth."

Oscar entered the room, folded himself into the chair opposite his wife, and crossed his legs.

"We were just speaking of Tuscany," Fran informed him. "Don't we love it?"

"The food is especially good," Oscar noted. "I recommend the focaccia with *Podere Sagna*, an olive oil, made right there on the premises."

"It's delicious." Fran turned to Tristan. "So. Tell me all about Chilton Crosse. We haven't visited in ages."

"Aunt Elda ordered me to shame you into coming soon," Tristan admitted. "She said to use whatever tactic would work—guilt, bribery…"

"That woman," Oscar muttered.

"Oh, Oscar. It's just Elda being Elda. She'll never change." Fran shifted to Tristan again. "You're liking the village? You always sound so upbeat when you ring me up to talk about your week."

"The villagers are great. Some are kind of… quirky, but most are super genuine. They've been really kind to the new kid. I think I might stay there, actually. Indefinitely. It's starting to feel like home."

Julia hadn't yet heard this from Tristan. She knew he'd felt comfortable in Chilton Crosse but knew nothing about his extended future plans. Not past the summer, at least.

"Well, thankfully, it's not *too* far from us." Fran shifted to Julia. "And Tristan has told us all about your father. He sounds so colorful. He sits outside your bakery every day?"

"Yes, as long as the weather's agreeable. He loves to be out in the community. It was his idea, actually. He started handing out bite-sized scones or biscuits or cakes, luring in potential customers. At first, the sampling was just an hour a day, but he enjoyed it so much, he decided to expand it. Every day, for much of the day, if he's up to it. He's become a bit of a celebrity."

"And I told you about the anniversary coming up," Tristan added. "Forty years."

Fran asked Julia more about her role in the bakery. Thankfully, the safe-and-easy topics that Julia could handle effortlessly. With each passing minute, Julia became more comfortable in her own skin.

Be yourself, her father had insisted. So far, it seemed to be working.

Half an hour later, they all sat at the dining table in another grand room. One wall was filled with expensive-looking paintings and another contained a picturesque window that showed off the serene meadows and hills outside. With a couple of trips from the kitchen, Oscar and Fran brought out the plates, each piled with mouthwatering food: pork roast slices in a delicate sauce, new potatoes, grilled asparagus, and warm, buttered rolls.

Fran admitted she'd also found the recipe for most of these dishes online. "Tristan helped me find a couple of the best sites," she confessed before they tucked in.

"It's all delicious," Julia confirmed in between bites of tender pork.

Tristan sat beside her on one side of the table, while Fran and Oscar sat opposite them. They hadn't yet run out of all their conversation in the parlor and were now on the subject of Fran's growing estate agents company. In fact, she had an unexpected showing of one of her properties later this afternoon.

Oscar was silent through most of the meal, thoughtfully chewing his food. He nodded politely now and again, whenever his wife would ask for his input. But he never initiated conversation, not until the end of the meal.

He had apparently been waiting for a rare lull to ask Tristan, "So. How's this business of yours coming along?"

The air in the room seemed to go stale, as Julia worried where this line of questioning might take Tristan and his father. She pierced her last bite of asparagus with her fork and waited for Tristan's response.

"Very well, in fact. I heard from an investor only yesterday. Duncan

Newbury. You might've read about him. Lives in Chilton Crosse, but owns a prestigious investment firm in London."

"Newbury." Oscar cut a piece of pork. "The name seems familiar."

"Well, he's decided to become my main investor, and my software prototype is nearly completed. I'm just working on a few of the bugs in the code..."

Not *quite* what Tristan had told Julia this morning in the car about Duncan merely looking over the project with no decision yet made. She knew the inflated details were strictly for his father's benefit, to stave off any judgment that might come his way. But to hear exaggerated truths so effortlessly dropping from Tristan's mouth surprised her.

Oscar waved his fork in the air. "I'll never understand all that technical mumbo jumbo. Even with an investor on board, it's still a risk, isn't it? This venture of yours."

"Well." Tristan wiped his mouth with a napkin, and Julia saw his hand clench into a fist in his lap. She reached over to wrap her hand around his and felt the fist loosen a little. "Any new business is a risk, Father. Look at Mum's. It took her several years to get her estate agent company off the ground, and now business is booming."

"Well. That's not a fully accurate comparison, is it?" Oscar sipped his water, his steel-blue eyes focusing on Tristan. "For one thing, selling properties isn't breaking completely new ground, whereas this... software thing of yours... is. And your mother's investor was me. She had that to fall back on. What's your safety net, son, if Newbury backs out, gets cold feet?"

At this, Fran placed her napkin beside her plate and pushed back her chair. "Julia, there's something I need to show you."

Julia wanted to stay, to keep her hand securely on Tristan's and give him at least a measure of physical support. But it would be rude to refuse Fran's offer. There was no way out.

"Certainly." She squeezed Tristan's hand, abandoned her napkin, and prayed she wouldn't return to see the two men in a shouting match. But this was Tristan's issue, his own relationship with his father, something she couldn't wedge herself in the middle of or heal by being in the room. This conversation obviously came with years of baggage and past disagreements attached. Tristan would have to handle this on his own terms, no other way.

As she followed Fran out the door, Julia heard the steady male voices, the low tones back-and-forth in an exchange, but the further she and Fran moved away from the dining room, the less specifically she could hear the actual words.

Fran walked steadily toward the staircase and began to climb it. Julia followed, surprised when Fran paused midstep. She pivoted carefully and pointed to the wall filled with family photos that Julia had been too distracted to notice before.

"I wanted to show you something." Fran clasped her hands at her waist. "I'm sure Tristan is too modest to ever mention it."

It was clear that Fran wasn't about to address the elephant in the room, the tense discussion going on downstairs between her husband and son. So Julia played along. She pivoted, too, straddling two steps as she followed Fran's gaze toward the wall. In the middle of all the various-sized photos was a black-and-white newspaper clipping, framed in dark wood.

Julia leaned closer to see the print but realized she'd forgotten to bring her glasses. If she squinted, though, she could just make out the larger headline—"Local Boy Saves Child from Drowning"—but not any of the smaller-print details.

"When Tristan was fourteen," Fran explained, "he rescued a little girl at the lake. Tristan and his brother were swimming there one afternoon and heard a scream and lots of splashing. Tristan was closest to her, so he swam over to save her." They stared together at the accompanying photo, a teenaged Tristan, crouched down on his knees with his arm around the little girl's waist. "He didn't even hesitate. I was so proud of him."

"That's amazing. I've never heard this story, but I'm not surprised. You've raised a real gentleman. I see it every day. Tristan has this... kindness about him. He likes to help people. Little gestures, but they mean a lot. He already has such a good reputation in our village. Everyone's just crazy about him."

"Thank you for saying that."

When Fran looked at her, Julia saw tears glistening in her eyes.

"The past few years have not been easy for this family."

"Because of Corbett."

"You know about the accident?"

"Tristan told me." Julia placed a hand on Fran's arm.

Fran sucked in a breath, and Julia knew she was trying to be brave. She wondered if Fran ever talked about Corbett these days, whether her husband ever *let* her talk about him.

Fran cleared her throat. "Here's my favorite picture of the two of them, Tristan and Corbett. I took it about a year before the accident. They really were each other's best friends."

She pointed beside the news article to a framed image of Tristan, eyes shut and laughing while Corbett pointed at something the camera couldn't see. It was the only candid shot on the entire wall, the only one not polished or posed. Julia could see why it was Fran's favorite. Squinting again, Julia noticed the oblong shape of Corbett's slender face, even the hairline. He favored his father.

"I can't even imagine losing a child…" Julia couldn't possibly find the right words to comfort Fran but at least wanted to try.

Fran nodded, still gazing at the photo. "At first, Corbett's absence left this hollow ache inside me. But then, later, after the hardest waves of grief softened, it was the future days I mourned. I wouldn't get to watch him become a physician like his father. I wouldn't see him getting married, having a family…" She stopped short. "I'm sorry. I shouldn't be burdening you with this…"

"Oh, please, don't apologize. I'm glad you've trusted me with it."

"You're very kind." Fran wiped a tear before it fell. "Well… I suppose we should get back to the table. Time to serve up those delicious-looking maple scones."

When they re-entered the dining room, they found a thick silence. Tristan and his father each had heads bowed, focusing on mostly empty plates. Their discussion, it seemed, had ended.

"I'll get the dessert," Fran offered with a clap of her hands.

"I'll help," Julia said.

They returned with the plates of scones, and Julia assumed they would be picked at half-heartedly in sullen silence. But when Julia sat down, Tristan had apparently chosen to end the meal on a high note and cheerily asked his mother about her vegetable garden, which was enough of a time-filler to get them through dessert. Fran discussed in great detail the aphids and rabbits that had become her greatest nuisance, as well as the gorgeous tomatoes that had become her favorite crop.

After a final bite, Oscar wiped his beard with his napkin and announced he had an important call to make. He departed for his study with a polite apology while Fran, Tristan, and Julia cleared the table.

"I have a cottage to show at three," Fran told Tristan as she stacked forks on top of a plate. "I was hoping you'd stay for tea?"

"We can't, thanks. I was going to take Julia on a quick detour, and then we've got to get back to the village. Aunt Elda wants me to do inventory tonight."

"My sister, the slave driver."

Tristan chuckled and followed Julia and his mother to the kitchen, setting his plates down by the sink. "And Julia needs to get back to her father and set up for poker night." He stared at Julia with wide eyes, as though he'd just accidentally spilled an enormous secret.

"It's fine," she mouthed then explained to Fran. "My ninety-year-old father has established a weekly poker night at the bakery. A bunch of his mates from the village come to play and exchange silly gifts as prizes. All in good fun. It's supposed to be this little secret, but I think everyone in the village is well aware of it."

"I would love to meet your father someday. Tristan has nothing but good things to say about him."

"I'm sure he'd love to meet you, too."

But in reality, the image of Julia's father meeting Tristan's mother was a bit too much for her. Julia was still a little wobbly from making it through this daunting meet-the-parents afternoon. She needed time to get her bearings before they all met each other.

Tristan gave his mother one last tight squeeze before she walked them to the door.

"I wish you could stay," she said. "It's never long enough."

"I know," Tristan replied. "But maybe it's best we leave now."

"I think your father might be off the phone by now. Do you want me to go and check, so you can say goodbye?"

"No, no. We said everything we needed to say. Don't bother him. Just give him my best. It was good to see you." Tristan planted a kiss on his mother's cheek then opened the front door.

"Thanks for everything," Julia told Fran. "It was lovely to meet you."

"Likewise." Fran leaned in for a cheek kiss. "Please come again soon. Anytime."

Fran leaned against the doorframe until Tristan and Julia climbed into the Toyota, clicked their seatbelts, and drove away.

"Sorry you didn't get a proper tour of the house," Tristan told Julia. "I meant to take you around after lunch, but things got a little… weird."

"It's okay. I saw enough of it. It's beautiful. And I'm not just saying this because I have to, but I really like your mother. She's so genuine."

"Yeah, she's amazing."

But in the very next moment, Julia saw Tristan tighten his lips as he turned onto a new road. For the next few miles, he was brooding and quiet, deep inside himself. She knew he had likely shifted from thoughts of his mother to the conversation with his father. Julia had never seen him this way before, sullen and silent. It unnerved her a bit, but part of her was also relieved. Tristan wasn't pretending for her sake. He wasn't putting on a face to make her comfortable. This was the real him. This afternoon, they had reached some deeper level together, moving beyond trying to impress each other.

She leaned closer to massage his shoulder gently. It was tense and taut. "Tell me."

Tristan blew out a sigh and blinked. "I'll never be good enough for him. My father, I mean. He'll never change. I can't do anything that would satisfy him. I guess it's pointless to try anymore. I think I had an epiphany back there, at the dining table. My father's eyes were just… vacant. Cold. He didn't *want* to give me the benefit of a doubt or to have faith in my choices. He wants to see me fail. Or at least, he expects me to. He's already given up on me. And so, maybe it's time for me to do the same. To give up on trying to please him. I need to let it go. I need to not care anymore." His palm tapped the steering wheel for emphasis.

"But how do you do that after so many years of trying to make your choices matter to someone?"

Julia moved her hand up to comb gently through Tristan's hair. "I think you said something really important. He won't change. I mean, he lost a son. You'd think he would cling to the other one, appreciate you more or admire how you pushed through pain and all the surgeries to beat the odds and walk again. If that didn't impress him, I can't imagine anything that would. I think he's decided to cling to bitterness so that it's colored everything now. He doesn't seem like a joyful man."

"Spot on. He was always pretty formal and distant, to me, to my mum. But never to Corbett. They just got each other on this whole different level. I guess, when Corbett died, the distance Dad felt toward me and Mum got worse, not better."

"Grief does weird things to people. I almost think he's afraid."

"Of what? Trying to build a relationship with me?" Tristan scoffed.

"Yes. Maybe in his mind, twisted by grief, accepting you as his only son means he has to let go of Corbett, admit that he's really gone. And I don't think he can do that. I'm not excusing your dad. He's made a choice to treat you this way. But you might try pitying your dad instead of being angry. He's got a loving, supportive family right there in front of him, but he pushes them away with both hands. I pity him for not seeing you the way I do, the way your mother does."

"How's that?"

"Kind. Brave. Heroic. And it's his loss for missing out on that."

Tristan rested his free hand on Julia's knee and gave it a tender squeeze. "You're good at talking me down. How do you know what I need to hear?"

"I don't. I'm just winging it, crossing my fingers something will stick."

"Well, that's reassuring." Tristan chuckled and squeezed her knee again, smiling for the first time since they'd driven away from the house. "So you're gambling with my emotions, eh?"

"It's worked so far."

Tristan pulled onto a remote, unpaved country road and slowed the car.

"Where are we?" Julia asked.

"I wanted to show you something. I hope it's okay."

He pulled over near a stone wall and switched off the engine. Julia followed his lead and got out of the car. She watched him open the back door and reach in for the flowers. She'd forgotten all about the third bundle. Julia joined him around the front of the car, and Tristan reached down to hold her hand. The road was empty, not a car to be seen, only some cattle mooing in the distance. A turquoise sky had cracked open through the clouds, and a ray of sunshine beamed down on them.

"This is near where the accident happened. See that cross?" He pointed across the road, and Julia saw a dark cross shape emerging from the grass.

"I see it."

"I erected it a few months after the accident. In Corbett's memory."

Julia squeezed his hand, almost to comfort herself more than to comfort him. She suddenly realized the weight of this moment. Tristan led her over the road, and they stood before the knee-high cross.

"I actually come here instead of going to his grave." Tristan's eyes held pain as they focused on the memorial cross. His voice was soft, barely above a whisper. "I didn't attend the funeral, but Mum pushed me in a wheelchair up to the grave site after I got out of the hospital. I haven't been back there since. It's too hard. Too spooky. I don't like picturing him under the ground, inside a coffin. That's not where he belongs. But here..." He gestured toward the cross. "For some reason, this is comforting. This isn't exactly where the accident happened. It's about a mile south of here." He pointed down the road. "I wanted to mark the spot before the accident, to remember those few happy minutes we had before everything changed. I come here to honor that moment. His life. Not the moment where he died."

Tristan leaned forward to lay the flowers near the cross then returned to Julia's side. Julia moved her hand to Tristan's wrist and realized she was touching the blackbird tattoo devoted to Corbett.

She decided silence was the most reverent response to this moment, so in her mind, she said a prayer for the family, for a grieving mother and father and a fractured relationship, and for Tristan, who would experience the impact of that one moment in time for the rest of his life. As he stood beside her in silence, she wondered if he might be praying, too.

"We're here," Tristan whispered, waking Julia from some misty dream she'd been having on the ride home.

She opened her eyes to see her cottage outside the car window. They were back in Chilton Crosse. "How long did I sleep? The whole two hours?"

"Just about."

Julia stretched her sore back and rubbed at her eyes. "What time is it?"

"Almost five. Earlier than planned."

"That's good." Julia suppressed a yawn. "It'll give me enough time to get things ready for poker tonight. I wish you could come."

"I might be able to sneak in a game at the end. I'll try."

She looked up at Tristan and rested her cheek against her seat. The euphoria of an unexpected nap hadn't worn off.

"You're really cute when you're sleepy." He grazed her lips with his fingers then leaned in to kiss her.

She reciprocated then smiled up at him.

"Thanks for going with me today. I know it wasn't all fun," he acknowledged.

Julia's mind stretched back into her sluggish memory to recall vividly the lunch with his parents, the awkwardness of Oscar's grilling of Tristan at the table, the flowers at the crash site. "I'm glad I was there. For all of it."

Tristan stroked her cheek. His dark eyes stared deeply into hers with an intensity she hadn't seen from him before. "I want you to know something. I'm really falling for you, Julia Bentley."

She stared back at him and whispered, "Likewise."

Chapter Nineteen

"A bakery specializes in comfort food. People love bread puddings, muffins, and scones that soothe, that are good for the soul. They dull the sharper edges of life. Put a plate of biscuits and tea between two people having a serious conversation, and they'll relax a little."

Julia held the tart in one hand and flipped through her mother's cookbook with the other, in search of the recipe she'd earmarked earlier.

"Where *is* it?" she muttered, desperate to find out where she'd gone wrong.

Two hours ago, after the lunch rush had died down, Julia had decided it was time to try another new recipe, so she settled on "Blimey Bakewell Tarts" and followed the recipe to the letter. Or so she'd *thought.* When she took a bite to test the final result, she cringed and spat it into a napkin. Something had gone horribly wrong.

"Here it is... Bakewell Tart." Julia peered through her glasses at the recipe and scanned the directions. She went back in her mind to review the process she'd followed: roll out the pastry, blind-bake it, add the jam, make the filling... "Lemon zest, eggs, caster sugar..." She paused. "That's it! How in the world did I forget the sugar?"

Julia shut the book then chucked all the tarts into the rubbish bin. They were much too bland to serve to customers, even dressed up or disguised with some sort of icing. *Too much extra trouble to try and save them now.* Sometimes, it was better to quit altogether than salvage a recipe.

Julia sat on the corner stool then removed her glasses and rubbed her eyes. It wasn't the first time she'd ruined a recipe, but those occasions were incredibly rare. She was always so careful. But since she'd awakened this morning, Julia hadn't felt like herself. She was off kilter, off balance. Something wasn't right, which was confusing since the London trip with Tristan yesterday had turned out better than she'd ever expected.

In hindsight, the trip should have been a total disaster, given all the ingredients: the meeting of parents, the awkward witnessing of deep-seated rough patches of a father/son relationship, the somber visit to the crash site where Tristan had nearly died. Any of those had the potential to alter a new relationship permanently, to move it in the entirely wrong direction.

But those moments had only served to strengthen her bond with Tristan. In fact, when Tristan had dropped her off at the cottage last night, Julia had sailed through the rest of the evening in a lovely, tranquil haze, thanking Mildred for her help, seeing to her dad, setting up for poker night, catching up on some bakery paperwork, going to bed without a single care in the world. The afterglow of Tristan's touch had lingered with her.

But by this morning, that afterglow had mysteriously worn off. Julia had gotten a late start, missed an appointment, forgotten to pick up her father's pills at the chemist's, and now—the tarts debacle.

The pressure of Mildred's recent text hadn't helped. *How did things go yesterday?* Julia knew Mildred was salivating for every possible detail. They hadn't had time to talk yesterday when Julia had returned home. She had replied to Mildred's text with: *Very well. Details soon. Promise.*

Details.

Sitting on the stool, faced with a rare moment of peace and quiet, Julia finally pinpointed the exact source of her discomfort. The only one that really mattered, in the end, was Tristan's weighty comment last night in the car. "I'm falling for you," he had said, with an unwavering certainty in his voice.

Falling. "In love" was always the unspoken phrase tacked on at the end, wasn't it? As intoxicating as it was for Julia to hear him imply those words, it was equally as nerve-wracking recalling them today because she was falling in love with him, too. "Likewise," she had replied, and she had meant it.

Julia couldn't hide behind her excuses anymore. The time had clearly come for the talk. About a future, about her inability to have children. Tristan, the man falling in love with her, deserved to know what a future with Julia might look like. The "it's too early in the relationship" and "I never thought this thing would last" rationale fell incredibly short today. Because with London, things *had* changed. She and Tristan were clearly moving toward something special, something potentially lasting. And the thought of her ripping that right down the middle with this impending talk nauseated Julia.

But it had to be done. She pressed the button on her mobile that dialed Tristan's number and waited. He picked up on the second ring.

"Hey," she said, her voice as light and carefree as she could make it. "Am I interrupting anything?"

"Nope. Just finished milking the goats. On my way to have a shower. What's up?"

"I just wanted to see you tonight. I know it's short notice, but maybe we could do something special? Go out to dinner, maybe even drive to Bath or make a reservation at the manor's restaurant?"

Someplace without people we know or extra distractions, was what she really meant. Julia figured she could either have the serious talk over dessert or, if she chickened out, over a nice isolated stroll in the manor's gardens or on a long drive back home.

"Sounds fancy. Any special occasion?"

"Not really. I just thought it would be a nice change of pace."

"Oh. Bollocks. The meeting."

"What meeting?" Even as she said the words, she remembered. The all-important, simply-can't-miss committee meeting with Mrs. Pickering, to finalize every last detail of a party now only six days away.

Julia sighed. "Oh. *That* meeting."

"Maybe tomorrow night for our date?"

"Sure, one more day won't hurt."

"Won't hurt?"

"I just mean... postponing will be fine."

"Maybe we can do something after the meeting?" Tristan offered. "A long walk back to your cottage for some tea?"

"Okay."

"See you tonight. Can't wait."

Tristan clicked off, and Julia thought, *I can*. Because when she hung up, something became very clear. Julia couldn't postpone one more day. Their talk had to take place tonight, on the walk toward her cottage, or she might lose her nerve forever.

A knock on the bakery's back door interrupted her anxious thoughts. Curious, she rose from the stool to answer.

"Mac! Hello."

"Hi, lass." He wore his usual tweed cap and a light jacket. A small smile emerged through his graying stubble. "I was wondering if I could show you something. I need your input. 'Twould only take a minute or two."

Mac had never needed her opinion on anything. Typically, Julia was the one getting his opinion on plumbing issues, on kitchen equipment repairs, on troubles with the van.

"Sure," she agreed. Nobody at the bakery would miss her for a few minutes. "I need a good distraction anyway."

She let Brandy know she'd be gone for a quick errand then followed Mac outside to his pickup. It was parked behind the pub, where he was probably finishing up some repair or other.

"It's on my property." He opened his passenger door for her. "'Tis a gift for your father."

Curiouser and curiouser.

He drove in silence. Mac was never much of a small-talker, for which Julia was particularly grateful today. She cracked the window to breathe in the fragrant summer afternoon.

As Mac's pickup ambled along the narrow path behind the shops, Julia noticed the sun shining brightly on the limestone buildings, creating shadows in their craggy crevices. Mrs. Wickham, the flower shop owner, waved to Mac as they drove by, and Mac nodded his cap in return.

When they arrived at Mac's property behind the village, he drove past his cottage and turned toward a large work shed. She'd never been here before. Mac parked and switched off the pickup then led Julia to the shed. He cleared his throat as he opened the door and switched on the light.

Even among the clutter of tools lined up along shelves and the various equipment standing about, the first thing Julia noticed was a chair. The comforting, sawdusty smell of fresh wood told her the chair was newly built and newly sanded. It stood in the center of the room, waiting for Julia's approval.

"For the anniversary?"

"Aye."

Julia inched forward, taking in every detail: the sturdy build, the engraving at the head, which resembled an eternity symbol, the carefully crafted arms that looked just the right height. "You made this?" She knew that Mac did a bit of woodworking from time to time, but she had no idea he made furniture.

"Aye. I measured your father's chair when he was gone one day. The dimensions should be the same."

Julia touched the chair's arm. "It rocks!"

"Your father had mentioned that he wished his chair were a rocker. I should've asked you first, lass, but I wanted it to be a surprise. Do you think he'll warm to it?"

"Oh, yes. His old chair is so weatherworn. I think he'll be very grateful."

"Some folk get attached to things, though. They avoid change… I hope Alton will be open to something new."

"No worries. I'm positive he'll love it, especially the rocker aspect. In fact, I wouldn't be surprised if he was hinting at wanting you to build him a chair all along. 'Cause he's never mentioned it to me before."

Mac chuckled. "Aye. 'Tis possible. Alton's no fool…"

"And if he's just too stuck in his ways and wants to keep using his old blue chair, we can always move your rocker to the inside of the bakery. It could be his inside chair during bad weather days." Julia ran her fingertips along one of the chair's arms. The wood had been lovingly sanded, smooth to the touch. "How long did this take you?"

Mac shrugged and rubbed his beard. "Oh, several weeks, I guess."

"It's really beautiful."

"Have a go."

"Really?" Julia stepped in front of the chair and lowered herself down. She rocked back and forth, imagining her father doing the same.

"It needs paint," Mac said. "Do you think your father would prefer the same blue? Or maybe a different color?"

Julia knew immediately. "Blue. No doubt in my mind. It's always been his favorite."

Mac nodded. "Blue it is, then."

She stopped rocking and looked up at Mac. "You're such a dear friend to my father. For all these years."

"Over forty years." His Scottish accent trilled his *r*'s. "Your father is one of a kind. The glue of this village, to be sure."

"Well. It's mutual. He's said the same about you many times."

"I just thought he needed a proper chair to last him the rest of his days. May they be long and healthy."

Julia stood, walked the few steps between them, and tentatively put her arms around Mac. Just as he wasn't a small-talker, he wasn't a hugger either. But she felt him returning the hug.

"Thank you for the chair. You're a treasure, Mac MacDonald. My father is lucky to have your friendship."

"I'm the lucky one, lass."

Chapter Twenty

"Always be a little on guard when you bake. You can never be fully relaxed during the process because something could go wrong at any turn. Anticipate mishaps or unexpected situations. Be prepared for them, as best you can. It can save you some heartache in the end."

"NOW, FOR OUR FINAL ITEM on the agenda." Mrs. Pickering cleared her throat, peered at her list, then looked up at the full room.

At the end of the meeting, after all the precise arrangements had been made—the food, the decorations, the parade, the banner-carrying plane—one thing remained: the scheming to produce the moment of truth, the surprise.

"Who would be willing to concoct a reason to keep Mr. Bentley behind for a few moments after the church service while we're all scrambling to surprise him at the bakery? Suggestions, please." She stared from face to face.

After some muttering and consideration among the committee members, Rachel, the vicar's wife, raised her hand with confidence. "I can do it. Michael and I could devise some important question to ask him. He and Michael usually chat after the service, so it wouldn't be anything out of the ordinary."

Mrs. Pickering gave a satisfied nod. "Agreed. Well then." She sucked in a breath and surveyed the room with a tight smile. "That's the end of things, I suppose. It's all come together rather well, hasn't it? If there's nothing else..."

"Actually..." Julia decided to stand up and face the members. She clasped her hands together as she pivoted to see everyone. "I'd like to say something." She hadn't actually planned out *what* to say, but something compelled her to address the group on this last, significant meeting. "I just... wanted to thank you, all of you, for your hard work over these weeks. I've watched the way everyone treats my father with such respect and care. Not only in the last months, but for all my life... And it's, well, it's appreciated. I know my father will be so pleased with this celebration, with everything you've planned for him."

"This is *your* celebration, too," Mildred spoke up from the chair next to Julia and tugged at her sleeve for emphasis. "You both mean so much to this village."

Julia saw a ripple of nods in the room and heard some scattered, "Mm-hmms." Tristan winked at her from two rows away.

Julia found herself unable to speak. She touched Mildred's hand and squeezed it, whispering, "Thanks," as she sat down.

"I'd say that's an appropriate ending to this last gathering. Meeting adjourned!" Mrs. Pickering cracked her gavel on the counter a final time.

In hindsight, the lengthy meeting *had* been as important as Mrs. Pickering had insisted it would be. The members had finalized crucial details, such as who would hang the anniversary banner and when (Mac and Joe and Tristan would do the job before church), how the decorating committee would gain access to the bakery (Julia would open it for them the night before), whether gifts should be brought (gifts were optional, but cards were strongly recommended), and when exactly the parade would take place (one o'clock, on the dot), with the plane flying high over the village at precisely one fifteen.

Mildred told Julia goodbye, and they made plans to have tea the following week. They still hadn't talked about the London trip, and right now wasn't the time or place. As members filtered out of the meeting, Julia tapped on her mobile, hanging discreetly behind to wait for Tristan, who chatted with his aunt about something.

Finally, they were alone in the room. "Hey," Tristan whispered, approaching Julia. She stole a quick kiss.

"Hey back."

"So everything's coming together."

"It really is. And I keep picturing Dad's face when he realizes what we've all done."

"He'll be gobsmacked."

"Which will make every single moment of these meetings worth it. That's what I keep telling myself..."

"Oh, before I forget, I talked to my mum today. She said to let you know how much she enjoyed yesterday."

"That's sweet of her."

"She said you had a particularly good chat on the stairwell. You didn't mention it. Mum sounded like it was a bonding moment."

Julia nodded. "It was."

Tristan tilted his head. "What don't you want me to know? What secrets did she spill about me?"

Julia remembered the tears in Fran's eyes, the admission of grief, the comfort Julia tried to provide. That moment felt too sacred to share, even with Tristan.

Julia leaned in. "Only your deepest, darkest ones." She kissed him. "Really, though, it was just some girl talk. She showed me some of your childhood pictures, and we chatted for a bit."

"Well, as long as you two don't start ganging up on me. You hungry?"

Julia shrugged. "Not particularly. I had a sandwich before the meeting. You?"

"Not particularly. Wanna go for that walk? There's an amazing full moon out tonight."

A moonlight stroll in Tristan's arms was the only thing Julia wanted right now, even if it might entail a serious talk about their future with inevitably strong ripple effects. Julia steadied herself and forced a smile. "Sounds perfect. Dad's been fed and assured me he wanted an early night with his book, so he's all set."

That settled, Tristan followed Julia into the pub's main room, still lively at this late hour with raucous young men having a darts game, a group of ladies enjoying shepherd's pie at the table near the fireplace, and a couple of old mates at the bar sharing a pint along with a story or two.

Tristan and Julia rounded the long mahogany bar together, but Tristan came to a sudden dead halt, as though an invisible wall had just been erected, and he wasn't allowed to continue forward. Confused, Julia stopped, too, and stared at him with a frown.

"Tristan?"

But his eyes weren't on Julia. They were locked straight ahead.

Julia followed his stare to the front of the pub, where a beautiful, raven-haired young woman returned Tristan's gaze. Her hand was clasped over her mouth, which covered a broad smile. She lowered her hand and said with delight, "Tristan?" She rushed to approach him.

Julia was forced to step aside, invisible, as the woman stretched out her arms for a generous hug from Tristan. His expression still hadn't recovered from the shock of seeing this woman, but his arms hesitantly wrapped around her in response. He didn't even have to bend down—she was nearly his height.

Finally, he backed out of the hug. "What are you doing here?"

The woman, dressed in a form-fitting blue skirt and top, kept her hand on the crook of Tristan's arm. "We thought we'd surprise you. It was all Gavin's idea, I promise."

Gavin. The university mate of Tristan's. The one with a twin sister...

So. This is Cynthia. Tristan's ex.

Cynthia whipped around, nearly stepping on Julia's foot without even noticing, and gestured toward the front door, where two young men stood. Julia hadn't seen them until now. Neither one resembled Cynthia, so it wasn't immediately obvious which one was Gavin.

"If Tristan can't come to the reunion," one of them proclaimed in a loud, booming voice, moving forward, hands extended, "the reunion *must* come to Tristan." He leaned in to Tristan for a tight hug, accompanied by one of those cursory backslaps that men sometimes felt obligated to add at the end.

By now, Tristan's overwhelmed expression had started to warm. "Blimey, Gavin. I can't believe you're all here. When did you get in?"

The other young man—James?—spoke up as he vigorously shook Tristan's hand. "Just now, mate. We booked a couple of rooms here at the pub. Thought we'd go for a tour of your quaint little village and hope to bump into you somewhere. Result!"

Tristan ran a hand through his wavy hair, his eyes moving from face to face.

"What has it been, almost eight years?" Tristan mused, his attention resting on Cynthia. "And you look exactly the same."

"So do you." Cynthia's smile widened.

Julia watched Cynthia, studied the long, dark hair reaching down to her ample cleavage, the brick-red lipstick against white teeth, and eyes so light blue that they were nearly translucent. She might as well have stepped into the pub directly from the pages of a fashion magazine.

"Pardon me, folks." Miranda held two filled-to-the-brim pints. "Oh. Hi, Julia."

"I didn't know you worked here," Julia said.

Miranda seemed sheepish. "I hope it's okay. Just making some extra money on the side. A teenage daughter can be expensive. But I promise it won't interfere with the bakery."

"Oh, I'm not worried about that. Only surprised to see you."

"Lizzie mentioned she needed some help, now that she's being more cautious with her pregnancy, just lifting trays and chairs and such. She gets tired so easily and wanted a back up to call on. She hired me yesterday."

"That's great. I'm glad she has some extra hands."

"Oh, we're in your way." Tristan moved aside.

"Well." Gavin clapped his hands together. "How about we get totally out of the way and find ourselves a table? I'm famished! How's the food here?"

"The best," said Tristan.

"Pints all 'round?" Miranda whispered to Julia.

"That would be perfect."

Julia had been inching further and further backward, away from the boisterous reunion, until she bumped up against a nearby table.

"Sorry," she whispered to the couple, wondering where she should go, what she should do with herself. She could easily slip out the back door. Her exit wouldn't even be noticed. Not even by Tristan, at this point, it seemed...

Tristan's mates had already found a table near the front window when Tristan stopped them. "Wait a sec." He looked behind him and motioned for Julia to join them.

No backing out now. Julia flashed a cursory smile, as though she was completely fine with this entire situation. She realized as she walked toward Tristan that she was dressed in bakery attire. She hadn't changed clothes all day, hadn't felt the need to, so she wore jeans and a comfortable cotton top, nothing fancy. A stark contrast to these immaculately put-together people she was about to be introduced to.

"This is Julia Bentley." Tristan placed his hand at the small of her back. His mates had already made their way around the table, preparing to sit, but they paused when Julia appeared.

She gave an awkward little wave. "I'm a friend… of Tristan's."

"I'm Cynthia."

"Gavin, here."

"And I'm James."

"Julia runs the bakery next door," Tristan added.

"Join us," James insisted, pulling out a chair for her.

"No, I really can't. But thank you. I've got some work to do."

"Nonsense," said Cynthia. "It's much too late in the evening for anything but revelry. Join us. Please. Work can surely wait."

Cynthia eyed Julia with the same intensity Julia had eyed her with moments before, likely assessing her, making mental judgments and assumptions.

"Please?" Tristan added with a private wince, pleading with his eyes, and Julia knew she had to cave for his sake.

"Well, just for a bit." She sat in the chair James had pulled out for her. Tristan sat on her other side with Cynthia beside him.

Miranda approached the table with a tray full of pints and distributed them. "While I'm already here, will you be ordering any starters? I can go ahead and put the order in for you."

The table looked toward Tristan for guidance, so he ordered his favorite, sausage rolls.

When that was done, Tristan said, "Catch me up. What's been happening since university?"

Julia wondered if this initial moving-of-the-spotlight toward his mates was on purpose, so that Tristan could have more time to get his bearings. She wished she could read his mind.

"I'll start." Gavin took a sip of his pint. "I've just accepted a job at a London firm. My first real solicitor job."

"Cheers." Tristan lifted his mug in support. "I remember how you wanted to go into law."

"It's a good position," Gavin acknowledged. "Real possibility for upward mobility. Makes me a real grown-up, taking a job like this."

James gave the next update, the complete opposite of Gavin's. "Let's see. Just returned from backpacking 'round Europe. Out of work at the moment, but on the hunt for something insanely lucrative with the minimal amount of actual effort." He grinned widely then raised his own pint. "Cheers to me."

The table chuckled, and it was Cynthia's turn. When she spoke, her full attention went to Tristan. "After nearly eight years in New York, I'm back in the UK for good. I have a new job as a consultant for a public relations firm."

"In Cornwall?" Tristan asked.

"Yes. Back home. You know, it's funny. I couldn't run away from Cornwall fast enough after university."

"I remember." Tristan confirmed this with a distinct nod, and Julia recalled that Cynthia had sprinted away to New York for a job, leaving Tristan—and their relationship—to disintegrate.

Cynthia made crescent-shaped indents in the cocktail napkin with her fingernail as she continued. "I assumed New York would be so glamorous, would give me something I couldn't find here. The energy, the people, the rush of a foreign city. Turns out it wasn't so glamorous. That city can eat you alive if you're not on your guard. Cornwall is a breath of fresh air. Quite literally. I missed the salty sea..."

Miranda appeared with the two plates of starters, and everyone politely tucked in.

"Your turn," Cynthia insisted, her attention moving to Tristan.

He cleared his throat. "Well. Where to begin..."

Julia wished she could pipe up, smooth things over, come to his rescue. His life path was so completely different from the rest of his mates'.

"After university, I did some soul-searching, I guess. Entered the Royal Navy."

"Seriously, mate?" When James leaned over Julia to speak to Tristan, she smelled the alcohol on his breath. He was already on his second pint. "Subs and aircraft carriers, and the like? Bloody exciting stuff!" With his gesture, his fingers came dangerously close to brushing Julia's chest. Julia discreetly shrank back in her chair to give him more room.

"Yeah, well." Tristan grinned. "I was on a sub for a few weeks at a time as a communications tech. The job didn't feel very important, just clicks on a keyboard, but I did have some very sensitive information passing through my fingers. It turned out to be pretty meaningful, when I look back on it. At least I made a contribution."

"Did you find yourself?" Cynthia asked.

James had finally backed away, but his hand remained on Julia's chair arm.

"Not then. Not yet." Tristan's gaze grew distant. "It took something else, later on, to help me do that. I was... well, I was involved in an auto accident, with my brother. Years ago. He died."

Tristan's mates gasped across the table as they issued soft condolences under their breaths.

"I had no idea."

"Hadn't heard..."

"So sorry, mate."

"I was injured, but I recovered. It's not the easiest thing to talk about, so. Yeah. There it is. That's been my life so far." As though sensing that he was the only one who could lighten the mood under the circumstances—and as a possible attempt to neutralize any awkward pity coming from his mates—Tristan shrugged. "Life takes unexpected turns. Case in point: Here I am in Chilton Crosse, trying to start my own software venture, and you blokes show up. Who would've thought?" He looked out across the table. "But does anybody ever really find themselves?"

"Cheers to *not* finding yourself." James raised his glass a third time.

"Hear, hear." Gavin joined in, clicking his mug with his sister.

James decided to shift the conversation by suggesting they order a meal. "I'm still famished!" he proclaimed then offered to go to the bar with all their orders. By the time he'd arrived back at the table, the topics had moved on to less serious, less introspective ones, mostly about the friends' shared experience at university, as they swapped endless memories and stories.

During this walk down memory lane, Julia quietly ate her sausage roll, feeling excluded. This, more than any other social setting, was always her least favorite—being in a mix of strangers who knew each other well and shared a long history together. It rendered her helpless, completely unable to participate in the conversation, not having known any of the major players in these stories. Julia had nothing to contribute. All she could do was nod, smile, and act as though these stories were completely entertaining when they were actually quite boring. These people might as well have been exchanging plots of novels that she'd never read or a film she'd never seen. It felt the same way. Empty.

"Remember the time..." Gavin would start, and James would finish his statement with the rest of the story as the entire table burst out in laughter. Except Julia. She (thankfully) hadn't been there when Gavin was so pissed that he tripped and fell and broke his nose outside a pub. She had never witnessed the hilarious prank they played on Professor Peterson. Or the rugby game that had won them the championship, thanks to James' amazing technique.

In the middle of a story, Miranda had brought out the food, giving Julia a socially acceptable reason to be preoccupied.

"How about the kayaking incident?" Cynthia placed a hand on Tristan's arm then giggled at the memory.

"Oh, I heard about this one." Gavin raised his eyebrows and popped a crisp into his mouth.

"Kayak?" Tristan seemed not to remember until his eyes widened. "Oh. Yeah. Wasn't that the day before you left for New York?"

"Our last date," she confirmed.

Cynthia must've noticed that Julia was, once again, clueless, so she took it upon herself to fill in the gaps. She leaned over Tristan and spoke straight to Julia, who was now forced to pause her eating out of politeness. "So. Tristan had set up this elaborate, romantic date for the two of us. Picnic at the riverside, kayaking afterward. But Mother Nature had other plans."

"That's an understatement," added Tristan.

Cynthia described, in elaborate detail, the angry dark clouds above as she and Tristan picnicked on homemade sandwiches and tarts at the riverside during a break from exams. Then she told about taking shelter in Tristan's car, waiting out the storm. Then the kayak.

"We weren't going to let a little storm get us down, were we?" she nudged Tristan.

"Certainly not."

"We took advantage of the one bit of sunshine that finally peeked through, and we folded ourselves into the kayak. It was this two-seater. I asked Tristan if he'd ever done this before, and he said..."

"'Of course I have. I'm an expert kayaker.'"

"Right. Which I suspected was a lie."

Tristan smirked and nodded.

"Anyway, off we went. It took us ages to balance ourselves, get the hang of it. Finally, we had a rhythm going with the paddles. But soon, I realized my brand-new shoes were soggy. I look down to see water, rising fast!"

Julia did her very best to react in the expected manner: eyes wider, mouth ajar. But picturing Tristan kayaking with his ex was becoming intolerable.

By now, the entire table was giggling in tipsy unity, including Tristan, who had downed nearly three pints in the last hour, probably due to nerves.

Cynthia was barely able to finish the story through her gasps and giggles. "We tried to... shovel out the water... using our shoes! But nothing worked. We were sinking!" Cynthia tossed back her head in a light, airy laugh. "But Tristan, ever the hero, waded to shore, with me clinging to him, piggyback. I didn't even get my hair wet. We just sort of slipped into the river and let the kayak sink on its own. It was a wonderful day, wasn't it?" She squeezed Tristan's arm.

"A raging storm and a capsized kayak?" Tristan said. "Don't know if I'd call it wonderful."

"Well, it was. Only because we managed to laugh our way through it."

"True," Tristan agreed.

Julia's sudden urge to shove back her seat and run far, far away from this whole scene was trumped by her desire not to let anyone at the table notice her bubbling jealousy. She couldn't let them know she was uncomfortable or insecure, hearing a beautiful ex talk about a date with *her* boyfriend, having to visualize every single detail. To leave now, right at this particular moment, would make it too obvious, especially to Tristan. Julia wasn't that type of girlfriend, easily jealous. At least, she didn't *want* to be.

She clenched her nails into her thigh and reminded herself that these were old mates, and that Tristan was, essentially, trapped. He hadn't *asked* these people to visit Chilton Crosse. In fact, he had turned down their reunion multiple times. They had taken him by surprise tonight and interrupted his date-walk with Julia. What choice did he have but to sit and listen to their memories and participate? He couldn't be rude and walk away, not when they'd taken the trouble to travel here, track him down, bring the reunion to him. In reality, Julia felt a bit sorry for Tristan, having to sit here between his current girlfriend and his ex, not free to fully reminisce under Julia's watchful eye.

She took a sip of her own pint, the half-filled mug she'd been nursing the whole time, and let out a chuckle. "Well, that *is* a great story." She tried her best to mean it.

When Miranda brought yet another round of drinks, it gave Julia an opportunity to leave. She had stayed entirely too long and was exhausted from all the pretending. The last thing she wanted was to sit around and watch them all get even more sloshed, tell even more stories. They would have to carry on without her. And she had no doubt they would.

"Another pint for you, Julia?" Miranda asked.

"No, thanks. I can't stay."

In a moment of rare quiet, while Gavin and Cynthia talked to each other and James was preoccupied with ordering a dessert, Julia whispered to Tristan, "I really need to go. My father's probably waiting on me now." She reached for her wallet to pay her share, but Tristan placed his hand over hers and squeezed it.

"I'll get this." His eyes held an apology. "Our lovely walk was ruined. But I'm glad you stayed here with me. Thanks for that."

Julia tried her hardest to be gracious and understanding. "It's okay. There will be other times, other walks."

She pushed her chair back and gave the cursory "Nice to meet you… sorry I have to leave" statement that Tristan's mates acknowledged with waves and "So lovely to meet you."

Cynthia added an unexpected, "We should do this again," before Julia slipped out the door of the pub and into the crisp night air, a stark contrast from the boozy scene inside.

This wasn't how the evening was supposed to go, walking home alone in the moonlight while Tristan shared laughs with old mates inside the pub for half the night. She wondered how the evening would have gone if she and Tristan had taken their walk instead, had missed seeing his mates by a matter of seconds, whether she would've had the courage to bring up the "baby" issues and what he might've said. But now, that all seemed so far away, so out of reach.

On the walk home, Julia scarcely noticed the paper-thin gray clouds passing over a brilliant moon in the night sky. She barely heard the nightingale's beautiful tune from a faraway tree or the rustle of leaves. All she could see in her mind's eye on the walk home was Cynthia. *Beautiful Cynthia. Model-thin Cynthia with the crystal-blue eyes.*

How long would she be staying in the village? Long enough to rekindle something with Tristan? That was her obvious goal, wasn't it? Julia wondered if Tristan realized this or whether he was buying the notion that this was an innocent reunion of old mates.

Julia hugged herself in the night air and pushed away the deeper fear that it wasn't Cynthia, per se, she should be worried about. It was what Cynthia represented. Not just beauty, but youth. Someone from Tristan's generation, reminding him of how it felt to socialize with people his own age, people who knew all his youthful stories and had youthful things in common.

An instant, natural compatibility occurred with people of the same age. A simple fact.

When Julia envisioned the pub right now, that specific table, those specific mates of Tristan's, she knew the conversation probably ebbed and flowed in a way that even she and Tristan had never really shared. And even though Julia had convinced herself, all these weeks, that age wasn't a factor between them, tonight, it seemed like the only factor.

Chapter Twenty-one

"Don't let anyone tell you that baking is an easy task. It takes time, dedication, and plenty of muscle. Kneading dough, lifting around heavy trays, lugging enormous bags of ingredients. There's physical labor involved. But once you see the smiles on the customers' faces as they try one of your tarts or scones or breads, you'll know it was all worth the effort."

Julia grunted as she adjusted the paper bag in her hands, wishing her father would take her up on the e-reader idea she'd suggested a couple of months ago.

"Hundreds of books, all in one place, right in the palm of your hand!" Julia had told him with a gregarious, hopeful smile. But her sales pitch had fallen flat.

"I could never learn to use it," he'd countered with a chuckle. "You can't teach an old man new tricks, love."

Feeling the ache in her lower back as she opened the door of the bookshop, Julia decided she would repeat her pitch to him once more and soon. An e-reader would eliminate this type of grandiose clear-out of books, the kind they'd done last night, which ultimately ended in her lugging all the unwanted novels to Holly's shop today. She foresaw many such trips in her future.

Her father was remarkably unattached to the books he devoured. Once he'd read them, he was finished with them and wished for them to "go to a new home."

"Set it free," he had told her last night before she'd placed another book onto the growing stack. "May those who read them after me experience the same pleasure I did in finishing them." She half-expected her father to give the sign of the cross for some sort of blessing, but instead he paused, picked up another book, and added it to the stack.

Holly's bookshop, located at the end of Storey Road, smelled of rich, decadent coffee and held the peaceful hush of a library, except for today, when Mary Cartwright was offering her children's hour book reading in the deep corner nook. From here, Julia could see the edge of Mary's sleeve as she turned a page. Mary pointed to the illustration. "And here's Mr. Mole, talking to the Otter."

Wind in the Willows, an old favorite of Julia's. Her father had read part of it to her every night before bed when she was a little girl. She could still hear his gravelly voice, even now, trying to act out all the characters with various accents and personalities.

"Hi, Julia." Holly approached her and immediately reached out for the bag. "Let me help with these." Holly had recently set up a used book section at the back of the shop and offered a couple of pounds for a book, sometimes more, to those who wanted to discard theirs.

"Thanks." Julia felt the relief in her back almost immediately as Holly took her bag. They walked to the back of the shop where Holly set her load onto the counter.

"There's one more bag in the van." Julia turned toward the front door.

"I'll get it for you, no trouble. Why don't you help yourself to a coffee?" Holly suggested.

"That would be great, actually. The van is still open." Julia went to the coffee station, poured the piping black liquid into a paper cup, and blew on its surface to cool. Before she took her first sip, Holly had reappeared with the second paper bag and set it down on the counter next to the other one.

"The wedding is getting so close," Holly mused while unpacking the books to determine their prices. "Less than three weeks away. I'm so nervous." A perfect auburn curl dangled near her cheek as she flipped through a Louis L'Amour book.

"I'm sure it will all come together fine. Is there anything I can do to help?"

"Not that I can think of. Just baking me a gorgeous wedding cake will be plenty."

Julia heard the tinkle of the front doorbell and saw Fletcher, Holly's fiancé, making his way toward them. He gave Julia a quick wave then met Holly behind the counter.

"Hey, you," he told her in his Texas accent then kissed her.

That was Julia's cue. She looked away to give them privacy, taking a couple of steps in the other direction to browse bookshelves. She heard them whispering back and forth, something about Fletcher's concern over his curriculum for the next term.

As Julia moved between the shelves with her coffee, Holly laughed at something Fletcher said. Julia thought about them as a couple—one of the sweetest, most compatible couples in the village. Same age, same interests. In fact, books were really what had brought them together last year, when Holly hosted an *Emma* book club, and Fletcher came to the village as the scriptwriter/consultant for the *Emma* film production. Their love story was something out of a novel.

"A match made in heaven. The perfect fit," Mildred had said about them once. "Meant to be." All the clichés that anyone in a new relationship wanted to believe about their own relationship.

Could Julia believe it about hers, though? Could she ever be sure? She certainly would never call herself and Tristan a perfect fit. There were just too many complications, too many unknown variables and challenges ahead. She envied Fletcher and Holly's sweet display of affection in public—something she wondered if she and Tristan could ever do…

Julia sipped her coffee and pulled out a random novel from the used book section. Her father had read that one before. She moved on to a different aisle, soothed by the classical music playing lightly in the background, and thought about Tristan. He had texted her this morning, just to say "hi," and she had glanced at his text, intending to respond later. She wondered how long he and his mates had stayed at the pub last night or what they'd done afterward.

Julia had no idea how long the twins and James would be staying, how long this reunion of theirs might last. But she knew one thing. She didn't want to be part of it. Last night's meal told her that. Julia couldn't suffer through another awkward meal, watching Tristan's ex explore old memories. She wouldn't put herself through that again.

Let them have their time, their fun, their reminiscing. She didn't begrudge them anything, but Julia didn't fit into that world. She would wait until they said goodbye and then would try to pick up with Tristan where they'd left off. If that were even possible.

By the time she'd entered the cottage's front door with her new bag of books, Julia's lower back was angry with her. More than angry, it was positively livid. She plunked the bag at the end of the sofa, where half of the contents spilled out, then straightened her spine and raised her hands above her head, groaning in misery as her lower back continued to spasm.

She had thought that being wise enough to take the van to Holly's would have protected her from a back injury. But a moment ago, when she'd retrieved the new bag of books from the van's backseat, she felt a sharp, painful twinge as she lifted them out.

Slow stretching helped the pain a bit, and the spasms lessened. But the deep ache was still there. Julia vowed to pop a couple of pain meds and use a heating pad before she returned to the bakery later this afternoon. If she was very careful, the pain would probably be cut in half by this evening. She'd gone through this before—overdoing, carrying something too heavy or carrying it the wrong way then regretting it immediately. But her back seemed to heal fairly well, sometimes within twenty-four hours, as long as she took gentle care of herself. She hoped this was one of those times.

Julia turned slowly to sit down, carefully arranging herself on the sofa, and lay down with her back flat on the cushions, knees up. But the spasms returned, more painful than before, as though someone had a strong grip on her lower spine and was squeezing her muscles then releasing, squeezing then releasing. Breathing even hurt at this point. It was worse than she'd thought. She stared at the beamed ceiling and wished the pain away.

Last year, when this had happened, she'd suspected a pinched nerve and asked Mildred to drive her over to Dr. Andrews' office for an x-ray. But the tests showed something unexpected: arthritis in her lower back, along with the formation of some small bone spurs. Nothing to be done for them, except some daily physical therapy exercises, which she usually forgot to do.

Julia clinched her fists and cursed the back pain, cursed how it made her feel, not just physically, but emotionally. Back pain of this intensity had the ability to stop her in her tracks, to change all her plans. But even worse, the pain made her feel old, less capable than she was, weaker. Times like these, she desperately missed her youthful self, the one that was able to bend effortlessly over a sink to wash dishes, roll out a pie crust, or walk with a bag of books without an ounce of pain. But this—a forced, slower pace, with careful decisions about how to lift or carry objects—was apparently becoming her new normal. A tear rolled down the side of her cheek, and she didn't even have the energy to wipe it away.

"Is that you, love?" her father called from his bedroom.

Julia cleared her throat and tried to yell back her answer without moving her body. "It's me. I'm in the living room."

She heard his slippers shuffling on the slate floor toward her. She caught a glimpse of him rounding the sofa, and he stopped short when he saw her.

"Are you all right?" He touched her knee.

"I'll be fine. Just resting my back for a bit."

He shifted his attention to the spilled-out books at the other end of the sofa, near her feet. "Did you lug these all the way from the bookshop?"

"I took the van, but I guess lifting them in and out was more stressful on my back than I'd realized."

"Can I get you anything? Medication, water?"

"I'm fine for now. I just want to lie here, be still. Feeling better already…" That wasn't entirely an untruth. The spasms had slowed down to a tolerable pace. Maybe they were phasing out.

Her father moved his hand from her knee to the stack of new books and perused their titles. "These look good." He picked one up. "I haven't read this before. It's his newest, isn't it?"

"Uh-huh," she said, without even knowing which book he held. As she stared at the ceiling, focused on the dark wooden beams, Julia's back muscles began to relax. Miraculously, suddenly, she could barely feel the pain. This was deceitful, though. She knew that lying still in this position only masked the pain. It was still there, lurking, and the minute she moved, it would return, stabbing and relentless. Ideally, she should stay immobile for about three days. She rolled her eyes at the ridiculousness of that thought. *Taking three whole days off, just for herself?* What nonsense.

She felt her mobile vibrate in her trouser pocket and assumed it was Tristan again. She was too knackered to reach for it and see, so she ignored it.

Her father grunted and sat on the table next to her. "I wanted to talk to you about something."

"Sounds serious." Julia pivoted her neck carefully to face him.

He held a book to his chest, and his fingers tapped on it as he played an invisible tune. "No, not serious. It's about the bakery. Do you realize that the anniversary is coming up? Forty years since it reopened."

"Forty years, already. How is that even possible?"

"Time flies. But I can still see your mother so clearly, wearing that flowery maternity dress and holding her belly—you—as she watched the new awning raised with her name in big, bold letters. It was a total surprise to your mother. She didn't know about the name change until the awning arrived. In fact, it was the first change we made to the bakery before all the renovations. I wanted to let your mother feel included in the process and to build some excitement in the village."

"Must've been quite a sight."

"Oh, it was. That awning became a symbol, I think, of high expectations and big dreams." His gaze shifted from the air in front of him back to Julia.

"This old man gets too caught up in the past sometimes. How tired you must be of my rattling on this way." He reached for her hand to squeeze it. "You're still in pain. I can tell. I'm going to get you those pills from the kitchen cabinet. It might take me awhile, but I need to stretch my legs anyway."

"Dad, you don't have to..."

"Julia Rose. No arguing," he said with a half smile. "Let me do this one thing for you. You do so much for me." He released her hand and pushed himself up with a grunt. "See? I can still manage. I'm not useless yet."

"You'll never be useless to me."

She heard him chuckle as he shuffled toward the kitchen. She was worried about him tripping or falling on the way back, clutching two pills in one hand and a glass of water in the other with no free hand to support himself. But there was no use debating it with him, stubborn as he was. His mind was set on his mission. So Julia closed her eyes and dutifully waited for his return.

Julia heard tapping, soft at first, then louder. She opened her eyes to realize she'd been asleep, probably for the past couple of hours, and that the tapping came from the cottage's front door.

Earlier, when her father had brought her some pain medication, Julia had called Brandy to let her know that she and Miranda should take over the lunch crowd. Miranda had also agreed to stay well past her shift to help close up. That done, Julia and her father settled in for an unscheduled rest. He took a book to his room and probably fell asleep in the middle of a chapter, while Julia shifted, finally finding a semicomfortable position on the sofa with her heating pad. She had wisely switched the settings to the lowest heat level, because she fell asleep on top of the pad almost immediately.

Julia heard the tapping again. The visitor wasn't going away. With a groan, she carefully moved her body sideways before rolling up into a sitting position. The medication and heating pad *had* helped a great deal. Her back still held tension and soreness but nothing compared to the searing pain of hours ago.

"I'm coming!" she said to the door then muttered, "Eventually," to the air. She rose and steadied her grip on the sofa then put one foot in front of the other, feeling very much like her ninety-year-old father, shuffling around the cottage. When she opened the door, Tristan stood, beaming, on the other side, hand raised to knock again.

"Oh. Hi!" She managed to return his smile, genuinely glad to see his gorgeous, stubbled face. He wore jeans and her favorite form-fitting navy blue jumper. He looked healthy, cheery, and ready to embrace life, the polar opposite of how she felt.

"Did you get my texts?" he wondered as she stepped aside to let him in.

She shut the door and faced him, trying not to resemble an invalid. "I'm sorry. I've been occupied all day... haven't had a chance to check my messages."

"Everything okay?" He took a step toward her, but she placed her hands on his arms, creating a little barricade before he could swoop her up in a strong hug.

She hadn't decided whether she should reveal her back troubles to him or not, but now she had no choice. "It's my back. I was carrying something too heavy, and it sort of gave out. It does that sometimes, just gets strained."

Tristan's eyes widened in concern. "I'm sorry. Back injuries are the worst. I injured mine during a rugby match at university, and I was laid flat out for a week."

Julia nodded, touched by his empathy. His thumb caressed her forearm. "Yeah, you take for granted those particular muscles until you can't use them anymore. Standing, sitting, lying down—nothing helps right now."

"Can I do anything for you? Get you anything?"

Julia shook her head. "It's all covered, thanks. Dad's taking good care of me. And I do feel better after resting. We both decided to take the afternoon off. I was napping on the sofa, and he's sleeping in the other room." Even as she said the words, she heard a loud snore coming from her father's bedroom.

"And here I am, disturbing you..."

"You could never disturb me. I'm always glad to see you. So what was in your texts? Anything wrong?"

"No, I just missed you and hoped you could join us tonight for dinner."

"Us—your mates from school?"

"Yeah, I had to work all day at the farm." He lowered his voice in a mutter. "Not easy after a bit of a hangover." He raised it back to normal volume. "Anyway, I haven't seen them all day, and they wanted to have dinner. I suggested the manor on your recommendation. Can you come?"

Julia winced at the thought of sitting—anywhere—in a hard-backed chair for two or three hours of revelry. She wasn't glad for her back problem, but was suddenly grateful that it would provide her with the perfect excuse. She wouldn't have to lie when she turned him down. "I really can't. Sorry. I need to keep resting so I can be a hundred percent for tomorrow, back to work. Or at least, ninety percent…"

"Okay. I understand. I don't like it, but I understand." He grinned. "I wanted you there with me tonight."

The thought of spending another minute with Tristan's mates was almost as excruciating as her backache, but Julia warmed at the thought that Tristan had tried to reach her all day, that he wanted so badly to include her in his plans.

"How long are they staying?"

Tristan shrugged. "They haven't said yet. A couple more days, likely. I know you're probably sick of hearing their old stories, but maybe if you feel better tomorrow, we could all do something together…"

"Maybe. But I'll have to catch up at work, so I need to play things by ear."

"Of course."

"You're really glad they're here, your mates…"

Tristan paused, as though analyzing his feelings. "Yeah. I think I am. I mean, I didn't expect to see them again—ever again—but the minute we started talking about those university days, I entered a sort of time machine. This weird, familiar flashback to another time in my life. Before the accident. Plus, since they already know me, I don't have to try too hard. You know what I mean. Seeing an old mate is like… this reminder of who you were back then, versus who you are now, and the two of them meet. Does that sound daft?"

"Not daft at all. Very philosophical."

Tristan carefully leaned forward without pulling her in, sensitive to her back woes. He closed his eyes and came in for a warm kiss. Any pain in her body seemed to yield to that kiss.

"Mm, I needed that," she whispered when he backed away. "Good medicine."

"Get some good rest. I'll talk to you tomorrow."

"Have fun tonight," she said as he opened the door and went through. *But not too much*, she wanted to add.

As he waved and closed the door behind him, Julia wondered if she was being naïve. Most girlfriends would want to stick like superglue to the side of their boyfriend while he had nightly dinners with his beautiful ex. But where was the trust in that?

In Tristan's kiss, in his visit, and in all those texts she still hadn't read, Julia didn't sense any particular nostalgia for an old flame. Tristan was enjoying the collective company of old friends, nothing more.

At least, that was what Julia told herself as she ambled gingerly back toward the sofa for another soothing nap.

Chapter Twenty-two

"Some foods contain a magical quality, taking us back in time. For instance, eat a bite of a favorite childhood treat—taste those familiar flavors, smell the familiar scents—and you're suddenly transported to your childhood, just for a moment."

"WHAT CAN I GET FOR you?" The young man at the counter hovered his index finger above the till's keys, waiting for Julia's order.

She nearly responded with "Blue Moon Curry" but stopped short. It wasn't an *actual* item on the menu, just her private joke with her father. He seemed to want curry on a weekly basis, but it was much too spicy for his digestive system. Dr. Andrews had warned him against it, but after much begging and cajoling from her father, the doctor agreed to letting Alton have his curry "once in a blue moon." The name stuck, and that was what her father always called it whenever he craved one. "Could you get me one of those Blue Moon Curries that the doc said I could have?"

If Julia ever balked, her father would deftly play the sympathy card. "But I'm an old man. Humor me. You never know if this will be my very last curry..."

So today, after a gentle back-and-forth with him, she had caved. He wanted curry for lunch, so curry he would have. Thankfully, Chilton Crosse's Indian restaurant offered all different levels of heat with their signature curry: mild, medium, hot, extra hot, and their special "eat at your own risk—scorching hot."

Julia ordered a mild curry with chicken, and the young man tapped in her order. As she handed over her money, she almost wished she'd gotten something for herself. Curry wasn't her favorite, but the delicious scents and spices wafting through the restaurant were starting to give her hunger pangs, even though she'd already grabbed a quick sandwich an hour before.

In the five minutes it took for the order to be filled, Julia checked her mobile for the hundredth time today, hoping for a reply from Tristan. This morning, she'd sent him a brief "How was last night?" text, but he hadn't responded. She assumed he was busy, catching up with work after another late night with his mates.

She hoped he would take a break and either pop round to see her, or at least return her message. But nothing so far. Julia clicked off her mobile and sighed.

After the plastic bag was handed to her, Julia stepped outside into the brilliant sunlight. It spilled over her shoulders and onto the brick pavement, creating strong shadows. This wasn't a day to spend indoors in a windowless kitchen, but she had too much to catch up on at the bakery after yesterday.

She had awakened today after nine straight hours of sleep with stiffness in her back, but nothing else significant. No jabbing pains, no soreness. Still, she insisted on moving slowly, methodically prethinking every movement, what she could and couldn't lift, how she could and couldn't twist her body. She couldn't afford to have a relapse. She'd even asked Miranda to roll out the bread dough for her this morning, not wanting to risk another back spasm. *So far, so good.*

A peal of cackling laughter hit the air, and Julia snapped her head up to see a group exiting Joe's pub, a few doors down. They were all caught up in the same laughter, which echoed down the street. One of them stumbled into a tourist walking nearby, who scowled at the troublemakers—"Look where you're going!"—then went on his way.

Julia squinted to see who the main source of the laughter was. *Cynthia. Along with James and Gavin.* Tristan was there, too, grinning from ear to ear. They hadn't noticed her yet, so Julia paused in her tracks and pretended to window shop at the emporium while she eyed Tristan and his mates with occasional side-glances. She couldn't hear what they were saying, but it was obvious they were entirely in their own world.

This was the time machine Tristan had mentioned. Julia was observing it from the outside, staring at a uniquely younger version of Tristan—jovial, carefree, even possibly a bit reckless. And yes, maybe even tipsy, after a pint or two at a pub lunch, in the middle of a workday. Julia assumed he had finished his morning shift then taken a long lunch or maybe skipped work altogether, played hooky.

During one of her subtle glances, Julia saw Tristan use his hands to gesture wildly while saying something. Seconds later, his mates burst out in laughter once more. She hadn't seen this particular flavor of Tristan. Sure, he could be funny and could make Julia laugh. He did it every day, quite easily. But his sense of humor with her was subtle, more nuanced and witty, not raucous or loud. She wondered which version of him was the authentic one. Could they both occupy the same space?

When it seemed the group had made the decision to cross the street together, Julia switched her attention again to the emporium's window. She could see the group's reflection and waited until they were all safely inside the art gallery before continuing her journey to the cottage with her father's curry.

She hoped Tristan and his friends wouldn't embarrass themselves inside the gallery, usually a tranquil, almost-sacred environment for those wanting to meditate on beautiful art. Likely, Tristan was just showing them around the village, giving a tour. But Frank would surely shush them or even suggest they leave if they dared to carry their tipsy laughter into the gallery.

As she rounded the edge of Storey Road toward home, Julia realized something. If she had seen Tristan and his mates today and not known them at all, not been acquainted with them in the least, her face probably would've held the very same scowl as that tourist, upon viewing such an obnoxious, immature, self-absorbed group.

Moving up the stone pavement toward the cottage, Julia worried about the impact on Tristan. His mates would be leaving soon—hopefully, soon—but would the ripple effects of their visit stay behind? Would they rub off on Tristan long-term? As Tristan had told her, these friends reminded him of a different self, a different time in his life. So why wouldn't he experience a sense of regret, a void, whenever they finally left town, as though a piece of him had gone with them? Would Julia or their relationship be enough for him after that?

"Keys, mobile, umbrella..." Julia gathered all the items she thought she would need for the afternoon shift at the bakery then massaged her back with her free hand. An hour ago, after she'd served her father's curry and driven him to his post outside the bakery, she felt her lower back throbbing again and decided to make a quick trip back home for a pain pill. Maybe it would be enough to see her through her final shift.

That done, she opened the cottage's front door to leave again but noticed someone walking briskly up the path toward her. "Mildred!"

"Hi, love." Mildred paused a few steps away. "Oh. You're going out. I was hoping to catch you..."

"What's the trouble?"

"No trouble." Mildred looked well rested and happy—as she always did, these days—wearing a classic cardigan, a scarf, and a bright expression. "I was just hoping we could talk. Brandy said I could find you here. Do you have a minute?"

Not really. But making time for Mildred was more important than making scones. "Remember this—people should *always* come before work," her father had often spouted when she was growing up, realizing young Julia had a tendency to want to hide away in the kitchen.

"Absolutely. Come in." Julia held the door open and then closed it behind Mildred. "Can I get you some tea?" she offered out of habit, realizing she didn't exactly have time to make it *and* to have a conversation. She only had time for one or the other.

"No, no. I'm just here for the scoop." Mildred's eyes sparkled as she pushed her hands deep into her cardigan's pockets and rocked back on her heels. "About Tristan."

"Tristan?"

"And London! Your trip—the details? You never told me anything, so I thought I'd finally come and get them myself, be nosy and wriggle them out of you. I hope that's okay." She looked squeamish, as though worried she'd crossed some sort of line.

"Of course it's okay." Julia set down her mobile, keys, and umbrella into a nearby chair. "I've just been so busy with work. I completely forgot to ring you back. I'm sorry. It's been a few days now, hasn't it?" The London trip—that special closeness she'd experienced with Tristan—seemed so far away now. "Here, let's sit down, and I can fill you in." They moved to the sofa, and Julia was careful to sit slowly and find a comfortable, back-friendly position.

"Where do I start?" Julia had to manually draw her memory back to that day, put herself there again. London.

But soon, she rolled through the details, hitting the main points: meeting Tristan's parents, the warmth and friendliness of his mother, the stilted and formal personality of his father. Julia slowed down a bit when she reached the part about the tense father-son argument at the dining table with Fran whisking Julia away to the staircase. Finally, she relayed the unexpected visit to Corbett's memorial site.

"Did I tell you his brother died? In the accident?"

"You mentioned an accident and some sort of injury Tristan sustained but nothing about his brother dying. I'm sorry to hear about it. What a trauma for Tristan to endure. And he took you to the memorial site?"

"Yes, it was heartbreaking. But it seemed to bring me closer to Tristan. Almost like he was sharing a secret with me, something he hides from other people. I'm glad we went." She continued on about the rest of the trip, including the "I'm falling for you" comment Tristan made in the car, at the end.

At this, Mildred raised her eyebrows. "As in… falling in love?"

"I *think* that's what he was hinting at."

"And? How did you respond?"

"Well, basically, that I felt the same."

Mildred cupped her mouth then removed her hand so she could say, "This is big. Isn't it?"

"I think so. It scared me a little, honestly. Things are moving fast."

"This was, what, four days ago? What's happened since? You should be glowing. I'm looking at you now… and I don't see a glow."

Julia shifted her position with a small grunt. "There's been a tiny complication." She explained about the night of the big committee meeting, her intent to tell Tristan about her hysterectomy, and how their walk was interrupted by an unexpected visit from Tristan's mates, including Tristan's ex.

At this, Mildred gasped slightly. "His ex is in town? What's she like?"

"Beautiful. Young. Perfect. I had dinner at the pub with them that first night. I got cornered into it."

"Does she have her sights set on him?"

"It's actually hard to tell. I'm sure some sort of old feelings have been stirred up. I'd be more worried if it was just Cynthia visiting. But her brother and friend provide a sort of buffer, like 'old mates in town for a reunion.' That's what they keep saying. But really, even if it did bother me, what can I do? I don't want to be that type of girl, who hovers or nags or gets easily jealous."

"But you are... jealous?"

"A little bit. Yes. But not just of Cynthia. Of his friends, too. And how they make Tristan feel. They seem to have this... different connection with him that Tristan and I don't share. It's an easy chemistry."

"Oh, well, that's easily explained. It's how old friends are with each other. You know, reconnecting, reminiscing. It just happens that way. They're stuck in the past, though. *You* are his future."

It was a good reminder, but the doubts were too strong. "I'm not so sure that's true anymore. His friends, their presence here... well, it's shined this weird spotlight on my old insecurities, and I can't shake them. I can't stop comparing myself to Cynthia. She's carefree and young and has no real responsibilities outside of her new, fancy job. I'm practically her opposite in every way. I'm middle-aged, and I can't have children. Plus, I take care of my aging father and work six days a week at the bakery. Realistically, where can a future with Tristan fit into all that? I just think sometimes that we're kidding ourselves."

"Oh, my dear..."

"It's true. The odds seem stacked against us. What was I ever thinking—dating a man Tristan's age? And Mrs. Pickering's nephew, to boot! It's ridiculous, really. Was I flattered by his attention? Bored with my own life? Is that why I fell so easily, so fast? Maybe he was just some beautiful distraction."

"You know it's more than that. When you first told me about him, I could see it in your eyes. You were smitten. And from every indication, he's smitten, too. Remember how close London brought you together."

Julia nodded, looked down at her hands, and lowered her voice. "I know deep down that my feelings for him are real, but... is that enough? To sustain something lasting?" She made eye contact with Mildred again, almost hoping to convince herself of what she was about to say. "I just... need to start being logical. Rational. To use my head more than my heart. I didn't realize it until now, but this week has been a sort of wakeup call for me, I think. It has me asking the tough questions. And I can't ignore them anymore. On top of that, we still haven't had our talk, which could be the actual deal breaker."

Mildred pursed her lips and shook her head. "Well, I would love to tell you that love conquers all and that those childhood fairytales are true. But we both know that not every story has a happy ending. Ultimately, this is your choice, to move forward—to have faith in you and Tristan and explore what this can become. Or to put the brakes on and do some serious thinking. But my one piece of advice is this: Don't make the decision for him. That's not fair. At least give Tristan a chance to weigh in on things, hear your concerns, and to tell you his own. He deserves that."

"Yes. That's a good point. And I intend to do that—if I can ever reach him. He's pretty preoccupied these days."

Mildred chuckled then clasped Julia's hand and squeezed it. "I'm so glad we chatted. You needed to get some important things off your chest."

"I did. But I didn't even realize it. Thank you for being my sounding board. I get a little too much inside myself sometimes. I needed this."

Julia risked a little back pain to lean in for a gentle hug. Mildred patted her lightly. "Don't you worry. It will all work out the way it's supposed to."

Julia only hoped she was right.

Minutes later, at the edge of the cottage's pathway, they said their goodbyes, and Julia felt the buzzing of her mobile in her pocket. A text—finally—from Tristan.

dinner at pub w/ gang – you in?

It didn't even sound like him—clipped and hurried, almost obligatory. Maybe James or Gavin wrote it for him.

Earlier this afternoon, while eating her sandwich at the bakery, Julia had actually contemplated going to dinner with Tristan and the crew if he only would've asked. But he hadn't, until now, when the rest of her day had already been set in stone. She was merely an afterthought to him right now.

She texted back. *Too busy, sorry.*

Julia slipped the mobile back into her pocket, glad that she wouldn't have to be chained to her device the rest of the day, anxiously waiting to hear something from Tristan. She had work to do.

Chapter Twenty-three

"Baking can sometimes make the darkest of days a bit more bearable. Taking a treat to a grieving friend, bringing fresh-baked sandwiches to a sick relative, or offering a biscuit to a sad child can produce a tiny ray of sunshine on a bleak day."

JULIA ROLLED THE VAN TO a lazy stop behind the bakery and heard a faraway crack of thunder. She was lucky it hadn't rained a drop in Bath for the past couple of hours. Julia had been at the farmers market collecting some essentials for upcoming recipes. She found her mobile and decided to give Tristan another ring. He hadn't answered her first call this morning, so she'd left what she'd hoped was a cheery voicemail. But that was a few hours ago and, still, nothing from him.

The moment she poised her finger to click on his number, her mobile vibrated in her hand, startling her. An incoming call from Tristan. Frazzled, Julia tried to answer, to make the vibrating stop, but she accidentally tapped the wrong button, "Decline."

She grunted her frustration and started to ring him back, but he beat her to it. The mobile vibrated again, and this time, she slowed down and tapped the correct button.

"Hi." She heard another crack of thunder in the distance.

"Hey, you." His voice was upbeat and relaxed.

"I accidentally hung up on you," she confessed. "I was in the middle of trying to ring you."

"I got your voicemail from earlier. Sorry I've been MIA today. I saw my mates off this morning then went right to work. Mr. Elton had a long list for me. I'm afraid I've had some catching up to do after my active week..."

"So they've gone, then? Your mates?"

"Back to Cornwall. And to London." A pause. "How's your back doing?"

It was the first time he'd asked since he'd visited her at the cottage a couple of days before.

"Better. Nearly a hundred percent."

"That's good. Listen. I've... missed you. I haven't seen you for ages. Can you come to the farm?"

"That's why I was calling. I wanted to see you, too. But I didn't know what your schedule was."

"Great. I'll grab a quick shower now. Can you come within the hour? I'll be at the cottage. I can use my lunch break to see you. I've got some good news."

"Sure, I'll be there soon."

That would give her enough time to unload her produce from the market, speak with Miranda about tomorrow's lunch specials, and mull over how she would shape this all-important conversation. Tristan had no idea what was coming.

They said goodbye and clicked off, and Julia watched the heavens pour open, dousing her van with pounding rain. Thank goodness she'd checked the forecast earlier and had moved her father inside the bakery instead of letting him greet visitors outside. She would check on him, though, just to make sure he was safe and dry.

By the time Julia had driven to Elton's farm, the intense and driving rain of twenty minutes before had whimpered into a light pitter-patter on her windscreen. Misty vapors hovered on the warm ground as Julia drove through the mud-soaked roads to reach the farm. The gate was already opened for her, so she drove through and continued on her way toward the cottage, her wipers creating a soothing rhythm.

As she switched off the engine, Julia marveled at how calm she felt, almost completely detached. She had purposely stayed busy with work and the farmers market today, keeping Tristan's image at arm's length.

Maybe she was just trying to neutralize her emotions so she could face this conversation in the most rational way possible, clearheaded and matter-of-fact. That's how she hoped things would go, whatever the outcome.

Stepping up to Tristan's cottage, she raised her fist to knock on the door and heard Maggie barking on the other side. Seconds later, he opened the door with Maggie panting at his feet.

"You're a sight for sore eyes." He grasped both her hands and led her inside. He shut the door with his foot and pulled Julia in close, swept her away. "I've really missed you." He moved in for a kiss, and Julia couldn't resist. When she felt his warm lips on hers and the strength of his arms holding her, an electric current crackled between them. No matter her recent doubts or reservations—valid as they might be—their chemistry together was undeniable. And distance had only made it stronger.

Julia heard whining and whimpering then felt a pressure on her feet. She broke from the kiss and peered down to see Maggie trying to wedge between Julia and Tristan.

"Someone's jealous again," Julia noticed.

"She should be." Tristan ignored Maggie and reached to move a stray hair from Julia's cheek. "You're the only one in the room as far as I'm concerned..."

Julia's resistance melted once more as Tristan nuzzled her neck, his stubble grazing her skin. She clasped his broad shoulders as he wrapped his arms around her waist in a gentle hug.

"I've missed you, too," she whispered. And it was true. Even as she'd faced serious doubts about their relationship over the past few days, she'd also experienced the sting, deep inside, of not seeing his face every day, of not being this close to him. She belonged here, in his arms.

But—she hadn't come here for this, to renew their bond. She had come to question it, explore it, face it head-on so that they *could* hopefully move forward, stronger than ever.

Perhaps Tristan could sense the change in her body language, the sudden shift in her train of thought, because he backed away and looked into her eyes.

"What is it?"

Julia wished so badly she could continue with the delusion, pretend everything was okay, go on as they always had. On an impulse, she moved her hand up to the scar above Tristan's eye and traced it gently with her index finger, as though seeing it for the first time.

Lowering her hand, she told him, "Well. I've been doing some thinking the past few days..."

"Uh-oh." Tristan frowned, but his grasp on her waist remained secure. "Sounds serious."

"It... well, it might be."

"You know you can tell me anything."

Julia nodded.

"Let's go sit."

"Oh, wait—you said you had good news," Julia reminded him. "When you rang."

Tristan dipped his head and grinned. "I got it. The investor. Mr. Newbury has agreed to back my project. I found out this morning."

"You must be chuffed to bits! I'm so happy for you!"

"Now I can relax, focus on the program knowing that it's got a backer. No more struggling, no more wondering. It's really happening."

"And... it's validation." She almost added, "to someone like your father," but stopped short.

"Definitely." Tristan grasped her hand and led Julia around to the sofa with Maggie at their heels. As Julia sat beside him, she noticed a crushed can of ale peeking out from beneath the table—probable remnants of a party the night before with Tristan's mates.

"What's the trouble? Something's on your mind..."

She wriggled out of her raincoat, suddenly feeling flushed and nervous. *So much for detached and calm.* This felt nothing like she thought it would. Tristan helped her with a stubborn sleeve, and then she turned to face him.

"I need to talk about London, to start." Julia couldn't just blurt out all her reservations at once. She needed to give Tristan some sort of context or background explanation for this mess of doubts she'd been trying to sort through. "It was wonderful. Meeting your parents, visiting the memorial site for your brother. I've never felt closer to you."

Tristan put his hand on her knee. "Same here. We reached a new level or something."

"Yes. Which, honestly, was a bit scary for me. I haven't done this in a while… had a real relationship, cared about someone, let someone in this way. So, back to London—the next day was your aunt's committee meeting, and we were supposed to have a walk together, remember? But then…"

"My mates arrived."

"Right. And the evening shifted. And things started to change for me…"

"Why? Because of my mates? But you acted okay about them being here. You encouraged me to see them, spend time with them."

"That's true. And I meant it. I wanted you to have a good time. They're your friends, and you just lit up when you saw them. But—when we all had dinner together that first night at the pub, it made me realize some things. Seeing you with them, the rapport, the memories you shared. It just brought back some… old insecurities of mine."

"How do you mean? Are you talking about Cynthia? I know she's my ex, but you have *absolutely* nothing to worry about. I should've made this clear to you days ago, set your mind at ease. In fact, she and James are in a relationship! They told me after dinner—after you'd left the pub."

Julia raised her eyebrows. "That's a surprise." Julia recalled that pub dinner—James on her left side and Cynthia on Tristan's right with no indication that they were anything other than friends. "But this isn't about Cynthia. I'm not jealous of her, specifically. I guess I'm a little jealous of something else, though. Sitting there, with people in their twenties—it made me feel old. Well, old*er*. I had very little in common with your conversations. University was so long ago for me, but it was practically yesterday for you. And sitting at that table, it wasn't you and me with your friends. It was you and your friends, and then… me. Separate. Apart."

"I'm sorry we made you feel that way."

Julia put her hand on top of his and squeezed it. "No, no. You're missing the point. It wasn't anything you or they did. Nobody's in the wrong here. They were perfectly polite to me. It was just an observation that hit me. But then it had a chance to snowball in the past couple of days." She fought to find the perfect words to make him understand.

"We've never really discussed this, but you and I are eleven years apart, Tristan. I mean, we're not even in the same decade. And although I'd put the age issue behind me a while ago, it just came tumbling back, watching you with your friends."

"But it's never bothered me. The age thing."

Julia craned her neck a little, looked him deeper in the eyes. "Really? I mean, truly, you've never thought of it, never been concerned about it? Not even once? I'm *forty* years old. You're still in your twenties."

"Not for long," he countered then shrugged. "I'm just not spooked by the age difference. You're Julia to me. Not a number."

This wasn't going as Julia expected. The conversation was a jumble of points, all misunderstood. She needed to stop circling and move closer to the heart of the issue. It was time. "Okay, well, age isn't the primary issue anyway. It goes deeper than that." She cleared her throat and found her bearings. The clock on the mantle seemed to tick louder during her pause. Had she ever noticed it before? "So. On the walk that we didn't have after the committee meeting, I was planning to reveal something about myself that I'd been holding back from you. The timing never seemed right, and it's ... a serious subject that's not easy to talk about."

Now that she was about to say the words, her mind froze. But she'd come too far. She had to keep going. She remembered Mildred's advice: *He deserves to be told.*

"When I was married, I told you that we tried to start a family..."

"I remember." Tristan squeezed her hand.

"Well, I actually had a couple of miscarriages."

"Oh. Blimey."

"And there's something else..." She couldn't look him in the eye anymore. She needed to focus on their hands clasped together in order to nudge out the words. "The miscarriages were a symptom that something was wrong. With my body. After the marriage ended, I started having these horrific pains. Female issues. Suffice to say... I had to have surgery. This was five years ago. I had a hysterectomy." She managed to glance up, curious to see his expression. So far, it was unchanged. "Tristan, I had a *full* hysterectomy. I can't have any children. That possibility is completely gone."

She could see his lips part a little, his eyebrows raise slightly.

"I'm sorry you went through that," he finally said. "It must've been pretty devastating."

"I think, at the time, I was a bit relieved because the surgery took away my immediate symptoms, solved that particular problem. No more pain. And I wasn't married, wasn't focused on having a family, so it didn't seem like a great loss. In time, I learned to accept that children wouldn't be part of my life."

"But... there's adoption. Did you ever consider it? As an option?"

Julia gave a small shrug. "There wasn't really a need to. I mean, sure, it has crossed my mind once or twice over the years. But my focus has been the bakery and my father as he's gotten older. I never thought about adoption seriously. I just... had no real reason to."

Tristan looked away, likely trying to process everything.

Julia felt sudden tears at the corners of her eyes. The longer he stared off into the air, mulling things over, the more it confirmed her greatest fear—that if they stayed together, she would be keeping something from him, holding him back from what he wanted. *A child. A family of his own.*

"Hey." He returned his gaze to her. "What are the tears for?" He wiped one gently away from her cheek.

"Because it's just so clear to me now, sitting here, saying it out loud. I can't give you what you want—at least the option of children in your future, if things ever moved in that direction for us. You deserve that option. You would make an incredible father. And it's something I couldn't offer, realistically. But Cynthia can..."

Tristan frowned. "What does Cynthia have to do with this? I don't want her. I want you."

"I just mean, in theory. Someone *like* her—someone young and able, who could give you a future, a family. But I'm not able to. And I don't see how we can go on..."

Tristan stared, unblinking. "Julia. What are you saying?"

She shook her head, fighting tears. She hadn't planned this far ahead, hadn't considered the messy aftermath of her confession. "I'm not really sure what I'm saying. There's just this... fork in the road. We can't go back from it now. We can't pretend it's not there."

"What if I'm okay with it, though? What if I don't care about having kids?"

She studied his face. "I'm not sure that I'd believe you. What if you're saying it just to be kind? To make me feel better..."

"But what if I'm not? I might be perfectly okay with it. But would you be?"

"What do you mean?"

Tristan stood up and ran a hand through his still-damp hair. "You just keep mentioning all these insecurities—age differences, Cynthia, not having children—but what if they're only excuses? What if you're using them to run away from us? I mean, you've waited until now to even mention them..." The brimming anger in his tone punctuated each sentence.

Julia felt her own frustration rise. He wasn't listening to her. She decided to do it, to release her innermost thoughts, uncensored, unfiltered, unrehearsed. "I *tried* to tell you about the miscarriages, the hysterectomy. That's why I wanted to share a walk with you, the night after the meeting. I had every intention of telling you, but then your mates came to town, and the opportunity was gone. I'm sorry I didn't tell you sooner. I should have. But, Tristan, these aren't empty, made-up excuses. This is the harsh truth about my life. I'm forty years old. I have arthritis in some of my joints. I have a bad back that gives out sometimes and makes me feel a hundred years old. I have to wear glasses because my eyesight is fading. I barely know how to work an iPhone or search the Internet. Plus, I'm taking care of an elderly parent and running a bakery on my own. To top it all off, I can't have children. These are huge roadblocks that factor in to a relationship, to a future together. These are valid complications, not excuses."

"Fair enough. But who says they can't be overcome? You just..." He began to pace a little. Then he stopped and looked at her. "It sounds like you're giving up on us. Are you?"

Julia couldn't answer him. This conversation had gone completely off the rails. It wasn't supposed to happen this way.

Tristan continued, his voice a little softer. "I think, bottom line, you're just scared. I think your fear is making you look for things to break us up."

"That's ridiculous." Julia's heart raced faster in her chest. The sofa was suddenly confining, so she stood up with the coffee table between them. Maggie whimpered at Tristan's feet, clearly aware of a change in the atmosphere. "These are legitimate issues, Tristan. I'm trying to be logical here. I'm trying to do the right thing—sparing you from a future..."

"Without kids."

"Yes. Exactly. It's easy to say it now—that you're fine with not having kids. But years from now, you could easily change your mind. And then you'd resent me for it. You might even leave me..."

Tristan put his hands on his hips and searched the floor. Then he made eye contact. "Julia, we only have today. If my accident taught me anything, it taught me that. Why are you fast-forwarding our whole lives, presuming you know what will happen or how I'll feel years from now? You've practically mapped out the future for us..."

"I'm just trying to spare us both pain, that's all. I want to be rational. Mature."

Tristan huffed out a sigh. "Implying that I'm being *im*mature. Yeah, I get it. I'm apparently too young to understand what all this means. But that's rubbish. There's a bigger issue here. Despite the children issue, the age issue, the whatever issue. You don't have any faith in us. That we can last. And you probably never did."

The truth was out. He'd said it more bluntly than she'd been able to say it to herself. Her greatest fear.

Tristan moved his gaze to Julia and held it there. "And *that's* why you've kept us a secret all this time. Isn't it? This wasn't about keeping me all to yourself or having privacy away from the gossips in the village. You were afraid we would never last. So why bother telling people about us, eh?" His voice was thick with frustration. "Where's your faith in me? In us?"

Julia tucked her hair behind her ears. She didn't know what to say. "This isn't getting us anywhere," she mumbled under her breath. The clock ticked louder, filling the silence.

"I think it is." Tristan had softened his voice, but the strong intensity in his eyes remained. He wasn't backing down.

"This is all getting… too complicated," Julia said quietly, deliberately. "I need some time to think. To understand things."

"Are you breaking us up?"

She studied his face—that handsome face that had been branded in her mind since the first day they met, when she'd spilled the flour all over the floor. "Don't call it that. I just need time, that's all. And you need time, too. This will be good for us." The detachment had returned, uninvited. Julia's tone felt flat as she said the words. She had poured out every last ounce of herself to this conversation, and there was nothing else to give. She was empty.

"Time." Tristan rubbed his chin and nodded. "Sounds like a breakup to me."

"Just call it a pause, then."

"Same thing." His anger was palpable.

"I'm sorry," was all she could manage. She stared back at him, took in his perplexed expression, his rigid stance, the makings of the new beard forming along his jaw. She wanted to memorize everything about him, even his anger.

Robotically, she found her coat and moved toward the front door in a daze. As she opened it, she heard rain pounding on the ground and knew she'd have to make a quick dash to the van. She closed the door behind her and understood the terrific irony. She was, quite literally, running away.

But right now, she was incapable of doing anything else.

Chapter Twenty-four

"There can't be a party without a grand cake. If you're commissioned to bake it, take that responsibility seriously. Spend time on the details: the texture of the icing, the accuracy as you pipe the flowers on top. Besides flavor, presentation is everything. The cake should be the notable centerpiece of any celebration."

Julia unlocked the door of the bakery's kitchen then flicked on the light, as she had done nearly every morning for eleven years. But this time, she paused as she shut the door behind her. Something felt distinctly different.

She scanned the kitchen, roaming over the gleaming stainless-steel island, the large sinks, the ovens, the tall cooling racks, the refrigerator. Everything in its place. Even her stool was in its usual position in the corner. As Julia moved forward to set down her bag and coat, as she always did, she realized—nothing in the kitchen had shifted, but something inside of her had.

All these years, this four a.m. hour had been her solace, a refuge, something she craved and enjoyed. Most people would've hated it—walking through a pitch-dark morning to the bakery, unlocking the door to prepare for work while everyone else stayed fast asleep in their cozy beds.

"Isn't yours a lonely occupation?" Julia was occasionally asked.

But she'd never thought of her work as lonely. Solitary, perhaps. Grueling sometimes. But never lonely.

At least, not until this morning. The sky outside was inky black, and the quiet hush inside the bakery, normally peaceful, now seemed stifling and bleak.

She could easily trace this shift back to yesterday's events. When she had left Tristan's cottage, Julia decided to busy herself the rest of the day, blocking him out. And she'd been mostly successful. But this morning, when her alarm bleated and her eyelids flew open to stare into the darkness of her bedroom, she had remembered. Everything. The confusion in Tristan's eyes, the tangible frustration between them, the pinch in her chest as she drove away from his cottage in the rain, wondering if it would be for the last time.

And along with the memories came haunting questions. What had she done? Had she really let him go? She played over every detail of their conversation, trying to remember the exact words, attempting to pinpoint the pivotal moment when everything changed between them. Even now, as she moved toward the island to prepare for her day, no clear answers presented themselves. She was as lost and confused as the moment she'd slammed the door and left Tristan behind.

How do you go back to a "before" part of your life? How do you un-know someone?

She needed something to fill the silence, so she tapped her mobile to play the music Abbey had recently shown her how to access. Classical music felt appropriate, something soft and formal, so she propped her mobile on the island and selected a familiar piece by Bach. Shifting into baker mode, Julia recalled her first order of business this morning, planning out the shortbread biscuits for a children's party. The mother had ordered five dozen of them with pink and purple icing for this afternoon.

Yesterday at the farmers market, Julia had spotted a bag of cookie cutters hanging from the side of a baker's stall, an assortment of animal shapes perfect for a children's party. She opened the bag now, spilling the cutters onto the island, deciding which ones to use. Spreading them out, she saw an array of animal possibilities: elephant, giraffe, dog, cat, horse, rabbit. Julia stopped at the rabbit and picked it up, examining the long thin ears, the cotton-puff tail. It triggered a memory of another rabbit, long ago, one she'd had as a child.

Her father had brought it home one day, when Julia was nine years old. He held a cardboard box and set it on the floor of the cottage. Little Julia peered inside and gasped with joy, seeing the rabbit twitch its whiskered nose.

"Mr. Elton's grandson has been raising some rabbits in the barn," her father had explained. "They were abandoned by their mother. They're old enough now to be apart from each other, and Mr. Elton is giving them away. I thought you might want one as a pet."

With no fear of being bitten, Julia reached inside the box and lifted the creature out then cradled it inside her arms. The fur was the softest she'd ever felt in her life and was white as snow. She stroked the fur then nuzzled her nose into it.

"Thank you, Daddy!"

"What will you name it?"

After a beat, Julia said, "Hare."

"Hair?" Her father scrunched up his nose. "Like the hair on your head?"

Julia giggled, still stroking the bunny with her free hand. "No, like hare. A rabbit, a hare."

"Ah, very clever. Leave it to my Julia to name it something unusual, not Peter or Brer. Well then. Hare it is."

For the next whole year, Julia took great care of Hare, feeding him, playing with him, telling him her nine-year-old troubles, reading to him. He even slept in her bed most nights. Her father drew the line at having Hare eat with them at the kitchen table.

One pristine summer day, Julia had shared a picnic with Hare in the front garden. She'd set up a plate for him with baby carrots and lettuce. Later, the warm sun—and a tummy full of teacakes—had made her drowsy, so Julia lay down for a nap, watching Hare sniff the ground and move along the edges of the quilt.

When she awoke, he was gone. *Gone*. At first, Julia assumed he was nearby. She bolted up and called out his name, scouring the entire garden with her eyes. But there was no sign of him. Panic rose as she called his name louder, which brought her father rushing out of the cottage to see what the trouble was. They spent the next two hours searching for Hare. But he had hopped away forever, and Julia never found him.

For the next week, she'd been inconsolable, weeping every time she felt the pull of each daily habit, now pointless—preparing snacks for Hare or cleaning out the cardboard box in her bedroom or telling him goodnight. It took a full month before she finally stopped searching the countryside around the garden, hoping he would hop his way back home.

One night, after one of those fruitless searches, her father sat Julia down for a chat. His warm hands encircled hers as he looked at her with softness. "My darling. I know you miss Hare. I'm so sorry that he's gone from us. I know how you loved him, took care of him. But I think it's time to accept it. He won't be coming back. He's probably found a new family, maybe some other rabbit friends. I'm sure he's quite content and cared for."

"Do you really think so?"

"I very much do."

Julia imagined Hare with a group of other rabbits, hopping around the countryside together. Her smile dipped into a frown as she searched her father's face again. "But why did he leave? Was he unhappy here with us?"

"No, no. I think he got curious about the outside world. He felt like exploring. But he loved you. I saw it in those beady little eyes of his."

"I still miss him."

"But sometimes, those we love have to leave us. And sometimes, there's no clear answer why. We just have to accept it. But remember this. All that time you spent with him wasn't in vain. It was precious. And those moments you shared together will never be lost. They will stick right here." Her father tapped his index finger to the side of Julia's temple. "Here, inside your memory. Forever. A treasure chest to open up, anytime you want."

Julia hadn't thought about that conversation in years. But looking back on it as an adult, she knew her father wasn't talking about a rabbit gone missing. He had been talking about his wife, Rose. About living with the ache of losing someone precious—with no good explanation or reason—sooner than you're ready.

Those moments will never be lost.

Five hours later, after making the shortbread biscuits as well as her usual batch of scones, bread loaves, and teacakes for the morning, Julia was more than ready for a break. It was time to give her father breakfast. And she would force herself to take a long nap today, in order to have some stamina for this evening. The anniversary party was tomorrow, so the decorating committee would be at the bakery tonight to set up after closing. Julia would use that time to make the sheet cake. She was grateful for the flurry of activity that lay ahead.

A knock on the bakery's back door startled her out of her thoughts.

"Come in."

The door opened, and Hamish peeked his sandy-blond head through. "Mornin'!"

"Well, hi. It's been a while. How's that leg of yours?" Julia remembered it had been broken in three places in his fall from Mr. Elton's barn.

"Got the cast removed yesterday. I'm back on duty." This meant that he would take over Tristan's egg-delivery duties from now on. The timing seemed awfully suspicious.

"The usual place?" Hamish asked. "For the eggs?"

"Yes. I've cleared a shelf for them already." She grabbed her bag. "Can you lock the door when you leave?"

"No problem."

He held the door while Julia walked through into a bright, warm day. She hoped the weather would be this lovely for tomorrow's festivities—the parade, the party, the airplane circling with a banner. She wondered if Tristan would be there or whether he would be relinquishing that duty as well...

Julia placed her hand on the cottage's front doorknob and froze, tilting her head to listen. Finally, there it was, another deep, loud snore floating from her father's bedroom. The coast was clear. He had finally fallen asleep reading his chapter. She twisted the knob and quietly sneaked out of the cottage, hoping he wouldn't awaken and wonder where she was. She'd said goodnight to him an hour ago. But just in case he did wake up, she had left her father a note saying she'd forgotten something at the bakery and would be right back. Partly true. She *would* be at the bakery but not because she'd forgotten anything.

Rather than enter the bakery through her usual back door, Julia made her way to the street entrance, where a cluster of women had already gathered, chattering and waiting on her. A nearby streetlamp lit up the cobblestone road in golden tones and created shadows over the women's faces. But as Julia came closer, she recognized Mrs. Pickering, Mary, Holly, and Lizzie huddled at the door.

"You ladies look like you're up to something," Julia teased as she unlocked the door. "Sorry I'm late."

"This will be fun!" Mary proclaimed, holding her bulging paper bag filled with decorations. "Does your father suspect anything?"

"Thankfully, no," Julia said. "At least, not that I can tell. He thinks I'm fast asleep in my bed right now."

"We are *so* sneaky," Lizzie whispered. "I love a good surprise!"

Julia let them into the bakery, and they got right to work.

"I'll make us some coffee. And tea," Julia offered. "It's a chilly night!"

She already knew the ladies wouldn't allow her to help out with the decorating. Mrs. Pickering had given strict instructions that Julia wasn't to lift a finger in all of this, except to bake the anniversary cake she'd insisted on making. Julia decided to bake it tonight in order to focus completely on her father tomorrow.

Over the next two hours, another three women joined the busy group, and Julia served generous portions of tea, coffee, and biscuits to give the ladies sustenance and energy. She worked steadily on the cake in the kitchen, propping the door open with the stool so she could feel a part of the preparations and hear whether anyone needed anything from her.

Mrs. Pickering, of course, oversaw the activities, and Julia heard her barking orders at the ladies. "Move that up a little higher." "Straighten this out. It's crooked." "No, no. That won't do at all. Push it over to that side." "I don't like that color. Do you have something else to replace it?"

Julia pictured her in a police uniform, directing traffic.

By the time the cake was ready to be iced, the ladies had completed their duties and had asked for Julia's approval of their handiwork.

She stepped inside the bakery's main room and gasped. "Oh, look at this. It's marvelous."

A homemade *Happy Anniversary* banner hung from one end of the room to the other with balloons, streamers, and party hats placed strategically on all the tables. Seeing everything come together, Julia was glad she'd decided to close the bakery for the entire day tomorrow. She had let her employees know they would be compensated—and invited to the party. This event was too special, too important to crowd it out with work and customers. The focus should be on her father alone.

"Here's the gifts table." Mrs. Pickering used a broad gesture to show Julia. "And I thought we could put your cake here." She pointed to the table beside it, already decked out with napkins, plates, and silverware.

"It's brilliant." Julia beamed. "He will love this. All of it."

A knock at the door startled Grace—who'd made a full recovery from her illness—standing closest to the front door. "Who could that be at this hour?" she asked with wide eyes.

Julia suddenly remembered she was expecting a visitor. "Oh. I know who that is!" She moved to the door and opened it to see a blue rocking chair and then the carrier of the chair as he inched his way inside.

"Mac!" Grace exclaimed.

Julia stepped backward to give Mac enough space. He carried the chair delicately through, careful not to bump it on the doorframe.

"You picked the perfect color," Julia said.

"Where would you like it, lass?" he grunted.

"Here, in the corner." Julia had already made room for it after Mac texted her that he would bring the chair by this evening. "My father can sit in it tomorrow for the festivities. Best seat in the house."

The ladies oohed and ahhed over Mac's handiwork as he held his cap in his hand, clearly uncomfortable with the chorus of female praise. Julia noticed that a white ribbon had been carefully taped to the top of the chair. *The finishing touch.*

"So ten thirty tomorrow, then?" he asked Julia quietly. "For putting up the banner?"

"That would be perfect, yes. Thank you, Mac."

"Ladies." He nodded toward the group, replaced his cap, and slipped out the front door.

Julia began collecting empty teacups and mugs, and Holly offered to help.

"I'll take you up on that, thanks," Julia said. "I still need to decorate the cake and try to get some sleep."

The rest of the ladies said their goodbyes, leaving Julia and Holly in the kitchen to work. Julia appreciated the company. She didn't want to bookend her day with more time spent in an empty kitchen, alone with her thoughts.

"I think the party will be a smashing success." Holly reached for a dirty cup. "I'm so glad you have your father. I mean, you two have a real bond. It's so obvious. It's special."

Julia poised her icing bag over the cake. "I agree. And he'll love the party, I'm sure."

"I just... I know what it's like, taking care of someone," Holly mused as she created suds with her rag inside the cup. "Well, three other someones. And I've probably never told you this, but I... admire you. For how you take care of him, your father. It's not easy, giving up so much of your life to look after someone else."

Julia looked across at Holly, who kept busy at the sink, her focus turning to another dirty cup. She and Holly had never really talked, had never really *had* a chance to talk about family, about fathers, about much of anything besides books or wedding cakes.

"Thank you. I admire you, too," Julia replied. "I always have." And she meant it. She had watched Holly in the village over the years, taking excellent care of her three younger sisters after their mother died. Holly knew firsthand about sacrificing her life for someone else's. She had quit university to become a mother figure to her sisters at age twenty-one with no complaints or qualms—well, at least, none that she would let anyone know about.

Holly glanced over at Julia to exchange a smile then finished her task as Julia returned to her icing bag and added purple flowers to the cake.

"That's it, then," Holly said after a few moments, wiping her hands on a dishtowel.

"Thanks again for sticking around."

"Tomorrow's going to be wonderful. A day to remember." Holly waved good night, leaving Julia to put the final touches on the cake, flick off the lights, and grab her bag to head home.

Chapter Twenty-five

"Sometimes in baking, things don't go the way you've planned. But every now and then, things go perfectly. Every element comes together, precisely on time, precisely the right way, and magic happens."

"WHAT'S THE OCCASION?" ALTON STEADIED himself, sitting at the corner of his bed as Julia looped the new tie around his neck. She'd bought it for the anniversary party but, of course, couldn't say so.

"Do I need a reason to give my father a gift? I saw this in a shop window yesterday and thought of you. It's time you had a spiffy new tie for church. That's all."

"It's royal blue." Her father peered down as Julia finished straightening the tie. "My favorite color."

"Made just for you."

"Is this a new dress?" He touched the fabric of her sleeve.

She backed away and did a little turn. "As a matter of fact, it is." Julia had grown tired of cinching up her skirts. She'd met her weight goal last week and rewarded herself with another trip to Mrs. Bennett's shop, where she'd purchased three skirts, four pairs of jeans, and a couple of dresses for church. This one was sea-foam green, a color she normally steered clear of, but Mrs. Bennett convinced her it "suited her beautifully."

"Speaking of gifts," her father said, "would you hand over something to that fellow of yours, to Tristan? Tell him it's from me. It's on that bookshelf—the large hardback sticking out."

Julia walked over to retrieve it. "This one?"

"That's it. About submarines in World War II. I thought he might enjoy the history of our Royal Navy. We were talking about it a couple of weeks ago." He frowned. "Where *is* that young man these days? I haven't seen him around lately."

Julia held the book at her side. "Well, he had some university mates come 'round last week. And since they left, he's been… busy. With work, you know. Catching up."

"I miss our chats. Tell him he must come by and see me. Soon."

Julia could only nod, believing that an "okay" would be too much of a verbal lie. She hadn't planned to say anything to her father about her pause with Tristan, most especially not today.

"We're going to be late for church if we don't leave," she prompted.

"Yes. Mustn't make the Lord wait on us…"

It had all come down to this—the months of planning and meetings, the top secret emails and texts between committee members, the baking of goodies, the decorating, the hanging of the anniversary banner, even the ten-minute diversion by the vicar after church—all of it for this one moment, when Alton Bentley would shuffle into the bakery to be met with hearty cheers from all his good mates from the last four decades.

Julia had been instructed to lead her father through the back entrance for the best possible impact—and to avoid his seeing the anniversary banner hanging out front. The white lie she'd made up was that she needed his opinion on a new recipe she had baked before church.

"Surprise!"

Everyone shouted it in unison the very moment Alton swung open the door to the main room. Holly, in charge of taking photos, stood up front and snapped Alton's picture at the perfect moment, capturing it forever.

Julia steadied the door with her foot and held her father's elbow as he took a step backward in surprise, open-mouthed, facing a sea of people with smiles and cheers.

Julia looked at him and whispered, "Are you all right, Dad?" She had earlier asked that people cheer softly so as not to give him too much of a fright.

After a beat, her father's gasp morphed into the broadest smile she'd ever seen. He nodded. "I'm positively gobsmacked. What's all this?"

Mrs. Pickering stepped forward as the cheers died down. "Mr. Alton Bentley. We are here, united, in celebration of this, the fortieth anniversary of Rose's Bakery."

Someone broke out into a rousing chorus of "For He's a Jolly Good Fellow," and every voice joined in. As Alton scanned the packed room and heard his friends and patrons singing to him, Julia noticed a glistening of tears in his eyes and had to fight off her own. This *was* the moment they had all hoped for.

He applauded as the song ended then turned, shifty-eyed, to his daughter. "Julia Rose. Were you in on all this?"

"I certainly was." She grinned. "It's been months in the making. You're not an easy person to keep a secret from, you know."

He patted her hand then spoke to the crowd in the loudest volume his gravelly voice could manage. "Well, now. One man doesn't possibly deserve all this..." He waved one hand in a sweeping gesture. "Thank you, my friends. Thank you all."

Julia scanned the room and saw nearly everyone she knew. Even some faces she hadn't seen in weeks or months had come out to celebrate. At least fifty people in total, she assessed. Perhaps more. And one of them, the most familiar of all, stood a head above the others in the background. Tristan. They made strong eye contact for a beat, then she glanced away, not knowing what else to do. He had come after all.

"Well, we have a whole party planned. Follow me, please." Mrs. Pickering directed Alton Bentley through the crowd, which parted like the Red Sea as they made their way to the far corner. Along the way, with Julia right behind, Mrs. Pickering pointed out the obvious details to him. She spoke slowly and loudly, as though she were instructing a five-year-old child. "Here's the gifts table for you, with cards and presents. And here's your cake, which your daughter baked lovingly last night. And later, there will be a parade in your honor, and after that, something *extra* special..."

"What's this?" Alton paused as he approached the new chair.

"A present from Mac." Julia looked around for him. Mac stood nearby, cap in hand. "He made you a new chair, crafted it by hand. Look, Dad! It rocks!"

"Is that one of those youthful expressions of yours?" her father said with a grimace.

"No, no. Literally. It rocks. It's a rocking chair, just like you wanted." Julia briefly left his side to demonstrate, tipping the chair gently with her hand.

"Well, would you look at that. Help me into it."

The guests milled around, some watching Alton settle into his new chair, others starting to gather at the refreshments table as Mrs. Pickering directed traffic. Joe poured champagne while Lizzie helped cut the cake. Holly stayed at a respectful distance, documenting all the important moments with her digital camera.

Alton Bentley rocked gently in his new chair and closed his eyes. "Heaven. It's so smooth." He opened his eyes. "Where's my friend? Where's Mac?"

On cue, Mac appeared, and they shook hands.

"My old mate," said her father, the wrinkles bunching around his eyes as he smiled his widest smile. "Thank you. I'll treasure this."

"Happy anniversary." Mac gave another nod then backed away again.

"Why don't we go ahead and have him start unwrapping gifts?" Mrs. Pickering peered at her watch. "There are quite a few to get through. There'll be just enough time, I think..."

The guests gathered in various clusters, as partygoers eventually do, chattering away with each other, the volume waxing and waning as people told stories, laughed, and caught up with each other's lives. Julia had lost sight of Tristan and wondered if he'd left the party.

Some guests had wandered closer to observe Alton in his brand-new chair as he opened his gifts. Before he began, he patted his chest, looking for something. "There they are," he said to himself, reaching for his reading glasses. "I want to be able to see what it is I'm opening."

Julia stood by his side, and Brandy handed her a couple of rubbish bags for the discarded wrapping paper. As Julia jotted down the gifts, she pictured herself over the next couple of days, writing dozens and dozens of thank-you notes.

The gifts were thoughtful—a fancy pen, a desk clock, a small

Wedgwood plate—and some, from his poker mates, were gag gifts. Julia was saving her own gift to him for the end. Noelle's painting of the bakery sat patiently, wrapped in gold paper, behind her father's new chair.

After half an hour, Julia offered her father a small break from the festivities, in the form of a piece of cake, but he opted for a cup of tea instead. "I'll have a piece a little later. I have no doubt it's delicious," he told her with great confidence.

Next, Mrs. Pickering handed Alton a flat, large square wrapped in blue tissue paper. He read the attached card, "From… Tristan Hannigan." He raised his eyes to scour the crowd. "Where *is* that boy? Come out from the shadows."

Julia finally spotted Tristan, threading his way through a few people to get to the front. When he came to a halt in front of her father's chair, steps away from Julia, he slipped both hands inside his jeans pockets and steadied his gaze on her father. Julia was apparently invisible. Close up, she saw dark circles under Tristan's eyes as well as his days-old beard.

"Happy anniversary, Mr. Bentley," he said.

They shook hands. "Thank you, son." Alton returned to the package. "Help me unwrap this, will you?"

"Certainly."

He and Tristan worked together to remove the tissue paper and reveal the gift—a hardwood picture frame. Alton tilted it toward him and peered through his glasses. "Would you look at this…"

Julia gazed over her father's shoulder and saw a collage of photos. Special photos, private family photos. She recognized all of them. In the center was a faded photo of her pregnant mother, holding her belly with one hand and wrapping her arm around Alton's with the other. They stood proudly beneath the "Rose's Bakery" awning out front. Other photos circled around it—little Julia baking in the kitchen with her father, an employee from years past standing at the till, her father perched in his original blue chair while chatting with a stranger, and one more of little-girl Julia, sitting on her father's knee.

"How did you…? Where did you…?" Julia started.

A light dawned for Alton, who said to Tristan, "*That*'s why you asked to take the box of photos with you." He craned his neck upward to see Julia as he explained. "The ones you found in that upper flat. Tristan had asked to borrow them, weeks ago. He instructed me not to tell you. Very mysterious."

"Guilty as charged," Tristan said. "I wanted to keep my project a secret. I still have the original photos. I've placed them in an envelope behind the counter for you. Those are the copies."

"Well. This is a treasure," Alton said. "Isn't it, Julia? Very thoughtful." His attention moved back to the frame he held, as he browsed each picture.

"Yes. Very thoughtful," Julia whispered, looking up at Tristan. But he still wouldn't make eye contact with her. His eyes remained on the frame.

"Tristan, that's *such* a lovely present," his aunt gushed loudly for all to hear. Suddenly, she gasped. "It's almost time for the next portion of our celebration." She tapped her watch and found the next gift on the table. "We'd better speed this along..."

Julia took the frame gingerly from her father and saw Tristan slipping away into the crowd and toward the front door to leave.

Two gifts later, it was Julia's turn. She placed the gold-wrapped present on her father's lap. "Here. From me. Happy anniversary, Dad."

"We're sharing this day, you know? This is for you, too."

Julia watched him unwrap the gift.

"Such fine, heavy paper," he commented. Julia saw Mrs. Pickering tapping her foot, eager to move things along. But this couldn't be rushed, not even for a scheduled parade.

"I know what *this* is." He removed the final bit of wrapping paper. Julia helped him hold the painting steady so he could see it properly. "This hangs in the gallery, doesn't it? It's a painting of our bakery."

"It can hang here now, Dad. At the bakery. I bought it. It's yours." She caught Noelle's eye in the crowd and smiled.

"It's perfect. It's beautiful." He held the frame steady with one hand and turned to find Julia's free hand. He raised it to his mouth and kissed it. "Thank you, love. For everything. All of this."

She bent to kiss his cheek.

"Let's see it!" someone in the crowd called out. Julia removed the painting from her father's grasp and lifted it high.

When the applause faded, Mrs. Pickering took the opportunity to announce that the parade was about to begin. Mac and Fletcher stepped in to help Alton move outside, taking the brand-new chair with them. He would have the place of honor.

Julia lagged behind, picking up the remaining bits of discarded rubbish, stacking the gifts out of the way, then looking around for her next task. Busy work. She wasn't terribly interested in the parade and would probably view most of it through the window.

"Are you coming?" someone asked.

Julia looked up and saw Mildred pointing toward the front door.

"I'll be there in a minute. Just straightening up."

Mildred came closer. "The party has been a raging success, I think. But you seem a bit… melancholy. Are you all right?"

Mildred could always read her. Julia heard the brassy sounds of a children's marching band through the nearby window.

Before Julia could answer her question, Mildred crossed her arms. "You had the talk. Didn't you? With Tristan."

Julia nodded.

"It didn't go well?"

Julia shook her head. She didn't want to talk about it. Not here, not now. *Maybe not ever.* Mildred seemed to hear her actual thoughts and produced a sympathetic smile, understanding without a word. She placed a hand on Julia's elbow. "This is your day. Your day and your father's day. Nothing else matters. Join us outside when you want. Take your time. I'll cover for you if Mrs. Pickering asks your whereabouts."

"Thank you."

Julia, left alone in the bakery, continued to pick up plates and wadded napkins. She combed the cake crumbs from the dessert table, stacked up clean silverware, then paused to look around. Forty years. A staple of the community, a centerpiece, a gathering place, this bakery. How many important conversations had taken place between these walls—politics or family troubles or life-changing decisions? How many long-term friendships, or even romances, had formed or even ended here? How much laughter or how many tears had been exchanged through the years? It wasn't just about sugar and butter and flour. This place was about people. It always had been. Julia wondered if her mother knew, even before the doors had officially reopened, what the bakery would represent. How vital it would be to the village.

Julia heard exclamations through the window. She abandoned her tasks and walked outside just in time to see the small plane buzzing overhead, pulling behind a long sign that read, "Happy Fortieth Anniversary. And Happy Forty More." Just as Mrs. Pickering had dictated all those weeks ago.

The celebration thinned out significantly after that, with only Alton and Julia's core friends and committee members joining them inside. Mac brought Alton's new chair indoors, where he sat and rocked, telling stories of the old days of the bakery. Some stories Julia had heard a million times, and some she'd never heard. As she continued the cleanup process, Julia listened with amusement, knowing *this* was her father's actual favorite part of the whole day—not the refreshments, the presents, or the parade. Her father had a captive audience while telling stories. He was in his element.

An hour later, the crowd had thinned again, and only a handful remained, mostly Alton's poker mates, along with their spouses. Julia offered to make the group sandwiches, and they took her up on it. The atmosphere had shifted since Mrs. Pickering *finally* left a few minutes ago. No more orders, no more planning or schedules or routines. Just old friends, reminiscing.

"Oh, I brought something for you," Julia told her father before heading back to the kitchen. She retrieved a small case from behind his chair. "I thought you might want to play something for your friends."

Her father gave a shy grin. "Oh, honey, I don't know. I haven't played in public in years."

"But this isn't public. These are your good friends on a special day."

"Aye," Mac prodded. "Let's hear a tune, then."

Alton shrugged and opened the case on his lap. He put together the various parts of his clarinet with nimble fingers. *How many times had he assembled his instrument over the years? One thousand? Two?* He could probably do it in his sleep, even with arthritic hands.

She left him to his clarinet and heard the first few notes of a warm-up scale float past her as she headed for the kitchen to assemble turkey sandwiches and crisps. She hummed along as her father launched into "April in Paris."

Only one thing was absent from this serene scene. Tristan belonged here, as part of the relaxed festivities, the inner circle, listening to her father's clarinet. He might have even grabbed Julia's hand halfway through the song to lead her inside the kitchen for a private dance, just the two of them…

But a scene like that was set in another time, a different world, an age ago. Julia reached for the fresh head of lettuce and began to peel back the crisp layers beaded with moisture, letting her mind wonder what Tristan was doing right now.

Chapter Twenty-six

"Timing is everything in baking. A minute too long or too short can ruin an entire recipe. And then you have to chuck it out and start all over again."

JULIA SHOOK OUT THE CRAMP in her hand and glanced over at the tall stack of thank-you cards she'd managed to write during the past hour with another tall stack still to go. She had chosen several pat phrases to write on each card, depending on the person and situation: "Your kindness is appreciated." "Thank you for the lovely ___." "We're so glad you were there to celebrate with us."

She had saved a separate batch of cards to write to each committee member as well. It was the least she could do for all the time they'd spent to make yesterday's party such a success.

Julia set down her pen and glasses, reached for her tea, and took a long, leisurely sip as she gazed out the kitchen window. She watched a bird tap against it, trying to enter. Realizing it couldn't get inside, it flew away. Spending an empty, serene afternoon relaxing on her afternoon off between book club and poker night would usually serve as the perfect balm for Julia's busy, difficult week. But something had been agitating her all morning, nagging at her. Something stirred inside, and she couldn't identify it specifically. Anxiety? Sadness? Anger? Frustration?

Julia had managed to push aside thoughts of Tristan—mostly successfully—in the days before the party, citing her father as her only priority. But today, the party was behind her, and her day was mostly empty. It was time to deal with the Tristan fallout. But she didn't even know where to begin.

"What's all this?" Her father's gentle voice broke her thoughts and brought her back to her original task. He stood before her in his striped flannel pajamas and yawned after his long afternoon nap.

"Oh, just writing out a few thank-you notes." She set down her cup and picked up her pen, moving on to the next card.

Her father gripped the chair across the table to steady himself. "A few? That looks like a mountain. I should be helping you."

"I don't mind. You can sign them, though, if you feel up to it. But there's no rush. Maybe do a few at a time over the next couple of days."

Her father cleared his throat. "I've had an idea. I think you deserve a genuine day off. I'm postponing poker night until tomorrow evening so you can rest tonight, have the whole night to yourself!"

"Dad, you don't have to do that..."

"Nonsense. It's already done. After the party last night, I asked Mary Cartwright to spread the word to the men about the change to Tuesday."

"You're sneaky! Well, that was sweet of you. I admit, a real evening off would be a treat after a busy weekend."

"It's settled then." Her father tilted his head. "Is everything all right? You don't seem yourself today."

A perfect opening for her to spill the news about Tristan. But she still couldn't bring herself to burden her father with it. Not yet. So she shrugged. "Just a bit knackered, I think. From the party."

Her father smiled. "It was a perfect day. Wasn't it?"

"It was."

Looking back, she wouldn't have changed a single detail. The party had been everything she'd hoped for. At least something in her life had actually gone the way it was planned.

"What's the matter?" Abbey stood at the swinging door of the bakery's kitchen, empty basket in hand.

Julia glanced up, realizing how she probably looked—scowling, staring at her mobile through her glasses, hand on her hip, endlessly frustrated with technology.

"Oh. Hi." She softened her expression. "Well, maybe you can help me with something."

Abbey set her basket down on the empty stool and came to stand beside Julia.

"Holly just emailed me all these photos," Julia explained, "from Sunday's party. And I don't know how to do anything with them. I want to save them somewhere, maybe even print them off later to show my father. But I can't get them past the email. I'm stuck."

Abbey nodded confidently and took the mobile from Julia. "Oh, that's easy! Here. Just hold your finger down until it gives the option." Abbey demonstrated as Julia leaned in to watch over her shoulder. "Now. Select Save. You've just saved that picture to your main photo album, so you can access it anytime."

Julia adjusted her glasses and frowned again. "Album. Hmm. Where's that?"

"Here. This is your album." She tapped a few more times—too fast for Julia to follow. "You already have a few pictures stored. See?" Abbey scrolled backward to demonstrate. "Aww. What's this one?"

She clicked a photo and it expanded to full-size, crisp and clear—the selfie that Tristan had taken of Julia and himself during their Chatsworth garden picnic. Their first official date. Tristan looked so happy in the photo. So did she.

Julia hadn't noticed that Abbey was staring at her, gauging her reaction. "You really fancy him, don't you? Tristan."

"Yes, actually. I do. He's a good man."

"I hear they're hard to find..."

Grinning, Julia bumped Abbey's arm with her elbow. "You're a wise young lady, you know that?"

"Mildred says that to me all the time."

"Well. She's spot on."

Abbey finished placing the rest of Holly's party photos into the album as Julia returned to her last batch of scones for the day's final shift.

When Abbey left a few minutes later with her wages from the sandwich deliveries, Julia glanced at her mobile again and noticed that Abbey had somehow posted Tristan's selfie as the main wallpaper background. "Sneaky little bugger," Julia muttered, knowing she'd never be able to figure out how to change it without Abbey's help. And knowing that Abbey probably realized that when she set it up...

Tristan stared back at her, his eyes squinting in the sunlight. His head was tilted toward Julia's. She remembered how close he had scooted toward her to get that shot, their shoulders and hips and legs touching. And how, minutes later, they shared a lingering kiss at the end of the road before walking away to their separate jobs, to return to real life. She could still feel his lips on hers if she tried.

Julia clicked off her mobile. This was what a break was supposed to be like, she reminded herself. What else had she expected?

The oven timer dinged, so Julia tugged the mitt onto her hand and retrieved the scones. Her next mission was to clean up her station and check on Brandy, make sure she had everything she needed for the next couple of hours. But all Julia wanted to do was leave. Maybe it was opening the oven to a wall of oppressive heat—as she'd done dozens of times in any given day—but her body was suddenly on fire. Was she getting sick? She placed her hand on her forehead, but her temperature felt normal.

Abandoning the messy island, she peeked her head through the swinging door and caught Brandy's gaze. "I'm going out. Be back in a bit."

"Right, boss." Brandy returned to the customer she was helping.

Julia abandoned her mobile on the island but grabbed her keys and bag and headed out the back door. She needed to get away, to drive, to go somewhere, anywhere.

Julia jogged uphill to collect her van from the cottage, got in, and started the engine. The late-June day was pristine and sunny with enormous, puffy clouds floating above. Windows down, she drove along the back street of Storey Road toward the countryside. She let the van take her wherever it wished, bumping down the dirt road. She wanted to be alone. To think. *Or maybe not to think at all.*

By the time she reached Chatsworth Manor, her breathing had slowed back to normal, and she felt refreshed. Perhaps she'd experienced some sort of panic attack. She'd read about them, heard about them, but never experienced one before.

She parked at the very edge of the lot, on the outskirts of the manor. From that spot, she could see the approximate place where she and Tristan had picnicked all those weeks ago. Eating, laughing, talking, building something between them. No matter all her doubts or reservations—they *had* built something real.

However, nothing had changed since their talk. The issues couldn't be resolved. They simply weren't fixable. The break was indeed for the best. And someday, Tristan might even thank her for letting him go.

In the greater scheme of things, she wondered why she had met Tristan at *this* time in their lives. Why not years later, when the age gap, or even the children issue, might not have been an issue at all? For a fleeting, bitter moment, she almost wished they'd never even met that day in the bakery. What if Hamish hadn't been a fool, hadn't broken his leg in the first place, leaving Tristan to make the deliveries? Or what if Tristan had met Brandy first, fallen head-over-heels for her before Julia even had a chance to lay eyes on him?

"Timing is everything," her father always told her when he was teaching her how to bake. "A minute too long or too short can ruin an entire recipe. And then you have to chuck it out and start all over again."

Julia puffed out a sigh, drumming the steering wheel with her fingertips. This wasn't helping, sitting here, wondering about things she couldn't control or change. It was all completely pointless. Her frustration began to transform into something else—a sort of urgency that originated at the center of Julia's chest and branched out to the rest of her. She experienced a sudden, overwhelming desire to put it all on the line, to seek Tristan out and fix things, to try to reverse the damage and tell him her deepest thoughts. *I miss the subtle cleft in your chin, your deep laugh, your wavy hair. I miss you. I think I even love you. You've left this gaping hole inside me, and I don't know how to fill it. Maybe I was wrong, stepping away from us. Maybe you were right—it was my fear talking. Maybe we can work things through. This break was a mistake. It's only reminded me of how my life felt before you walked into it. Incomplete and hollow. Please say we can try again. Please, please...*

Julia shifted the van's gear with resolute purpose. She drove along the tree-lined drive of the manor and took the turn heading toward Mr. Elton's farm. But with every passing mile floated a new doubt. Although he made a brief appearance at the party, Tristan hadn't tried to contact her since their talk, not once. What if he had seen sense? What if, during these days without Julia, his *own* doubts and insecurities had surfaced? This break had made her want him more, but what if the break had made him want her less? That was why he hadn't fought for her, hadn't contacted her. That was why he'd left the party so early. Maybe he had come to his own conclusion that they didn't belong together. Was it all just a mirage?

By the time she'd arrived at the gate at Mr. Elton's farm, Julia was deflated. If Tristan had missed her the way she was missing him, he would've reached out to her by now. He wouldn't have let pride get the better of him the way Julia had done. He was probably still angry with her. Or worse. Perhaps she had done such a fine job during their talk of convincing him that they were wrong for each other that he had actually started to believe her.

Julia squinted through the windscreen, looking far past the rolling pastures and meadows of the farm, to see the tiny outline of Tristan's cottage in the distance. His car wasn't where it normally was, parked against the side. Even if she'd wanted desperately to speak with him, even if she still had the will to do it, he wasn't even there. She didn't know where to find him. And maybe it was best not to try. Maybe this was all for the best.

Drained and defeated, Julia jerked the steering wheel around for an awkward U-turn on the narrow dirt road and headed to the bakery. Back where she belonged.

Julia leaned against the counter and moved her pen around the notepad, drawing scribbles and circles and figure eights where she *should* have been writing out tomorrow's specials.

After closing, the bakery had been quiet tonight, except for soft Nat King Cole music in the background and the shuffle of cards in the men's hands. The sudden eruption of cheers and jeers, another game won, broke Julia from her doodling. She looked up and saw Adam with his victor's fist in the air as the other men grumbled and grunted.

"Nice one, Adam."

"Good on ya."

Tristan had been a no-show at poker night. Though it was possible he had been out of reach when Mary had called him about the change to Tuesday night, Julia knew he wouldn't have come anyway. Why would he? So Julia had decided to press on with things, dispensing snacks and drinks to the men as though this were any other poker night.

"Julia, would you like to join our final hand?" her father called from the table.

She straightened up and found her smile. "No thanks. I'm really busy with work, here, Dad." She pointed to the pad with her pen and shrugged.

"Okay, men. Who's going to win the big prize?" Her father asked as he gathered the stray cards together in a sweeping motion.

Silence again after the shuffle as the men received their cards and mulled them over, which to keep and which to play.

Julia abandoned the notepad and tapped on her mobile, purposely ignoring the Tristan selfie and making a mental note to figure out on her own later how to remove it as her wallpaper. She brought her mobile closer and clicked on Holly's newest email, containing more party pictures. At the bottom of the bunch was one of Tristan shaking hands with her father, who had just opened his lovely gift. Julia tried to click the photo to make it bigger. But something happened, and the photo disappeared. Holly's entire email, in fact, had disappeared. Julia let out a little gasp.

"Something wrong?"

She looked up and found her father staring at her. She whispered, "Oh. No. Nothing. Sorry for the interruption."

Her father nodded and focused again on his cards. Julia clicked her mobile off with a firm press of her thumb then turned the device on its face before flipping to a fresh blank page in her notepad.

Chapter Twenty-seven

"In the end, baking is a way of life, but it isn't life. Other elements—friendships, family, health, faith, education—these are the things that make life worth living. Always keep your priorities in the right order."

Julia spritzed a generous layer of disinfectant on the kitchen's island and wiped it clean a second time, for good measure. The lemony scent made her sneeze. This was her final task of the day before heading home to serve her father dinner. She mused over the meal as she cleaned. Perhaps a takeaway from the pub might be a nice change of pace for him, a shepherd's pie or maybe fish and chips...

The workday had been unusually long and grueling. Three days after the anniversary party, there seemed to be more customers than ever. In fact, people had to stand and wait for tables at one point during the afternoon, and Miranda stayed for a second shift to help Julia with the baking. Miranda had assured Julia that after the additional tutorials they'd recently had, she felt confident enough to bake a few items on her own, which helped greatly during the unexpected crunch. Julia suspected that the party had been the primary reason for the surge in customers, piquing the interest for many villagers who hadn't visited in a while. As well, some of the traffic could've been attributed to Tristan's website and the bakery's new online presence. Even the hampers had been a recent success, and Julia had ordered another dozen of them just yesterday. She might have to consider hiring extra help for all this new business...

Julia's back ached, and she reached around to rub it. In the corner,

Enzo washed dishes and mouthed the lyrics to something blasting from his ear buds.

When Julia pivoted to put away the disinfectant, an odd crackling sound caught her attention. She paused to listen. *There it is again. Strange.* She stared hard at the ovens, where the sound had originated. Maybe she'd forgotten to switch one of them off, and the heat inside was creating the crackle.

Julia set down the bottle and moved toward the oven to check it. But a louder *pop* startled her, and she halted midstep, heart thumping faster. That noise wasn't from the oven, which she could see *was* switched off. This new sound seemed to come from somewhere higher, inside the wall. Julia's eyes widened as she tried to figure out what was going on...

"Enzo!" she called, but he continued to move his hips to the music, oblivious.

A hissing noise emerged from the wall, followed by another, louder *POP!* A small flame sparked above the oven, growing in size with each passing second.

"Enzo!!" Julia's voice cracked under its own volume. She kept her eye on the flame, still growing, now making its way up the wall and branching out in all directions. She backed away, half paralyzed with fear, but forcing her feet to move.

Enzo finally swiveled around, reaching for his ear buds. His mouth shot open when he saw the fire devouring the wall. "Fire!"

"Get the extinguisher!" Julia ordered, pointing at the swinging door. "Under the counter. Go!"

Some oddly calm part of Julia's brain kicked in, pushed her ahead, reminded her of the other extinguisher, located under a cabinet nearby, collecting dust. As she crouched to open the cabinet, she heard more fizzing and hissing and crackling from the wall. The flame had grown wider and bolder, leaving a charred-black trail behind it then continuing its scattered path, up toward the ceiling.

Julia found the extinguisher and grunted, fumbling with the canister and begging her mind to remember how to use it. She had read the instructions and watched an Internet video on how to use an extinguisher a while back but had never actually used one. Not until now. Panic threatened to overtake her as the flames continued to grow, as she pictured the entire bakery burning to the ground. These next seconds were critical.

"P.A.S.S." somehow came to mind—Pull, Aim, Squeeze, and Sweep. She said these words over and over out loud as she struggled to hold the extinguisher upright.

By now, Enzo had returned, holding his own extinguisher. When he saw the fire, he resembled a bewildered little boy with wide eyes. Julia noticed thick, gray smoke was beginning to plume at the ceiling. They were running out of time. She knew they might have to evacuate, but Julia *had* to try this first. She had one shot at it, and she would take it.

"Watch me!"

Breathless, she yanked the pin out of the cylinder with all her strength then grabbed the nozzle. She guided it closer toward the fire, gulping in fear at the angry, licking flames traveling faster. The powerful heat on her cheeks was stronger than any she'd ever felt.

She pressed the lever tightly to release the firefighting chemicals. A wide spray of yellowish powder spewed powerfully from the nozzle with a loud shushing sound. At first, Julia's aim was poor, but she quickly corrected herself, dousing some of the flames.

Enzo joined her and took over the tallest parts of the fire while she focused on the bottom section. Together, they spewed the lifesaving powder onto the fire, covering it, fighting it, killing it. Julia breathed in heavy pants and gulps as she continued to aim, knowing that she and Enzo alone were responsible for saving the bakery.

Finally, miraculously, the fire sputtered into oblivion, until all Julia could see was a thick layer of gold, all over the wall, all over the ovens. The fire had been contained.

It had happened in about four minutes' time, but for Julia, it had seemed like four hours. Gasping, heart pumping, weak at the knees, she dropped the empty extinguisher to the floor with a *plonk* and stepped away, leaning her full weight against the island. She felt light-headed and wondered if she might pass out. The strong scent of pungent smoke permeated her senses, nauseating her.

She coughed deeply to try and eradicate the toxic chemicals and smoke from her lungs. Enzo was coughing, too. He had the good judgment to rush to the back door and open it wide, welcoming in the fresh evening air. Julia heard crickets chirping outside. Such a strange, serene contrast from what was going on inside the kitchen.

Julia felt a hand at her elbow. "Are you all right?" Enzo asked, still breathless.

She nodded, and a little of her strength returned as she fully realized the end result of their efforts. They were safe. And so was the bakery.

"Yes. How about you?"

"Okay." He sputtered and coughed again.

Julia cleared her head to figure out what to do next. "We should shut down the electrical box. Just in case."

She pushed herself up from the island and started to weave. She managed to glance back at the wall and cringed at the sight—black streaks and thick powder that looked like pollen covered most of the back wall, with smoke still lingering thick in the air. Her kitchen. Her sanctuary. She wanted to cry. *How had this happened?*

"Go get some fresh air," she instructed Enzo. "But leave the door open. Keep an eye on that wall. Make sure the fire doesn't return."

Julia went off to find the hardly ever visited metal box in the storage room, opened it, then flipped off the main breaker with a loud *thunk.* Instant darkness. She hadn't thought to bring along a torch to light her path. She felt her way along the walls, back to the kitchen, thankful for the faint light of dusk coming through the open door.

What next? She'd never been through anything like this before. The only person she could think of to call was Mac MacDonald. He would know what to do.

She couldn't remember where she'd set her mobile. Her thoughts were fuzzy and far away, as if she moved inside some awful dream in slow motion. Enzo stood in the doorframe, leaning forward to catch his breath. They were both still coughing but lighter now.

She found her mobile on the stool and joined Enzo outdoors, switching places with him at the doorframe to keep a careful eye on that back wall. She wouldn't feel safe until someone inspected it.

Mac answered his phone, and Julia poured out the details in jumbled spurts. All Mac said in response was, "On my way. I'll call the fire brigade."

Of course. She hadn't thought to call the firefighters first, perhaps because the fire had already been extinguished and the imminent danger seemed over.

"Enzo, you should see the doctor. I'll call Andrews..."

"No, no." He waved her off. "I'm fine. I'll wait here with you."

"No need to wait. Really. Mac is on his way. And the fire brigade. I'll be fine."

"Only if you're sure."

"I am. I'll ring you tomorrow. And... thank you."

She smiled for the first time since the fire erupted and felt the slightest rush of relief. They *had* made it through. Together. He returned the smile then walked away toward home.

Julia sensed weakness in her legs again, so she sank down at the edge of the doorway and tried to breathe. *In, out, in, out.* Every tenth breath was in the form of a cough.

When a gentle breeze caressed her face, Julia smelled the smoke again, as strongly as before. She realized the scent was embedded in her nose, her senses. It was also in her clothes and hair—they were saturated with the odor of smoke.

From here, Julia could see her cottage. She pictured her father, yawning and stretching from a blissful nap, ready to take his second round of medication with dinner. How would she ever tell him about the fire? What words would she offer? They had only just celebrated the bakery's forty years. This would break his heart.

She thought about the timing of the fire. They were lucky, really. What if the fire had broken out *at* the party, with a bakery full of people, and it had gone unnoticed until it was too late? Or what if it had happened in the dead of night with no one there to stop it and the fire spreading to the other shops? Her thoughts jumped ahead to the bakery's future, wondering what would happen to it postfire. The immediate future was obvious—calls to insurance people, inspectors, employees. But the long-term future seemed unsure—renovations, expenses, shutting down the bakery for how long? And what about catering commitments already made? And Holly's upcoming wedding cake?

The thoughts piled on top of each other in rapid succession, making Julia almost as dizzy as the smoke had. She couldn't do this right now.

She attempted to focus on the quiet evening, the stillness after the panic. But she couldn't calm her mind.

Half an hour ago, Julia's greatest concern of the moment had been choosing which meal to pick up for her father from the pub. Incredible, what could happen in a few ticks of a clock. Priorities rearranging themselves, perspective forever shifted, the future creating a giant question mark. All in the span of a cricket's brief song. A darker thought hit her. *Why had the fire started? Was it somehow her fault? Something she did or didn't do?*

"Lass?" She heard Mac's voice reverberate in her head and saw him crouching nearby her. He had placed a hand on her shoulder. "You're trembling."

She hadn't even noticed.

"Mac. I'm so glad you're here." She leaned on him as she struggled to her feet. She coughed and let go of his arm.

"You should see a doctor," he insisted.

"I'm okay. Maybe later."

"Promise me, lass. Soon."

"I promise. It will be my next call." She'd never imagined Mac as the fatherly type, but right now it was what she needed, and she was grateful for his concern.

Mac poked his head inside the dark kitchen and clicked on the torch he'd brought with him, flashing the beam inside. "The fire started at the wall?"

"Yes. Above the oven." She didn't want to, but she relived every detail as she described the fire to him. He would need this information for an accurate assessment of things. He could pass along the details to the firefighters.

When she was finished, Mac nodded. "At least no one was injured."

"That's what I keep telling myself."

"You should let your father know."

Julia tucked a stray lock of hair behind her ear and realized her palm was covered with faint remnants of powder. "I know."

"Do you want me to go with you? For moral support?"

Julia shook her head. "I can do it, thanks. I'll go now. Best to get it over with."

"Aye. I'll assess things inside, stay here for the fire brigade, make a few more calls. We'll know more within the hour."

"You're the best, Mac." She wanted to kiss his cheek but realized she smelled disgusting and changed her mind. She squeezed his elbow instead.

The cottage's front door had always seemed a stone's throw from the bakery, an easy minute-long walk. But as Julia trudged the final steps up the stone path, coughing a few times along the way, it was taking an eternity to get there. She tried to rehearse what she would say, but it was impossible. She wished, in hindsight, she had brought Mac with her.

During the haze of the journey home, Tristan's clear, bright image floated briefly to the forefront of her mind, out of nowhere. His face brought momentary comfort. The frightened, little-girl part of herself wanted nothing better than to find him, tell him about the fire, rush into his arms, and let him comfort and soothe her. But he wasn't around anymore. She had made it just fine on her own for all these years without his help. This would have to be another of those thousand times she leaned on her own strength.

There was nothing he could do to make this better anyway.

"Dad?" she called as she opened the cottage door.

"In here, love."

Julia desperately needed to run upstairs and shower, change clothes, but there wasn't time for that.

She followed her father's voice to the kitchen and found him sitting at the table, hunched over with a pen clutched in his hand. He was attempting to sign his name to a thank-you card. He finished the *y* in "Bentley" with great flair then set down his pen and saw Julia. His relaxed expression quickly pinched into a frown of concern as he saw his daughter's condition. And surely, by now, he'd caught a great whiff of the smoke she'd brought along. She imagined it trailing behind in a cloud as she walked, like in some sort of cartoon…

"What *happened*?" He placed his hands on the table and tried to rise with a wobble. Julia moved forward to help.

"Dad, it's okay, you don't have to stand."

"Nonsense. I want to see you, eye to eye."

After a moment, he stood as tall as he could and faced her, holding the table for support. He looked her up and down as she held both his elbows to stabilize him.

"Dad, I don't want to alarm you. Everyone's safe, nobody got hurt."

He sniffed the air. "I smell smoke." He patted along her shoulders, down toward her hands, as though such a hasty and inadequate examination would reassure him that she was uninjured.

"I'm okay. There was a fire. In the bakery—the kitchen. Enzo was there, and we put it out together with fire extinguishers. Nobody was hurt," she repeated, hoping the emphasis would keep him calm.

"That's a great relief. How did it happen?"

"We're not sure yet. Mac's there now, waiting for the fire brigade, assessing the damage. From what I can tell, the fire only affected the back wall, above one of the ovens. It started there, I'm guessing due to a faulty wire..."

She wanted to spill more of the harrowing details, to tell him: *Daddy, I watched it spark and climb up toward the ceiling. It was hissing at me. And then it branched out, grew more powerful, and there was smoke. I wasn't sure I could stop it. I felt like a tiny soldier with a pebble, confronting a growing Goliath. That fire was the most frightening thing I've ever seen.* But she couldn't risk alarming him further. She knew his blood pressure might spike if he saw her upset.

"Do you want some water?" she asked him.

"Me?" He chuckled. "No, no, my dear. I'm fine. You're the one who probably needs water. And a meal. And some good rest. I'm okay. Just relieved you're all right."

He leaned in for a hug, but Julia protested. "I'm really stinky, Dad. Like, gross-stay-away-from-me type of stinky."

"I don't care about that." He pulled her in close and squeezed her tight, and she let him.

When he backed away, he gave a faint smile. "And Enzo?"

She tried to cover a small cough. "He's fine, too."

"Dr. Andrews should see both of you."

"He will. I promise. But I had to let you know about the fire first."

"I want to see it."

"Dad, it's not necessary. Mac's taking care of things. You can see the kitchen tomorrow maybe. If it's safe."

"I'm going now. I need to see it for myself."

Julia heard the stubborn tone in his voice that she'd recognized as a little girl. Once Alton Bentley's mind was made up about something, he couldn't be stopped.

Julia took a quick moment upstairs to wash her face and hands, to sweep her hair up into a tight bun, and to change, lightning-fast, into jeans and an oversized T-shirt before driving her father back to the bakery. When they arrived, they saw the fire truck and another car parked outside the back door. Julia helped her father out of the van and saw two men walking toward them—Mac and Dr. Andrews.

"Hope you don't mind, lass," Mac said as she and her father slowly approached. All the men exchanged handshakes as Mac continued. "I took the liberty of calling the good doc. Better safe than sorry."

"I heartily agree," echoed her father.

Julia was clearly outnumbered. "All right. But I'd like to hear Mac's assessment of the damage first."

Mac removed his cap and scratched at his hairline. By now, the sky was a dark blue, and only a streetlamp illuminated the area.

"The firemen are still inspecting, but they've already confirmed what I suspected. Good news and bad news. Which do you want first?"

"Good," Alton said. "Then the bad."

"Well, the damage could've been much worse. Your daughter saved the bakery with her quick thinking. If those fire extinguishers hadn't been used, the building would have easily been consumed. In fact, worst-case scenario was that the bakery could have been completely gutted with the fire spreading to the other connecting buildings."

"The pub and the emporium," Julia said.

"Aye. From what I can tell, both walls you share with them are undamaged. The fire seems to be limited to the back wall and ceiling."

"That's good," Alton said.

"So here's the bad news," Mac continued. "There's significant damage to that back wall and connecting ceiling, which includes the flat above. So we have some structural issues to consider, along with an inspection of all wiring and the repairs that go with it. The damage also extended to the oven and refrigerator. They'll have to be replaced after the repairs. All of this means..."

"We have to close the bakery," Julia whispered.

"For how long?" Alton kept his hand threaded through Julia's.

"Depends on how fast we can get the repairs done. I've already put a call in to an inspector I know, to give us a better assessment. And I have a couple of mates from other villages who specialize in this sort of repair. I'll ring them up next. And Julia will need to notify the insurance company."

"It's at the top of my list," she said.

Mac rubbed his chin. "It's clear to me—and the firefighter concurs—that this was an electrical fire, likely started by a faulty wire."

"But I really don't understand," Julia said. "I had an inspection done just last year. This shouldn't have happened."

"Aye, but these old buildings"—Mac glanced behind him and tapped the beautiful limestone of the bakery with the palm of his hand—"I assume this one's nigh four hundred years old, are unpredictable. They can be hazardous because of their age." He looked squarely at Julia without blinking. "Lass, this wasn't your fault."

Hearing Mac say the words sent a wave of relief over Julia. She needed to hear it.

"Is it safe to go inside?" her father asked. "I want to see."

"Safe enough. But only take a step or two inside for a peek. You'll need to cover your nose and mouth with this rag. I'll help you inside while Julia gets her exam from the doc." Mac winked at Julia, who smirked at him.

Her father squeezed Julia's arm and made eye contact. "It's going to be all right," he told her then reached for Mac.

"I'm all yours," Julia told Dr. Andrews. "Do we need to go to your office?"

"No, no. Here will be fine. I brought a portable oxygen tank with me in case we needed it. This should be just a quick assessment." He brought out his stethoscope and held it to her chest. "Breathe in for me."

Before she did, she asked, "Would you mind making a visit, after this, to Enzo's cottage? He fought the fire with me. I'd feel better if you looked him over, too. And send me his bill."

"Certainly. Now. Deep breath…"

Back home at the cottage an hour later—after Julia had received the all-clear from Dr. Andrews, given the nightly set of pills to her father, then rung up the insurance company—she took a long, hot shower and decided to make a simple dinner of tea and toast. Neither she nor her father had much of an appetite after today's events. They needed some light comfort food.

She moved aside the thank-you cards for another time—they seemed so unimportant now—and set the kitchen table. The absolute panic of two hours before had been softened by physical exhaustion. She couldn't wait to collapse into bed.

"It's ready!" she called to her father, who had gone to change into his pajamas.

She munched on buttered toast then took a long, restorative sip of hot tea. Nothing had ever tasted better! She sniffed the air and realized that even with a sudsy shower, washing her hair three times and changing into freshly laundered clothes, she still smelled faintly of smoke. Would she ever be rid of it?

Julia grabbed a pad and pen from the countertop and began scratching down a list of things to do, people she would still need to call. She underlined the few tasks that had to be done tonight before bed. The hardest—*Call Theresa, Miranda, Brandy.* She paused and thought it through. She would need to tell them not only about the fire but also that they were out of a job for the foreseeable future.

"This looks delicious." Her father approached the table, sat down carefully, and stretched his hand for the sugar to put in his tea. "What's that?" He pointed at her pad.

"Just a to-do list."

"That can wait for tomorrow, don't you think? It's been a long night."

"I know. But this helps, doing something, staying active. It gives me some structure. It's just…" She set down her pen and leaned back in her chair. "I feel like this fire happened *to* me tonight. Against my will. So

I guess making a list—as barmy as it sounds—gives me the illusion that I'm in control of something."

"Not barmy at all." He stirred his tea in slow circles then tapped the spoon against the cup. She watched him, his demeanor, his body language. Relaxed, content. Almost as though nothing had happened, as though their entire world *hadn't* just been altered.

"You're so calm, I mean, I..."

"What?"

"I don't know, Dad. I'm a ball of nerves about all this. But you almost seem... okay with everything."

Her father drank his tea, savoring the flavor. "Not okay with it, certainly. But..." He set down the cup and threaded his fingers together. "I suppose I've accepted it, to a certain degree."

"But how can you? And so soon?" Julia felt something similar to frustration start to rise—not at her father, but at that fire she could still see in her mind's eye, even now. Brazen, relentless, frightening, threatening. Intrusive. Still, she kept her voice steady. "I mean, the bakery nearly burned down tonight. And we have to close it up indefinitely. Our work, our life..."

Her father shook his head. "I've never seen the bakery as my life. Yes, it's important. Of course it is. But it's only a building, bricks and mortar. We still have each other. That's the most important thing. Am I sad about the fire? Yes. But I've lived ninety years on this earth. I've experienced a series of tragedies and triumphs. I've had great successes, but I've also lost people I loved. Life is an odd mixture of both good and bad, never all one or the other. We can rebuild the bakery. And with no injuries and no other shops being affected... well, I call that the hope in the storm. There can be unexpected blessings in the midst of tragedies. But we have to choose to see them that way."

Unexpected blessings. Julia wondered what specific part of his ninety years he was thinking of, and suspected she knew. Rose's death, the unexpected tragedy, and a new baby, the unexpected blessing that came with it.

Julia placed her hand on top of his and squeezed it gently. "I know you're right. But it will take some time for me to gain that perspective. I guess I'm just not that brave most of the time."

"You can't be serious." He raised his eyebrows as high as they would reach. "You stood in the face of danger tonight, my Julia. You didn't run from it. You stayed and fought the fire—valiantly—and won! I'd call that pretty damned brave."

Julia chuckled at the rare bit of profanity she'd ever heard her father speak. But it was surely warranted under the circumstances.

"My little warrior." He shifted in his chair. "Well, I believe our tea is getting cold."

Julia returned to her list, and as they spent the rest of their brief meal in silence, she mulled over her father's words. She couldn't quite agree to the "blessings in the midst of tragedy" philosophy. She was too mired down in the gritty reality in front of her, of people to call and things still to do. She was also staring ahead at an unknown path filled with endless question marks. She wondered when the bakery would reopen, if the insurance would cover the repairs, if things would ever feel back to normal in her life again, business as usual…

She decided to keep her thoughts to herself, to let her father bask in his Zen philosophy. Why should the both of them be anxious?

When she crawled into bed two hours later, Julia closed her eyes and tried to shut out the world. The earlier calls to all her employees had gone surprisingly well. Enzo had already informed them about the fire, so Julia didn't have to start at the beginning and relive the harrowing details. They each gave their sympathies in pleasant tones and said they were still interested in their same positions whenever the bakery reopened. But Julia knew they couldn't go without paychecks for four weeks, five weeks, more? They would have to seek out other employment.

Everything had changed.

Out of habit, Julia rolled to her side and reached for the clock then paused. No need to set her alarm for 3:30 a.m. Not tonight, or any night in the near future. Under any other circumstances, that fact would fill her with absolute joy. But tonight, it left her rolling back onto her side, clutching her pillow, and letting quiet tears melt away into the soft fabric.

Chapter Twenty-eight

"When you bake for someone who's ill or troubled, you become part of the healing process. Food can be restorative, energizing. Arriving with bundles of food on the doorstep of someone in despair is sometimes the only appropriate gesture in a time of crisis."

JULIA HAD ASSUMED SHE WOULD dream about the fire all night long, have nightmares about flames dancing, smoke rising, panic choking her. But instead, she only dreamed about Tristan, the same dream on a continuous loop, nothing at all to do with the fire. In the dream, Tristan was stuck in an empty, gray room with poor lighting. Julia could see him from above as he hit his fist against a locked door, shouting something unintelligible. Then she saw herself approach the door from the other side, struggling to unlock it. But the door remained frustratingly closed.

It occurred to Julia later, over breakfast, what the dream was about. The obvious interpretation was the breakup. They were out of touch, broken. But the dream went even deeper. It was about loss and lack of control, about not being able to get back something that was gone. Julia had endured loss with the bakery's fire, but she'd also endured it over the breakup. *All in the very same week.*

Though the dream hung over her like a cloud for the rest of the morning, it still didn't distract her from her to-do list as much as something else did, a frequent and steady stream of calls and visitors to the cottage. Apparently, news about the bakery's fire had spread rapidly around the village the morning after. The details—some greatly exaggerated—had brought a barrage of calls of support and sympathy, as well as visits. Women from the book club and men from Alton's poker nights appeared first, followed by more familiar faces and acquaintances.

As the morning rolled on, Julia saw the genuine concern in each face and realized this wasn't about the bakery. It was about her father. And about her. The villagers' interest in their well-being was overwhelming. Julia felt it in every word and gesture, in every offering of food they brought, one by one by one.

Her father enjoyed the visits at first, but Julia could tell he was tiring, so she offered to take over the greeting duties around midmorning.

At one point, during a rare moment of quiet, Julia completed one can't-wait item on her list. She rang Holly up to discuss her wedding cake. With the bakery being fully out of commission, it would be impossible for Julia to bake it. So she gave Holly the name of a bakery in another village, which Julia had already rung up. The baker had gladly agreed to help, even on such short notice, and even offered a sizeable discount.

When lunchtime arrived, Julia didn't even have to consider what to serve her father for a meal. She had a multitude of choices available with all the soups and cottage pies that neighbors and friends had brought. Julia didn't possibly have enough room to cram them all into their mini-fridge—and the bakery's fridge was no longer an option—so she asked if Mildred would store them at Foxglove House.

Mildred hadn't heard about the fire until noon—she'd been on an overnight London stay with her husband—and came rushing over to the cottage, panic-stricken.

She cupped Julia's face in her hands. "Oh my dear. You're all right. No burns or injuries?"

"None, thank goodness."

"A miracle. And your father?"

"Nowhere near the fire. He was at home, resting."

They didn't have time to continue the conversation. Cora and Grace knocked on the door next with smiles and heaping portions of food.

"I'll leave you to it," Mildred whispered. "Let me know if you need anything else. I'll check on you later."

Abbey, who had come along with Mildred, had already loaded up their car with food to store at the house. Julia would either end up freezing it or maybe even giving it to a homeless shelter. The villagers' good will wouldn't go to waste.

The only obvious person missing from the morning's stream of visitors was Tristan. Hadn't his busybody aunt told him about the fire by now? Surely, even with the painful breakup, Tristan would have contacted her father, at least, out of concern. But she remembered the hurt in his eyes during their last conversation, the accusations he'd made about Julia giving up on the relationship. Perhaps things were just too broken between them.

Still, curiosity gnawed at Julia to the point that she left her father with his lunch of shepherd's pie from Lizzie and Joe, who were still chatting with him in the kitchen, and drove the short trek to Mrs. Pickering's market. She had a few supplies to pick up anyway. Perhaps she would run into Tristan. Perhaps she wouldn't. But maybe her curiosity could at least be sated.

In the five minutes it took for Julia to browse the short, narrow aisles of Mrs. Pickering's market in search of necessities, it became clear that Tristan wasn't there. Julia hadn't heard him milling about in the storage room, hadn't caught a quick glimpse of him in the office, hadn't seen any trace or sign of him. She assumed he was at the farm, then, working hard.

Julia approached the empty counter and began placing her items onto it when Mrs. Pickering suddenly appeared at the till, startling her.

"Oh my GOODNESS!" Mrs. Pickering leaned across the counter to look Julia straight in the eye. "I heard about the FIRE. I haven't had a chance to step away from the shop yet and come for a visit. Was it horrible? Was it frightening?" Her eyes widened more with each new question. Her tone didn't contain the usual somber, quiet concern that all the other villagers had this morning. Mrs. Pickering's voice held an overly interested tone, a gossipy one, and Julia knew she was fishing for exclusive details to spread around the village.

Julia managed a thin smile. "Yes. It was frightening. But we're all safe, and there wasn't too much damage."

"You'll have to close, won't you?" Mrs. Pickering *tsked*. "Back in 1975, a shop across the street—antiques shop, I think—had water damage from a burst pipe. They had to close the doors for*ever*." She said this last word ominously. "Someone else eventually bought the shop. I believe it's Mrs. Bennett's now. But those poor people—they couldn't afford to rebuild..." Another *tsk*.

Eager to leave and completely regretting her wasted trip here in the first place, Julia set the rest of her items onto the counter with haste, hoping Mrs. Pickering would take the hint. But she didn't.

"I rang Tristan this morning," Mrs. Pickering said, which made Julia pause. "About the fire."

"You did?" Julia wasn't sure why Mrs. Pickering was telling her this.

"Oh, yes. It was very clear to me at the party how fond he was of your father—with that darling picture frame he gave as a gift. So I wanted to make sure he knew about the fire."

"And... did you reach him?" Julia tried to sound casual.

Mrs. Pickering shook her head and picked up Julia's first item, a jar of jam. "I left him a—what do you young people call those things? A voice message. I told him no one was harmed in the fire. That's what Mrs. Cartwright told me this morning when I saw her. He's been gone for almost three days, you know. Tristan left the night of the party, said he was going 'off the grid,' whatever that means, and not to worry. But I do worry, of course."

"Of course."

Mrs. Pickering tapped the price of the jam into the old-fashioned till. "It's curious. I've rung him every day but haven't been able to reach him."

Julia wondered if that was because his mobile was turned completely off or because he kept seeing the multiple calls from his aunt and was ignoring them on purpose.

"He might be in Cornwall," Julia said, more to herself than Mrs. Pickering. Perhaps he went to visit James and Cynthia.

Mrs. Pickering stopped midtap and stared across the counter at Julia, still holding the jam. "What an odd thing to say. Why in heaven would you suspect Cornwall?"

"Oh, well..." Julia stammered, trying to cover. "It's just that his mates were here recently. They're from Cornwall. I believe."

"How do you know so much about Tristan's friends? Or Tristan's life?" Mrs. Pickering continued, one eyebrow raised. "In fact, why should it matter to you where my nephew is? I wasn't aware you knew him *that* well."

The nasty implication in Mrs. Pickering's tone and the condescension in her eyes stirred something inside Julia. She felt the heat rise to her face.

"Actually, I know him quite well. And it does matter to me. Because *he* matters to me," Julia heard herself say, heart beating faster, voice growing louder as Mrs. Pickering's eyes continued to widen. "I care very deeply about him. And we... we've been secretly dating these last several weeks."

And there it was, out in the open, for all the world to hear.

Rather than fear the fallout of her admission, Julia felt positively free. The blood pumped faster, warming her entire body as she watched Mrs. Pickering's face pucker, as though she'd just eaten a lemon whole.

"I can't... I just..." Mrs. Pickering, possibly for the first time in her life, was without words.

"Tristan has become important to me." Julia's voice grew bolder. "It was my idea to keep us a secret. Your nephew wanted to tell the world. But I let my fear of the gossip in this village keep me quiet. You don't think I've heard your opinions about me over the years? The cruelty of your judgments and the lies about my life? But I have. Loud and clear. And I've let it bury me into this cocoon, where I'm afraid to live my life in front of the village for fear of what others will think. But no longer. I have nothing to be ashamed of. Tristan and I have done nothing wrong!"

Before Mrs. Pickering had time to collect herself and offer a scathing retort, Julia pivoted on her heel, abandoning her items on the counter and nearly bumping into three villagers—Mary, George, and Dr. Andrews—who had heard the entire exchange.

Instead of frowns or gasps, they issued broad smiles and nods as Julia walked through the market's front door and into the welcoming sunshine, wondering what on earth she'd just done.

Julia tied the belt of her dressing gown as she tiptoed downstairs, careful to avoid the squeakiest steps so she wouldn't wake her father. But it wasn't necessary. As she landed on the final step, she saw her father's shadow in the living room as he sat on the sofa, reading his new novel underneath a golden circle of lamplight.

"Dad?"

He looked up and removed his glasses. "Oh. Hello, love."

She walked over to his side of the sofa. "You couldn't sleep, either?"

"I tried. You?"

"Well, my days and nights are all mixed up now that I'm not waking up in the middle of the night anymore. Plus, this was such a busy day. I think my brain is still trying to process it." *Plus*, she could've easily added, *I'm still stirred up from my encounter with Mrs. Pickering a few hours ago.* She still couldn't believe how bold she'd been. But even now, she didn't regret a single word.

"Indeed." He patted the seat beside him.

Before she joined him, she asked, "Oh, do you want a cup of tea? I could brew us some."

"No, no. Perhaps later. I wanted to talk to you about something."

Curious, she sat down next to him and adjusted a pillow under her back for support.

"First, what did that inspector fellow tell you about the bakery?"

Julia had already told her father every detail of the inspector's report a few short hours ago, but he hadn't remembered. She gave him the quick version, the nuts and bolts of it: "He confirmed that it was an electrical fire, started in the wall. It will take a few days for his final report to be filed, but we should hear something soon about the renovations, when we can start, how much money we'll have to work with. The upstairs flat will need repairs as well. Mac has offered to help us find the best workers when we're ready."

"Yes. That's right. You told me that earlier, didn't you? I've been doing some serious thinking all day about the fire, the future..." He shut his book and set it in his lap and shifted to face Julia squarely. "I think we're at a crossroads with the bakery. We have a choice to make. Or rather, you do."

"What do you mean? I assumed we would repair the damage and open the doors again as soon as we could. That was always the plan. Wasn't it? Are you having second thoughts?"

"No, don't misunderstand. I'm fine with the bakery reopening. But it's not my choice to make. The bakery is yours. To renovate, or even..."

"What?"

"Or even to sell. If that's what you wish."

She stared at him, studied his face, wondered where all this was coming from. "I don't understand. The bakery has been in your family—in our family—for four generations, counting me. Why would I ever sell it?"

"Well, that's a question for you to answer. Don't let the weight of the past stop you from pursuing other things. We could perhaps retire the bakery during *this* generation. I've always worried in the back of my mind if I pressured you into taking it over—whether it was what you really wanted, deep down. So this is a chance for you to make sure, to explore your options. To follow a dream, perhaps, or another career you've always wanted to try. People change careers all the time."

"But, I don't want to change careers. We sort of had this conversation a few weeks ago." But maybe he didn't remember... "You asked me if I was happy here, at the bakery, and I told you I was."

"But at that time, we didn't have this second chance staring us in the face. Indulge your old man. This fire could end up being a rare gift. It could be a moment in your life that you decide what your future looks like. A fork in the road, of sorts."

Julia didn't know what to say. She had no idea her father felt this way.

"Of course, on the other hand, you could choose to stay and reopen the bakery, but start fresh with it. A clean slate."

"Start fresh?"

"You know, a blank page. You could use the insurance money to make the repairs and then use some of my savings to spruce up the place, renovate completely—new color scheme, different flooring. You could even rearrange the main floor if that's what you wanted."

"I would never take that money from you, Dad."

"But I've invested well. And it's *your* money, anyway, in the end. It doesn't matter to me when it comes to you—now or when I'm gone. What's the difference? Just think about everything. Roll it over in your mind. You have some time to consider it. And if you do keep the bakery, you could even rename it. *Julia's Bakery*."

Her first instinct was, "No, I would never change the name." But she could tell that a quick no wasn't the answer her father wanted. He was serious about this, asking her to consider every possibility while she had time, while the bakery's future was in limbo.

He leaned over to pat her hand. "Life is so much shorter than you think it's going to be. You suddenly look back on all your days and wonder where they went. Poof. Let this decision be your heart's desire, whatever that is."

"Okay. I'll consider everything. I promise."

"That's all I ask." He returned his hand to his lap and cleared his throat. "Tell me, did you see Tristan today? He didn't stop by the cottage with all the others. I was hoping to see him."

His question felt out of the blue here, but she'd actually been expecting it all day.

"He's out of town for a bit."

Not a lie, but not the entire truth. A couple of times since the party she'd nearly told her father about the breakup. But after the fire, Julia wanted to spare him more disappointment. Besides, she had no idea what the future would end up looking like, whether Tristan, after a while, would come around to visit her father and maintain their steady friendship, or whether he might leave the village permanently. Tristan had always said he could do his job, the software program, from any location. Until she knew more, Julia thought it wise to say very little.

"I see." Her father stifled a yawn. "Well. It seems this old, tired brain is finally ready for bed."

Julia stood up, offering help. As they shuffled along toward his bedroom, Julia wondered what the coming days would hold for the both of them. They had already been through so much in the past week. She wasn't sure how much more she could handle.

Chapter Twenty-nine

"Rely on others for recipes—those are tested, tried, and true—but don't be afraid to rely on yourself. Listen to your instinct, your gut. You know best, whether an ingredient or technique is working or not. Be confident in your own skills. Trust yourself."

IT WASN'T UNTIL THREE FULL days after the fire that Julia experienced all the ripple effects involved. Her quiet kitchen mornings, her work staff, her customers, her afternoon naps, her whole routine... All of it was gone. She didn't realize how heavily she had leaned upon that routine as a safety net, something to depend on. Even the weekly poker nights would vanish. Hopefully, the guys could take their game to another venue, maybe even to Julia's cottage. But it wouldn't be the same.

Julia sat on the crest of a hill outside the village, a place she used to visit as a teenager whenever she had anxiety or heartache over a boy or simply needed to escape life for a bit. This spot was the most isolated in the area. Anywhere she turned, she could only see manicured pastureland, stone walls, grazing sheep, thick trees, peaceful deer. No people, no cars. Only nature.

She had left her mobile at the cottage. It needed a good charge anyway, and Mary and George had stopped by for a visit with her father, so he wouldn't need Julia for a couple of hours. She'd brought with her a pad and pen, prepared to make another list. This time it wasn't about the fire but about her father's proposal regarding the bakery. Perhaps writing her thoughts down would help clarify them.

Julia's gut response to her father's offer was to keep the bakery. She wasn't restless or eager to leave. She hadn't been secretly searching for other job openings in the area. She didn't have a deep-seated longing to do something other than what she was doing.

But she'd promised her father she would consider her options.

Julia started back in her memory from the beginning, tried to recall what her original little-girl dreams were. But she came up empty. Most of her friends wanted to be models or TV hosts or wives and mothers. But Julia wanted to be like her father. A baker.

Today, thirty-something years later, did she have any dreams left? She couldn't pinpoint them easily. But Julia knew one thing for sure. She could never leave her father. Yes, it was because he needed her, relied on her, but she needed him, too. She would stay in Chilton Crosse indefinitely. It was home.

But what was stopping her from seeking an online degree and eventually having a new career within the village? That option was entirely possible. The problem was—what career was appealing enough to pull her away from the only job she knew?

This wasn't helping.

Julia set her empty list aside and pushed off from the patch of grass where she'd been sitting. She dusted off her jeans and began to walk. She needed to move. The clouds had created broad, slow-moving patches of shadow over the endless countryside, and as she made her way down toward more level ground, she slowed her pace and took in every detail of this glorious day—the deliciously scented summer wind, the melodic birds, the puffy gray clouds holding the promise of rain.

Perhaps it would help more to reflect backward instead of jumping ahead to her future. Maybe she could find some clarity as she analyzed her bigger, life-changing moments. She started by detailing her major decisions, starting with her youthful days, then on to her adult years up until this moment. And as she sifted through her choices, one by one, she discovered something incredible. They weren't really her choices at all.

It had been her father's idea for her to work in the bakery as a teenager after school. It was also her father's idea for Julia to leave Chilton Crosse for university, to branch out, find herself. Julia probably would've been content simply standing in place. But at her father's urging, she'd gone to London.

Even then, on her own for the very first time, Julia couldn't make a decision about a field of study. So she'd chosen it randomly. She'd scanned the list of degree choices, closed her eyes, and let her finger point the way. Sociology? She knew nothing about Sociology, but it sounded as good as anything else on the list. Decision made.

Even Julia's marriage hadn't technically been a conscious, definitive choice. One night at a pub, Braeden, tipsy, had told her, "Hey we should get married," and Julia had said, "Why not?"

Years later, Julia wasn't brave enough to make the decision to leave her husband. The divorce had been initiated by Braeden after he'd fallen in love with someone else. And when the marriage ended, Julia's father had been the one to recommend a return to the bakery, to Chilton Crosse. At the time, Julia had been working in a dead-end job as a clerk at a Tower of London gift shop. The bakery was heaven in comparison.

And what about Tristan? Originally, he had been the primary instigator of their earliest conversations. Julia had resisted him until he gently pursued her, and she went along, bit by bit, despite her reservations. Even the breakup—that *seemed* like her choice—had been more about running away from a decision than actually making one. Had Tristan been right? Had Julia used her insecurities as an excuse to push him away, to avoid the hard choice of staying together?Maybe she'd even kept her inability to have children private all that time, not out of nervousness about his reaction, but out of pure self-protection. Maybe Julia didn't trust that their relationship had any staying power. Why tell someone an intimate secret if that person probably wouldn't be in your life for very long?

Looking back, had Julia ever consciously, deliberately made a major life decision all on her own? She had let situations happen to her, guided by other people's opinions. She hadn't really ever chosen the bakery. She just grew up in it then returned to it, a safe spot to lick her wounds, when she had no other place to go. It was her backup plan, her port in the storm, her default.

No wonder it was important to her father that Julia take time to stop and think, to make an actual, deliberate choice on her own. He'd watched her, all her life, fall into things, floating around and letting things happen *to* her. She was never the proactive force. For the first time, Julia saw her life from an entirely different angle. Her usual perspective tilted on its axis. Maybe it was because of the fire. It had shaken her, awakened her. Tristan had accused her—rightly so—of letting fear guide her. Looking back, had she done that all her life?

Julia felt a significant shift deep inside—a boldness, a new strength building. It had been growing more intense the past couple of days, but she hadn't recognized it until this moment. Maybe she *was* the little warrior who had faced a fire, fought her fears, and won. And maybe she could start doing that in all the other areas of her life as well.

"I haven't been choosing my life," she said loudly to the birds, the trees, and the sheep. "It's been choosing me."

Julia no longer needed a paper and pad with a pros and cons list. She had discovered her answers, right here on a hilltop, inside the whispers of a breeze. She knew exactly which decisions she would make about her future with the bakery and with Tristan. Nothing had ever been clearer.

Julia entered the cottage out of breath from her brisk walk down the hill. She had already spent the last ten minutes rehearsing what she would say to Tristan when she finally got ahold of him, somewhere, somehow. She had to let him know about her hilltop epiphany, to talk to him about risks and second chances. Julia was ready to try, to talk about the hard things, and even to compromise a little. To explore *all* the options, eyes wide open. To stand and face this man she loved rather than walk away and risk losing him entirely. She only hoped it wasn't too late.

Before sprinting upstairs to retrieve her mobile, she wanted to check on her father. She found him sitting at his bedside, struggling to remove his watch.

"Dad. I'm here. I'll help. Mary and George left?" She gently rolled his wrist over to view the band.

"A few minutes ago. And I have something else to tell you—" He looked up at her. "You seem… flushed. Your cheeks are pink."

Julia gently threaded the wristband back through the clasp, careful not to pinch her father's delicate skin.

"I was on a hike, of sorts. I did some much-needed thinking, and I've come to some decisions. But, you go first. What did you need to tell me?" The wristband came loose, and she placed the watch on his nightstand.

"Well, you had a visitor while you were gone. Tristan came to see you. About an hour ago."

Julia sucked in a breath. "He's here? In town?"

"You're surprised."

Julia sat in the chair across from him and dipped her head. "Dad, I've been dreading telling you this, but Tristan and I been having some issues. We broke up, actually. Well, I broke things off with him. Before your party. I let my insecurities get the best of me."

"Why didn't you mention it?"

"I didn't want to worry you, especially on the day of your party. And then the fire happened, and I couldn't find the right time to tell you. But the last few days have forced me to stop and look at my life, to see what's important. And, Dad... Tristan is important to me. I want him in my life. I want to fight for him."

"That's my girl." Her father winked. "Did I ever tell you that I broke things off with your mother? Right before we got engaged?"

Julia's eyes widened. "No. Why?"

"I don't actually recall all the reasons. They seem so distant now, so pointless. Maybe it was our age gap. Or maybe I wanted to spare her from the solitary life of a military wife. I'm quite sure I thought I was being noble at the time. But now, I look on it as foolishness."

"What happened? After the breakup?"

Her father chuckled, his eyes focused on something far away, as though searching for a memory. "Your mother, bless her. She wouldn't hear of it. She refused to accept the breakup and wore me down with her letters. She convinced me, in no uncertain terms, that we were meant to be together. And it turns out she was right. I can't imagine what my life would have been without her." His eyes refocused on Julia. "My precious daughter, once you've found a love this great, you can't let it go. Don't be a fool like your old man. Go after what you want. Be bold."

Julia nodded. "I will. I have to try, at least. Tell me more about Tristan's visit. What was his demeanor?"

"He seemed serious."

Julia had no idea how to take that. What did it mean? Serious?

Her father continued. "I told him you were out, but I wasn't sure where. He had tried reaching you, but your mobile wasn't on."

"I left it upstairs charging." Julia rose from the chair, feeling a renewed urgency to check her messages.

"Was Tristan the decision you were talking about earlier, when you first came in?"

"Oh. No, I also wanted to speak with you about the bakery. But it can wait. I'll go see Tristan first, and then I'll come back, and we can talk." She had an irrational notion that unless she sought Tristan out this very minute, found out what he wanted to say, he might run off again, and she would never find him. "I'll bring you some dinner from the pub. How does that sound?"

"Scrumptious."

Julia leaned over to kiss her father on the cheek. "Thank you. For everything."

"I want the best for you." He patted her hand. "Only the best."

"I love you, Daddy."

Julia scurried upstairs and switched on her mobile to see several text messages from Tristan: *Need to talk. Can we meet?* Then later, *Where are you? I went to the cottage. You weren't there.* Then finally, *Text me back. It's important.*

She knew that her impatient, fumbling fingers would take forever to text a message, so she opted for the old-fashioned route and rung him up.

"Julia?" he said on the second ring.

Tristan's voice had never sounded so familiar, but still far away.

"Dad said you were here, at the cottage. I was actually on my way to find you. But I didn't know where to start. Your aunt said you were out of town."

"Yeah. I came back this morning."

She couldn't read between the lines or tell what he was thinking from these clipped responses. They needed to meet in person.

"I really need to see you. Can we meet somewhere?" she asked, overly aware of the pleading tone in her voice.

"I'm at the farm. We could meet in the middle? On that path..."

"Where the roads branch off toward the manor?"

"Yeah."

"I'm leaving right now."

She clicked off and did a quick mental assessment of her appearance. The last person she'd planned to see today was Tristan. She couldn't even remember if she'd put on makeup this morning. The day had been so hectic with a thousand more calls to make, another stream of visitors with food to the cottage, and another stop at the bakery with Mac to talk over the renovations. Her break on the hilltop was the only one she'd had all day.

But Tristan didn't care about her appearance. He wanted to see her. That was the only thing that mattered.

"Bye, Dad!" she hollered before closing the front door.

As Julia walked toward the fork in the road, she was almost grateful not to see Tristan standing there yet. She needed a moment to catch her breath, to order her thoughts. A hard task, considering she had no idea what she was walking into—his frame of mind, his perspective, his view of the future. But she would stick to her script and tell him about her revelation on the hillside. He needed to know.

Within seconds, she saw his tall frame in the distance, walking toward her. She let the breeze soothe her as she waited, trying not to stare at him. It would make her too nervous. She paid attention instead to the rustling leaves above. The rich canopy of tree branches created a shelter from the warm sun.

"Hey," Tristan said when he got within speaking distance. He lifted up a hand in a weak wave.

Her father had been right. Tristan's face looked serious. *A poker face, giving nothing away.* It could mean a thousand things. Maybe he'd come to believe that Julia had been right to break things off. Maybe he was here to say goodbye.

"Hi," she said with a half smile, her hands clasped in front of her.

She could tell he hadn't shaved in days, probably not since the party. His full beard made his eyes and hair look even darker, even more handsome, if that were possible. Like the first day they met. He stopped at a safe distance from her, not too close, not too far.

"I heard about the fire." He tucked one of his hands into his jeans pocket. "I'm glad you weren't hurt. Your dad said you were a beast putting out the flames." One side of his mouth rose in a hint of a grin, giving Julia some hope.

"Yeah, it was surreal. I'm just glad I was there to stop it. With Enzo. He helped. And Mac says we can repair things in a couple of months, maybe, but the bakery will have to close in the meantime." Julia realized she was rattling off details that didn't matter right now. She wasn't here to talk about the bakery. "So you've been out of town?"

"London. To see Mum. My father was at a conference, so it was just the two of us. After your dad's party, I..." Tristan ran a hand through his unkempt hair. "I just couldn't stay here. In the village. Knowing you were here, that I could bump into you anytime. So after the party, I packed a bag, put Maggie in the car, and we just took off. But when I heard about what you said yesterday... at my aunt's market..."

Julia winced at the memory, at Tristan hearing his aunt's overinflated and probably inaccurate version of events. She assumed Mrs. Pickering had found a way to contact Tristan immediately afterward—probably by ringing up her sister—in order to grill Tristan about this secret relationship.

"What did your aunt tell you?"

"She called it an 'extraordinary outburst' on your part. She said you outed us. It really surprised me." Tristan grinned. "Wish I could've been there to see it."

"I don't know where it came from," Julia admitted. "But I guess I was tired of pretending. Tired of hiding from everyone."

This was her moment to let it all spill out, to take the great risk, even not knowing what Tristan might think. She had to jump off this cliff, no turning back.

"I've been making some decisions recently. About my life. The fire sort of... shocked me, made me examine everything. My choices, my future. And here's the blunt truth. When I look at my future, I can't picture it without you there, Tristan. I just can't." Hot tears formed in her eyes, and she blinked them away. "I honestly don't know if that future has children in it or not. But I'm at least willing to discuss the options and not close myself off from the subject. These past months, you've opened up my heart, my world, and I want to be open to everything. No more closed doors."

Tristan took a step closer as Julia continued, "You were right about me. Fear has guided how I live my life and where I've ended up. I see that now. But I want to be braver, like when I stood up to that fire. I fought my fears because the bakery was important to me. And *you're* important to me. I don't want to lose you."

Tristan closed the gap between them and clasped her face tenderly in his hands. She saw his warm smile through his beard. "I don't want to lose you either."

He leaned in to kiss her, softly, slowly. Then he backed away and reached down to hold her hands.

"When my aunt told me what you said in the market, I thought… I hoped… there was a slim chance for us, that maybe you were changing your mind. That's why I came back to find you." Tristan's eyes remained locked on hers. "When you broke things off, I was blindsided. And so my first reaction was anger. I mean, I thought we were in a good place. So that conversation shocked the hell out of me…"

A car drove up the road from the manor, and Tristan nudged Julia gently out of harm's way, guiding her to the edge of the road. Someone inside the car waved at them. When the car had passed, Tristan reached for Julia's hands again, squeezing them sometimes for emphasis as he spoke. "I did a lot of thinking, too, in London. About us."

"And it helped?"

"Yeah. I saw the situation from your perspective—my mates' visit, the issue about children. I understand it now, your doubts about us. But I'm ready to conquer them together, commit to a future with you, whatever that future looks like. The bottom line is—my life doesn't feel the same without you in it. And if I'm sure about anything, it's this. I love you."

A smile spread wide across Julia's face. "I love you, too." Saying the words aloud was easier than she'd ever imagined because she meant them with her whole heart.

This time, Julia stretched up on her tiptoes to kiss Tristan. His response was immediate as he held her waist and pulled her forward, pressing their bodies together, kissing her deeply.

No other kiss they'd shared before had held this kind of intensity. Insecurities melted, fears vanished, doubts subsided. There was safety inside that kiss—reassurance of a hope and a future. It felt like home.

Chapter Thirty

"There is nothing more satisfying in life than a day spent with good mates and good food."

FOR MOST OF HER LIFE, Julia had hidden away in her father's bakery, kneading bread, measuring out baking powder, icing cakes. But on a sun-drenched day in late June, she sat in Mildred's garden, very much *un*-hidden with her father at her right side and Tristan at her left, to watch Holly and Fletcher exchange wedding vows in front of their loved ones.

By now, several days after she and Tristan had reconciled, the entire village knew about their relationship. Villagers had seen the new couple holding hands as they walked down the high street, eating together at the pub, or sitting together at church. Mrs. Pickering had been the only one to openly gawk when she saw them together for the first time. Tristan had given Julia a light kiss in front of a shop window while Mrs. Pickering was walking past.

"Hello, Aunt," Tristan had said with a smirk then turned to walk the other way with Julia trying to contain her laughter at his side.

Julia wondered if Mrs. Pickering would ever get over Julia's outburst or would ever accept Julia as Tristan's girlfriend. But her new philosophy was to care a little less about what people thought, especially people like Mrs. Pickering.

Julia's father, of course, had been more pleased than anyone about Tristan's return to the fold. He had clapped his hands together that evening when Julia and Tristan had brought him dinner after their reconciliation. "I *knew* you two would work this out, make it right again."

He'd sat down comfortably with them at the cottage's kitchen table to eat. That was when Julia announced to her father that she was choosing to reopen the bakery. It *was* her heart's desire. After congratulations were issued, her father and Tristan fell easily back into their lengthy chats about books or music or the Navy. Everything was as it should be.

Tristan leaned in to find Julia's hand as the vicar finished calling out the vows for Holly and Fletcher to repeat. Holly absolutely glowed, rosy-cheeked, and only had eyes for her handsome groom, who choked back tears a couple of times.

Julia's favorite moment of any wedding wasn't the fancy dresses or the procession down the aisle. It wasn't even the music or the ring exchange or the tearful vows between a couple in love. Her favorite part was always at the end, the moment the vicar announced the new couple to the crowd: Mr. and Mrs. So-and-So. The ceremony had begun with two separate people with two different last names, and by the end, they'd become legally and spiritually united. Like magic.

In these past few years, Julia had attended many weddings of Chilton Crosse couples: Lizzy and Joe, Noelle and Adam, Mildred and Duncan, and now, Holly and Fletcher. Mostly all young couples in their twenties. Julia had always believed the notion that weddings were reserved for a certain age group. But sitting next to Tristan, feeling his thumb rub gently against the palm of her hand, she knew her views were starting to change.

Two months later...

If Julia had thought the baking profession was exhausting work, it hadn't even begun to compare to the grueling hours involved in renovating a bakery. Aside from the actual repairs, which were challenging enough, decisions had to be considered—paint colors, floor textures, appliance brands and sizes, table and chair selections, a new menu board. And Julia was the ultimate decision-maker. Whenever she would ask her father's opinion on something, he would shake his head and wave his hand with a chuckle. "No, no, love. This is all yours."

But finally, after weeks and weeks of meeting with designers and craftsmen and laborers, it had all come down to this. Julia stood beside her father's blue rocking chair inside the new bakery and gazed at the end result. Buttery-yellow walls, an off-white tiled floor, dark wood tables and chairs, framed recipes from her mother's cookbook lining the walls, and up front, a fancy new till, espresso machine, and a newly expanded glass display case for all the treats: her vision, brought to life.

Julia had tried out the new kitchen yesterday for the very first time, the top-of-the-line industrial ovens, the roomy refrigerator, the expanded kitchen island, the tall cooling racks. She'd even helped design a lovely slim crisscrossed window to let in the outside light. And this time around, she welcomed some company in her kitchen. Brandy and Miranda, both of whom jumped at the chance to be re-employed at the new bakery, had already expressed interest in being taught more of Julia's baking secrets. They could be a great help, she decided, apprentices who could lessen the excessive burden on her shoulders and could even pass along Julia's recipes and techniques and baking philosophies to future generations.

But Julia still insisted on claiming those precious before-dawn hours. The early morning would forever be her shift.

"It's beautiful!" Mildred proclaimed, beaming at the new interior.

She, along with Julia's other favorite people, had been invited to come see the new bakery early, before the grand reopening, to share those breathless moments before the doors would open again for the first time in nearly three months. All the employees were there—Theresa, Brandy, Miranda, and brothers Enzo and Marco—as well as Mildred and Abbey, Holly and Fletcher, Lizzie and Joe, Mary and George, and Mac. Even Tristan's mother had made the journey from London for this special reopening day. Her sister, Mrs. Pickering, had been invited, too. In the last few weeks, she hadn't exactly given her blessing to Tristan and Julia, but she had been surprisingly cordial to Julia, which was a good sign at least.

And of course, there was Tristan.

"It's perfect," he whispered into Julia's ear as he came to stand beside her, then he kissed her cheek. "It's everything you wanted."

Her father, who hadn't stopped smiling since he'd been helped into his chair this morning, reached for Julia's hand and clasped it. "My dear, your mother would be so very proud of you."

"I wish she were here," Julia said.

"She is," he reassured. "She is here."

Even with all the crisp newness of the bakery—the scent of fresh paint still lingered in the air—Julia's favorite piece in the room was something she had framed and hung last night, beside the counter so that everyone could see it. A photo of her eight-year-old self, standing tiptoe on a stool beside her father in the old kitchen. They were making scones together, likely her first batch. Little Julia mirrored the look of concentration on her father's face, and his hands guided hers. That photo, more than any other part of the bakery, represented precisely why Julia had decided to reopen. The bakery was about tradition and heritage and, ultimately, family, including the broader family that the village had become.

"Okay, I think it's time," Mrs. Pickering said. True to form, she'd been standing at the front door, keeping a strict eye on the clock, making sure the bakery opened precisely at its scheduled hour. "Ready?" She looked over at Julia.

"We're ready. Aren't we, Dad?"

"Right we are. This is the moment."

Mrs. Pickering opened the door to a host of eager customers, who'd been anticipating this day for weeks. Some were tourists and strangers, but many others were familiar faces, nodding and waving to Julia, congratulating her.

"Oh!" Julia said a minute later. "There's one thing we forgot."

"What's that?" Tristan asked.

Julia took Tristan's hand and led him out the front door after the last customer had been ushered in. When they were alone outside, Julia stood near the window at the corner of the bakery then handed her mobile over to Tristan. "Would you do the honors?" She pointed at the new awning. "In the bluster of the last week, I forgot to take a picture of this. I want to mark the occasion."

"Certainly."

Tristan stepped backward into the empty street. "Tell me when you're ready."

Julia squared her shoulders and smiled at Tristan. Her father was right.

She could sense her mother's presence, right here in this same spot where she'd stood, herself, over forty years ago, under a brand-new awning.

Tristan snapped the picture then stepped forward to show Julia the image he'd taken.

"Can you zoom it a little?" Julia had forgotten her glasses again.

Tristan spread his finger and thumb over the screen, and the new awning came into clear view—along with the bakery's new name: *Julia Rose's Bakery.*

Other Books by Traci Borum

Painting the Moon (Chilton Crosse #1)
Finding the Rainbow (Chilton Crosse #2)
Seeking the Star (Chilton Crosse #3)

Acknowledgements

To my family—particularly Mama, Maw, Grammy, and Karen. Your support means everything and your encouragement keeps me strong and motivated.

To Daddy and to Pappy, who would've been so supportive of this new book. I miss them every day.

To my dearest friends, and to those who continue to be supportive of my writer's journey: Augusta Malvagno, Sandy Graham, Becky Bray, Karen Peterson, Doris Lininger, Sue Willis, Sheree Webb, Deanna Markham, my TJC friends and colleagues, and my beloved Commandos.

To Linda Bratcher, for using her eagle eye on this manuscript. Your support and friendship is so appreciated!

To Kate Manning, who read through the book to double check the British-isms. Also thanks to Rich Sawrey and Ellen Ervine for their input on all my British questions.

To Mike and Debbi Miller for helping confirm details regarding firefighting procedures in the story. Your input was so appreciated!

To Claudia Bazan Hill, owner of Chez Bason in Tyler, Texas, for answering all my baking questions. I enjoyed our chat and felt much more confident in my research after speaking with you.

Special thanks to my publisher, Lynn McNamee, whose professionalism, knowledge, and ambition have helped to create an amazing publishing company that produces high-quality books. I'm honored to be on board with Red Adept. Also special thanks to my content editor, Suzanne Warr and to my line editor, Karen Allen. Their careful input and guidance has heightened the quality of the book in every way.

To the entire Red Adept team, but especially Jessica Anderegg, Streetlight Graphics (particularly Glendon Haddix), and all the acquisitions editors and proofreaders and formatters. This novel is what it is because of your diligence and dedication and talents. I'm so grateful to you.

To Clint Jones at Motophoto for my author photo.

Finally, all thanks to God, who makes everything in this life worthwhile. He is the Source.

About the Author

Traci Borum is a writing teacher and native Texan. She's also an avid reader of women's fiction, most especially Elin Hilderbrand and Rosamunde Pilcher novels. Since the age of 12, she's written poetry, short stories, magazine articles, and novels.

Traci also adores all things British. She even owns a British dog (Corgi) and is completely addicted to Masterpiece Theater–must be all those dreamy accents! Aside from having big dreams of getting a book published, it's the little things that make her the happiest: deep talks with friends, a strong cup of hot chocolate, a hearty game of fetch with her Corgi, and puffy white Texas clouds always reminding her to "look up, slow down, enjoy your life."

CPSIA information can be obtained
at www.ICGtesting.com
Printed in the USA
LVOW11s2026140917
548743LV00007B/1010/P

9 781940 215914